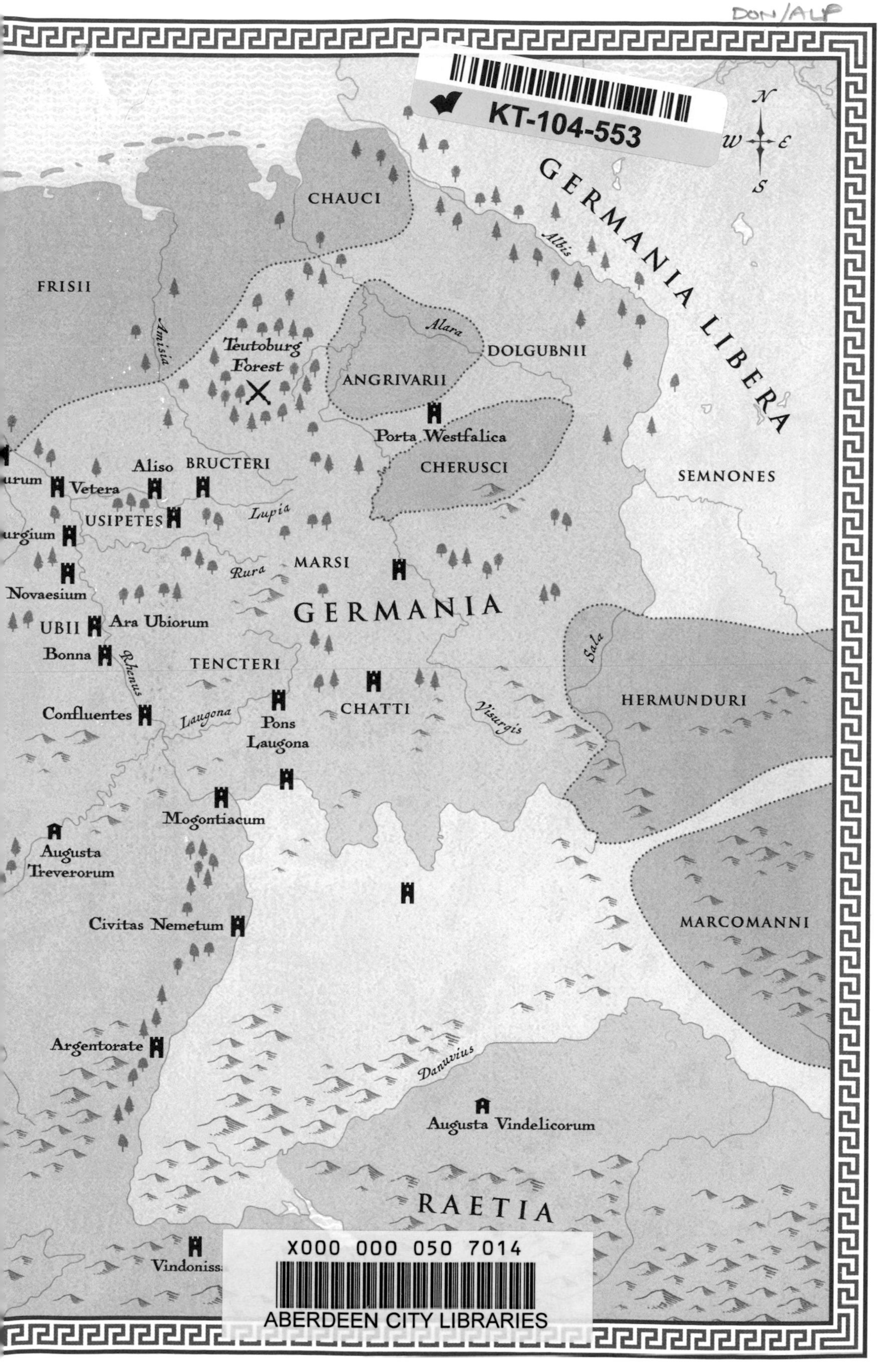

GERMANIA LIBERA

N
W E
S

CHAUCI
Albis
FRISII
Amisia
Teutoburg Forest
Alara
DOLGUBNII
ANGRIVARII
Porta Westfalica
CHERUSCI
SEMNONES
Aliso
BRUCTERI
urum
Vetera
USIPETES
Lupia
urgium
MARSI
Rura
Novaesium
GERMANIA
UBII
Ara Ubiorum
Bonna
Rhenus
TENCTERI
Sala
HERMUNDURI
Confluentes
Laugona
Pons Laugona
CHATTI
Visurgis
Mogontiacum
Augusta Treverorum
MARCOMANNI
Civitas Nemetum
Argentorate
Danuvius
Augusta Vindelicorum
RAETIA
Vindoniss

Eagles at War

Also By Ben Kane:

The Forgotten Legion
The Silver Eagle
The Road to Rome

Spartacus
Spartacus: The Gladiator
Spartacus: Rebellion

Hannibal
Hannibal: Enemy of Rome
Hannibal: Fields of Blood
Hannibal: Clouds of War

Eagles at War

BEN KANE

preface

3 5 7 9 10 8 6 4 2

Preface
20 Vauxhall Bridge Road
London SW1V 2SA

Preface is part of the Penguin Random House group of companies whose addresses can be found at global.penguinrandomhouse.com.

First published by Preface in 2015

www.randomhouse.co.uk

A CIP catalogue record for this book is available from the British Library.

ISBN 978 1 84809 404 8

Map illustration on endpapers by Darren Bennett, DKB Creative.

Penguin Random House is committed to a sustainable future for our business, our readers and our planet. This book is made from Forest Stewardship Council® certified paper.

Typeset in Fournier MT by Palimpsest Book Production Limited,
Falkirk, Stirlingshire

Printed and bound in Great Britain by Clays Ltd, St Ives plc

This book is for my readers – every single one of you. You come from all over the world, from every continent bar Antarctica.* Your loyalty gives me the freedom to be a full-time writer, and to do a job that I adore.

For this, you have my heartfelt thanks.

* If you've worked in Antarctica, and read my books when there, please let me know!

'Quintili Vare, legiones redde!' 'Quinctilius Varus, give me back my legions!'

Cassius Dio's record of the Emperor Augustus' reaction to the news of Varus' fate

Prologue

Germania, 12 BC

The boy had been fast asleep, but the insistent shaking of his shoulder woke him at last. He opened gummy eyes to find a figure stooped over him. Profiled by the weak lamplight behind, his father's face – bearded, keen-eyed, framed by braids of hair – was frightening, and he recoiled.

'It's all right, little bear. I'm no ghost.'

'What is it, Father?' he mumbled.

'I have something to show you.'

Behind the powerful figure that was his father stood his mother. Even in the gloom of the longhouse and fuddled with sleep, he could see that she was unhappy. His gaze returned to his father. 'Is Mother coming?'

'No. This is something for men.'

'I'm only seven.'

'No matter. I want you to see this. Out of bed. Get dressed.'

His father's word was law. Slipping from under the warmth of his bear pelt, he shoved his still-stockinged feet into his boots, which sat by his low bed. Rummaging for his cloak, which doubled as a second blanket, he threw it around his shoulders. 'I'm ready.'

'Come.'

As they passed his mother, she reached out. 'Segimer. This is not right.'

His father whirled. 'He *must* see it.'

'He is too young.'

'Do not question me, woman! The gods are watching.'

With pursed lips, his mother stood aside.

The boy pretended that he hadn't heard, or seen. Following his father, he slipped past the forms of sleeping slaves, the glowing fire, the cooking pans and wooden storage chests. The two doorways in the longhouse were opposite each other, in the middle of the building. From the other end, currents of warm air carried the rich odours, and the sounds, of their cattle, pigs and sheep.

His father set the lamp down as he went outside. He looked back. 'Come.'

The boy moved to the doorway. Stars glittered overhead, but the night was still dark and intimidating. He didn't like it, but his father was beckoning. Out he came, taking a deep breath of the cool, damp air. It chilled his nostrils, reminding him of the winter that was already nipping at autumn's heels. 'Where are we going?'

'To the forest.'

The boy tensed. He loved being among the trees in the day, when he could play with his friends at hunting, or see who was best at finding deer tracks. He'd never been there at night, however. The forest would be a shadow world now, full of spirits, fierce animals and the gods knew what else. He had been woken many times by wolves howling at the moon. What if they met some?

'Hurry!' His father was already a distance along the path that led out of the settlement.

In that moment, being left alone outweighed the boy's fear of what lay beyond the houses, so he chased after his father. He wanted to ask if they could hold hands, but he knew what the answer to that would be. Pacing by his father's side was better than nothing. Segimer's long sword, which marked him out as a wealthy man among their people, was also reassuring, knocking off his thigh as he walked, and reminding the boy that his father was a fearsome warrior, the equal – or better – of any in their Cherusci tribe.

His courage somewhat returned, he asked, 'What are we going to do?'

Segimer looked down. 'We shall witness an offering to the gods, such as you have never seen.'

Excitement mixed with the fear in the boy's belly. He wanted to know more, but his father's stern tone, and the fact that he was striding ahead at a great speed, made him hold his tongue. Keeping up was what mattered. Mud squelched beneath their boots as they traced their way between a score of longhouses. A dog yapped as they passed one dwelling, setting off a chorus of others. Despite this noise, the village remained still. Everyone was asleep, the boy realised. It was late indeed. He grinned, thrilled. Staying up to watch a wedding feast with his friends, say, was one thing, but to go out in the depths of night, even to the forest, *that* was a treat. The fact that he was with his father, whom he idolised, made it even better. Segimer wasn't unkind or cruel, as some of his friends' fathers were, but he didn't have much to do with him. He was a distant man. Aloof. Always busy with other nobles; or hunting; or away, fighting the Romans. This time had to be enjoyed, the boy decided.

Their path led into the forest that sprawled to the south of their settlement. There were woods throughout the Cherusci's lands, Segimer had told the boy, but around the larger villages, much of it had been cut down so that the ground could be used for agriculture. To the west lay the river, a source of water and many types of fish. To the east and west, a patchwork of little fields produced grain, vegetables and grass for their livestock. The trees to the south provided wood for the tribe's fires, deer and boar for their tables, and sacred places for the priests to consult with the gods.

They had to be going to one of those spots, thought the boy, his unease returning. He was grateful that his father could not see him shiver. He had never dared to enter a grove. Once, he and his friends had ventured far enough to see the entrance to one. The horned cattle skulls nailed to the trees had tested their courage to the limit, and they had skulked back to the village in silence. Tonight, no doubt, they would be going beyond that point. Sweat trickled down his back as they entered the forest. Be brave, he told himself. You can show no fear now, or later. To do so would bring shame on his family, and on his father.

For all of his resolve, he jumped when a figure stepped out from behind a tree. Cloaked, armed with a spear, he raised a hand in salute. 'Segimer.'

'Tudrus.'

The boy relaxed. Tudrus was one of his father's most trusted warriors, and a man whom he'd known since he was tiny.

'You woke the little bear.'

'Aye.' Segimer's hand brushed the boy's shoulder, a touch for which he was grateful.

'Are you ready, lad?' enquired Tudrus.

The boy didn't know what he was agreeing to, but he nodded.

'Good.'

Segimer peered at the path which ran in from the west to join the one he'd taken from the settlement. 'Are there any more to arrive?'

'They're all here. Warriors of the Bructeri, Chatti, Angrivarii and Tencteri. Even the Marsi have sent noblemen.'

'It will please Donar that so many have chosen to come,' Segimer pronounced, eyeing the sky. 'We'd best hurry. The moon will reach its zenith soon. That's when the priests said they must die.'

Tudrus rumbled in agreement.

When they must die. Stifling his unease at what the words might mean, the boy concentrated on keeping up with his father.

BOOOOOOO!

The boy started forward with fright. He regained control fast, but beside him, he caught Tudrus smiling. His father frowned, indicating with his eyes that he was not to move again.

BOOOOOOO! BOOOOOOO!

The boy didn't stir this time. The bizarre sound *had* to be from a horn, blown by a priest, but it felt as if it were a demon, or a god, announcing his arrival in the grove. Ten heartbeats skipped past, then twenty, and still no one appeared. The boy's gaze slid from left to right, over the shadowy space, which was even more intimidating than he had imagined. The path into it had been frightening enough, a winding, muddy affair bounded on both sides by marsh. The entrance, a crude wooden archway decorated with cattle skulls, had been no better. But it was the sacred circle of oak trees, fifty paces across, in which he now waited with his father, Tudrus and a large group of warriors, which had set his guts to churning.

In its centre stood a pair of altars, enormous slabs of stone that looked to have been hewn by giants. On top of one, a pyre had been built; ominous dark red-brown stains marked the surface of the other. Before the altars, a large fire burned, the only source of light in the grove. One of two tables beside it was covered in an impressive array of bladed and serrated instruments, probes, tongs and hammers. The second was bare-topped. Ropes dangled from its four legs, testimony to its purpose.

The boy had expected to see animals tethered here. Religious ceremonies he'd attended in the settlement had seen cattle and sheep offered to the gods. Once, he'd witnessed – had his ears bombarded by – a boar being sacrificed. He could hear its screams still.

BOOOOOOO! BOOOOOOO! BOOOOOOO! The sound originated from behind the altars.

'Here they come,' whispered his father.

Curious now, the boy stood on tiptoe, craning his neck to see.

A procession wound its way out of the trees. First came two robed priests, blowing long cattle horns. Next were two magnificent white mares, led by acolytes, and pulling a chariot in which stood an old, stooped priest. His head was bent, and the boy knew that he was listening to the sounds made by the sacred horses. Important messages from the gods could be ascertained from their whinnies and nickers. Behind the chariot walked four more priests blowing horns, but it was the miserable figures who shambled after that really drew the boy's gaze.

Eight men, roped together at the neck and wrists. Seven of them wore belted, off-white tunics that ended above the knee. The last's garment was red, and he alone wore a helmet, which bore an impressive transverse crest of red and white feathers.

'Romans,' the boy whispered in awe. He'd seen bodies of his people's enemies once before, left behind after a patrol had been ambushed by his father and the tribe's warriors. These were the first Romans he'd seen alive. They weren't unharmed, however. Even at a distance, and in dim light, the bruises and welts that covered the prisoners' bodies were obvious. Behind the Romans paced a dozen strapping acolytes, armed with long spears.

A queasy feeling rose from the boy's belly. Whatever happened to these men, it wouldn't be good.

His father seized his shoulder in a grip of iron and bent to his ear. 'See those bastards?'

He nodded.

'The Romans stand for everything that we do not, boy. Their empire stretches further than a man could walk in a year, yet they're not content. They seek always to conquer new lands. For decades now, their leader, *Augustus*' – his father spat the word – 'has desired to be emperor over us. Over our brethren, the Chatti, the Marsi and Angrivarii. He wants to make us his subjects, to be ground forever beneath the heels of his soldiers. He must never succeed!'

'Never, Father,' agreed the boy, remembering what had happened when the Romans had come to the area before. A nearby settlement had been torched; many had been slain, including his aunt and two cousins. 'We will stop him.'

'Stop him we will, *and* his cursed legions. So I will swear, with these other warriors. Donar will be our witness.' He gave the boy a rare smile. 'You will take the oath too.'

Wonder filled him. 'I, Father?'

'Yes, little bear. That is why you are here.' Segimer placed a finger on his lips, and then pointed.

Moving to the sides of the altars, the horn-blowers fell silent. All eyes watched the old priest as he dismounted from the chariot and shuffled to a position at the fire. The horses were led away, and the prisoners shoved forward by the acolytes until they stood by the tables.

'We give thanks to you, Great Donar, for watching over us.' The priest's voice was strong for all his apparent frailty. 'Your thunderbolts protect us, and your storm clouds bring us the rain without which our crops would wither and die. When we fight our enemies, your strength aids our struggle, and for this we are always grateful.'

Throughout the gathering, men were murmuring in agreement, rubbing hammer amulets, whispering prayers.

'Of recent years, we have had need of your aid every summer. Vermin such as these' – the priest stabbed a long fingernail at the prisoners – 'come in their thousands to visit destruction on our lands. No one is safe from the Romans' depredations, their bloodlust. Men, women, children, the old, the sick are slain or enslaved. Our villages are burned, and the crops and livestock stolen.'

Warriors made angry comments. The boy's father's knuckles were white upon the hilt of his sword. He felt his own fury surge. His aunt and her sons – his cousins – had been his favourite relations. These Romans had to be punished.

'We gather tonight to make you an offering, Great Donar,' intoned the priest. 'To ask for your help in fighting these invaders. To ensure that they flee, defeated, to the far side of the river they like to call the *Rhenus*. To ensure that once there, they *never* return to your lands, and ours.'

'DONAR!' shouted Segimer.

'DO-NAR! DO-NAR! DO-NAR!' roared the warriors in reply. The boy joined in, but his reedy tones were lost in the deafening chorus. 'DO-NAR! DO-NAR! DO-NAR!'

'Make your oaths,' ordered the priest when the noise had died down.

Pride filled the boy as Segimer stood forward first.

'I, Segimer of the Cherusci, swear before Donar never to rest until the

Romans have been driven from our lands forever. The gods strike me down if I ever stray from this path.'

The priest watched in silence as, one by one, the warriors pledged to toil without rest until their enemies had been vanquished and thrown back over the river. The boy's turn came last. Nervous before so many men, his voice faltered a little, but to his relief no one laughed or looked angry. The priest even gave him a nod of approval, and his father squeezed his shoulder when he returned to stand with the rest.

The priest gestured. Four acolytes seized the nearest captive, a short Roman with a round face, and hauled him forward, kicking and struggling. Without ceremony, he was slammed down on to the empty table and his limbs tethered.

A reverent silence fell, allowing the Roman's whimpering to be heard.

Still the boy didn't quite believe what was about to happen. Yet when he glanced at the faces around him, which had grown hard and cruel, the cold certainty of it could not be denied. His eyes were drawn back to the table, and the victim stretched upon it.

The old priest selected a curved iron probe and held it aloft. 'Without eyes, the Romans will be blind. They will not see our warriors' ambushes, or their secret camps.'

A hungry *Ahhhhh* rose from those watching. Surely he isn't . . .? The boy shuddered.

Two of the acolytes held the Roman's head immobile as the priest approached. His wailing intensified.

A deep voice began shouting in a tongue the boy didn't understand. It was the Roman in the helmet, who had pushed forward as far as his bonds allowed. He aimed his words at the priest, at the assembled warriors, at the acolytes.

'What's he saying, Father?' asked the boy in a whisper. 'Tudrus?'

'They are soldiers,' hissed Segimer. 'Honourable men, who do not deserve to be treated like animals. He is asking that they be slain with respect.'

'Is he right, Father?'

Segimer's eyes resembled two chips of ice. 'Did they kill your cousins with honour? Or your aunt? Or the scores of unarmed villagers who also died that day?'

The boy did not know how his relations had died. Neither had he understood everything that the older youths had said about the Romans' atrocities, but he *was* certain that gutting a pregnant woman was an evil thing. He hardened his heart. 'No, Father.'

'That is why they will die like beasts.'

They deserve nothing better, thought the boy.

The Roman's shouting came to an abrupt halt as he was beaten to the ground by several acolytes. A gag was tied around his mouth. When that had been done, the priest stooped over the man on the table. A hideous shriek shredded the air. It rose higher than the boy would have thought possible. The priest placed something small, red and wet by the man's side, and his screaming eased a little. A heartbeat later, it returned to its previous level, as the priest used his probe to delve into the man's second eye socket.

Holding two small globes high with a scarlet-coated hand, the priest faced the warriors. 'Blinded, the Roman cannot see us! Accept this offering, Great Donar!'

'DO-NAR! DO-NAR! DO-NAR!' the boy yelled until he felt his voice crack.

Sparks flared as the priest tossed the eyeballs into the fire.

'DO-NAR!' roared the warriors.

Replacing the probe, the priest selected a long-bladed knife. Dark blood gushed over his hands as he poked around in his victim's mouth. A burbling scream rose, and the man thrashed about on the table.

'Without a tongue, the Roman cannot speak his lies!' A piece of flesh flew from the priest's hand into the flames.

The boy closed his eyes. The prisoner has to die, he thought. He could have been the one who slew my cousins. A sharp jab from his father's elbow forced him to observe once more.

'DO-NAR!'

The priest plunged his blade into the Roman's chest. With business-like intensity, he twisted it to and fro. The staccato rhythm of the man's heels on the table went faster and faster, but then slowed right down. By the time the priest had discarded his knife in favour of a saw, they had stopped moving altogether. Before long, he had cracked open the man's ribcage and freed his victim's heart from the network of vessels that surrounded it. He brandished the small, bloody globe at the warriors like a battle trophy. 'Without a heart, the Roman has no courage! No strength!'

'DO-NAR! DO-NAR! DO-NAR!'

The boy was grateful for the shouting. Despite his hatred of the Romans, the spectacle was turning his stomach. He watched through half-closed eyes as the victim's body was heaved on to the pyre and set alight, and as the second, third and fourth Romans were dispatched in similar manner to the first.

At length, Segimer noticed. 'Observe everything!' he snapped.

He obeyed with reluctance.

Segimer's breath was hot in his ear. 'Do you know how one of your cousins died?'

The boy wanted to answer, but his tongue felt like a plank in his mouth. He shook his head.

'He had been trying to defend his mother, your aunt, from harm. He was only a boy, of course, so the Romans disarmed him with ease. They held him down, and one of them ran a spear up his arse. Right up, inside him. The whoreson didn't shove it in far enough to kill him straightaway, though. He lingered on while they murdered his brother and violated his mother in front of him.'

Hot tears – of rage, of fear – ran down the boy's cheeks, but his father wasn't done.

'Your poor bastard of a cousin was still alive when we reached the village that evening. It was left to his father, your uncle, to end his life.' Segimer pulled the boy's chin up, forcing him to meet his gaze. 'These are the kind of creatures that the Romans are. D'you see?'

'Yes, Father.'

'Would you want something like that to happen to your mother, or your younger brother? To your grandmother?'

'No!'

'Accept then that giving the Romans to Donar in this way is a good thing. A necessary thing. With the thunder god's approval, we cannot fail to defeat them.'

'I understand, Father.'

Segimer's eyes searched his, but the boy did not look away. At last his father nodded.

He watched every moment of the rest of the gory ceremony. Runnels of clotted blood coated the sacrificial table, and the air filled with a cacophony of screams and the cloying smell of burning flesh. Whenever the boy's stomach protested, he made himself think of his cousin, impaled on a spear, watching his mother and brother being abused and tortured. Those images drove all else before them. They made him thrum with rage, made him want to grab the priest's knife and stick it in Roman flesh.

I will remember this night forever, he pledged to himself. *One day, as Donar is my witness, I will teach the Romans a lesson that they will never forget.*

I, Ermin of the Cherusci, swear this.

PART ONE

Spring, AD 9

The German frontier

I

Arminius sat astride a fine chestnut horse, watching eight *turmae* of his cavalry canter to and fro across the vast parade ground outside the fortified camp of Ara Ubiorum. It was a fine morning, cool and crisp. The last signs of winter had vanished, and the fertile landscape around the camp was a bright shade of green. Skylarks swooped and darted overhead, but their delicate cries were drowned out by the pounding of horses' hooves on the packed earth, and the shouted commands of Arminius' junior officers.

Like his troops, his dress was a mixture of Roman and German: a mail shirt and silvered cavalry helmet contrasted with a tribesman's wool cloak, tunic, patterned trousers and ankle boots. A fine *spatha*, or long cavalry sword, hung from a gilt-decorated baldric over his shoulder. He was in the prime of life, large-framed and striking-looking, with intense grey eyes, black hair and a bushy beard of the same colour.

His five hundred Cheruscan warriors formed the *ala*, or cavalry unit, attached to the Seventeenth Legion. They served as scouts, and provided flanking cover to marching legionaries, but they could also be used in battle. This necessitated training on a regular basis, and Arminius was here to supervise his men to do just that. He had watched these exercises countless times, and knew every move inside out. His well-trained riders made few mistakes, so it wasn't long before his mind began to wander. The previous day, he'd had his ear bent by a chieftain in a village on the far bank of the River Rhenus. The man had made vociferous complaints about the new imperial tax. It wasn't the first time Arminius had encountered such resentment. Here in Gaul, the only Germans were auxiliaries in the legions, well-paid men who were content with their lot. On the other side of the river, among the tribes, it was a different story.

Governor Varus and his contemporaries were oblivious to the discontent, Arminius thought. In their minds, the Romanisation of Germania was proceeding just as it should. There were numerous permanent and temporary military camps scattered throughout a vast area more than three hundred miles deep and half that across. At least half the region's tribes were allied to the empire, or had made treaties with it. A few skirmishes aside, peace had reigned for several years. The legions' engineering works each summer meant that an increasing number of roads were being paved. One settlement – Pons Laugona – was well on the way to becoming the first Roman town east of the Rhenus, with its forum, municipal buildings and sewerage system. There were other communities eager to follow this example. Even in the villages, it was becoming common to hold a regular market. Imperial law was permeating into tribal society; magistrates from Ara Ubiorum and other camps west of the Rhenus now made regular journeys over the river to adjudicate in land disputes and other legal matters.

These social changes had angered some tribesmen, thought Arminius, but a good number had been happy enough, in the main because living standards had risen. Legionaries required vast quantities of food, drink and clothing. Farmers who lived near the camps could sell livestock, grain and vegetables, wool and leather. Their women were able to peddle clothing, and if they desired, their hair. Prisoners taken in clashes with other tribes could be sold as slaves, and trapped wild animals – for use in the military camps' amphitheatres – fetched considerable sums. Young men could join the Roman army, escaping their mundane lives on farms. Enterprising individuals opened taverns and restaurants beside the military bases, or found employment inside them.

Yes, there were many benefits to being part of the empire, Arminius admitted to himself, but they came at a high price. First among these was having an absolute ruler, a so-called *emperor* – Augustus. A man to whom everyone had to pay obeisance; a man who had to be venerated almost as a god. Germanic tribes did have leaders, but they were regarded in a different manner than Augustus. They were esteemed, thought Arminius. Feared – likely. Revered – perhaps. Loved – possibly. But superior to all others? Never. A chieftain who acted as if he were better than others would not last long at the head of a tribe. Warriors followed him out of respect, and if for some reason their high opinion of him changed, they walked away, or began backing another chieftain. As a leader of the Cherusci, Arminius was mindful of the need to retain this support, in particular because he spent the majority of his time away from home, with the legions.

The second price of being part of the empire – Arminius' lips quirked, because it was just that, a price – was its damnable taxes. This summer, the collecting of tax was to be extended beyond the Rhenus for the first time. While imperial officials would gather the money and trading goods that many would use in lieu of coin, it would be the legions' presence close by that ensured its payment. The chieftain who had approached Arminius – regarding him as trustworthy because he too was German – had been incandescent. 'The tax is an outrage! I can afford to pay, but many of my people will find it difficult to come up with goods to the value of the coin that has been spoken of. Why should we pay anyway?'

Arminius had muttered various platitudes about the protection offered by the empire, and the benefits to all and sundry that it brought, but his heart hadn't been in it. He suspected that the chieftain had seen this too. The contentious tax issue didn't just apply to the tribes who lived in the border zone that comprised the thirty miles east of the Rhenus, but to all those who lived under Rome's influence. The tribes further afield were accustomed to sending their sons to serve with the legions, and they were becoming used to other aspects of Roman society. Accepting these things was one matter, thought Arminius, but the imposition of tax was altogether different. The old anger came to life in his belly, the resentment towards Rome that fuelled his very being.

Hooves hammered the ground close to him, and Arminius' attention was drawn to his men. Over and back the riders went, practising the same moves again and again. In close formation, they rode straight at a pile of training equipment. This was the 'spear', the pointed shape designed to smash open an enemy line. Their next move, a loose, upside-down 'V', was meant to do the same, but to unprepared foes who hadn't had time to tighten up their position. The third move was the simplest: it consisted of a long line of charging horsemen, riding close to one another – almost ankle to ankle.

As they advanced, the trumpeter in their midst sounded his instrument with all his might. *BOOOOOOO! BOOOOOOO! BOOOOOOO!* This, the most common attack against enemy infantry, worked almost every time. Whether it was daring, a desire to impress him or just poor control by the officer in charge, Arminius wasn't sure, but his riders thundered to within a hundred paces of a cohort of training legionaries. The Roman troops would have known that the cavalry were friendly, but that didn't stop their lines from bending away from the horsemen. Angry shouts from their centurions – directed towards the riders as well as their own troops – soon saw the soldiers re-form and resume their training, but there could be no denying the move's efficacy, or the irritation it would have caused the legionaries' officers.

It worked, thought Arminius with considerable satisfaction, because it was so terrifying. Many of his men were wearing silvered cavalry helmets that were less ornate than his, but similar in design. The hinged frontpieces of each had been shaped into human features, to resemble the individual wearing it. Like the rest of the helmet, the 'face' had been covered with a thin layer of silver foil. When pulled down, the wearer's field of vision was much reduced, meaning only the most skilled riders could make use of them. Yet the masks' effect – turning the wearer into an unearthly-looking creature that might have been from the underworld – made this sacrifice worthwhile. A massed charge with even a few such riders, accompanied by the blaring of trumpets, sent terror lancing into the hearts of the bravest foe.

Arminius had been around long enough to have had to use all the tactics he'd just seen. He knew the effectiveness of each, and which one to choose at what moment. The cavalry were yet another part of the impressive Roman military machine, the centrepiece of which was always the damn lines of armoured legionaries. Again his grey eyes wandered towards the unit that his men had intimidated.

It still felt odd to regard the Romans as allies. It had been so since the first day he'd served with the imperial army, eight years before. The campaigns and battles he'd taken part in – on Rome's side – meant that he had a healthy respect for its soldiers and their officers. Their bravery, discipline and ability to stand firm against an enemy were remarkable. On more than one occasion, he and his men had been saved by the intervention of one such unit or another. He had endured lengthy marches with the legions, got pissed with their officers, and even whored with some of them. His loyalty to the empire had seen him first rewarded with citizenship and then elevated to equestrian status, the lower rank of Roman nobility.

Despite these experiences and honours, Arminius felt less kinship with the Romans than might have been expected. In the main it was because he continued to regard himself, with pride, as German. The Romans' superior attitude didn't help either. Despite his exalted status, he was to many little more than a fur-wearing savage. He and his men were good enough to fight – and die – for Rome, but not to be recognised as equals. This had been hard enough to take during the years Arminius had served elsewhere in the empire, but being close to his homeland of recent months had accentuated his aggrieved feelings. Not two miles hence, on the eastern bank of the Rhenus, the tribal lands began. His people, the Cherusci, lived far away, yet he still had far more in common with the nearest tribe – the Usipetes – than he did with the Romans. He held the same values, spoke a similar tongue, and worshipped the same gods.

Arminius remembered the night in the sacred grove so long ago, and a line of sweat ran down his back. When the legions crossed the river to punish tribes who had risen against the empire's rule, those they slew were not Dacian, Illyrian or Thracian. They were German. Like him. Like his warriors. Like his long-dead aunt and cousins. They were people who had a right to live their lives freely. Why should they be subjects of Augustus, who lives many hundreds of miles away, in Rome? Arminius asked himself. Why should I?

It had been twenty-one years since he had stood among the trees with his father, but the words of his oath were as vivid in his head as they had been the first time he uttered them. *One day, as Donar is my witness, I will teach the Romans a lesson that they will never forget. I, Ermin of the Cherusci, swear this.*

His eyes rose to the blue arc of the heavens, which was decorated with a scattering of lambswool clouds. The sun was warming, but not too hot. The skylarks yet trilled from on high, a sign that spring was passing. Summer would arrive soon, and when it did, Publius Quinctilius Varus, the governor of Germania, would lead his army east. Over the Rhenus, where his troops would collect taxes as far as the River Visurgis. Only the Romans could have come up with fucking taxes, thought Arminius. The tribes' hard-earned silver would go towards gilding yet more statues of the emperor, and building paved roads upon which his armies could tramp. Great Donar, he prayed, I have waited long years to fulfil my oath. To wreak vengeance for those of my tribe slain by Rome. I ask that you let the right moment be this year.

This summer.

'Greetings!' called a senior centurion. Wearing scale armour and sporting a helmet with a transverse crest of red feathers, he was hurrying across the parade ground in Arminius' direction.

Like as not, he was the officer in charge of the unsettled cohort, thought Arminius in amusement. He didn't look happy.

'Centurion.' Arminius inclined his head, but not much. As an equestrian, *he* was of higher rank, and the centurion knew it. Arminius could tell from his posture that this difference was not something that sat well with him.

In his eyes, no doubt, Arminius was a jumped-up barbarian. The great effort that he'd put into winning over every senior officer worked with many, but it wouldn't with this one. Bitter memories flooded in, of when his father had sent him to Rome, aged ten. Like Arminius' subsequent enlistment in the legions, it had been part of Segimer's plan. Arminius was to be immersed in the Roman way of life, learning everything there was to know – while never forgetting his tribal roots, or his true loyalties.

To the high-born Roman youths he'd been thrown in with, however, he had been little better than a slave. After several bloody fights, not all of which Arminius had won, they had learned to respect his fists and boots at least, and to keep their lips sealed when he was around. Despite their fear, few had been prepared to extend to him the hand of friendship. Arminius had learned to be self-sufficient, and mistrusting of all.

He caught the centurion's eyes on his chin. Once more he gauged the thought before it had reached the man's eyes. You're so superior, aren't you, you whoreson? He made a point of stroking his beard, to the Roman a mark of an uncivilised nature, but to him a symbol of his culture. 'Can I help?'

'I'd appreciate it if you'd keep your men under better control.'

'I have no idea what you're talking about,' lied Arminius with relish.

'Your troops charged a moment ago. They all but closed with my soldiers! It caused great . . .' The centurion searched for a word that didn't imply fear. '. . . confusion.'

'They didn't go *that* close.'

'It was close enough to panic . . .' Again the centurion thought. '. . . some of the new recruits.'

Arminius raised his eyebrows. 'Panic? Since when did legionaries of the Seventeenth *panic*?'

'It's a normal enough reaction for men who haven't seen charging cavalry before,' replied the centurion, bristling.

'The next time you open your mouth, you will call me *sir*,' retorted Arminius, his own temper rising.

The centurion gaped, swallowed, muttered, 'Sir.'

'I paid no attention to your overfamiliarity at first, centurion, because I'm not one to stand on ceremony. When someone is disrespectful, however, I remind them that *I* command the ala attached to the Seventeenth. I am no simple Roman citizen – like you. I am an equestrian. Had you forgotten that?' Arminius pinned the centurion's eyes with his own.

'No, sir. My apologies, sir,' replied the centurion, flushing.

Arminius waited for several heartbeats, driving his superiority further home. 'You were saying . . .?'

'Some of my men aren't used to cavalry, sir. Yet,' added the centurion quickly. 'If your riders could refrain from coming too close to them, I'd be most appreciative.'

'I can promise nothing, centurion. I suggest instead that you move elsewhere, and expose your men to cavalry more than you have done up to this point. Otherwise they could be routed the first time they face them in battle,' said Arminius with a cold smile. 'Dismissed.'

'Sir.' The centurion somehow managed to convey his dislike with his salute. It was a clever stroke, stripping Arminius of much of his gratification. By way of retaliation, he had his riders repeat the manoeuvre that had scared the cohort's new recruits. After the third charge, the centurion conceded defeat by leading his soldiers to another part of the parade ground. Arminius watched them go with cold pleasure. The move would win him no new friends among the centurionate. If the prick complained to the legate, he might receive a rap across the knuckles. Arminius didn't care. It had been worth it, and the centurion wouldn't cross him again.

Several hours later, Arminius was in his quarters, still brooding over his best course of action. Time and again, he paced the floor of his simple office. Ten paces from wall to wall, and back. A scowl at the bust of Augustus, placed there to give the impression that he loved the emperor as much as the next man. Every so often, his eyes would stray to the map unrolled on his desk, its corners held down by clay oil lights. A thick ribbon marked the Rhenus, running north to south; smaller, winding ones the waterways running through Germania. Inked-in squares showed the positions of the Roman camps and forts throughout the region. There were fewer east of the Rhenus than to the west, as was natural, but things were changing, thought Arminius angrily. With every passing year, Rome's influence spread, and the chances of rebellion grew slimmer. If it doesn't happen this summer, it never will, he decided.

It was time to sound out the chieftains of the other tribes, and gauge their loyalty. He had the perfect opportunity to do so in the coming days. Varus, the governor of Germania, had summoned him to Vetera, some sixty miles to the north. Rather than travelling along the faster, paved roads west of the Rhenus, he could do as most auxiliaries, and make the journey on the other bank. A diversion to visit his family on the way to Vetera, as the ordinary soldiers did, would take too long. The Cheruscan lands lay far to the east. Instead, he would meet with tribal leaders whom he hoped to win over to his cause.

His plan wasn't without risk. Any lowlife chieftain with a need to show his loyalty to Rome could inform on him. The instant that Varus or any other senior officer believed such a tale, his life would be forfeit. Damn the risks, thought Arminius fiercely, picturing his aunt and cousins, slain in the cruellest fashion by the Romans. Their shades would haunt him in the afterlife if he hadn't avenged them. It was a shame that his own brother Flavus didn't feel the same way, but there was nothing to be done about that. Several years younger than Arminius, Flavus had always been a tempestuous character. They had never got on, even as boys, so perhaps it wasn't so surprising that Flavus was loyal to Rome, heart and soul. Arminius had revealed his hatred of the empire's grip over Germania once, some years before. Flavus' violent reaction meant he had never mentioned it since; nor would he now.

Thump. Thump. Thump. The heavy raps on his door brought him back. 'Who is it?'

'Osbert.'

Even if the name hadn't been Cheruscan, the man outside could not have been Roman. He hadn't said 'sir'. If one of his men had addressed him so, Arminius would have fallen over with surprise. It was another of his people's ways, one which many Roman officers tended to look down on. They couldn't see it for what it was, thought Arminius: that chieftains did not treat their followers as inferior. 'Enter.'

In came a warrior with a beard that matched his own. Short, barrel-chested, prone to drinking and fighting, Osbert was one of his best men. 'Arminius.' He stalked up to the map without ceremony, grunted and dragged a stubby finger along the road that led east. 'Thinking about the journey?'

'Aye.'

'It should be routine enough, Donar willing.'

'Aye.' But not if I have my way, Arminius thought, reining in his desire to let Osbert in on his plan. 'What brings you here?'

'The priest Segimundus is sacrificing at the altar, in honour of Augustus. He's happy to accept offerings when that's done, so a group of us are taking some rams. I know you're not a great one for seeking favours of the gods, but the men will be pleased to receive Segimundus' blessing before we leave the camp.'

Attending the ceremony would be good for morale, Arminius decided. 'I'll come. There's no harm in knowing that the gods are on our side.'

The great altar to Rome and Augustus had been erected by the order of Lucius Domitius Ahenobarbus, the first official governor of Germania, some eight years earlier. To commemorate its elevation to a cult centre, the settlement had changed its name from Oppidum Ubiorum to Ara Ubiorum. The great rectangle of stone sat upon a plinth carved with scenes of Augustus and his family presenting sacrifices to the gods, and dwarfed the usual daises seen outside temples. It was so large that the shrine building to Augustus, which stood behind, looked small by comparison. Yet this too was built on a grand scale, with six mighty columns forming its frontage.

The religious sector, a vast area enclosed by a low wall, sat outside the town, close to the Rhenus. In addition to the main temple and the great altar, there were smaller shrines, living quarters for the priests, classrooms for the instruction of acolytes and stables for livestock. There was even a lodging house and tavern for pilgrims who had travelled from afar.

The place was packed with worshippers.

Accompanied by Osbert, a score of his men and three young rams, Arminius worked his way through the multitude towards the side of the altar. In front of it were several hundred legionaries and officers, including the legate, watching the priest Segimundus conclude the offerings to Augustus. There were numerous similar celebrations throughout the year. Arminius attended only the ones he had to, when an official invitation came from the *principia*. The sacred days were a clever ploy, helping to reinforce Augustus' authority and to foster the notion that he was a divine being.

Most men would be happy as absolute rulers over half the world, thought Arminius, irritated as usual by the state propaganda. Why does he have to play at being a god too? Arminius suspected that many Romans held views close to his own, but he'd never heard anyone say so. It didn't do for *anyone* in imperial service to badmouth the emperor.

Nearer to the priest, Arminius realised that something was wrong. None of the assembled soldiers looked happy. Men were cupping hands and whispering in one another's ears. At first glance, the pile of ram carcases – six at least – in front of the altar told him nothing. The emperor's importance required large-scale offerings, after all. Segimundus, recognisable by his shock of unruly blond hair, was stooping over another ram, which was being restrained by a pair of acolytes. A number of others stood behind, held by more trainee priests. Blood gouted as Segimundus drew a blade across the ram's neck. Its legs beat out a frantic rhythm on the ground as it died.

'The beast met its end in fitting fashion,' intoned Segimundus. 'That bodes well.'

'You said the same damn thing about the others,' Arminius thought he heard one of the officers say. 'Get on with it. Look at the liver,' said another.

With the ease of experience, the acolytes flipped the ram on to its back. Segimundus knelt at once and worked his knife into its belly, opening it from pelvis to ribcage. The scent of abdominal contents – thick and cloying – reached Arminius' nostrils a few heartbeats later. Segimundus' position blocked him from seeing the slippery loops of bowel and the grey-skinned stomachs, but he had butchered enough animals to be familiar with their appearance. In general, priests paid them scant attention, moving on to the most important organ, the liver. Its location, under the ribcage, snug against the diaphragm, was harder to access than the rest of the belly's contents.

Segimundus hadn't had time to do that, however. He kneeled back on his haunches and gazed at his audience. 'I see signs of disease in the intestines,' he pronounced.

An unhappy *Ahhhhh* rose from the officers.

Despite his lack of belief in augury, Arminius' heart beat a little faster. The rapt expressions on Osbert's and the others' faces told their own story. Although he was from another part of the tribe, Segimundus was also Cheruscan, which meant they placed great store by his words.

As Segimundus resumed his examination of the ram's insides, the legate strode up to the altar. A calm type in normal circumstances, he now looked rather irritated. 'Hades below, Segimundus, how can this be? For one ram, even two, to be unhealthy would be one thing, but all of them?'

'I can but tell you what I find,' replied Segimundus in a grave voice. 'See for yourself.'

'I hope – and anticipate – that this beast's liver will prove to be unblemished,' said the legate, breaking with custom and peering over Segimundus' shoulder.

Segimundus worked his blade to and fro; then he raised a bloodied hand high. On his palm sat a glistening, swollen lump of tissue. The legate started, recoiled. There were cries of dismay from the officers. Arminius blinked. Instead of the normal deep purple-red colour, the liver in

Segimundus' grip had a mottled, pale-pink appearance. Only a liar – or a madman – could claim it to be normal.

'What does this mean?' demanded the legate.

'I cannot be sure,' replied Segimundus, 'but it does not augur well for the emperor, the gods preserve him forever. Or perhaps it's his empire which is at risk.'

The legate's expression grew combative. 'Bullshit! I say that these rams come from the worst flock for a hundred miles. Kill another. Keep killing until you find me one with a healthy liver.'

'As you command, legate.' Segimundus bowed his head. 'Bring the next one forward.'

Arminius eyed the gathered officers and legionaries. Although the legate's attempt at reassurance had settled them, many still looked unhappy. When the next ram's liver also proved to be diseased, and the next, their disquiet grew ever plainer. Arminius could see from his own men's faces that they too were placing weight on Segimundus' findings. A small part of him felt the same way. What were the chances of so many rams being unhealthy?

Segimundus declared the omens from the final sacrifice to be good, but that wasn't enough for the enterprising legate. He summoned the farmer who'd sold the sacrificed beasts to his officers. Seeing the man, Arminius' rational side overpowered his nascent superstition. Ill-dressed, filthy and as scrawny as a plucked chicken, he looked a poor stockman from head to toe. As the legate humiliated the farmer by loudly accusing him of providing his officers with poor-quality beasts, the mood lightened.

Yet Segimundus' face remained troubled, and a flash of inspiration struck Arminius. His own kind were as superstitious as the Romans. What better way had he of winning tribes to his cause than to relate what had happened here? To make the story convincing in its entirety, he only had to leave out the farmer, and the last, healthy ram. This, this was the sign he'd needed. Thank you, great Donar, he thought. It would be useful to sound out Segimundus too. He had always been loyal to Rome and, by tradition, his section of the Cherusci tribe did not get on with Arminius', but his support – if Arminius could get it – would prove useful indeed.

Arminius' certainty that the time was ripe to act solidified further as the rams brought by him and his men were sacrificed. The three beasts died without protest, and were each revealed to have healthy organs. The coming months, Segimundus pronounced, would be fruitful ones for their unit, and their families. Arminius' men were delighted, and clustered around the priest, thanking him.

Arminius used the opportunity to load the purse he'd brought with a great deal of extra coinage before he too approached. Pressing the bulging bag into Segimundus' hand, he said, 'I am grateful for your findings.' More than you could imagine, he added inwardly. 'The gods will be good to us this summer.'

Assessing the purse's weight, Segimundus smiled. 'You are generous indeed, Arminius.'

There's no time like the present, thought Arminius. If Segimundus would be prepared to spread the word among the tribes that the gods were angry with Rome, his wish to defeat Varus' legions could become more than a burning desire. He jerked a thumb at the diseased rams. In a low voice, he said, 'Can your findings really be put down to the owner's poor stockmanship?'

Segimundus threw him a sharp glance. 'Why do you ask?'

'You seemed uncomfortable when the legate laid the blame at the farmer's feet.'

Segimundus indicated his acolytes and the others present with his eyes. 'If we are to discuss the matter, I would rather some privacy. Come into the temple.'

Arminius had been inside the shrine numerous times, yet it never failed to impress. Oil lamps on bronze stands lined the walls, filling the long, narrow interior with a golden-orange glow. As with the altar, the quality of the decoration and the statues was second to none. The grandest, a figure of

Augustus, was more than twice the height of a man even without its waist-high plinth, and was reputed to be one of the most lifelike depictions of the emperor that had ever been carved. Augustus was dressed as a general, bareheaded, in an ornate cuirass, with *pteryges* and calf-high boots. His slight frown, direct gaze and steady jaw completed the look that the emperor was a born leader, a man capable of leading armies into battle and winning victory at any price. A god, almost.

Scorn filled Arminius. Augustus no longer looked like that. The likeness must have been taken a generation ago. He was an old man now, and like as not needed hot stones in his bed at night to keep the winter chills away.

It was clear that the room was empty, but Segimundus peered up and down before he was content. 'Despite the legate's protestations, even the least skilled farmer can raise animals that thrive. Would you not be concerned if every beast but one that you offered to the gods was unhealthy in some way?'

'I would indeed,' Arminius admitted. 'I also fail to see how the healthiness of the last ram wipes out the ill omens that you determined from the others.'

'It's simple. It cannot.'

Arminius took a deep breath. He had reached a fork in the road. One path would see his plan to fruition, and the other to discovery by the Romans. The only way to determine which was the right route – or the wrong – was by revealing his hand. Then it came to him that Segimundus might have the same concerns as he – for all the priest knew, *he* was true to Rome. Realising the irony, Arminius laughed.

Segimundus cocked his head. 'What's funny?'

'Here we are, dancing around each other, trying to gauge the other's opinion, trying to see what the other really thinks.'

'Is that what we're doing?'

'You know it is, Segimundus.'

A chuckle. 'Perhaps I do.' He paused. 'I wonder how the legate would react if I told him of my dream last night.'

'Go on,' said Arminius, intrigued.

'I saw a golden eagle, a standard like the one each legion possesses.' Segimundus appraised Arminius before he added, 'It was being consumed by fire.'

Hope stirred in Arminius' heart. 'That is a powerful image indeed. Was it a sign from the gods, do you think?'

'I feel sure that it was. It came to me in a sacred grove belonging to the Sugambri. Yesterday I was on the other side of the river, on official duty,' Segimundus explained. 'The hour had grown late before my business was concluded, and the settlement's priest invited me to stay. As night fell, I decided to spend some time in the grove, to see if Donar would commune with me. I went alone, as I always do, and prayed to the god. I drank some barley beer. At first, nothing happened. Some time passed, and I fell asleep.'

Arminius could feel a pulse beating at the base of his throat.

'The dream of the burning eagle was so vivid, so intense, that I woke from it. I was covered in sweat.' Segimundus' eyes were alive with passion. 'Donar sent me the vision. I know it. The rams today are further proof.'

The two men studied each other for a long moment.

Arminius spoke first. 'It gladdens my heart to hear you speak so. Too long have I served Rome. Too long have I done nothing while the empire mistreats the different tribes. Are we Cherusci not kin to each other, and to the Chatti, the Marsi and the Angrivarii? We share more with one another than we ever will with the Romans.'

'I cannot fault your logic,' said Segimundus. His expression grew serious. 'Have you a plan?'

Segimundus' words made Arminius throw caution to the wind. 'I plan to forge an alliance of the tribes. We will drive Rome's legions west of the river once and for all.'

Segimundus looked surprised, and wary. 'No modest aim, then.'

'My part of the tribe is with me. I hope that soon the Chatti and the Usipetes will be too. It's possible too that the rest of the Cherusci could be won over. If you were by my side, or better, elsewhere, spreading the word of your dream and what happened here today, we'd be sure to convince others to join us. What do you say?'

Segimundus did not reply. Arminius' heart hammered out a few unhappy beats, and he found that he was clenching his fists. Perhaps he had misjudged the priest? Damn it, he thought, his anger rising. I'll shut him up rather than let him squeal to the legate. Quite how he could get away with murdering Segimundus in the temple, he had no idea. A surreptitious look to either side, and down the room, told him that they were still alone. Turning a little so that Segimundus could not see, he let his right hand creep towards his sword hilt.

'Donar must have sent you.'

The fervour in the priest's voice was unmistakeable. Letting his hand drop to his side, Arminius faced Segimundus. 'Really?'

'Why else would things happen in such close succession? The dream, the diseased rams, and then you telling me of your plan?'

'So you'll help?'

'As Donar is my witness,' replied Segimundus, solemn-faced.

'I am grateful,' said Arminius, shaking his hand hard.

'We can talk tonight, in my quarters.'

Arminius felt a broad smile break out. 'I look forward to that.'

He walked out into the warm sunshine. Like his first ally, it seemed to have been sent by the thunder god himself.

Win over the chieftains of the various tribes next, he thought, and I will have an army.

Real excitement filled Arminius at that prospect. As for a time and a place to ambush Varus' legions, well, he had those in mind too.

Gods, but he could not wait until his plan came to fruition.

II

Senior centurion Lucius Cominius Tullus stood on the side of the road, close to the main, arched gate of Vetera. A rectangular, fortified camp, some nine hundred paces by six hundred in size, it was home to his legion, the Eighteenth, and had been a Roman base for more than twenty years. His wasn't an old unit by any means – it had been founded by Augustus half a century before, during the civil war that had brought him to power. The Eighteenth's first period of service had been in Aquitania. Just a few years later, it had been transferred to Vetera on the River Rhenus. When Tullus had been promoted to the centurionate fifteen years ago, he had been transferred into the Eighteenth from his old legion.

Tramp, tramp. The soldiers of Tullus' century marched past. Led by the standard-bearer, they were six men wide, twelve deep – a unit was never at complete strength – with his *optio* Fenestela near the back.

As each man passed Tullus, he took great care to square his shoulders and keep his shoulder-carried javelin at the right angle. Keen-eyed, expressionless, Tullus observed how good their equipment looked, and whether it showed any signs of wear, or damage. He'd spotted most of the problems when the legionaries had assembled outside their stone barracks: a loose armour plate here; a helmet cheekpiece missing its iron tie ring there. As then, none of it mattered enough to halt their progress. They'd been chastised, he thought, and would fix their kit upon their return. That, or they'd feel his *vitis*, vine cane, across their shoulders.

Now and again, Tullus' attention strayed to the camp's impressive fortifications. His home had been within for a decade and a half, and he wasn't yet tired of appreciating the defences. Everything about them exuded confidence, permanence and the power of Rome. First came the deep double ditch, with the spiked branches at the bottom of each. Behind those was the earthen rampart, built with the spoil from the ditches. It was taller than the loftiest cavalryman. The stone wall that sat atop it was even taller, and ran around the camp's entire perimeter.

Flashes of sunlight marked the sentries pacing to and fro on the rampart's walkway. Those who were in the twin towers spanning the gate observed Tullus with a faint air of superiority, their height and his patrol duty giving them immunity to any potential reprimand. Tullus' lips twitched with amusement. He'd acted much the same way as a young low-ranker, a lifetime before. As long as the sentries remained alert – and they appeared to be – he didn't care.

Even in these peaceful times, outside a camp containing a legion, it paid to be watchful. That was how he approached life, how he approached routine duties such as this. No one had had a problem with tribesmen this side of the river in years, but every time his legionaries marched beyond the walls, on duty, they – and he – were armed and equipped for battle.

Tullus was a solid man; middle-aged, but in excellent physical shape. Under his centurion's crested helmet and the felt liner that sat beneath it, he had short brown hair. A long jaw didn't stop him from being good-looking; nor did the pattern of scars that marked his body. He jerked his head as his optio, Marcus Crassus Fenestela, drew level. They paced together to the front of the unit, their gaze roaming over the tramping legionaries.

As Tullus walked, he studied Fenestela sidelong. It amused him that he and Fenestela were such physical opposites. Where he was solid, Fenestela was thin; where he was brawny, Fenestela was wiry. Fenestela's auburn, curly hair was longer than regulation cut, and his features were, as Tullus liked to joke, uneven. His ugliness wasn't helped by his bushy red beard. Tullus didn't give a shit about Fenestela's appearance, however. He and his optio had served together for many years. They had saved each other's lives on numerous occasions, and trusted each other inside and out.

'Happy?' Tullus asked at length.

'Aye, sir,' Fenestela replied, his keen eyes darting over the column. 'They look all right.'

'Even the green ones?' asked Tullus as they drew alongside two ranks of newish recruits. He was amused: although the soldiers' helmets and kit shone from polishing, and their gait was satisfactory, they were careful not to catch his eye.

'They're coming along,' Fenestela murmured.

'Look at Piso. He's got mismatched feet, or I'm no judge.' Tullus watched the tall soldier in the second rank of recruits. Despite the fact that he was furthest from Tullus, it was easy to spot his rolling step, the shield hanging at an awkward angle on his back.

'He's learning, sir,' said Fenestela. 'Another few months and he'll pass muster.'

'Aye.' Content that Piso, who'd made it through the tough initial training, would go on to become a decent soldier, Tullus' gaze strayed to the shining silver band that was the Rhenus. The river came from behind them to the right and ran parallel to the road at a distance of a couple of hundred paces. Half a mile onward, it flowed past the *vicus*, or civilian settlement, that served the massive military camp – their legion's base – to their rear. The watercourse's span was interrupted close to the vicus by large islands covered in trees, making it impossible to see the far bank, as they could from their current position. Germania Magna began on the other side, and it was where they were heading.

Discerning the direction of his gaze, Fenestela scowled. 'I don't like going over there, sir,' he muttered.

'You always say that, Fenestela. Any tribes still hostile to Rome live a hundred miles to the east, or more. The ones who live closer know better than to resist our rule. They've been taught enough lessons over the last twenty years.'

'Aye, sir.' Fenestela's tone revealed his doubt.

Tullus didn't comment. It was a topic that they had argued over countless times. According to Fenestela, he was overly trusting. Tullus thought his optio far too cynical. The longer Rome's rule lay upon a land, the less likely it was that there would be trouble. There hadn't been a major uprising close to the Rhenus for almost five years. If it continued, he mused, he could end his career in peacetime. That prospect appealed now more than it ever had – the price, perhaps, of seeing so many of his soldiers die in battle.

Despite the attraction of retirement, Tullus knew that he would sometimes miss the insanity of combat, when the blood pounded in his ears, and the men around him felt closer than brothers. He increased his pace, indicating that Fenestela should walk with him.

'Are we taking the usual route today, sir?' asked a soldier from the depths of the ranks.

'We are. Over the bridge at the vicus to the other side. Out the east road, alongside the River Lupia for about ten miles, and back again.' Tullus saw the sideways glances of the legionaries, and heard the low grumbling that followed. 'I make it just over twenty miles. An easy march,' he added, winking at Fenestela.

Fenestela returned the wink. 'Without their full kit they'll want to run it, sir.'

More muttering.

'That's an idea,' said Tullus. 'Maybe we'll double-time it back to the camp.'

As he'd expected, someone took the bait. 'There's no need for that, sir, surely?' called a voice from another rank, rendering the speaker invisible.

'I don't know,' declared Tullus, with a glance at Fenestela.

The faceless soldier and several others groaned.

'Don't give me reason to insist on it,' warned Tullus as Fenestela chuckled.

The complaints died away fast.

Tullus wasn't going to force his men to return to the camp at that pace, but there was no harm in them thinking it *might* happen. The uncertainty kept them on their toes. The last ranks of the century marched past once more, and he conferred with the *tesserarius*, the most junior of his officers. No one was lagging. Content, he and Fenestela trotted back up the patrol, resuming their positions in turn.

The straggling development of houses, businesses and stables that formed the outskirts of the vicus drew near. They harked back to the settlement's humble beginnings. Nowadays, most wanted to forget those rough times. The council talked of little but knocking the shacks and brothels to the ground, of grand new building projects and of a wall around the settlement's perimeter. Part of Tullus would be sorry when these inevitable changes came, because any sense that this was the frontier would depart with them. This part of Germania would be no different to anywhere in Italy, or Hispania, and the idea that one day citified dandies might look down their noses at him from the tables of a pricey inn stuck in his throat like a fish bone.

If the damn bridge over the Rhenus had been built in a direct line east of the camp rather than just outside the settlement, thought Tullus, such a thing could never happen. Yet the camp's position on high ground, back from the vicus, made tactical sense. As a result, soldiers had no option but to pass through it each time they had to venture over the river. And that, despite an officer's best intentions, meant an inevitable slowing in their pace. The instant that legionaries were spotted, every shop and restaurant owner, every trickster and wild-eyed soothsayer, every whore and vendor of trinkets, thronged to the side of the road, where they harangued the passing business. He could see them gathering already, could hear a red-cheeked woman bellowing about her delicious, fresh-cooked sausages.

Senior centurion and cohort commander Tullus might be, but he didn't have any legal jurisdiction over civilians. Nevertheless, he readied his vitis. In practice, he could do as he wished. If someone got too enthusiastic, he wouldn't hesitate to administer a sharp clout.

In they tramped, hobnails clashing on the paving stones, past the miserable shacks in which the poorest of the poor lived. Snot-nosed children in rags watched the armoured legionaries with wide eyes. 'Spare an *as*?' shouted the most confident one to no one in particular. The call was like the first drop from a raincloud. The urchins darted forward, yelling, running alongside the soldiers with outstretched hands. 'Got any bread, sir?' 'A coin, sir, a coin!' 'Want to screw my sister, sir? She's beautiful!'

Few men were interested in this first wave. Used to Tullus' close monitoring, they kept moving, giving as good as they got. 'I haven't got two *asses* to rub together,' Tullus heard Piso say. 'I wouldn't waste my money on little tykes like you,' declared another soldier. 'Your sister?' retorted a third. 'If she's got your looks, she's got webbing between her fingers and toes!'

Hurling insults, but quietly – they knew well the pain a kick from a studded sandal could deliver – the urchins withdrew.

As the next flood of hopefuls descended, Tullus sighed, and readied his vitis once more.

'Fresh bread, hot from the oven! Who'd like some?' 'A cup of wine for any of you brave men? I sell only the best vintages!' 'Look at you strong, handsome boys! One of you must have time for a little knee-trembler! Three *sestertii*, and I'll even let you kiss me!' The whore who'd made that offer wasn't as raddled as most in the settlement, and Tullus sensed the step of the legionaries nearest her waver. Wheeling out of rank, he was on her in half a dozen strides.

'They have other business right now. Clear off.'

She leered and pulled down the neck of her grimy robe, exposing her still pert breasts. 'A fine centurion like you must have the money to buy a feel of these – and more!'

'Go on, piss off!' Tullus' eyes appraised her chest even as he raised his vitis.

With a knowing pout, she retreated to the door of her hut, where she continued to entreat his men to come inside.

Tullus let her be. Fenestela, who was in the tenth rank, and the tesserarius, at the back, would ensure that no one dared to break formation. If it hadn't been for his other officers, however, he wouldn't have put it past one of his men to try and have a 'quickie'. It had been done by soldiers in other units before, without the centurion noticing, or so the gossip around the fires went in the evenings.

In the event, he didn't have to use his stick. The swarm of locals eased as they entered the vicus proper, where homes and businesses of a better class were situated. This was where many of the camp's legionaries, and not a few of the officers, had common-law wives. Invitations to come and eat, to drink wine, to buy weapons or trinkets for their girls, continued to rain down, but their path wasn't impeded. Laughter broke out among his soldiers when a pair of hefty tribeswomen with braided hair, sisters perhaps, spotted their common-law husbands in the century's midst and rained a barrage of abuse on both, complaining that neither man had given them as much as a *denarius* for the previous month. The miserable bastards needn't come back over the Rhenus, the women squawked, or set foot in their houses, until they gave them some money. The soldiers' muttered excuses that they hadn't yet been paid brought down further abuse. Hoots and jeers from their comrades added to the clamour.

'Keep moving!' roared Tullus, quelling his men's noise, if not that of their wives. He marched on, grateful to be free of such nagging. At times, he missed having a woman, but running his own soldiers as well as a cohort of six centuries more than filled his time. When the need came upon him, which was less often than it used to, he visited the best whorehouse in the settlement. Upon his retirement, there would be time to find a young bride, to raise a family. Until then, he was wedded to the army.

The buildings close to the vicus' forum were proud affairs, the homes of merchants who'd grown rich on the trade that flowed to and fro across the Rhenus. Studying a grandiose house, Tullus considered whether he'd have been happier selling wine, pottery and silver platters over the river in return for cattle, slaves and women's hair – the goods that Rome desired from Germania. He'd have made a fortune – could have owned a large property with central heating, private toilet facilities and a courtyard. Then, from the pavement, a veteran in a faded military tunic gave him a proud salute – with the stump of his right arm. Tullus returned the gesture, ashamed that he might consider anything other than being a soldier. The comradeship granted by a life in the legion was beyond price. Money came second to that – and it always would. Besides, his centurion's pension would be plenty to live on, and a sight more than the poor bastard with one hand received. He fumbled with the purse at his belt and tossed the man a denarius. Loud blessings followed him down the street.

Jupiter, Greatest and Best, grant that I see my final days out whole in mind and body, Tullus prayed. If that is not to happen, I wish for a swift death. In reflex, he rubbed the phallus amulet that hung from his neck. Why this dark mood? he asked himself as they took the street that ran towards the river. There's no call for it on this fine day.

'Off on patrol, sir?' called the lead sentry, one of eight legionaries outside a small building by the side of the crossing. The position was manned day and night.

'Yes. Lucius Cominius Tullus, senior centurion, Second Cohort of the Eighteenth.'

'Today's password, sir, if you please.'

'Roma Victrix.'

With a salute, the soldier stood aside.

Tullus led the way on to the stone arched bridge, which was wide enough for two carts or eight legionaries to pass abreast, and which spanned a section of the river that was a hundred and fifty paces wide. Beyond it, in midstream, was a narrow island, dotted with thickets of crab-apple trees. A party of off-duty soldiers joked with one another as they fished from the bank nearest the vicus. Further off, a crane perched by the water's edge. A paved road led straight across the islet to another island, via another, bigger bridge. Beyond that, a third bridge took the road to the eastern bank. The last one had been a bitch to construct, Tullus remembered. The river there was deep and fast-flowing. A number of men had drowned before the massive wooden piles that formed the foundations had been manoeuvred into place. Halfway across, a plaque commemorated the unit that had built it, and venerated Augustus with the words *Pontem perpetui mansurum in saecula* – 'I have built a bridge that will last forever'. You didn't build it, thought Tullus with a trace of anger. We did, with our sweat and blood. The names of the dead legionaries ought to have been inscribed on the stonework, but that was not Rome's way, or the army's, worse luck.

A second sentry post stood some five hundred paces away, over the widest section of the river. Being on the German side, it was a good deal larger than its fellow on the near bank, and held half a century of legionaries. As Tullus drew near to the bridge's end, an ox-drawn cart hove into view. The pair of beasts pulling it seemed most unhappy, bellowing and refusing to walk in a straight line. His view was obstructed as a trader leading two wagons full of dead-eyed slaves passed by. By the time he could see again, the cart driver – a soldier by his appearance – had been forced to take his vehicle off the road. Some of the men from the sentry post had gathered to watch. Their rude comments reached Tullus' ears. 'Call yourself a legionary?' 'You can't even control two damn bullocks!'

'Piss off!' retorted the man. 'It's not me that has them agitated, it's the smell of the damn bear.'

Tullus could feel his legionaries' gaze moving, as his was, to the rough-hewn cage that was tethered to the cart. The soldier and his companions were *ursarii*, whose job was to trap bears that could be used in the wooden amphitheatre which stood outside the camp. Beast hunts were an ever-popular form of entertainment for the garrison. To ensure a regular supply of animals, it had long been the practice to delegate soldiers to catch bears, wolves and deer in the forests east of the river. In Tullus' mind, hunting was far more enjoyable, but the displays were an easy way to keep the troops happy, and that mattered.

'Come on, Jupiter, the bear can't touch you. Easy, Mars!' said the *ursarius*, rubbing the bullocks' heads in turn. 'Nearly there. Just three bridges, and the vicus, and you'll be back in your pen.'

Tullus forgot the ursarius' woes as he greeted the officer in charge of the outpost. Their conversation had only just begun, however, before it was interrupted by the bawling of oxen.

'Excuse me,' said Tullus. He took a couple of steps towards the cart. 'Soldier!'

Despite the clamour of his beasts, the sweating ursarius heard him. He threw off a quick salute. 'Yes, sir?'

'Name?'

'Cessorinius Ammausias, sir. Ursarius to the Eighteenth.'

'Why in Hades' name are your oxen so panicked?'

'These are a new pair of oxen, sir. It's their first time with a bear in the cage. They'll be all right after a little rest, after I've talked to them.'

Several comments were hurled about Ammausias' relationship with his cattle, and he bunched his fists.

It wasn't the ursarius' fault, thought Tullus. 'Enough,' he cried, raising his vitis.

The jibes died away.

Ammausias threw him a grateful look. 'The bear will put on a good spectacle, sir. The brute is half again as big as any I've seen.'

'In that case, it should impress,' said Tullus, wondering how dangerous it would have been to hunt the bear.

A clatter of hooves on the road announced the arrival of a troop of German horsemen perhaps sixty strong. Cloaked, bearded, armed with shields and spears, they trotted towards the bridge in a disorganised mob. The behaviour wasn't uncommon, and Tullus rolled his eyes at the guard officer. 'They can wait until I get my men off the bridge. It's our road, not theirs.'

'I'll stop them, sir,' said the officer, stepping forward.

Before he could say a word, events took on a life of their own. This time, it wasn't the oxen that grew alarmed, but the bear. As some of the tribesmen rode up to the side of the cage for a better look, it launched itself at the bars, snapping and growling. Jupiter and Mars took instant fright. The lead rope was ripped from a startled Ammausias' hands and he was thrown to one side as the oxen barged down the gravelled embankment by the roadside. Their angle of descent forced the cart to take a different path to theirs, which unbalanced it at once. Within a few heartbeats, it had overturned. Wood splintered, oxen bellowed and Ammausias cursed in vain.

For all that he was in full armour, with almost eighty legionaries at his back, Tullus' heart skipped a beat as the bear burst free from the wreckage of the cage. Ammausias had not been exaggerating. It was a magnificent beast, with dense brown-yellowish fur and a large, rounded head with small ears. Yet for all its size, the bear wanted nothing more than to escape. Ignoring the oxen, and the crowd of watching soldiers, it lumbered down the slope towards the nearest stand of trees.

'Damn tribesmen,' Ammausias cried.

Fresh laughter broke out among those on the bridge, and Tullus smiled despite himself.

'Fetch the nets and ropes,' Ammausias called to his companions. 'We might still have a chance of catching it.'

Rather you than me, thought Tullus. Chasing down a large, angry bear, and then trying to restrain it, was a fearsome prospect. Even if the hunters succeeded, there was the tricky matter of transporting the beast to the camp. The cage was smashed beyond repair.

He hadn't expected the German horsemen to do anything other than look on in amusement. Urged on by their leader, however, a broad-shouldered man with a black mane of hair, they broke up and rode after the bear.

'This is more entertainment than I get in days of sentry duty, sir,' said the guard officer, chuckling.

'It's more than I get too,' replied Tullus. 'But it doesn't seem right that we're standing by while the Germans help to catch the creature.'

'They're the ones that scared the bear, sir.'

'All the same, it reflects badly on us if we do nothing.' Tullus turned his head. 'Fenestela! Get up here.'

Leaving his optio in charge of the patrol, Tullus led fifteen men off the road, following the direction taken by the bear. To his surprise, the Germans had already cornered the beast by the time they had caught up. The riders had driven it out of the shelter of a group of birch trees, and surrounded it in a loose circle of horses and inward-pointing spears. Every time it tried to flee, it was driven back by fierce charges from the warriors. Growling with rage, the bear roamed to and fro, probing their defences to no avail. Ammausias was conferring with the Germans' leader; his companions stood by, nets in hand.

Tullus stalked up, unnoticed.

'Can you catch it?' demanded the German in accented Latin.

'We've done it once, so we can do it again,' asserted Ammausias. 'It's roping the brute tight enough to carry it as far as the amphitheatre that will prove dangerous.'

'I can always order my men to back off,' said the German with a smile.

'No!'

'I jest with you.'

Ammausias let out a rueful chuckle.

Tullus cleared his throat. 'Can I be of help?'

Looking pleased, Ammausias glanced from Tullus to the German, who smiled, and back again. 'Yes, sir, thank you, sir. Your men could strengthen the circle, using their shields to fill the gaps between the horsemen.'

'Very good. You'll do the rest?'

'We'll net him as soon as your soldiers are in place, sir,' replied Ammausias, watching the bear. 'Best move fast, though. Soon he'll charge his way out, or get speared as he tries to do so.'

Tullus issued orders to his soldiers. 'Do your best not to get injured, brothers,' he urged, eliciting nervous laughs. Unslinging his own shield and stepping into the ring of men and horses, Tullus threw back his shoulders. They were here now. They would get it done.

To his relief, the bear was soon trapped. The moment that everyone had taken up his position, Ammausias and his comrades went into action. As one man distracted the bear by taunting it with a spear, the others crept in on it from behind. An angry charge at its tormentor was brought short by a well-flung rope that landed around its neck. That was drawn taut. A large weighted net followed, covering the bear from head to foot. It snapped, and ripped at the netting with its front paws, but soon entangled itself. Several men darted in, more cords in their hands. Tullus watched in amazement as they seized first one back paw and then the other, slipping loops of rope over the bear's limbs and securing them with running knots. One soldier got clawed on the arm, but his was the only wound suffered as the bear was trussed up like a giant hen for the pot.

Ammausias regarded Tullus and the German chieftain with satisfaction.

'You know how to restrain a beast,' said Tullus with respect.

'Aye, sir, I have to. My thanks to you both for your help. Once we've chopped down a few large branches for carrying poles, we can hump him back to the road. I'll commandeer a wagon to carry him back to the camp.'

The warrior's gaze fell on the bear. 'My people hunt these beasts, but in the wild. I do not understand why you would trap a creature only to kill it before thousands of people.'

Ammausias looked scornful, but was prudent enough to say nothing. With a salute, he left them to it.

'It is the Roman way,' Tullus explained. 'I too prefer to hunt, but the majority like to watch such spectacles from the safety of amphitheatre seats. There must be men of your kind who would do the same.'

The German laughed. 'You speak the truth. I may surround myself with warriors, but not everyone in my tribe is a fighter.'

Close up, the German was an impressive specimen. Muscles rippled under his wool shirt, and his thighs were as thick as small tree trunks. The fine silver brooch pinning his cloak at the shoulder and the yellow tassels on the garment's border revealed his high-born status. 'What tribe are you?' asked Tullus.

'Cherusci,' came the proud answer. Then, a wink. 'From the part of the tribe that's friendly towards Rome.'

'Ha!' said Tullus. Certain branches of the Cherusci had been indomitable enemies of the empire just a few years before. 'You're not one of Arminius' men, by any chance?' A centurion friend of Tullus had a high opinion of the Cheruscan officer, in the main because of his valour in the three-year Pannonian war, which was still dragging on.

There was a loud chuckle, and Tullus realised. '*You* are Arminius.'

'One and the same.' He leaned down, extending a hand.

'Lucius Cominius Tullus. Tullus.'

Arminius jerked a thumb at Tullus' helmet. 'Senior centurion?'

'Aye. You're an auxiliary prefect, I understand. I should call you "sir", by rights.'

Arminius chuckled again. 'There's no need for that. We're not on parade, are we?'

Tullus found himself warming to Arminius' informal and genial manner. 'Where are you stationed?'

'I command the ala that's attached to the Seventeenth, at Ara Ubiorum.'

The great base at Ara Ubiorum, home to two legions, was more than fifty miles away. It was also on the west bank of the Rhenus, but Tullus was used to German tribesmen taking the longer route north, via the opposite side. 'Been on leave?'

'We have been, me and my boys. The camp commander let us go ten days ago. Told us to meet up with the Seventeenth again here, before the summer march into Germania.'

Tullus nodded. That made sense.

'Varus wants to talk to me.'

Publius Quinctilius Varus was the governor of Germania, and the commander of five legions. He'd been in the Eighteenth's camp for some time, preparing for the campaign ahead. Tullus knew him by sight, and had heard him speak on a number of occasions, but he had never been introduced to the man. 'You know Varus?'

Arminius shrugged. 'We get on well, aye.'

Tullus felt a flicker of irritation that a German chieftain should be a friend of his supreme commander, when he, a veteran Roman officer of more than twenty-five years' service, was not. It wasn't altogether surprising, though. Arminius' cavalry detachment was similar in size to a cohort. He was a high-ranking noble of his tribe, a Roman citizen and, as everyone knew, an honorary equestrian. The last detail rankled a little. Just a little. 'Well, when Varus has finished with you, come to my barracks. We can share a jug of wine.'

'I will take you up on that offer,' said Arminius, grinning. 'Until then.' So that was Arminius, thought Tullus, watching the Cheruscan ride away. He tries hard, but he seems like a good sort.

III

Publius Quinctilius Varus was sitting at a desk in the office of the legate Gaius Numonius Vala, a room that he had commandeered since his arrival. Although his red tunic was of the finest quality, he was an unremarkable-looking short man with thinning, curly grey hair and a slight paunch. Despite his luxurious surroundings – heavy wooden furniture, expensive busts of the emperor, an ornate candelabra – the office felt to him like a prison.

'Are we nearly done?' he asked, knowing from the heap of documents and tablets on the desk that they were not.

His secretary Aristides, a rotund Greek slave who'd been with him for longer than he could remember, let out a practised sigh. 'No, master. We have worked our way through perhaps half of them.'

Varus rubbed a hand across his weary eyes. 'If I'd known that my life would be ruled by paperwork, I never would have started this career,' he grumbled.

Aristides, who was standing behind his left shoulder, said nothing.

'Don't give me that look,' said Varus, whipping his head around.

Aristides' face was a blank. 'What look, master?'

'The disbelieving one, when you lift an eyebrow.'

The corners of Aristides' mouth moved a little. 'I'm not sure I know what you mean, master.'

'Liar. I just didn't catch you.' Varus smiled. 'You know me too well, Aristides.'

A trace of smugness entered Aristides' expression. 'After this long, master, I would be a fool if I didn't.'

'I have no real reason to be unhappy,' admitted Varus. 'After returning to Rome from Syria, I spent my time moaning that I had nothing to do. When Augustus offered me the governorship of Germania a little more than two years ago, I was overjoyed. I am governor of one of the most important provinces in the empire. Better these, here' – he slapped a hand on to the documents – 'than having to sit on my hands, listening to my wife's complaints about the prices that her dressmaker charges.'

'You are happier when you're working, master.'

'Yes, I am,' declared Varus. 'Fetch me some of that Gaulish vintage I like, and we'll get through the rest of these papers in no time.'

Despite his master's robust words, it was telling that he should ask for wine when it was just after midday. Ever discreet, Aristides kept his thoughts to himself. Calling for the slave who stood by the door to the office, he ordered wine to be brought.

By the time that Varus had finished his first cup, they had dealt with a bundle of letters from Lucius Nonius Asprenas, the legate based at Mogontiacum, two hundred miles up the river from Vetera. Asprenas, Varus' nephew, was an able administrator and commander, and his communications consisted of reports and straightforward requests that were easy to deal with. Varus dictated his replies to Aristides, who scribbled notes in cursive on a waxed wooden tablet, to be written out in full later. This done, Varus tackled the next pile of documents, which consisted of grievances from German tribal leaders locally and further afield, and appeals for a surgeon from the camp commander at Aliso, and for supplies of iron and bronze from the senior officer at the fort of Confluentes. A merchant in Bonna complained about extortions he'd been forced to pay to soldiers when transporting his goods through the settlement. 'When I protested,' the merchant wrote, 'I was beaten on the street, like a stray dog. I went at once to the camp commander, who laughed in my face. In desperation, I, a Roman citizen, write to you,

Publius Quinctilius Varus, representative of Augustus himself. I ask for nothing but justice.'

'Gods above,' said Varus, frustrated. 'What can I do to remedy this?'

Again Aristides said nothing. Like as not, the merchant was telling the truth. It was standard practice for soldiers guarding the empire's roads to extract tolls from passing traders, and to manhandle those who objected. He knew it. Varus knew it.

Varus thought for a moment. 'Write to the fort commander in Bonna. Tell him that he is to receive this merchant with respect, and listen to his accusations for a second time. If the man's charges can be proved, he is to return what was stolen, using monies from the garrison's pay chest. If they cannot, he is to give his soldiers an unofficial warning not to be so damn greedy. You are also to send word to the merchant, expressing regret that he is unhappy with the treatment he received from my troops. Be careful not to admit that there has been any wrongdoing. Inform him that I have instructed the commander to meet him and hear his complaint again, with an impartial ear.' He waited until Aristides had finished scribbling on his wax tablet. 'Got all that?'

There was a little sigh. 'Of course, master.'

'Good.' Varus threw a baleful look at the stack of correspondence, which was still substantial. 'Although I'll miss the comforts of a permanent camp, it will be good to leave this place behind.'

'You mean our summer march to the east, master?' This time, Aristides made no attempt to conceal his distaste.

'Yes. Three months of good weather and hunting, during which official letters will find it difficult to find me. There'll be bookkeeping to be done, but it will be nothing compared to the volume I receive here. You'll be able to deal with most of it. When we return in the autumn, a mountain of documents will cover this desk, but I don't care.' Varus saw Aristides' expression, and chuckled. 'You shall have your hot baths while we're away, from time to time at least. Slave you might be, but you cannot say I do not look after you.'

'You do, master, thank you,' said Aristides, his frown easing. 'I am ever grateful.'

'I haven't forgotten my promise to you either. When my term as governor is up, you will receive your manumission. You've served me well; it's the least I can do.'

'Publius Quinctilius Varus, you are the finest master that a slave could wish for,' said Aristides, beaming from ear to ear. He bowed. 'Gratitude.'

'Are you now content to travel into the wilds of Germania?' asked Varus with a smile.

'Will there be any fighting, master?'

Varus didn't look down on Aristides for being afraid. He was a scholar, not a soldier. 'I doubt it. Things seem to be quiet on the other side of the river. Besides, more than ten thousand legionaries will be accompanying us. No hostile tribesmen in their right minds would come within miles of our camp.'

Aristides looked pleased. 'Very good, master.'

'Back to work then.' Varus picked up a wooden tablet and broke the seal on the string that held its two parts together. Opening it, he began to read. 'Ah. This is from the commander at Fectio. His news is good, and he asks for nothing, which makes a change from most of these wretched communications.'

'What does he say, master?'

'Almost his entire fleet – triremes, biremes and troop transports – is seaworthy. He places them at my disposal for the coming months, and awaits any orders.' Varus rubbed a finger along his lips. 'It's a shame that I won't have reason to call on him this summer. Still, never mind. Better to have ships that I don't need rather than the other way around.'

'True, master. Do you wish to reply?'

'Yes. Congratulate him on his fleet's readiness. There are no special plans for the fleet at this time, so the normal patrols of the seas and the local waterways are to continue. Inform him that I will be marching east for the summer, taking legions Seventeen, Eighteen and Nineteen. Once the taxes have been collected, and the harvest is in, we will return to the Rhenus and winter quarters. He can expect a visit from me soon after that.'

Varus was still waiting for Aristides to finish writing down his instructions when there was a rap on the door. 'Come,' he called.

One of the two legionaries stationed outside marched in and saluted. 'The new tribune is here to see you, sir.'

Varus' eyebrows rose, and he shot a look at Aristides. 'Again?'

Aristides gave a faint, diplomatic shrug.

'Send him in,' ordered Varus.

A moment later, the tribune entered. He marched to within a few steps of Varus' desk and stood to attention. 'Senior tribune Lucius Seius Tubero, sir!'

'Tribune.' Varus studied Tubero's blue eyes, blond curls and chiselled chin. His breastplate and boots had been buffed beyond even parade standard. Good looks and shiny kit don't make you a soldier, Varus thought. Be fair, he told himself a heartbeat later. This is the boy's first military posting. He's young and enthusiastic, and wants to prove his worth. I was like that once.

'Did I come at a bad time, sir?' Tubero glanced at the mounds of paperwork.

'There's never a good time for a governor; perhaps you'll learn that one day.' It was Varus' practice to find out everything possible about his new officers before they arrived. Tubero was only seventeen, young indeed to be a senior tribune, but his breeding was good. More important was that his father was a friend of Augustus, which explained his posting to the Eighteenth as its second-in-command. If Tubero kept his nose clean, and showed some ability over the next decade of his service and more, and if his family didn't fall from favour, there was every chance that he might end up as the governor of a province. Varus hoped that Tubero would prove 'easy to manage'. He had enough to do without having to nursemaid yet another spoiled brat.

'If it's not convenient now, sir, I—'

'Stay,' ordered Varus. 'A short break from my administrative duties is always welcome.'

'Thank you, sir.'

'What brings you to my door?'

'I've been here for a few days, sir . . .' Tubero hesitated.

'Are you settling in? I trust that your quarters are satisfactory?'

'Everything's fine in those regards, thank you, sir.'

'Is the legate giving you a hard time?'

'No, sir. He's been very helpful, instructing me in my duties.'

'Has one of the centurions been insolent?' This was a common occurrence. Veteran centurions often took a dim view of the young aristocrats who swanned in from Rome to command them. 'Or one of the junior tribunes?'

'It's not that, sir.'

Varus' interest was piqued. 'What is it then?'

'It seems quiet, sir. There's no . . . trouble.'

Here we go, thought Varus in amusement. 'That's a *good* thing, tribune. Peace is something to be valued. It means that the empire's business can carry on without interruption.'

'Of course, sir, it's just that I . . .'

Remembering his early years in the army, Varus asked, 'You want to see some action?'

'Yes, sir!'

Varus ignored Aristides' little *phhhh* of contempt. 'Your posting here will be for at least a year, tribune. In other words, there will be plenty of time for you to draw your sword in anger.'

Tubero's nod was unhappy.

'Oh, for the eagerness of youth,' said Varus, thinking: There's nothing wrong with humouring him in this matter. He's well connected, after all. 'What would you like to do – lead a patrol over the river?'

'That would be wonderful, thank you, sir,' replied Tubero, his face lighting up.

'Fine. You can take my latest orders to the camp commander at the fort of Aliso. It's two days' easy march to the east, on the River Lupia. You'll pass a number of settlements as you go. Venturing that far into Germania should give you a feel for the land and the tribes. There shouldn't be any trouble. After you've delivered the letters and received the commander's replies, you will return.'

'My sincere thanks, sir.'

'A cohort should be more than sufficient. I'll have a word with Vala. He can ensure that the senior centurion in charge of the men is a solid type.'

Tubero flushed a little. 'I don't need anyone to hold my hand, sir.'

'Let me be the judge of that, tribune. That the imperial peace should continue in Germania is my responsibility, not yours.'

'Yes, sir,' said Tubero, the reluctance loud in his voice. 'Had you anyone in mind?'

'As it happens, I have – a senior centurion called Tullus. Have you come across him yet?'

'No, sir.' Tubero somehow conveyed in the two words his scorn for those lower in rank than he.

Varus began to grow a little irritated. 'Two things, tribune. The first is that it behoves you to make the acquaintance of every cohort commander in the Eighteenth. In an ideal world, you would also get to know every centurion. It's not been long since you arrived, yet you ought at least to have heard of Tullus. He's a highly decorated, well-thought-of officer, with more than twenty-five years' service under his belt. Everyone esteems him, from Legate Vala to the lowest ranker. I've heard it said that he's one of the best-loved officers in the legion.'

Like so many youths, Tubero could affect a disinterested look to perfection, thought Varus, his temper rising. 'You will treat Tullus with the respect he deserves. Clear?'

Tubero cleared his throat. 'Yes, sir.'

'Secondly, a word of advice. Going about with your nose in the air while you're here will earn you few friends, and more than one enemy. Those of lower station have to obey you, but if you treat them like dirt, they will make your life difficult. Orders will be followed at the slowest pace possible, or "forgotten", or misplaced. Do you understand?'

'I do, sir,' muttered Tubero.

'Good. You'll receive your orders for the patrol by nightfall. Dismissed.' Varus' acknowledgment of Tubero's salute was curt. When they were alone, he looked at Aristides. 'The young always know best, eh?'

'It has ever been thus, sir.'

Varus sighed. 'I was the same, I suppose, and so were you. If he's tempered in the right way, Tubero will probably make a fine soldier.'

'Indeed, sir.'

'I'll dictate Tubero's and Tullus' orders later. For now, we had best finish with this damn lot' – Varus slapped the stack of documents – 'or we'll still be here at dawn.'

Late-afternoon sun bathed the clearing where Arminius and his men had stopped, a short distance from the road that led east from Vetera to the fort of Aliso. The unit's hobbled horses were grazing beyond the cluster of lean-tos and tents. Piles of equipment were stacked close by: standards, helmets, mail shirts, swords, spears and shields. Some of the warriors sat about on their blankets, talking and cooking, while others wrestled with one another or gathered fuel and water. From a nearby birch, a blackbird shrilled its indignation at the intruders on its territory.

Arminius was sitting with several men by the fire outside his lean-to when a sentry arrived, looking excited. 'Maelo is here,' he announced.

'Bring him to me.' Arminius had been expecting his second-in-command, who had left Ara Ubiorum a few days after him. The warrior hurried off, and Arminius leaned over the cauldron that was suspended from a tripod above the flames. The venison stew within was from a deer that he'd brought down with an arrow some hours before. Its butchered carcase was still hanging from a branch on the nearest tree.

'Ho, Arminius!' called a voice. Maelo stalked up, and he and Arminius embraced. The other warriors didn't rise, but they greeted him with respect. Brown-haired, Maelo was of medium build, but he was as solid as a block of stone. He leaned over the pot. 'It smells good. What is it, venison?'

'Aye. We've been hunting.' Arminius indicated the carcase.

After a little talk about the day's sport, Maelo's expression grew serious. 'Which chieftains did you manage to speak to?' he asked in a low voice.

'Only those of the Chatti and the Usipetes,' Arminius replied.

'There'll be time enough to talk to the other tribes later, once the legions march east. How did you fare?'

Arminius' eyes flickered at the others present, and back to Maelo.

Maelo took his meaning. 'Let's take a walk.'

'Yes.' Arminius stirred the stew, before tasting a spoonful. 'It's good. Don't let it burn,' he ordered one of his men. He scooped up two lengths of fishing line and hooks from the entrance to his lean-to. 'Follow me,' he said to Maelo. 'There's a stream not far off where we might catch some bream, even a salmon if we're lucky.'

'Salmon *as well as* venison? Lead on,' said Maelo.

They walked a distance from the men before Arminius spoke again. 'You shouldn't have said a word until we were alone. They mix with Roman soldiers all the time!'

'Every one of them is a warrior of your own damn clan, Arminius,' protested Maelo.

Arminius' frown eased, but then returned. 'Imagine, though, what might happen when we're on the other side of the river, and they're on the piss in the inns and catching the pox in the whorehouses. A man's tongue loosens when he's got a bellyful of wine, or a whore has sucked him dry. Most people don't pay any attention to drunken gossip, but it would only take one filthy Roman to hear something suspicious for word to reach Varus. All our hard work would be undone, just like that.'

'I won't mention it again.'

Arminius clapped him on the shoulder. He trusted Maelo as few others; the man had saved his life more than once.

Reaching the stream, they sat, baited their hooks and tossed the lines into the water. 'Tell me then!' demanded Maelo. 'How were you received? Do you bring good news or bad?'

'For the most part, it's good. The Chatti didn't take much convincing, which was no surprise. I think their chieftains might have been planning something. I was accused of being an upstart Cheruscan, and trying to steal their thunder. I kept calm, and praised them to the heavens as mighty warriors, and told them that they'd be free to do as they wished once the battle started.'

'Will they wait?'

'I think so. Their priests said that as long as the omens continued to be good, the Chatti would do well by rising against Rome with us. One of their oldest chiefs spoke in my favour, saying that I knew the empire's ways, and how its soldiers fought.' Arminius' grey eyes took on a darker, colder colour. 'That I would spring the best ambush, which would cause the most casualties.'

'And so you will, brother!' Maelo agreed. 'Varus likes you. He trusts you. When you fill his ears with tales of a tribal uprising, he'll lead his army off the Roman road just as we have talked about.'

'I need at least four tribes on our side first,' said Arminius, chewing a nail. 'Varus won't march east of the Rhenus without two to three legions at his back.'

'We have three tribes already.'

'Two.'

'The Usipetes weren't convinced by your plan?'

'I thought at first that the chieftains would agree, but when they took a vote, the majority voted against joining us.'

'Pah! Was it because of their dislike of the Chatti?'

'That was part of it only. I persuaded them that they need not have anything to do with each other. They could camp apart, and fight in different areas. It was more because their lands run right up to the bridge to Vetera.'

'When the legions cross the river in anger, it's their people who die first, and their settlements that are burned.'

'If there was a way to guarantee victory, one priest said, they'd be with us, but without that, it pays to be prudent.'

'Understandable. Nothing can be guaranteed in this life.'

'Except death, and Roman taxes.'

There was a bitter tinge to their laughter. 'If the Usipetes won't join us, the other tribes might not either,' Maelo said at length.

'Aye.'

There was a silence, during which Arminius' face grew stern and determined. When he spoke, his voice was granite hard. 'We have the priest Segimundus' support. His words, and his dream of the burning eagle, will convince many to join us. I *know* it.'

IV

Tullus strode up to the principia in the centre of the camp. Recognising him, if not by his face, then by his centurion's crested helmet, the sentries guarding the headquarters saluted and stood back to allow him entrance. In the passageway beyond, Tullus returned the greetings of first one officer he knew, and then another. He was further delayed in the courtyard, waylaid by one of the Eighteenth's tribunes, a talkative type who liked to do things by the book. Bored to tears by the tribune's droning, Tullus could do nothing but endure. He managed to extricate himself in the end, promising the tribune that he *would* order spare winter cloaks for his cohort at the first opportunity, and check that the other senior centurions had done so too.

It wasn't unknown for the tribune to remember other 'vital' tasks the moment one had left his company, so Tullus hurried to put a party of document-carrying clerks between them. Affecting a nonchalant walk, he made it to the safety of the colonnaded walkway before the clerks broke away, one by one, into various offices. At that stage, Tullus was far enough from the tribune to be able to saunter around the passage to the great hall, the front of which formed the courtyard's entire back wall.

The building's massive, iron-bound doors stood wide open, as they did every day from dawn to dusk. They were only closed during the hours of darkness, and when important meetings were being held. The sentries here were present more to reflect the hall's importance than the need for security. Tullus returned their salutes with a nod, and entered.

The vast room within was dominated by a double row of massive columns that ran from left to right, holding up the high roof. In the spaces between, larger-than-life-sized painted statues of Augustus and his immediate family had been placed. There were few people about. Three ordinary legionaries in belted tunics were sweeping the floor. A priest was praying before the largest effigy of the emperor. Puffed up with his own importance, a quartermaster stalked past, accompanied by two soldiers carrying a heavy chest. No one gave Tullus, a high-ranking officer, more than a cursory glance, which suited him well. He was not here for conversation, or to be accosted by those higher, or lower, in rank. As was his custom before going on patrol, he was here to pay his respects to his legion's eagle.

Placing his boots down with care, so that his hobs didn't make too much noise, he made his way across the mosaic floor to the back wall and the shrine. A pair of legionaries stood guard at its entrance, one either side of the double stone archway. They stiffened to attention. 'Centurion,' one murmured.

'Is anyone inside?' asked Tullus, peering in. It was often impossible, but unspoken protocol dictated that praying soldiers should be left alone within the sacred space.

'You're in luck, sir. The *aquilifer* has just left.' The soldier whose job it was to carry the eagle checked on the standard once daily.

Pleased to have the place to himself, Tullus walked inside. Light, cast by a multitude of well-placed oil lamps, glittered off the stuccoed walls and the ceiling, and reflected off gold and silver emblems – images of the emperor, discs, human hands, spear tips, laurel wreaths – on the dozens of standards that were propped up against the back wall. To the left and right of the standards were the embroidered cloth banners used by detachments from the legion, and the imposing cavalry standards. In the centre of all, with a space on either side to indicate its status, the legion's eagle had been placed in a special rosewood stand. A physical embodiment of everything that was noble about the Eighteenth, it was an awe-inspiring sight.

Compared to most, Tullus was not superstitious; much of the time, he didn't place a lot of faith in the gods either. In this room, he felt different. A sense of reverence fell over him now, as it did with each visit. The deep silence helped – no one spoke in the shrine unless there was great need – and so too did the dazzling light cast by the abundant precious metal on display. The standard of a man's century and his cohort were also causes for pride, as were the battle awards affixed to their staffs. Yet the main reason for Tullus to bow, and for the hairs to stand on his neck, was the overwhelming sense of majesty emitted by the eagle.

Cast from solid gold, and larger than a man could hold in both hands, the eagle was depicted lying forward on its breast. A golden wreath encircled its almost-touching wings, which were raised straight up behind its body. Its open beak and piercing stare gave off a real sense of arrogance. I know my purpose, and what I represent, it seemed to say. Do you, Tullus? Will you follow me, even unto death? Will you protect me at all costs?

I will, he thought, closing his eyes, as I would have done since the first day I enlisted. I live only to honour you, and my legion. I swear this by every god in the pantheon.

Tullus' heart thudded in his chest, ten, twenty, fifty times. There was no answer from the eagle. There never was, but a gradual sense of acceptance stole over him, as if his promise had been received, as if the eagle would watch over him on the impending patrol. He looked up.

You are a true soldier of the Eighteenth, the eagle's eyes seemed to say. You are one of mine.

That was all Tullus ever wanted to be.

Tramp, tramp, tramp. Scchhhkkk-thunk. Scchhhkkk-thunk. The comforting sounds, of hobnails striking the road surface, and of mail shirts knocking off the back of shields, filled Tullus' ears. He was riding alongside his century, which was positioned third along the column, a vantage point that allowed him to ascertain – should he need to – what was going on at the front and back, and to either side. Separated by strips of cultivation, German longhouses dotted the landscape. Boys stood watch over small groups of sheep and cattle. At the edge of a copse, a dozen bare-chested men toiled together, felling trees.

This was the second day of their patrol, and they were nearing Aliso. Things had gone well thus far. From the start, the new tribune Tubero had been as keen as a leashed hunting dog with the scent of game in its nostrils, but he had listened – albeit with reluctance – to Tullus' advice. Moreover, he had followed it, which had been a relief to Tullus. Varus had sent a note on the eve of their departure, ordering Tullus to ensure that 'nothing untoward' happened while they were gone. Despite Tubero's seniority, there was no doubt on whose shoulders the responsibility for the patrol fell.

Tullus didn't know where Tubero was at that exact moment. Although that meant he had no one watching him, that the potential for trouble existed, oddly Tullus did not care. There was something about Tubero that ruffled his feathers the wrong way. He couldn't decide if it was the tribune's condescending manner or the faint air of disbelief he exuded every time Tullus expressed an opinion – or whether it was something else altogether. When he wasn't about, Tullus could feel less irritated, even if he then grew a little concerned about what Tubero might be up to. Don't worry, he thought. The young cock's only riding about as if he's the emperor, impressing the natives with his finery while he makes derogatory comments about them under his breath.

After an uneventful first day, they had slept the night in a marching camp twenty miles from the Rhenus. Built during a long-since-forgotten campaign, it had been left in place for passing units to avail themselves of, and was popular among soldiers. Its solid earth ramparts and deep ditches meant an escape from their usual obligation of constructing a camp at the end of a day's march. These lighter duties, and an uninterrupted night's sleep, had ensured that the fourteen miles to Aliso had sped by. Using the regular stone markers at the side of the road, Tullus reckoned that they were exceeding four miles an hour. Being able to maintain that speed was expected of legionaries, but it wasn't often insisted upon, because it wore men out fast. Yet when high spirits drove them to act in such a manner, as it was right now, Tullus wasn't one to stand in their way.

He wouldn't have admitted it to a soul apart from Fenestela, but the fast pace made him grateful for his mount. Tullus had taken to riding of recent times, because of his aching back and creaking joints. He would have coped today, but he'd have paid for it later. Most of his legionaries were fifteen years younger than he, or more.

Horse or no, Tullus was looking forward to reaching Aliso. Like the marching camp they had stayed in, it was favoured among legionaries, because of its size, and empty barracks. It too had been constructed during previous campaigns and was large enough to house a legion, but the usual garrison nowadays comprised a single cohort and two *turmae* of cavalry. Even a second cohort, the troops assigned to Lucius Caedicius, the newly arrived camp prefect, wouldn't come close to filling the rows and rows of timbered barrack blocks. In Aliso, thought Tullus with anticipation, everyone could expect a bed for the night, and a solid roof over his head. Those small luxuries were to be appreciated, for on many patrols such things were a rarity.

'Look out, brothers. Here comes the senior tribune again,' announced a legionary several ranks in front.

Tullus felt a dart of irritation at the resulting straightening of backs, shifting of yokes and throwing back of shoulders. Tubero had been issuing reprimands of one kind or another at soldiers throughout the patrol, but he hadn't commented on Tullus' century. Yet. If it happened now, Tullus wasn't sure he'd be able to hold his tongue.

He watched as Tubero came cantering down the road, his mount's hooves throwing up little puffs of dust. His entourage of two staff officers and a scribe followed close behind. It was satisfying that he said nothing about Tullus' legionaries.

Tubero slowed up at last. 'Centurion.'

'Sir. See anything of interest?'

'We rode as far as the fort. It's an impressive structure, and built in a good spot. It's near the River Lupia, but high enough above it to have a range of vision all around.'

'You've got the right of it there, sir,' said Tullus, thinking a man would have to be blind not to notice its strength of position. 'They're expecting us then?'

'I told the sentry to inform Lucius Caedicius of our imminent arrival.' He cast an impatient eye at the ranks of passing legionaries, and his nostrils flared in the way that so annoyed Tullus. 'That is, if these shirkers can be bothered to march at a respectable speed.'

Tullus had to bite his lip before he answered. 'They're covering more than four miles an hour, sir.'

'Does the Eighteenth not pride itself on the quality of its soldiers?'

You pompous little prick, thought Tullus. 'It does, sir.'

'Then why aren't they doing more than that, centurion?'

'Because I haven't asked them to, sir,' replied Tullus. He didn't need to add, 'I'm the one who's really in charge here.' Even as Tubero's mouth opened in outrage, Tullus interrupted, so only the tribune could hear. 'It's two miles and more to Aliso still. We're on a routine patrol, sir, carrying non-urgent messages from Varus. There's no need to push them any harder. Imagine – the gods forbid – that an emergency were to arise and they were too tired to march off in response. I'd never forgive myself. Would you, sir?'

Tubero gave Tullus a petulant look. 'I suppose not. Leave them be then.'

'Wise words, sir,' said Tullus in a diplomatic tone.

An angry glance from Tubero. 'There's no reason why I should linger here. I'll return to the camp and give Varus' letters to Caedicius.'

'Very good, sir,' replied Tullus. *Good riddance.*

The legionary Marcus Piso and the seven others in his *contubernium* had been allocated a room at the far end of the barracks' corridor. It was furthest from the centurion Tullus' quarters, which pleased everyone. They wouldn't escape his scrutiny, but there would be some warning of his approach.

Piso, a tall man, came into the room last, having been the final member of the group to enter the building, which was situated some distance from Aliso's main gate. He dumped his weapons in the tiny room opposite their bedchamber and went to find a bed. To his annoyance, the only spot that didn't already have a soldier or some equipment on it was a top bunk. He rolled his eyes, and clambered up the two rungs to his bed. In the process, he knocked his head against the low ceiling, hard. Rolling on to the mattress, he groaned. 'Jupiter's sweaty arse crack.'

'Take off your armour first, stupid,' said one of his tent mates from the opposite bunk.

'I wanted to rest my legs for a moment,' Piso complained.

'You're tired after that short march?' asked Vitellius, the man below him. He was an acerbic individual whom Piso didn't like much, not least because Vitellius made him feel that he wasn't yet part of the contubernium, or even, he'd said once, a real soldier.

'That's not what I meant,' said Piso, bristling. 'The idea of a bed was appealing, that's all.'

'It is to me too,' came the reply. 'But I thought to lose my mail shirt before I lay down.'

Piso rubbed the swelling lump on the top of his skull. 'That was about the only part of me that didn't hurt.'

'Always complaining, aren't you?' jibed Vitellius.

Afer, one of four other veterans in the contubernium, and the one who'd been most decent to Piso since his arrival a few months before, weighed in. 'That's a little rich coming from you, Vitellius. I remember the time you caught crabs in Vetera's cheapest brothel. You spent months moaning about it, and keeping us awake with your scratching.'

The laughter drowned out Vitellius' sour rejoinder, and Piso gave Afer a grateful look. Afer, a hairy barrel of a man from one of the roughest parts of Mutina, winked back. Piso felt a rush of gratitude. He used the diversion of the general hilarity to get down from the bunk and return to the equipment store. He'd undone his belt and was attempting, without success, to shuck the mail shirt up on to his shoulders – from there it was easy to take off – when he sensed someone behind him. Thinking it was Vitellius, come to mock him further, he wheeled with bunched fists.

'Easy, brother,' said Afer, raising his hands.

'Sorry. I thought it was—'

'I know. Don't mind Vitellius. He's a bitter prick, but when it comes to a fight, he's a good man to have beside you.' Afer smiled at Piso's disbelief. 'It's true. He saved my skin in Illyricum once when I'd already seen the ferryman poling his way across the Styx to pick me up. Killed two tribesmen, he did, and got himself wounded in the process. And before you ask, it wasn't just because I was an old comrade. I've seen him do the same for new lads too. If you're in his contubernium, he looks out for you, same as we all do. He's just got an interesting sense of humour.'

'Interesting? Ha!'

'Here.' Afer held out his hands, and Piso heaved his shirt up again. This time, Afer was there to grab it and heave it up to the sweet spot, just below his shoulders. With a groan, Piso brought it up over his head. He was ready for the balance of its weight to shift, and moved his feet back as it spilled on to the floor with a loud *thunk*. 'Thanks.'

Afer was halfway back to the bunkroom. 'Got any wine?' he called over his shoulder.

'I wish.'

'Go and find some, eh?'

There was a loud chorus of agreement from the rest.

Piso wanted to lie down for a bit, but Afer's intervention had meant a lot. He tested the weight of the purse that hung from his belt and judged it held enough coinage to buy wine for them all. It had been a good idea to be careful with the advance he'd been given upon enlistment – the next payday wasn't for some time. 'I will,' he said, catching the empty leather skin that Afer flung out to him, 'but it won't be my turn again until each of you shower of shits has bought some too.'

Ignoring the whistles and insults that followed, he strapped on his belt, adjusted his tunic, checked that his dagger was in place. The abuse was to be expected. Being in the army wasn't that different to spending his entire time with a group of his boyhood friends in northern Italy. Checking that Tullus was nowhere in sight – he wasn't doing anything wrong, but the centurion always managed to find a fault of some kind with his appearance or kit – Piso sloped out of the barracks door.

There were plenty of legionaries from the patrol about. Some were lighting fires to cook their evening meal. Others had kit to repair and were doing it outside, where the light was better. Two men were playing dice in the dirt, watched by their friends. A pair with more energy than most were wrestling together, grappling and trying to throw the other to the ground. Wagers were being made on which of them would go down first. Piso was tempted to watch, even to gamble, but his thirst won out. 'Anyone found a place to buy wine?' he asked.

'Try the avenues around the garrison's barracks,' advised a legionary. 'There'll be someone flogging it around there.'

Muttering his thanks, Piso walked towards the main gate, where the resident soldiers lived. As he rounded the corner on to the *via praetoria*, an optio passed by. The man wasn't from Piso's unit; nonetheless, he averted his gaze and breathed easier when the officer had gone. Piso had always been a little clumsy, perhaps because he was so tall, but it had never mattered much until he had joined the army. Everything had to be done *just so*, and if it wasn't, officers like Fenestela and Tullus let him know about it in no uncertain terms. Still, he seemed to be getting the hang of most things at last. Keeping his clothing and equipment clean and ready for use, wearing his uniform in the correct manner, marching in step and weapons training were all routine tasks now.

In the event, it didn't take Piso long to find some wine. A white-haired Phoenician with deep brown skin – 'The only one of my race to trade in Germania,' he boasted at the top of his voice – was hawking an assortment of goods from a portable stall near the camp's entrance. He had fish sauce and olive oil in little pots, aromatic herbs, and exotic spices wrapped in twists of fabric – black pepper, coriander and cumin. What he was selling most of, however, was wine. Piso listened as the Phoenician recommended half a dozen vintages, all of which cost more than he could afford, before plumping for a skinful of the cheapest variety. Even that cost a deal more than it did in Vetera, but when he protested, the Phoenician gave an eloquent shrug. 'The stuff didn't walk here on its own. Travel costs, you know. Do you see anyone else offering wine of any quality, let alone the divine flavours I have?'

Piso snorted. The wine's resemblance to pure vinegar was astonishing, but the merchant was right. There was no one else to buy the stuff from – this centrally, anyway. The rogue must have an arrangement with one of the garrison's offers, he thought, handing over the coins.

'Can I tempt you to some pepper?' The Phoenician swept a handful of the spice under Piso's nose. His nostrils filled with the pungent, heady aroma that he hadn't been able to afford for months.

'Not this time.'

The pepper was withdrawn at once, as if he would steal it, and the Phoenician's toothy smile shrank. 'When you need it, my friend, I'll be here.'

Piso headed for his barracks, trying and failing not to think about the wonderful foods that had been available in the neighbourhood where he'd grown up. Spiced lentils, smoked ham, fresh fish, breads of every type imaginable, pastries and sweetmeats, and a dozen times as many spices as the Phoenician had had. The signature dish of one local restaurant had been veal escalope with raisins – Piso had only been able to afford it once, but his mouth watered at the thought of it. Distracted by the fantasy, he didn't see the burly legionary in his path. With a clash of heads, they collided. Piso stumbled back, clutching the throbbing lump on his skull; the other let out a string of oaths. 'Clumsy bastard! Watch where you're going!'

'My apologies. I wasn't looking.' Piso's heart sank as he saw that the soldier – one of the garrison – had two friends with him. As if on cue, they stepped to either side of their comrade, blocking the avenue.

'Damn right, you weren't,' retorted the legionary. 'You must have been thinking about your centurion shoving his cock up your arse.'

'There's no need for that,' said Piso, wishing that Tullus were close enough to have heard. But he was nowhere to be seen. Neither were his tent mates, or any of his unit. 'I said it was my fault. I'm sorry.'

'I don't care what you said, maggot.' The legionary leered. 'Me and my mates don't like you. Walking around here like you own the damn place, buying up all the wine.' Quick as lightning, he snatched the leather bag. Shaking it, he grinned. 'It's just been filled up, boys. Our luck's in, eh?'

'Give that back.' Piso reached out, but the legionary tossed the skin to one of his friends. Piso turned to the man but, like bullies who've taken a child's toy, he threw to the next one. 'I paid for that,' said Piso, his temper rising. 'It's mine.'

'Regard it as payment for being such a fool.' The big legionary spun on his heel with a chuckle, and Piso closed his eyes, wondering what to do. Trying to get the skin back would get him beaten up, but if he let the men walk away, his comrades – in particular Vitellius – would remind him of the humiliation for days to come.

He waited until the trio had all turned away before he charged. Arms outstretched, he managed to knock the legionary's comrades aside, but in the process slammed into the man's back faster than he'd meant to. Down they both went, Piso landing on top. There was an *oomph* of pain from beneath him. Surprised and relieved that he hadn't been injured, Piso grabbed the skin and clambered to his feet. One of the soldiers that he'd pushed sideways swung a wild punch; Piso ducked and it whistled over his head. 'Get him! Get the whoreson!' roared the big legionary from the ground.

He couldn't hang about. Piso darted forward, in the direction of his barracks. Eyes fixed on the middle distance, he didn't see the foot that had been stuck in his path. The dirt came up to meet him with sickening speed. His left shoulder was the first to hit it; next was the side of his face. Starbursts of agony went off in his brain. Half-stunned, he lay helpless as his enemies closed in. Piso knew the pain would be bad, but the shock of the first studded sandal connecting with his head was beyond anything he'd ever experienced. Another followed, and then it was kick after kick to the ribs and belly. Nausea swamped him, and he retched.

'Beat the shit out of the maggot, but do it quick,' said the man he'd walked into. 'Otherwise an officer will catch us.'

'Or I will,' said a voice that Piso, confused, couldn't quite place.

'One of his mates, are you? Fuck off, or we'll give you a hammering as well,' the big legionary retorted.

'Will you now?' The speaker laughed. 'Piso? Can you get up?'

The urgency in his saviour's voice penetrated the fog encasing Piso's brain. With an effort, he sat up, then stood. Dumbfounded, he stared at Vitellius, who was facing up, alone, to the three legionaries. The dagger in his hand explained their hesitancy; only one of them, the weediest-looking, was armed. Piso picked up the wine skin – he wasn't going to leave that behind – and scrambled away from his assailants, to Vitellius' side.

'Draw your blade,' Vitellius hissed.

Piso obeyed.

'Listen, you sewer rats! Me and my friend are going to walk away, with our wine. You are going to stay put, unless you want to end your days with a knife in your belly.' Vitellius edged a step backward and, taking the hint, so did Piso.

The big legionary glanced at his friends. 'Come on! We can take them.'

'Off you go,' the weedy one said. 'I'm not dying for a skin of wine.'

'Me neither,' said the third soldier.

'Screw the both of you!' shouted the big legionary at Piso and Vitellius. 'Don't let me catch either of you round here again, or you'll be sorry.'

'Fuck you too.' Vitellius shuffled backwards a dozen steps and more, all the while facing the legionaries. Piso did the same, waves of relief washing over him. A little further, and they'd be safe.

A moment later, the three made obscene gestures and began walking in the opposite direction.

'Are you all right?' asked Vitellius.

'I'm fine,' replied Piso, even as the light-headedness took hold. His vision blurred, and he swayed.

Vitellius drew one of Piso's arms over his shoulder and held it tight. 'Lean on me, brother. Those bastards won't come back. We can take it slowly to the barracks. We'll have a nip of wine in a bit to give us some strength, eh?'

It hurt to laugh, but Piso did so anyway. 'That sounds good. Were you looking for me?'

'Aye. You were taking so long that we were dying of thirst. I said I'd find you.'

'I'm glad you did. My thanks, Vitellius.'

Vitellius patted his hand. 'You're in my contubernium, and I'm in yours. We might hurl shit at one another, but we look after our own.'

At this, the pain that had been battering Piso's body faded a little into the background.

For the first time, he felt like a real legionary.

V

Evening had fallen over Aliso. The legionaries of Tullus' cohort had been allocated quarters some time since. While the five other centurions ate with the camp's officers, he and Tubero had been invited to dine with the camp prefect Caedicius and the fort's usual commander, Granius Marcianus, in the rundown *praetorium*. Caedicius' presence here was to ensure that the summer needs of Varus' army, which would pass the camp on its outward and return marches, were met. Tubero's behaviour thus far had been exemplary. After several cups of wine, Tullus was beginning to think that perhaps he was just another eager young officer keen to prove himself, and out to make an impression.

Their surroundings might have seen better days, but every part of the large building was still grander than Tullus' set of rooms at Vetera. The mosaic floors throughout wouldn't have been out of place in an equestrian's house in Italy. A fountain pattered in the central courtyard, and the mythical scenes painted on the walls of the larger chambers were as fine as he'd seen in any camp on the Rhenus. Caedicius and Marcianus were men who didn't stand on ceremony, however. The couches upon which the previous occupant's guests would have reclined had been stacked at the far end of the dining room, and a plain but serviceable table and set of chairs set up in their place. Tubero's face had registered surprise at the informal arrangement, but he'd had the wit to remain silent. The *primus pilus*, or chief centurion of the Eighteenth for many years, Caedicius was now a camp prefect. Technically, Tubero outranked him, but in reality it was a different thing. Not that Caedicius made a thing of that either. He had ushered them to the table as any host might and poured each man wine with his own hands, while Marcianus had passed round the cups.

The olives that they'd had to start hadn't been the freshest, but this far from Italy that was unsurprising, thought Tullus. The local cheese – and the wine, which was excellent – had more than compensated for their lack of flavour. So too had the leg of wild boar, roasted whole and served with garlic and rosemary. Silence had fallen over the table as the four officers set upon it.

Caedicius mopped up some of the juices on his plate with a piece of bread and popped it into his mouth. After swallowing, he sighed. 'Gods, but that tastes good.' He reached out and pulled another strip of skin from the joint. 'The crackling is always the best bit, eh?'

'Indeed it is, sir,' said Marcianus.

'It's my favourite too, sir,' said Tullus, helping himself to a piece.

'The meat's delicious,' added Tubero.

Caedicius chuckled. 'Not to your taste, is it, tribune?'

Tubero squirmed. 'It's a little gamey,' he admitted.

'Better get used to it. You'll find precious few dormice this side of the river.'

Marcianus laughed, and Tullus managed to bury his smile by swigging from his cup. 'I'm not effete,' said Tubero, the colour rising in his cheeks. 'I don't like dormice either.'

'I'm glad to hear it,' said Caedicius. 'I've never been able to understand why people eat rodents. Snobbery is what it is, if you ask me. You might as well cook up a rat – there'd be more feeding in it.' He eyed Tubero. 'If not boar, what's your choice of dish?'

'I'm fond of fish. I haven't tasted it yet, but I'm told that the salmon from the local rivers tastes wonderful.'

'I'll agree with you about that,' said Caedicius, smiling. 'The eels are good too. But enough of food. What news of Illyricum? Is it true that the war's over?' Everyone's gaze switched at once to Tubero, most particularly that of Tullus, who had served there for more than a year.

'It is, after three years. Word had just reached the capital as I was about to leave,' said Tubero, pleased by the attention. 'Tiberius and Germanicus vanquished the last rebels in Illyricum not two months since.'

'Excellent news,' declared Caedicius, raising his glass. 'To the emperor!'

Tullus echoed the toast, feeling a little disappointed that he hadn't been there to see victory. More of him was glad that he had survived, however. Recovering from the injury that had sent him back to Vetera and his legion had taken the best part of six months.

They all drank.

'Augustus is said to be delighted,' Tubero went on. 'Rather than taking the customary title of Imperator, he is allowing Tiberius to use the honorific. Tiberius is also to celebrate a triumph upon his return to Rome.'

'How times have changed,' commented Caedicius in an undertone, winking at Tullus and Marcianus.

Marcianus hid his mirth, but not well. Tullus was also amused, but he kept a neutral face before Tubero. He had no reason to think that the tribune was a spy sent by Rome, but when it came to the imperial family, it paid to watch one's mouth. He wasn't going to be the one who mentioned Augustus' previous dislike of his adopted son Tiberius. In a memorable damning of his now heir, the emperor had once been heard to say, 'Alas for the Roman people, to be ground by jaws that crunch so slowly.' For his part, Tullus liked Tiberius. Although not the type he'd want to go drinking with, Tiberius was solid and reliable and, most important of all, a general who cared for his soldiers. 'It's excellent that Augustus is recognising him in that manner,' said Tullus. 'He is a most able commander.' Tullus saw Tubero's blank stare, and added, 'Four years ago, not long after he'd been adopted by Augustus, he served as governor of Germania, and led our legions over the Rhenus for two campaigning seasons.'

Tubero looked embarrassed. 'Of course, of course, I remember.'

'We marched as far as the River Albis, and overwintered in Germania,' Tullus explained. 'The year after that we would have crushed Maroboduus, but the Pannonian revolt put paid to that plan.'

'Tiberius assembled ten legions, didn't he?' asked Tubero, his eyes glinting.

'He did, sir. Four of them from this province. It was a grand sight,' said Tullus, glancing at Caedicius. 'Remember, sir?'

'It stirred the blood, aye,' growled Caedicius. 'A damn shame that the campaign never happened. It was only five days until it began too!'

'What does Varus plan for the summer?' Tubero enquired of Caedicius. 'Will we go as far as the River Albis, do you think?'

'I don't think so. Porta Westfalica is where you'll make camp. Tullus?'

'That's what I've heard, yes, sir.'

'Are the tribes in that area restless?' Tubero's eyes swung from Caedicius to Tullus, Marcianus and back again. 'Is there any chance of fighting?'

Caedicius laughed. 'Quite the lion cub, aren't you?'

'This is what I've been hearing since we left camp, sir. He's keen for action,' said Tullus, adding for the sake of diplomacy, 'which is a good sign in a new officer.'

'It is,' Caedicius concurred. Tubero looked pleased until he added, 'You might be disappointed, however, tribune. As far as I'm aware, the tribes between here and the River Visurgis seem content. The army's main duty will be to collect taxes, while Varus holds court sessions and settles petty disputes.'

Aided by the wine perhaps, Tubero's restraint fell away. 'I didn't come to Germania to listen to court cases!'

Cheeky bastard, thought Tullus.

'With respect, senior tribune, you'll do as you're ordered,' barked Caedicius, all primus pilus once more. 'Whatever the duty may be.'

'Of course,' said Tubero, flushing. 'My apologies.'

Caedicius' fierce expression eased. 'If I've learned one thing in the army, Tubero, it's to expect the unexpected. You must always be prepared to fight, even if it looks unlikely. That way, when it happens – and it will happen to you sometime – you'll be ready.'

'I'll remember that. Thank you for your advice,' said a chastened Tubero.

Caedicius saluted him with his cup. 'Old I may be, but I know a thing or two about war. As do we all, eh, Tullus? Marcianus?'

'We'd be poor soldiers if we didn't, sir,' said Tullus with a smile.

Marcianus chuckled before saying, 'I've been meaning to tell you, sir. The tribune might find this interesting too. One of my officers mentioned a trader who passed the camp today. The man was talking about some trouble caused by the Tencteri.'

Tullus' ears pricked up. Tencteri territory lay some distance to the south of Aliso, but was still close to the Rhenus.

Caedicius frowned. 'What did he say, Marcianus?'

'It seems that a band of Tencteri has been cattle raiding among the Usipetes in the last ten days or so. According to the merchant, they started off on the fringes of the Usipetes' lands, but they've grown bolder. A couple of men were killed during their latest raid, and there's been talk of retaliatory attacks.'

Tubero looked confused, so Tullus explained, 'Cattle rustling is a perennial problem in Germania, tribune. It's a badge of honour for young warriors to steal beasts from another tribe. In recent years, the chieftains have been quick to step in before things get out of hand, but that doesn't always work. Sometimes our troops are needed to restore order.'

Tubero looked like a small child who'd been handed a pastry. He glanced at Caedicius. 'How far away is this happening?'

'Too great a distance for us to consider investigating without permission,' said Caedicius. 'I will advise Varus of this development, and if the governor sees fit, a detachment of troops will be sent to investigate.'

'Perhaps I could lead that unit,' Tubero suggested.

'Varus will be the man who decides what action will be taken, if any,' answered Caedicius.

Disappointment filled Tubero's eyes again. Tullus felt for him. Officers with initiative were a valuable asset to a legion. 'If Varus decides to send a patrol out, and you were to petition him for its command, he might grant your request, sir,' he offered.

'Let us hope so,' said Tubero. He lifted his cup. 'Fortuna grant that it is I who is sent to settle the dispute.'

By the following morning, Tullus was regretting the late night he'd had. True to form, Caedicius had insisted that they keep drinking after the food had been cleared away. Marcianus, a pisshead of the first order, had been happy to obey, and Tubero had still been keen to impress, so Tullus' protests had been in vain. His memory of the end of proceedings was hazy, but he was certain that the third watch had sounded as he fell into bed. The dawn trumpet, which sounded what seemed like moments later, had been most unwelcome.

Dry-mouthed and sweating, he'd gone straight to the baths and jumped into the cold pool. After a short spell, he had moved to the hot room, and then back to the *frigidarium*. Somewhat revived, he had forced down a few mouthfuls of water and pulled on his armour before inspecting the cohort. Prompted by Fenestela and the other centurions, it had already formed up in the wide space between the walls and the barracks, ready to march back to Vetera. As he stalked the formation, three centuries wide and two deep, Tullus noted that some men looked worse for wear, but most seemed fit and ready. Given his own state, he decided to say nothing. The soldiers could be assessed as they marched. As long as everyone kept up, he could overlook a few hangovers.

It was some consolation that when Tubero appeared – late – he was red-eyed and pale-faced. Tullus affected not to notice.

Caedicius came to bid them farewell. To Tullus' chagrin, he looked as spry as a man half his age who hadn't touched a drop. 'I'll see you in the summer,' he declared. 'May the gods guide all of our paths until then. Good luck, tribune.'

Tubero's response was more scowl than smile. 'Thank you, sir.'

'Ready, sir?' asked Tullus of Tubero.

There was a grim nod.

'You have Caedicius' letters for Varus?'

'My staff officer has them.'

'Very good, sir. With your permission, then?'

A weak gesture from Tubero indicated that he should continue.

Satisfaction filled Tullus. He'll be as quiet as a mouse on the way back, he thought. He gave the order to turn about face, and to move out in turn after the tribune had led off. Tubero and his followers rode past the front ranks of the cohort, towards the gate. In neat ranks, the centuries began to march after, each falling into line behind the next, standard-bearers at the front, and their centurions riding alongside. Tullus' soldiers were in first position, as before, but he did not join them yet. When the entire unit was moving, he saluted Caedicius. 'Thank you for your hospitality, sir.'

Caedicius chuckled. 'You look as if a couple more hours under the blankets would have helped. As for Tubero, well, they don't make them like they used to, do they?'

'I'll be fine, sir. Tubero too. The fresh air will clear our heads.'

Caedicius inclined his head. 'Farewell until next we meet, Tullus.'

'Farewell, sir.' Tullus urged his horse after the cohort, grateful once more that he did not have to walk.

The morning passed without event. Practised at dealing with hangovers, Tullus drank often from the two water skins he was in the habit of carrying. When the inevitable piss stops started to become necessary, he slipped from his horse's back and ignored the chorus of ribald comments that accompanied him down the bank off the road. In his mind, for soldiers to make fun of their commanding officer was acceptable in certain circumstances. If Julius Caesar had tolerated his soldiers chanting that the men of Rome should 'watch their wives, the bald adulterer's back home', who was he to care if his troops were amused by the small size of his bladder? What mattered was that they respected him, and that they obeyed his orders – both of which they did.

Tubero wasn't used to being the butt of ordinary soldiers' jokes, however. Some time later, Tullus was riding along, eyes closed, imagining one of his favourite whores doing what she did best, when the senior tribune's outraged voice dragged him from his reverie.

'Tullus! TULLUS!'

'Yes, sir?' Fully awake, whore forgotten, he regarded a puce-faced, sweating Tubero from no more than ten paces. 'What's wrong, sir?'

Tubero's cheeks went a shade rosier. He cleared his throat and pulled his horse's head around so that it faced forward again. When Tullus was alongside, he leaned in with a conspiratorial look. 'I'm not feeling well this morning.'

'Sorry to hear that, sir,' replied Tullus.

'I was feeling nauseous just now. I climbed off my mount by the side of the road, and was sick. I vomited.'

'My sympathies, sir. These things happen. Has it passed?' asked Tullus, holding in his amusement. He knew what was coming.

'I don't need sympathy, centurion.' Tubero glared at the passing legionaries, one of whom had snickered.

'No, sir,' said Tullus, adopting the blank, uncomprehending expression favoured by low-rankers pretending not to understand an officer.

'Your men mocked me! There I was, retching, feeling terrible, and all they could say was, "Too much wine last night, tribune?" or, "Typical. An officer who can't hold his drink!"'

Tullus put on a solicitous face. 'That's terrible, sir.'

'One even said, "I'd like to see you in combat, tribune,"' cried Tubero. 'It's insufferable. Outrageous!'

'Did you spot the soldiers who made the comments, sir?' asked Tullus, knowing full well what the answer would be.

'Do you think I have eyes in the back of my head?'

'No, sir.'

'You must do something,' hissed Tubero. 'Such contempt cannot be tolerated.'

'I didn't like it the first time it happened to me either, sir.' He smiled at Tubero's shock. 'It happens to all of us, sir, even Varus.'

'It's indiscipline of the worst kind!'

'Different rules apply on the march, sir. Stupid jokes don't harm anyone, and they pass the time.' Tubero did not look convinced, and Tullus added, 'The dogs have been ribbing *me* all morning because of the frequency with which I've had to piss. "Look! The centurion's at it again." "His bladder must be the size of an apple." "Keep out of the way, brothers. Tullus is about to flood the place again!" I tolerate it, sir, because it makes me human in their eyes. Let's be clear: they still have to follow orders – I don't give them a pubic hair's leeway on that – but it's part of the marching ritual.'

There was silence for a moment, and then Tubero nodded. 'So be it, centurion. I will overlook the men's attempts at humour – this once. Let it be known that if it occurs again, I will have the *whole* damn cohort on latrine duties, and worse, for a month. Do I make myself clear?' Despite the sweat coating his forehead, Tubero's stare was unwavering.

'You do, sir.'

'As you were, then.' Tubero gave his horse its head, and trotted off to the front of the column.

Tullus watched him go, thinking that perhaps his initial dislike of the tribune *had* been well founded after all. Despite this, what had just taken place wasn't entirely bad. It took considerable spine for a freshly commissioned senior officer to disagree with a veteran centurion. Tubero might yet develop into a fine leader. Marshalling what was left of his goodwill, Tullus told himself that *that* would be the case. It felt better to think that rather than the other things Tubero could turn out to be.

Patrol routine took over once more. Several miles down the road, Tullus judged that it was time to halt for a meal break. The front and rear centuries had to remain on duty on the road and eat where they stood. Meanwhile, the four from the column's middle spread out into a fresh tilled field, unslung their shields and devoured bread and olives. Tubero, who had returned, watched with clear annoyance, but did not intervene. 'I'm not hungry,' he snapped when Tullus offered him some food. It wasn't long before he took off again with his entourage in tow, shouting over his shoulder that he would keep scouting out the road ahead. 'Good fucking riddance,' Tullus heard one soldier say. Fenestela, who was sitting beside Tullus, chuckled. Tullus couldn't argue with the sentiments of either man, so acted as if he hadn't noticed a thing.

The food helped Tullus' hangover to recede, leaving torpidity in its place. He roused himself with an effort a while later. There would be time to sleep when they reached the marching camp. He ordered the legionaries back to the road. 'Eight more miles,' he remarked to Fenestela.

'We've broken the back of it, sir,' replied Fenestela. It was his stock phrase after the midday break.

As Tullus rode along, he began to daydream again about the whore in the vicus, but he did not entirely relax. Every so often, he studied the land to both sides, and the road in front and behind. He kept half an ear on his soldiers' banter too, and was content that they seemed in good humour.

An hour or more passed in this fashion.

Then, in the distance, towards Vetera, a man shouted. The panicked tone roused Tullus at once. 'Tell the optio to be ready for trouble. Pass the word back, all the way to the rear,' he barked at the nearest legionary. Ordering the trumpeter to follow, he drummed his heels into his horse's sides and rode forward at a steady canter.

It wasn't long before Tullus could see three riders hammering along the road towards them. Tubero was out in the lead, and it was he who was yelling.

'To arms! To arms!'

Although he could see no one behind Tubero, Tullus' stomach did a neat roll. What in Hades has happened? he wondered, reining in. 'Sound the halt,' he ordered the trumpeter.

The trumpet's blare had not finished before the ranks of soldiers had come to a stop.

'Front century, yokes on the ground, by your feet. Javelins ready!' shouted Tullus over his shoulder. 'Wait for my command.' He waited as Tubero galloped towards them. The tribune seemed uninjured; so too did his companions, which was one good thing.

Tubero sawed on his horse's reins as he drew near to Tullus. 'Ready the cohort for battle.'

'What's going on, sir?'

'Half a mile up the road, I came across a group of the tribesmen who've been cattle rustling. The Tencteri, was it?'

'That's right, sir,' replied Tullus, feeling the first traces of concern. 'Can I ask how you recognised them as Tencteri?'

A withering look. 'It was a group of young warriors, about twenty strong. They were driving cattle south. They didn't seem to like the sight of me, and shouted insults when I demanded to know who they were, and what they were doing. That was enough for me.'

Tullus' disquiet grew. Plenty of tribesmen disliked Romans, even more so if they were an arrogant young officer. 'How do you know what they said, sir?'

Irritation flared in Tubero's eyes. 'I don't. Now, I want two centuries to advance at the double. The tribesmen are still quite near the road. There's plenty of room for our men to deploy before we envelop them.'

Cattle rustlers didn't swan about in broad daylight, thought Tullus, but it wasn't for him to question the tribune too much. 'Front two centuries, prepare to advance,' he barked. To Tubero, he said, 'Will you ride alongside me, sir?'

'I will.' Tubero half drew his sword, allowing Tullus to note with horror that the blade was red with blood. Tubero laughed. 'You seem surprised, centurion.'

'Did they attack you, sir?'

'No. I rode down the nearest – the one that was shouting insults. I don't think he believed that I meant business until I cut him from neck to waist. By then it was too late.' A snicker.

Tullus' anger flared, but he swallowed it down. 'Did you kill anyone else, sir?'

'Sadly, no. Two of them lobbed spears at me. I judged it best to return to the patrol, and gather the men.'

Tullus offered up a quick prayer that the warriors were indeed Tencteri cattle rustlers. If they weren't, well, the gods only knew the repercussions that would result. Roman law lay lightly on many of the surrounding tribes . . . He quelled his concern. 'That was prudent, sir. Varus would not be happy if I came back without a tribune.'

Tubero sniffed. 'But he *will* be happy that the rustlers who have been troubling the Usipetes have been dealt with.'

'*If* they are the men responsible, sir' – Tullus ignored Tubero's indignant look – 'Varus will be the first to congratulate you.' If they're not, he thought, he'll be sending you back to Rome in disgrace, and serving me my own balls on a silver platter.

'Come on,' demanded Tubero. 'We need to move fast, or they might abandon the cattle and get away.'

'Aye, sir.' Tullus regarded the trumpeter. 'Find the centurion in charge of the third century. Tell him that the rest of the unit is to follow us at a fast pace.' To the legionaries behind him, he bellowed, 'First two centuries, with me – at the double!'

If the warriors hadn't realised that Tubero and his companions were part of a larger group, they soon would, thought Tullus. A hundred and fifty men in full armour, running, made a lot of noise.

It was no surprise, therefore, that when they reached the spot where the confrontation had taken place, the tribesmen were herding their cattle to the south at speed. Tullus' heart quickened. Whatever the right and wrong of it, they were quarry now. 'If one century moves to the left, sir, it should cut them off from those trees by the river. The other century goes to the right. Some might get away, but we'll soon run them down. If any are foolish enough to come back in this direction, they'll meet the rest of the cohort.'

'Fine,' replied Tubero. 'Try and keep a couple alive at least. They can be interrogated before I have them crucified.' Beckoning to his staff officers, he galloped off, straight after the warriors.

'Sir!' But the tribune paid him no heed. Impulsive fool, thought Tullus. It'd be just my luck for one of the tribesmen to fell him with a lucky spear. Despite his dislike of Tubero, he had no wish for that to happen, nor to suffer one of Varus' thunderous – and famous – dressing-downs. He issued his orders, deciding to take his century to the right while the other centurion and his men went to the left.

They charged down on to the pasture upon which the cattle had been grazing when Tubero arrived. The corpse of the man slain by the tribune stood out, a slumped figure on the green grass, surrounded by a circle of crimson. Tullus passed close enough to see that Tubero had almost cut him in two. He felt a little respect. The boy was no slouch with a sword. Within a short distance the grass gave way to a large swathe of barley, beyond which stood a couple of longhouses. Tullus cursed at the sight of them. The cattle had trampled much of the crop flat, and the passage made by his men would make things worse. Whatever the reason, the local farmers – Usipetes – would blame the Romans for the destruction of their precious barley.

He hadn't expected to be confronted the moment that he and his soldiers neared the longhouses. Two red-faced tribesmen stamped out to block their path. Bearded, dressed in dark homespun tunics and trousers, and unarmed, they shouted and waved their arms in evident fury, not at the disappearing warriors, but at Tullus and his men.

He sensed the legionaries behind him growing tense. 'Halt! Stay calm, brothers. They're farmers, just angry farmers. No one is to lift a hand unless I say so.' Although Tullus' fingers wanted to grip the hilt of his sword, he raised his right hand, palm showing, as he walked his horse towards the pair. Their ranting checked a little, but it did not stop, nor did they retreat. Tullus' understanding of the local tongues was decent enough, and what was being said was not complimentary. 'Calm yourselves,' he shouted. 'Tell me what has happened. Slowly.'

The older of the two, a greybeard with a weeping eye, batted at his companion, who reluctantly fell silent. At once a new tirade began. 'Ruined crops . . . starvation in the winter . . . cattle being chased . . . a man murdered . . . and for what?' Tullus heard. 'For what?' repeated the greybeard, spittle flying from his lips.

Tullus felt even unhappier. 'The cattle. They were stolen by those warriors. Tencteri rustlers.'

He received a contemptuous stare. 'Tencteri? Those are Usipetes, same as I am! They were driving the herd to new grazing when a lunatic Roman attacked them for no reason. Killed one of them dead. He was sixteen summers old. His body's over yonder.'

'You're certain that they're Usipetes?' asked Tullus, feeling foolish.

Another scornful look. 'Several are kin of mine. Or of his.' He jabbed his companion. 'Is that enough proof for you, Roman?'

Tullus clenched his jaw. Jupiter, I ask you to help this situation not to go all the way to Hades, he prayed. 'For the moment, it is, yes.'

'The Usipetes are at peace with Rome! Did the fool who attacked those boys not know that?' screeched the greybeard.

Tullus did not answer, but he was thinking that the reckless imbecile didn't bother to check. Someone had to ride after Tubero and stop him from killing more innocents – if he hadn't done so already. 'Damn you, Tubero,' Tullus whispered. *He* would have to do this. 'Did you catch any of that?' he demanded of the other centurion, a solid type called Valens, who had ridden up alongside.

'The important bit, sir, I think,' replied Valens, looking troubled. 'They're Usipetes, not Tencteri.'

'That's right. Follow as fast as you can. I'm going to try and prevent

Tubero from starting a tribal uprising all on his own.' Tullus cracked his reins over his horse's neck and set off in pursuit.

His worst imaginings had come true by the time he'd caught up. Tubero and his companions had cut down three more men, killing one and wounding the others so badly that Tullus doubted they would live. He had no doubt that if the remaining tribesmen – a group of fifteen or so fearful-looking youths, wielding spears – hadn't banded together in a loose circle, Tubero would have done for even more. While his staff officers watched, he was riding his horse to and fro, just beyond spear-throwing distance, hurling insults. 'You dogs! Scared of facing me, are you? Wait here, then, until the soldiers arrive. You'll all die soon enough. You're cowards and thieves, the lot of you!'

'Sir!' Although the staff officers saluted, Tubero didn't appear to hear his first shout. Tullus rode closer. 'SIR!'

Tubero's head turned. He smiled, like a wolf. 'Tullus. You can't wait to start shedding the enemy's blood either, eh? Never fear, I've left a few for you.'

Tullus rode in until his thigh touched Tubero's. He ignored the tribune's annoyed reaction. 'Sir,' he said in a low tone. 'These are not the cattle rustlers.'

'Of course they are, centurion!'

Tullus leaned even closer. 'No, sir, they are *not*. They're Usipetes, who were herding cattle to new pasture.' As you'd have discovered if you had bothered to ask, you stupid bastard, he wanted to add.

Uncertainty mixed with the anger in Tubero's eyes. 'How can you be sure?'

'I spoke to the farmers in the houses back there. They're kin to these youngsters.'

'There must be some mistake. They shouted at me; they fled when I rode towards them.'

Tullus ground his teeth. 'They must have panicked, sir, having an armed Roman charging them, shouting in a tongue they didn't understand.'

Tubero digested this in silence. After a moment, his face cleared. 'Oh well. A few less tribesmen in the world is no bad thing, eh?'

'The Usipetes are not at war with Rome, sir. The tribe's leaders will count this as an unprovoked attack. They'll say that the youths were murdered. Varus won't be best pleased either.'

Tubero's eyes glittered like those of a snake watching its prey. 'What will you tell him?'

I can't trust this one as far as I can throw him, Tullus realised. 'What happened, sir. Nothing more.'

'See that that's all you do, centurion.' Wheeling his horse, Tubero rode away, leaving Tullus to clear up the mess.

VI

It was a baking hot day, with few clouds in the sky. Arminius was sitting cross-kneed on the ground outside his tent, scratching patterns in the dirt with the tip of a dagger. Maelo squatted beside him. A third warrior stood over them, waiting. Around them, Arminius' troops' tents formed the long sides of an open-ended rectangle, with pens containing their horses taking up the short side. The 'open end' faced on to one of the many avenues in the sprawling temporary camp that had sprung up outside Vetera as Varus' summons was answered by the troops along the Rhenus. Despite the number of tents, it was quiet. Most of the men had headed for the inns and brothels the instant that they had been given permission.

'I want to hear every word of what you just told me again,' Arminius ordered.

'Some young Tencteri have been rustling cattle from the Usipetes over the last moon or so,' said the warrior. 'The Usipetes had begun to think about reprisals, but the Romans at Aliso heard about the latest raid before they had a chance to act. A patrol that was making its way back from there chanced on a group of Usipetes youngsters who were herding some cattle to fresh pasture. One of them – it sounds as if it might have been Tubero, a new senior tribune – assumed that the boys were the rustlers. He attacked them, killing several. A bloodbath was prevented only by the intervention of a centurion who'd discovered that the youngsters were not Tencteri.'

'Was any apology made?'

'Not as far as I know.'

'This is how they treat men from a tribe who are at peace with Rome?' spat Maelo. 'The dirty Roman bastards.'

'Peace, Maelo,' said Arminius, although his eyes remained ice-cold. He glanced at the warrior. 'My thanks. You're going for a drink now, I assume? Or two.'

A sheepish grin. 'Aye.'

'A favour. Go into as many of the taverns as you can before you get pissed. Make sure that every tribesman you meet hears the story.'

'You have my word, Arminius.'

When the warrior had gone, he regarded Maelo again. 'The deaths of those youngsters are regrettable, but they're also a godsend.'

'Their deaths will push the Usipetes to join us.'

'Indeed.' Arminius' smile was tight. Precise. 'I couldn't have asked for a better way for it to happen.'

'But—'

Arminius bent towards Maelo. 'I wish those youngsters hadn't been slain, you know that more than anyone. But if their deaths guarantee that the Usipetes join our cause, and that other tribes do too? Does that not make it worthwhile?'

There was a moment's pause.

'It does, curse it,' Maelo said with a shake of his head.

'Think about the blood price we will extract from the Romans when the time comes.'

'When the time comes,' repeated Maelo. 'It seems as if I've been waiting all my life for an opportunity to hit Rome where it really hurts.' He made a rueful face. 'As if you haven't too.'

'It's been a long time for us both,' Arminius agreed, 'but the waiting will soon be over.'

The sound of approaching footsteps brought their conversation to a close. Soon a young legionary appeared from the direction of the camp.

Sweat was running down his face, evidence of how hot it was to wear full kit in summer weather. His pace slackened at the sight of Arminius and Maelo. 'Sir,' he said with a perfunctory salute.

'Greetings,' Arminius replied, annoyed that even a low-ranker could indicate his disapproval with such ease.

'I'm looking for Arminius of the Cherusci, sir.'

'I am the man you seek,' offered Arminius, and was pleased to see the legionary's face redden with embarrassment. 'What brings you here?'

'Varus asks you to the principia for the start of the ninth hour, sir. He's to hold an enquiry into the incident with the supposed cattle rustlers.'

Maelo stiffened, but the legionary didn't appear to notice. 'Thank Varus,' said Arminius, 'and tell him that I will be delighted to be there.'

'Very good, sir.' With another salute, the legionary withdrew.

'*Supposed* rustlers? What were they doing then: stealing cattle from themselves?' hissed Maelo.

'Peace, brother. If Varus didn't keep up the pretence, he'd be as good as admitting that the tribune murdered innocent men.'

'Which he did!'

'You and I know that. The centurion who intervened knows it. Varus must do as well, but he's not going to hurl shit at one of his own, especially a senior tribune, before he's heard what happened.'

'I'll wager you my best sword that even when he has listened to everyone's story, and it's clear that the officer in question acted without good reason, Varus won't punish the whoreson. At least, not in the way he deserves. Being pressed face first into a bog by a wicker hurdle would be too good for him.' Maelo was referring to the common tribal method of executing criminals.

'You're right.' Arminius got to his feet and dusted down the backs of his trousers. 'But that doesn't mean I can't make Varus squirm, can't embarrass him into paying heavy reparations to the families of the dead men.' He added in a low voice, 'The Usipetes will be furious at the travesty of justice offered to their slain. Every last warrior of theirs will want to take part in the ambush.'

'Donar, but I can't wait for that day,' said Maelo.

'Patience, brother. It draws near,' said Arminius, his expression fierce as a hawk's.

Varus was irritated. Irritated by the meeting he was having to convene, irritated with Tubero, who was its cause, irritated by how long it was taking to get ready. He slapped his body slave's hand away from the pteryges on his left shoulder. 'By all that's sacred, you must be done by now!' The slave bowed his head and stepped back. With a critical eye, Varus stared into the tall bronze mirror that stood alongside the stand for his armour. He had bathed, and been shaved. His cuirass was gleaming; the red sash of his office was sitting in the correct place; his ornate sword hung at the right angle. He glanced at his feet, which were encased in a pair of well-polished calf-high leather boots. 'Well?' he asked, returning his gaze to the mirror.

'You look perfect, master,' said Aristides. 'The governor from head to toe.'

'Not quite,' replied Varus in a dry tone. He clicked his fingers. 'Helmet.'

The slave hurried forward again, felt liner and horsehair-crested helmet in hand.

When he'd tied the chinstrap in place, Varus checked the mirror once more, and then threw an enquiring glance at Aristides.

'You're the personification of Rome, master,' said the Greek.

'Ah, you could charm the birds down from the trees, Aristides,' Varus mocked, but was pleased nonetheless. 'I'd best get to the principia. It wouldn't do to arrive after the Usipetes. Is Vala ready?'

'He's waiting for you in the courtyard, master.'

'Good.' Varus brushed a hand over the statuettes on the little shrine by his bed. Ancestors, grant that this goes well, he asked. Pushing his unease deep inside, he walked to the bedroom door. Aristides got there before him, and opened it with a flourish. 'Master.'

Varus gave him a cordial nod, but his face changed as he stalked out into the corridor, becoming stern, even intimidating. When the legionary on duty outside saluted, he affected not to see. The legate Vala's cordial greeting he met with a small smile, but he did not respond to the honour guard of ten legionaries outside the praetorium, which stiffened to attention as the two emerged. Varus looked neither to left nor right as, preceded by the legionaries, he and Vala made their way down an avenue towards the principia. It was all deliberate. Until the meeting was over, he intended to be seen as the governor of Germania, a man appointed by Augustus himself, worthy of the deepest respect.

Reaching the headquarters, Varus strode towards the monumental front archway. The duty optio barked an order, and the sentries snapped to attention. Vala acknowledged the officer, but Varus had already entered. Within, the courtyard was its usual hive of activity. Officers stood talking in twos and threes while low-rankers and slaves hurried to and fro between the offices that lay to either side. Ignoring the salutes, calls of 'Governor!' and 'Well met, sir!' and other greetings, Varus made straight for the great hall.

Inside, Varus was pleased to note that the cloth screens concealing the shrine's entrance and the standards within had been pulled back, as per his instructions. Extra lights had been placed in the chamber, drawing men's eyes to the glint of silver and gold. It was natural that the golden eagle – the most precious talisman of the Eighteenth – attracted most attention. Everything about the bird, from its elegant form to its upturned wings and the thunderbolts it gripped, demanded respect, thought Varus. For it. For the legion. For Rome.

More than a dozen officers were standing at the foot of a low, central platform: the tribunes and ten most senior centurions, including Marcus Caelius, the primus pilus. Like Varus, they were all dressed in their finest uniforms. Tubero and Tullus were among them, and Varus wasn't surprised that they were standing at opposite ends of the group. Their written reports, which he had demanded soon after the patrol had returned, had intimated that there was some animosity between the two men. Varus felt his irritation towards Tubero recur. Despite the accusation of heavy drinking he had made against Tullus, it was as clear as the sun in the sky that the tribune's actions had been rash, and without basis. Moreover, four innocent tribesmen were dead.

Varus had a sour taste in his mouth just thinking about it. If Tubero were an ordinary soldier, he would have had him flogged, just to start. If a junior officer or a centurion, he'd have had him demoted to the ranks. Why does he have to be a senior tribune, whose father is friendly with Augustus? Varus fumed. If Tubero received anything more than a rap across the knuckles, he, Varus, risked censure from the emperor himself, and that was not a menace he wanted hanging over his head, dead tribesmen or no. The youths' families would have to be content with a hefty payment of cash, he had decided, and a promise that such a thing would not happen again.

Tubero attempted to speak as Varus drew near, but shut up when Varus gave a fierce shake of his head. 'If I order you to, you will agree that what happened was . . . most regrettable,' Varus muttered. 'It was a tragedy, and the men's families must be recompensed. Refrain from apologising, however. Do you understand?'

'Yes, sir,' Tubero replied. 'I—'

Varus waved him away. 'Tullus, a word if you please.' He took pleasure in the anger that flared in Tubero's eyes as the centurion joined him on the platform.

Tullus saluted. 'At your service, sir.'

Varus glanced him up and down, and liked what he saw. Tullus looked as solid and as dependable as the camp ramparts. He was brave too – the gold torques, the *phalerae* on his chest harness and the silver bands on his wrists were proof of that. 'I read your report.'

'I see, sir.' Tullus' tone was neutral.

'And Tubero's, of course. The tribune accused you of having drunk to excess the night before, and of being unfit for duty on the day in question.

He said fewer men would have died if you had responded to his orders faster.' Varus let his words linger in the air before asking, 'Is there any basis to this charge?'

'I had a reasonable amount to drink, sir, yes. We were guests of Caedicius, whom I think you know?'

'Indeed. He's a fine officer.'

'And a man who likes his wine, sir.'

Varus coughed. 'I won't argue with that.'

Tullus looked pleased. 'I will *not* admit to being unfit for duty, though, sir. Until the incident with the Usipetes, everything had been running as well as any other day on patrol. The other centurions will testify to that.'

Varus had spoken to several of the officers who'd been present, but he made no mention of it, or of the fact that their testimony agreed with that of Tullus. Varus hadn't been sure if they'd been telling the truth, or covering for their superior, to whom they felt loyal. 'Tubero also dined with you and Caedicius?'

'He did, sir, along with Aliso's usual commander, Marcianus. He was most excited when the cattle rustlers were mentioned.'

'Meeting them would be every unblooded officer's dream. Did he drink much?'

'I can't recall, sir.'

'I see,' said Varus, amused by the obvious lie. 'The following morning, how was he?'

'He seemed all right to me, sir.' Tullus' gaze was fixed on a point somewhere over Varus' right shoulder.

Varus came to a number of conclusions at the same time. Tubero had got as drunk as Tullus. Less likely to be a seasoned drinker than the centurion, he had been as sick as a dog the next day, whereas Tullus – no doubt practised at the art – might have been a little under the weather, but not much more. Tubero's accusations against Tullus were a crude effort to cover up his mistake. Despite the allegations, which carried with them the risk of being disciplined, Tullus was unprepared to respond in kind against the tribune. It was a mark of the character of both men, Varus concluded, how they had acted. 'Thank you, centurion. Dismissed.'

Varus had Vala, the Eighteenth's six tribunes and the primus pilus stand close to the shrine's entrance before the Usipetes' chieftains arrived. Tullus and the other centurions arrayed themselves in front of the dais. It was a display intended to impress and intimidate: watched by Augustus' statue, almost twenty senior officers in full regalia waited together, while half a century of legionaries from the First Cohort lined the chamber's walls and the standards glimmered from the shrine. Varus was pleased with his preparations. Battles were often won by the general who got to choose the battlefield, and who used the terrain to his advantage. Here, he had achieved both of those things. All that needed to happen now was for him to deploy his forces – in this case, words and, if the time came, a suitably humble Tubero – and victory would be his.

Not long after, the duty optio from the gate led in the Usipetes' leaders – and Arminius. The Cheruscan chieftain could not have made a balder statement of his intent, yet he continued to advance, right up to the officers before Varus. 'I thank you for your invitation today, governor.'

Wrong-footed, Varus managed only, 'Arminius.'

'The Usipetes are not happy,' Arminius said, low-voiced, in Latin.

'I will see what I can do to remedy that,' snapped Varus. 'Roman justice will be done.' Any chance to continue talking was prevented by the optio's formal presentation of the Usipetes' chieftains. Varus struggled to control his temper as Arminius strolled back to stand with the tribesmen.

'You are most welcome to Vetera,' Varus announced. 'I am Publius Quinctilius Varus, imperial governor of the province of Germania.' Catching the blank stares of more than one of the party, he added, 'Do any among you speak Latin?'

Only two of the chieftains nodded. 'I'll make sure the others understand,' said the nearest, a thin individual with a mane of red hair.

'I can interpret too, if needs be,' Arminius offered. 'From German to Latin, or the other way around.'

Varus seethed. He wanted to rebuke Arminius – 'Act like the Roman citizen that you are!' – but it would look bad, so he smiled instead. 'If it is necessary. Perhaps it would be best to begin by hearing what you chiefs have to say.'

The instant that his words were translated, several of the Usipetes began to shout.

Varus had been in his job long enough to have picked up some German. The words 'innocent' and 'murder' were repeated over and over, as were a number of choice swear words. He was pleased when Red Head managed to calm his fellows. 'I shall speak for us all, governor,' he declared.

Varus inclined his head, acting as if no insults had been hurled. 'Please begin.'

In a calm voice, Red Head explained how the twenty young Usipetes, who lived near the Roman road, had been instructed to move their fathers' cattle to fresh grazing. 'It's an easy job, driving the beasts just a couple of miles. The herders get paid in barley beer, so everyone wants to do it.' What should have been a pleasant task for a summer's day, the chieftain explained, had turned violent when a Roman officer – here he threw a pointed look at Tubero – had ridden up and started screaming in Latin at the herdsmen, all of whom spoke nothing but their own tongue.

Without warning, the officer had ridden at the nearest youngster and cut him down. Some of the group had retaliated by throwing spears, forcing the officer to retreat. In a panic, they had fled, to be pursued soon after by Roman infantry and riders. 'Three more men were slain or wounded so severely that they died. If not for a centurion with some wits, only Donar knows how many innocent lives would have been lost,' said Red Head, to growls of anger from his companions. 'What happened is an outrage! The Usipetes have been at peace with Rome for years. We sell our goods and our cattle to your merchants, and are shortly to pay our taxes. We give no trouble to the empire. And our reward is for four young men to be foully slain?'

'The murderer must die!' cried one of the chieftains in heavily accented Latin. His fellows shouted in agreement. 'Give him to us that he may receive justice!' demanded another.

Arminius said nothing, but his eyes darted to and fro, from Varus to the frightened-looking Tubero to the Usipetes and back again.

Varus raised his hands and the clamour abated. 'I thank you for your account,' he said to Red Head. 'I have also read the reports of the two most senior Roman officers who were present. I have been led to several conclusions. The intervention was made because the officer in question believed that the young men were Sugambri rustlers. By challenging them, he was endeavouring to capture wrongdoers – thieves.' Ignoring the incredulous expression on Red Head's face, he ploughed on, 'Their aggressive reaction to his challenge led him to conclude that they were indeed the cattle rustlers. After his initial attempt to force them to surrender failed, he sought out the main body of the patrol. It is unfortunate that several more of the "thieves" were injured or killed before it became clear that they were not Tencteri. In light of this most regrettable incident, I wish to express my sympathies to the dead men's families, and to offer substantial compensation.' Varus halted, to allow what he'd said to be interpreted.

There was pandemonium as his meaning became clear to the Usipetes' chieftains. None of them were foolish enough to lay hands to their weapons, but they shook their fists and spat obscenities at both Varus and Tubero.

Varus waited in stony silence until some level of calm had returned. 'Your companions are not pleased?'

The red-haired chief shook his head. 'This is no kind of justice, governor! What happened was cold-blooded murder, and the perpetrator must be punished.'

'He will be,' replied Varus, noting with satisfaction Tubero's continuing alarm. The boy's smug attitude needed adjusting. 'I shall see to it myself.'

'Hand him over to us.'

'You know that will not happen. He is a Roman noble, of high military rank.'

'That is your final word?'

'It is,' answered Varus with a cold look.

'There is one law for the Romans, and one for everyone else,' said Red Head with disgust. He translated for his fellows, who again gave vent to their unhappiness. He turned back to Varus. 'How much will you pay for each man's life?'

Before Varus could reply, Arminius stepped forward. 'I thought a figure of two thousand denarii per man might provide suitable recompense.'

Taken by surprise again, a furious Varus watched as Red Head relayed this sum, to great excitement. 'What else can we do but accept?' he thought he heard one man say. Varus' anger eased a little at this, and he held his peace. A dozen heartbeats later, Red Head declared, 'My fellow chieftains remain unhappy, but they will accept two thousand denarii for each of the dead, with one proviso. You must give an assurance that this will never happen again.'

Varus flashed his politician's smile, all polish and no substance. 'I give you my word as governor of Germania that all law-abiding Usipetes will be left in peace from this day forward. I will have the money drawn up at once, so that you may depart with it.'

Red Head gave a tight nod. 'So be it.'

As the Usipetes conferred, Varus addressed Vala. 'Dismiss the officers, but leave the soldiers on guard until the tribesmen have left.' He called next to Arminius, who was talking with Red Head and the rest. 'A word, if you will.'

Arminius joined Varus with a smile. 'That was a satisfactory result, don't you think?'

'What do you think you were doing?' hissed Varus.

Arminius' face registered wounded innocence. 'I don't understand?'

'You arrived with the Usipetes. What kind of message does that give them? You are a citizen ally of Rome. An equestrian!'

'My apologies, governor. My entrance was unintentional, I assure you. I was late getting to the principia, and I chanced upon them outside. We fell into conversation. The chieftains felt intimidated coming here, and concerned that they would not receive justice. I offered to accompany them inside, and said that you were an even-handed man, a man of integrity.'

'Neither was it your place to offer them two thousand denarii per man,' Varus snapped. 'That is an extortionate sum!'

Arminius bowed his head. 'Forgive me for being presumptuous, governor. I wanted the Usipetes to feel that they were being shown respect. They suspected that you would not hand over Tubero before they came in. Their pride had to be assuaged in some manner, and the only way that that seemed possible was to make them a generous offer.'

'It needn't have been that much. I'd wager they would have accepted half the amount.'

Arminius had the grace to flush. 'I can only apologise again, governor. I was trying to help, but I should have remained silent.'

Arminius' humility helped to ease Varus' anger. What made the real difference, though, was the knowledge that peace – the all-important peace – had been maintained for what, in the greater scheme of things, was a small sum. He sighed. 'Let's put the matter behind us, eh?'

'Thank you, governor.' Arminius cast him a stealthy look. 'By way of further apology, could I tempt you with a hunting trip on the other side of the river? My second-in-command has found an area with a rich concentration of boar and deer. It would make a fine day out, and an escape from your paperwork.'

Varus was about to reject the reconciliatory gesture, when he changed his mind. 'Damn it, why not?'

'Excellent. If you have no objection, I'll ask Centurion Tullus as well. Would two days hence suit?'

'It would,' replied Varus, smiling at last. 'Thank you, Arminius.'

'The pleasure will be mine, governor. I'll call at the praetoria for you soon after dawn.' Arminius half bowed and walked away.

Varus watched the Usipetes leaving the great hall in an unruly gaggle. If only all Germans were like Arminius, he thought. The world would be a more civilised place, and my life – everyone's lives – would be that much easier.

VII

Piso, Afer and Vitellius had found one of the best tables in the tavern that night. It was against the back wall, allowing them to set their backs against it as they drank, and to see everyone in the room. The establishment was popular with legionaries, in the main because it was owned and run by a veteran, a toothless reprobate by the name of Claudius. His goodwill towards serving soldiers went as far as extending credit, a practice that few other innkeepers in the vicus were prepared to emulate. As a consequence, Claudius' tavern was always heaving. It didn't matter that the wine was poor, and the food worse again, or that the whores were as rough as bears' arses, and the latrines full to overflowing. A soldier knew he could drink there, even if payday wasn't for another three months.

The three had been on the patrol, and heard since about Varus' interrogation of Tullus, and the confrontation with the Usipetes. They had been talking about little else since they had arrived. Well, Afer and Vitellius had been discussing it, and Piso had been listening. He was more accepted in the contubernium now, but when it came to discussing important issues, he yet preferred to keep his counsel.

'Varus is still more likely to take Tubero's word over Tullus',' said Afer for the third or fourth time. He scowled. 'It's a sad fucking day when a wet-behind-the-ears tribune gets believed before a career centurion.'

'It won't have been the first time, and it won't have been the last,' retorted Vitellius.

The close proximity of their nearest neighbours, a dozen legionaries seated around a long table, meant that despite the clamour, their conversation could be overheard. One of them, recognisable anywhere by a nose that had been broken so many times that it resembled a piece of baker's dough, turned around. 'Varus is wise to that jumped-up little prick Tubero, never fear.'

'Were you in the principia?' asked Piso.

'Aye. All of us were.' He eyed his companions, who were arguing over where to go next. 'Tubero tried to speak to Varus before the Usipetes got there, but Varus cut him off. He grilled Tullus hard enough – is that your centurion?' He glanced at the friends, who nodded. 'We couldn't hear what was said, but it seemed as if Varus believed him.'

'That's good news,' said Vitellius, his face brightening. Afer raised his cup in salute; so did Piso.

Broken Nose thrust out his hand. 'Marcus Aius, Second Century, First Cohort.' From nowhere, he produced a pair of worn bone dice. 'Any of you like to play?'

'Aius.' It was one of his companions.

'Leave me alone,' Aius growled.

'Don't say I didn't warn you,' said the legionary. He glanced at Piso and Afer. 'This man would gamble on two flies circling a fresh turd. Trouble is, he's wont to pick the wrong one.'

'Piss off,' said Aius, but in an amicable tone. He eyed the friends. 'Well?'

'I'll have a game,' said Piso, producing his own dice. 'Afer?'

'Why not?'

'Small change only,' said Aius, dumping a little pile of asses and other low-denomination coins on the table.

Vitellius went to refill their jug. Upon his return, he joined in for a short while, but after losing several bouts to Aius, withdrew. Afer was doing better, although by the time the wine had been finished, was down somewhat on where he'd started. Piso had fared similarly, yet when his friends suggested moving on to a different tavern, he shook his head. 'My luck will change,' he said.

'Of course it will,' agreed Aius with a wink.

Afer flicked his eyes at Aius' companions, and then the door. Piso understood that he meant it would be best if they left together. 'Six more rolls,' he said. 'Fortuna's in a good mood with me tonight.'

'She hasn't shown much sign of that so far,' said Afer, but he relaxed on his seat. So too did Vitellius. 'We're leaving after that,' he ordered.

'Let's raise the bet to five asses,' said Aius. 'One sestertius.'

Piso wasn't going to back down now. 'All right.' Blowing on the dice, he threw them on the table. 'Two sixes!'

Aius' eyebrows rose. He rolled, and got a three and a two. 'Here you go.' He slid five asses towards Piso.

A devilment took Piso. 'Double or quits?'

'Why not?' retorted Aius. 'I'll go first this time.' His dice spun and turned, coming to rest on a four and a five. 'Ha!'

Piso repeated his trick of breathing on *his* dice, and was rewarded with a five and a six.

With less grace than before, Aius handed over two sestertii. 'Same odds again?'

Piso glanced at Afer, who shook 'No' at him. 'Aye,' he said.

To his delight, Piso won that bout, and the next, and the next. His friends couldn't believe his luck – nor could Aius. His good humour – and his coinage – all but gone, he regarded Piso with a black expression. 'I'm starting to think that you're a cheating bastard. Those dice of yours must be weighted.'

'They are not!' protested Piso.

Afer leaned in close. 'Piso. Time to go.'

'It's all right,' said Aius, waving a hand. 'We have one more throw to play.'

'One sestertius?' enquired Piso. That was all the money Aius had left on the table.

'Damn it, no!' Aius rooted in his purse, and slapped down a pair of curved bronze fasteners, the type used to hold the shoulder doubling on mail shirts in place. 'These, against all your coins.'

The fasteners had been well made; they were graceful-looking but solid, and were worth a deal more than the money Piso had won. He turned one over, then the other. 'M AIVS I FABRICII' had been stamped on to one; 'M AII I) FAB' incised on to the other. They both said that the fasteners were the property of Marcus Aius, of the century of Fabricius, in the First Cohort.

'But if I win, and someone finds me with them, I'll get accused of being a thief,' objected Piso.

'You can scratch out my name easy enough, and have your own marked in on top. Don't worry about it, however. You're going to lose.' Shaking the dice in his fist, Aius flipped them on to the table. A smile spread across his face. 'Not bad. Two fours.'

Piso was about to throw his own dice when Aius offered his. 'Use these.'

It was clear that there would be a fight if he didn't. With a shrug, Piso accepted the bone cubes, shook them to and fro, and let fly. The first dice came to a stop at the edge of the table – a four – but the second fell to the floor. He glanced at Aius, who had an unpleasant grin on his face. 'Invalid throw,' he said.

'Very well.' Bending down, Piso was annoyed to see a six staring up at him. Cupping both hands around the dice this time, he rolled them about for a count of two and let go. His heart thumped in his chest as the dice skated over the surface, coming to rest by Aius' folded arms.

'A four and a five. With my own dice. What an old bitch Fortuna is,' Aius growled.

'It was bad luck, right enough. Maybe you'll fare better next time.' Piso picked up the fasteners and Aius' last coin, and feeling the need to avoid trouble, stood. 'See you around.'

Over the next hour or two, the three friends wandered the streets, devoured some greasy food from an open-fronted restaurant and had a couple more drinks. There had been no sign throughout of Aius or his comrades, and Piso had almost forgotten them. He had told his story multiple times, and was about to begin it yet again, when Afer could take no more. 'We were there, Piso, and saw you win, over and over. It was good fortune, but we don't need to hear about it for the rest of the damn night!'

'Fair enough,' replied Piso, a little put out. His disgruntlement vanished ten paces later, outside one of the better brothels in the vicus. A sign hanging over the entrance depicted a painted phallus, and one of its whores stood half-clad in the doorway, entreating male passers-by to come in. 'Got enough coin to go in here?' he asked his comrades.

'Aye – if you're paying,' retorted Afer.

Vitellius was quick to chime in. 'I wouldn't say no either.'

'Piss off, the pair of you,' grumbled Piso, turning away. 'I'm not wasting my winnings on you.'

His comrades' ribbing continued for a distance down the street. None of the three noticed Aius and several of his companions emerge from the brothel, recognise them, and summon the rest of their group from a restaurant opposite. Like a pack of dogs stalking a cat, they crept up behind the trio.

The first Piso knew of it was when Vitellius, who was a little way behind, let out a sharp cry. In the same moment, a carter steering an ox-drawn wagon laden with bricks walked out of a side street, cutting him and Afer off from their friend. Desperate to reach Vitellius – it was clear from the shouted curses and cries of pain that he was being attacked – Piso scrambled under the cart on his hands and knees, between its front and back wheels. All he could see beyond was a mass of legs, kicking at a prone shape. 'Vitellius!' Driving forward, Piso grabbed the nearest man round the lower legs and took him tumbling to the ground. Letting go, he swept another off his feet in the same manner and managed to punch another in the balls. Shouts and roars told him that Afer was doing some damage too, but their enemies had realised what was going on. Piso found himself surrounded by four legionaries. Light cast by the torches burning outside a tavern revealed one to be Aius. 'Thought you could take the piss out of the First Cohort and get away with it, did you?' Aius cried.

That was how he'd got his friends to come along so readily, thought Piso. Protest was futile. Resistance was futile too, but he couldn't just stand there. 'Fuck you, Aius!' he roared, and threw himself at the broken-nosed legionary. He landed two good punches, one to the belly and another to the face, when something hit him on the side of the head. Stars burst across his vision, and Piso felt his knees fold. At once the blows started to rain down. Before the pain took over, he had a brief thought that Vitellius had done a far better job of saving him in Aliso than he had of Vitellius here. Poor old Afer was getting it too, all because *he* hadn't just walked away from the damn dice.

A kick to Piso's solar plexus drove the air from his lungs in a mighty *whoosh*. A world of pain erupted then, in his head, through his whole being. He retched, brought up a mouthful of rancid wine, nearly choked on it. *Stamp*. One of his ribs broke. Someone raked their hobnails down his arm, and Piso felt his flesh tear open. If he'd been able, he would have screamed. Winded, almost paralysed by the blow to his midriff, he could do nothing but lie there, helpless as a babe.

Then, for no apparent reason, the punishment stopped.

Piso felt instant relief, but renewed terror that his assailants were planning something worse.

'What in the name of fucking Hades is going on?' roared a voice.

Piso rolled over, groaning with the pain that the movement caused. Opening his puffy eyes, he tried to focus, but could see nothing other than a sea of shuffling feet.

Crack. It was the unmistakeable sound of a vitis landing. A yelp followed. 'Answer, you maggot!'

Is that Tullus? Piso wondered, feeling a trace of hope seep into his foggy brain.

'It's just a fight, sir. Got a bit out of hand, that's all.'

Crack. The vitis connected again, eliciting another anguished cry. '"A bit out of hand," he says, when it's eight, nine – no, ten of you against three! What big fucking men you are!' *Crack*. *Crack*. *Crack*. More bawls and shouts of pain. 'Over there, against the wall – all of you! MOVE IT, YOU SHOWER OF CUNTS!'

The legionaries filed away. Piso rolled over, and was relieved to see Afer close by. Blood was running down his forehead, and one of his eyes was closed, but he was able to leer at Piso. 'Where's Vitellius?' asked Piso.

Afer pointed. Their friend lay a few paces away, unconscious. Piso was comforted to see that his chest was rising and falling. He might be badly hurt, but he wasn't dead.

'Gods above and below. I should have known it'd be you.' Tullus, solid as a tree trunk, was standing over Piso. He extended a hand. 'Can you get up?'

'I think so, sir.' Taking the grip, Piso managed to push himself up with wobbly legs. The world spun, and he grabbed Tullus' shoulder. 'Sorry, sir,' he mumbled, releasing it and almost falling again.

'Hold on to me, you fool.' Tullus' voice was gentler than normal. He guided Piso to the wagon. 'Lean against that.'

Piso clutched the planking as if it were a branch found at sea by a shipwrecked sailor.

Afer had managed to stand on his own. He weaved his way to Vitellius, and knelt.

'How bad is he?' asked Tullus.

'I'm not sure, sir. He's out for the count.'

Tullus' brow lowered further. He stared at Piso. 'What happened?'

'It was nothing more than a few games of dice, sir, with one of the soldiers. He really didn't like losing these, I think.' He pulled the bronze fasteners from his purse and handed them over.

'Swear to me that you're telling the truth.'

'I swear it, on my mother's life, sir.' There was a non-committal grunt, and Piso added, 'May Jupiter strike me down if I lie, sir.' He held his breath as Tullus peered at the fasteners, front and back. Then he watched, his nerves taut as a wire, as Tullus strode over to the legionaries, who were little more than a line of black figures outlined against the tavern wall.

'It turns out that the men you were beating are from my century. Your reasons for beating them better be fucking good, I can tell you,' Tullus threatened. 'My soldier here tells me this whole pile of shit is about a game of dice. He says that one of you took exception to losing his money, and these fasteners.'

'It wasn't that, sir,' protested one legionary. 'He was mouthing off about the First Cohort.'

'What did he say?' barked Tullus.

There was a short silence, and the legionary said, 'Err, not sure, sir. It was Aius here told us.'

'You're Aius?' demanded Tullus.

'Yes, sir.'

'Enlighten me as to what was said.'

Aius reeled off a list of insults, every one of which was credible as something that might be hurled at a unit: the First Cohort were all *molles*, arselovers. They were cowards too, men who would always run from a fight. They were a disgrace to the legion. 'I could go on, sir,' said Aius.

'That's fine, legionary,' interrupted Tullus. 'Tell me why three soldiers would say things like that when they were so outnumbered by the very legionaries they were insulting?'

'I-I couldn't say, sir. It must have been the drink talking.'

'The drink talking,' Tullus repeated. He stuck his face into Aius'. 'I could believe that of certain men, perhaps, but I know my soldiers quite well. Pissheads they may be, stupid too, to some extent, but they're not cretins!' He rammed the fasteners partway up Aius' nose and pulled them out again, leaving Aius groaning. 'These are inscribed "Marcus Aius of the First Cohort". That *would* be you?'

'Yes, sir.' Aius' voice was muffled by his hands, which were clutching his face.

'And you lost them in a game of dice not long ago, to that man over there?' Tullus pointed at Piso.

'Aye, sir.'

'How many years' service have you completed?'

'Twelve, sir,' replied Aius.

'If I've learned one thing as a centurion, it's that a soldier who gambles pieces of his kit, a veteran in particular, is a man with a problem. My gut is telling me that you're such an individual.' Aius did not reply at once, and Tullus bawled, 'Would I be correct?'

'I wanted to get my money back, sir,' mumbled Aius. 'And those fasteners.'

'I thought as much,' Tullus snapped. Moving closer to one of the torches, he produced a wax tablet and a stylus. 'Approach, one at a time. I want names, any distinguishing features, century, and your centurion's name.'

Piso watched with increasing pleasure as the ten legionaries filed past Tullus, giving their details and showing him the scars, birthmarks or tattoos that would identify them from other men. None dared ask what their punishment would be. When Tullus was done, he glanced at Afer. 'How's Vitellius?'

'He's come to, sir,' came the answer. 'Says he's not too bad.'

Piso could have sworn that relief flashed across Tullus' face. 'Lucky for you maggots that he's woken up,' he yelled at Aius and the rest. 'Piss off, the lot of you. Centurion Fabricius will be hearing about this in the morning.' With *thwacks* of his vitis, he drove them away. Piso took great satisfaction from the fact that the man he'd punched in the balls was walking with an odd gait.

His good spirits lasted as long as it took Tullus to determine again that their injuries weren't too serious. After that, he lambasted them from a height. 'What kind of stupid bastard starts gambling with a soldier who's got half his century with him? No legionary of mine should *ever* be caught fighting in the street either. What kind of lowlifes are you?'

Piso and the other two absorbed the tirade in silence. They didn't complain either when Tullus confined them to camp for a month, adding in latrine duty for the same period, nor when he promised them extra training marches the moment that the surgeon pronounced them fit. At length, he finished his rant. He gave them each a hard stare, which they met with reluctance. 'Out of my sight,' he ordered. 'Back to barracks.'

Supporting Vitellius on either side, Piso and Afer began to edge around the wagon. The dumbstruck carter, who had been watching from a safe distance, not yet certain that the trouble was over, ventured towards his oxen.

'Piso.'

Piso looked back.

'Were your winnings worth it?' asked Tullus.

Piso ached all over. His friends must too, he thought, in particular poor Vitellius. 'No, sir.'

'Think before you play dice the next time, eh? The First Cohort might be arrogant whoresons, but they're tough.'

'Yes, sir. We're grateful you happened upon us.'

Afer and Vitellius were quick to add their thanks.

'Just as well I did.' To Piso's amazement, Tullus handed him the bronze fasteners. He chuckled. 'After a fight like that, a man should hold on to what he won.'

VIII

Tullus and the rest of the party left Vetera soon after first light, every man relishing the clear sky, the crisp, fresh air and the dew on the roadside grass. Varus had dressed like Tullus, in a simple, off-white tunic and sturdy hobnailed sandals. Rather than a sword, he wore a dagger on his belt. Anyone who didn't know him would have had no idea that he was the most important man in the whole province, thought Tullus. That, he suspected, was something that Varus was relishing. No doubt he was also looking forward to – as Tullus was – a day without the grinding routine of army life. Today would be a chance to forget the drudgery, the aggravation of dealing with malingering soldiers, self-important quartermasters and arrogant officers such as Tubero.

Arminius had with him Maelo and a dozen men, two of whom were driving a cart that carried six caged hunting dogs. At Vala's insistence, Varus had brought along a century of legionaries, extra personal protection. It was awkward enough for men in civilian dress to pursue a boar through woodland, thought Tullus, let alone those who were in full armour, carrying javelins and shields, yet he wasn't against the idea of the escort. Arminius was a trusted Roman ally, but Tullus didn't know him well yet. Arminius aside, there were plenty of people east of the Rhenus who regarded Governor Varus if not as an enemy, then as an oppressor.

With the legionaries and tribesmen following, Arminius and Maelo guided Varus and Tullus to a forested area some eight miles from the bridge over the Rhenus. Tullus knew the location well – to see. He had passed it many times over the years, on his way to and from Aliso or further afield, but had never had cause to leave the road. If the truth were told, he'd always thought the forest a potential spot for an ambush. Left to his own devices, he would have had the beech trees cut back further from the road, reducing the chances of any attackers falling upon unsuspecting patrols. The location had been deemed 'low risk' by the legate, however, and Tullus had given up mentioning it. Despite the jovial atmosphere, therefore, and the fact that this was likely to be a good place to start the hunt, he felt a tickle of unease.

'How is it that the trees haven't been chopped down for firewood, or to increase grazing?' he asked Arminius. 'We passed a settlement not far back.'

'The Usipetes believe that it would bring them bad luck,' said Arminius, touching the little hammer amulet at his neck. 'This ground is sacred to Donar, the thunder god.'

Tullus spotted Arminius' reaction. 'Is he important to you?'

Arminius' grey eyes darkened. 'Aye, he is. Do you favour a deity?'

'No single one. I pay my respects to Jupiter, Mars and Mithras, but I don't rely on any of them to get me out of trouble, or Fortuna. I count on my soldiers, and this.' Tullus tapped the *gladius* that hung from his belt.

'A sensible approach.' If Arminius thought it unusual for a man to take a sword on a hunt, he didn't say. 'And you, governor?'

'I believe that the gods are all around us, but it's rare for them to interact with humankind. I've also found it best to depend on those whom I can see with my own eyes,' replied Varus.

'If this area belongs to Donar, is it wise to hunt here?' Tullus enquired.

'As long as we enter the trees with respect in our hearts, and make an offering of whatever we may kill, the thunder god will be content. So I have always been told by our priests.'

Maelo muttered something unintelligible in German. Never fond of not knowing what was going on, Tullus threw an enquiring glance at Arminius.

'Maelo said that it wouldn't be a good idea for us – or more particularly you Romans – to enter the sacred grove,' continued Arminius with a smile.

'I can understand that,' said Varus. 'And I have no wish to upset your god, Arminius. Let us ask that any quarry we find stays well away from it.'

'It's odd, but even the animals seem to give the place a wide berth.'

'Perhaps it's the smell of blood,' suggested Maelo, in Latin this time.

A look passed between him and Arminius, which Tullus couldn't read. It made his unease grow. 'Where shall we begin?'

'This is a good place,' answered Maelo. 'I've seen boar and deer tracks around here before.'

They dismounted and led their horses off the road. The legionaries came to a halt and waited for orders, while the cart carrying the dogs was last to trundle up alongside. A frenzy of whining and barking went up the moment that the vehicle's wheels stopped turning. The dogs leaped out, allowing their handlers to place leashes around their necks with the greatest reluctance. They were of two types: a tall, rangy trio with shaggy grey hair and deep chests, which would be excellent at chasing down deer, and three stocky-framed dogs with broad heads and massive jaws, bred to face charging boars.

'They're even more eager than we,' said Varus with a smile.

'Aye, sir.' The prospect of a chase was exciting Tullus too. He cast his eyes over the trees once more, and saw nothing. There's no one out there, he told himself, and we have a century of legionaries with us. Relax. Enjoy the hunt. 'What are we to do with the men, sir?' he asked Varus.

'I told Vala that they'd be useless in the forest, but he wouldn't listen. "Your position as governor requires you to have an escort, sir."' Varus was silent for a moment. 'We leave them here, and pick them up when we return.'

Tullus was thrown by Varus' casual attitude. Unbidden, Caedicius' words ran through his head. 'Expect the unexpected. You must always be prepared to fight.' Arminius only had a few men with him. And, thought Tullus, they were Germans, not Romans. Their loyalty could not be guaranteed. 'Beg your pardon, sir, but I agree with Vala. We should take some of them at least.'

'What could happen?' asked Varus, frowning. 'We're on Vetera's doorstep, and Arminius' warriors will be with us.'

'You need have no cause for concern, Tullus,' Arminius murmured.

'You mistake me. I'm not concerned. It would be a good idea, that's all,' replied Tullus, smiling to show he meant no offence. Inside, he was thinking: Ally of Rome you might be, but I'd rather have some of my own to guard my back, and the back of the most important man in Germania.

Finding a deep patch of shade under the branches of an impressive beech, Tullus stopped. 'Thirsty, sir?' He slipped one of his two water skins off his shoulder and offered it to Varus.

'My throat's as dry as a Judaean riverbed.' Varus wiped his brow with his tunic sleeve and paced over to accept the bag. Taking a long pull, he grimaced. 'Nothing like the taste of oiled leather, eh? It reminds me of being on campaign.'

'It's pretty foul, sir, but better—'

'—than nothing,' said Varus, interrupting with a smile. 'I know.'

Seeing that they had paused, Arminius also came to a halt. 'I hadn't expected it to be quite this warm.' He slapped at a biting fly, just one of clouds that hung in the muggy air, plaguing them at every opportunity. 'Perhaps it wasn't the best day to track down a boar.'

'Nonsense,' Varus declared. 'Here, I have no paperwork to deal with, no clerks with urgent requests. I am my own master. That, let me tell you, is something that money cannot buy.'

Arminius cocked his head. 'What do you say, Tullus?'

'Eh?' Tullus was watching the fifteen purple-faced, sweating legionaries, who were beginning to appear. The road was perhaps two miles to their rear, but the soldiers looked as if they'd just marched five times that distance.

'How are you bearing up?' asked Arminius.

'Better than those poor bastards.' He gestured at the legionaries, and added, 'I'll be content if we don't come away empty-handed by the day's end.'

'Maybe Donar doesn't want us to find anything,' offered Varus. 'Have you thought of that, Arminius?'

'He will reward us if we persist. This is perfect ground to find a boar.' Arminius pointed at a nearby fallen tree, the gnarly trunk of which was covered in exuberant growths of fungi. 'They love rooting around those, searching for insects and worms. There's a boggy area by a stream not far away too. During hot weather, they like to roll in the mud. Even if we don't find a boar, we're bound to see a deer.'

'Gods grant we bring down something. My belly's clapped to my backbone,' said Varus.

Arminius rummaged in the pouch at his belt. 'Here,' he said, proffering a dark strip of material.

Varus eyed it with some suspicion. 'What in the gods' name is that?'

'Dried bear meat.'

'There's a first time for everything,' said Varus, putting it in his mouth. Tullus, who had eaten bear before, watched with some amusement as his commander chewed and chewed. 'I'm glad I still have most of my teeth. It's as tough as old leather,' Varus said when he'd swallowed it. 'Tasty, though. Is it from a bear you killed?'

'Indeed it is.' Arminius thrust back and forth with his spear, miming. 'He was a tough one. Killed four of our dogs before I took him down.'

'You have my respect. Bears are formidable creatures,' said Varus. 'I have never slain one, and I am not sure I ever want to get close enough to try.'

'Your stout heart and steady spear would see you through,' declared Arminius.

Varus looked pleased, but the compliment made Tullus uneasy. Arminius is a born charmer, he thought. Some might even say arse-licker.

BOOOOOO! BOOOOOO!

Food, drink, idle chat forgotten, the three twisted to face where the horns had blown, to their front.

'They have found something,' announced Arminius. 'Best hurry, or it will have fled.'

'Follow as fast as you can,' Tullus ordered the nearest legionary, who nodded dully. As they outstripped their escort with ease, he worried again about an ambush. The recent trouble with the Usipetes brought them first to his mind. It wasn't impossible that a dozen well-armed warriors might jump out from behind those sessile oak trees, for example, or that massive beech. He and Arminius wouldn't stand a chance. The governor of Germania, dead, just like that. Tullus quelled the grim image. The Usipetes don't know we're here, he told himself. Relax.

Trampling the green-leaved wood melick that grew everywhere, the three ran towards the horns.

BOOOOOO! BOOOOOO! BOOOOOO!

Arminius was the youngest and fittest, and soon drew into the lead. In response, Tullus slowed until he was last. It felt better to watch Varus' back, and it let the governor determine the pace. They went down a sloping bank, trampled through a dry stream bed and up the other side, into a mixed area of sessile oaks and beech. Tullus cursed as the tip of his spear snagged against a low-hanging branch and wrenched his wrist to the side. There was no time to check if it was sprained: Arminius was shouting something about being quite close. Tullus ducked his head to avoid a whipping bramble caused by Varus' passage, but didn't see the second, spindly length that followed. Thorns tore all along his cheek, and then he was free. Tullus dabbed at his face, and his fingers came away red. He kept running.

Perhaps three hundred paces further on, Arminius halted to check his bearings. Despite the chorus of squeals and barks that was audible ahead, Tullus was grateful for a reprieve. The heat and the muggy forest air were more strength-sapping than he cared to admit. Varus, who had done well thus far, was in a worse way than him. Sweat was pouring down his bright red face, and his chest was rising and falling like a smith's bellows as it coaxes a fire to life.

'All right, sir?'

'I'll . . . be fine. Give me . . . a moment.'

Tullus walked a few paces back into the trees, unsurprised to see no sign of their escort. He found he was holding his sword hilt, but he let his fingers fall away as he turned back to the other two. It was better that neither see his unease.

Maelo had appeared by Arminius' side. 'It's a boar. A big male,' he announced. 'The dogs caught up with it, but it escaped. You need to hurry, or you've got no chance of a kill.' Both Cheruscans cast a look at Varus, who waved a hand. 'Lead on. I won't fall behind.'

'Just follow the noise.' With a grin, Arminius took off after Maelo. It wasn't long before their dark clothing blended with the trees, and they vanished.

'Where are the legionaries?' asked Varus, as if he had felt Tullus' disquiet.

'Coming along behind us, sir. They'll reach us soon,' said Tullus, who wasn't at all sure that they would.

'This is harder than I thought it would be.' Looking rueful, Varus mopped his brow. 'I need to exercise more. It doesn't take long for a man to run to fat when he's stuck at a desk every day. Best keep going, though, or we'll kill nothing. Lead on.'

In the event, things happened fast. The cacophony of barking, yelps and squeals grew deafening as they drew nearer. Men were shouting and, through the trees, Tullus could see figures running to and fro. 'Prepare yourself, sir,' he said. 'The boar could be coming back this way.'

'Look out!' It was Arminius' voice.

Tullus and Varus moved apart, their eyes searching the ground before them.

The boar burst into sight half a dozen heartbeats later. A blur of motion, it came at an incredible speed. Thick-bodied, with a hump at the shoulders and covered in a thick layer of hair, it was the size of a small cart, yet it tore through the trees faster than an athlete could sprint. The tusks jutting from the sides of its slavering mouth revealed it to be a male. Barking furiously, the three boarhounds came charging after, nipping at its heels.

Tullus laughed, half amused, half frustrated. The boar would pass within fifty paces of him, but unless it slowed, it might as well be a mile away. He was no slouch with a javelin, but he couldn't hurl a heavy spear with enough power or accuracy to bring down a beast of that size at that distance. The boar would disappear into the forest, and their pursuit would have to start all over again.

He hadn't reckoned on the hounds, or Varus, who found a hidden reserve of energy. As one of the dogs managed to catch hold of the boar's right hind leg, slowing its progress, Varus ran forward, his spear at the ready. Tullus blinked in surprise, and followed. In battle, a man who hesitated was lost.

Furious, the boar wheeled on its attacker. There was a loud yelp as one of its tusks connected, and the dog released its grip. Before the boar could flee, however, another hound had seized hold of its haunches. Squeals shredded the air, and the boar turned anew, gouging at the second dog's head and neck. Droplets of blood flew everywhere, but instead of letting go, the dog clamped its jaws even tighter. This was what its two companions had been waiting for. Hurling themselves forward, they sank their teeth into whatever part of the boar came within reach.

Tullus was still about fifteen paces from the spinning mass of flesh, but Varus had closed right in. He drove at the boar with his spear. Whether it was accuracy or blind luck, Tullus couldn't tell, but Varus' blade sank into the beast's neck rather than into one of the dogs. The weapon was almost ripped from his hands as the boar bucked and tossed in an effort to free itself, but Varus hung on. Tullus reached the maul and took a position several steps away. When his chance came, he too stuck his spear into the boar, taking him in the belly. Spitted on two shafts, the boar shrieked his distress, but he was far from done. With a vicious swipe of his tusks, he eviscerated one of the hounds, which fell away, yelping. At once the boar focused its attention on another of the dogs. Shouting encouragement at Tullus, Varus ran his spear even deeper into the beast's neck. Tullus emulated the governor, shoving his weapon so far in that he wondered if it would emerge on the other side. He was now far closer to the boar and its gore-tipped tusks than he would have wished. Its rank odour clawed at the back of his throat. If it broke either of their spear shafts, he thought, they could be injured or killed.

There was a heavy impact as another spear was plunged into the boar. Tullus wasn't ashamed to feel relief that Arminius had arrived. Even with three spears in its body, and two dogs hanging off it, the boar would not die. It wasn't until Varus' blade slid right into its chest cavity that that happened. Gouts of bright red blood poured from its mouth as it shuddered its way to oblivion.

Its dead weight was far too great to hold up. Tullus and the others released their spears as one, letting the boar collapse to the ground. Fierce grins split their faces as the reality sank in. 'Fine work, sir,' said Tullus.

'Yours was the first strike?' Arminius saluted Varus. 'You did well, governor. He must weigh as much as three men.'

'I didn't stop him. It was that poor creature.' Varus gestured at the gutted dog, which was being dispatched by Maelo.

'Nonetheless, it takes balls to charge a boar of that size, and to stay with him until another hunter can get to you,' said Arminius. He spoke a couple of sentences in his own tongue – Tullus heard the words 'first to blood his spear' – and the gathering warriors called out in appreciation. When Arminius pulled free his hunting blade and raised it, crimson-coated, to the sky, they joined in his shout. 'Varus! Varus! Varus!'

His concerns about the Usipetes set aside, so too did Tullus. Varus had a name for being a brave man, an individual who got things done, and this was proof of it. The governor *was* a man to follow, which made Arminius' continuous stream of compliments more likely to be genuine.

Tullus' disquiet about Arminius lingered, however. Life had taught him that people who worked hard to win others over always had an ulterior purpose.

What was Arminius' motive?

The sun was falling in the sky and the muggy heat had abated by the time that the party neared the Rhenus. Small boys clutching poles and strings of fish stood by the roadside, watching as the soldiers passed by. Scrawny pups by their feet yapped futile challenges. An old woman sat by a little stall covered with vegetables, crying in bad Latin that her produce was the best in all of Germania.

Tullus was riding at the front as before, with Varus, Arminius and Maelo. They had been sharing skins of wine since reaching the wagon, and Tullus was half pissed. It wasn't surprising. He'd had nothing to eat since dawn except a strip of Arminius' dried bear meat, and he had shed a bucketload of sweat during the long hunt through the forest. If he had been one of the unfortunate legionaries who had accompanied them, Tullus decided, or one of the warriors who had lugged the boar's gutted carcase back to the road, he wouldn't have made it to the end of the day. He was getting old, that was the problem. Stop it, you fool, he ordered himself. Some of your new recruits wouldn't have kept up today.

'Tullus.'

With an effort, he focused on Varus. 'Yes, sir.'

'You'll dine with me tonight,' Varus repeated. 'Arminius and Maelo will be there too.'

'I'd be honoured, sir.'

'I will need the company. Arminius is saying that because mine was the first spear into the boar, I must eat one of its balls.'

Tullus glanced at the Cheruscans in disbelief. 'It's our tradition,' said Arminius, grinning. 'The most courageous hunter has to savour the bravest part of the boar.'

'You'll both have a mouthful too,' warned Varus, also smiling. 'But the other bollock belongs to Tullus.'

Tullus, who had been drinking from the skin, spluttered wine everywhere. Arminius threw back his head and laughed. 'Sir . . .' Tullus managed.

'There'll be plenty of good wine to wash it down, you have my word,' said Varus.

'As our host today, you must have at least one mouthful of mine as well,' Tullus shot at Arminius.

Arminius grinned in acceptance. 'So be it.'

Tullus winked, glad to have paid Arminius back a little. In truth, he wasn't that bothered about eating a few mouthfuls of rubbery testicle. It was a small price to pay for the vintages that Varus had at his disposal.

Tullus' good humour faded soon after, however, when he spotted a horse and rider galloping towards them from the direction of Vetera. No one rode that fast unless there was an urgent reason, and in Tullus' long experience, it was seldom a good one. 'Messenger approaching, sir,' he said.

Varus' mouth turned down as he too spied the horseman. 'We're not even over the river, and already duty calls.' He urged his mount in front of the rest and, with an imperious wave, gestured that the rider should halt.

The man *was* a messenger, thought Tullus, spotting the 'SPQR' brand on the horse's withers. Augustus might be the first emperor, but the mark, a vestige of how things had been in the Republic, remained in use. Men such as these carried official news the length and breadth of the empire, renewing their mounts at the regular way stations. It was possible that whatever Varus was about to hear had come all the way from Augustus, in Rome.

The messenger looked none too happy at being stopped. 'I seek Publius Quinctilius Varus,' he cried.

'And you have found him,' replied Varus in a sardonic voice.

The messenger's face could not have fallen any further. 'My apologies, sir. I did not recognise you.'

Varus made an impatient gesture. 'Who sent you, and what news do you carry?'

'Vala said I should find you with all speed, sir. Reports are coming in of a band of Usipetes that have crossed the river, some distance between here and Asciburgium. They have sacked numerous farms, and are moving westward.'

Varus let out a ripe oath. 'How many?'

'It's not clear, sir. Several hundred at least.'

'Anything else?'

'Vala said that it was too late to send out any troops, sir. He knew that you were returning from a hunt, and would want to decide on the best response.'

Dismissing the messenger with orders for Vala to organise a meeting of his senior officers, Varus regarded Tullus with a faint smile. 'The Usipetes were unhappy with my ruling after all. They will have to be taught the error of their ways.'

'Aye, sir,' replied Tullus with a grim nod.

'Refrain from drinking any more wine. You too, Arminius.'

'You'd like me to be part of the retaliatory force, governor?' asked Arminius. Tullus glanced at him, wondering if he had sensed a tinge of reluctance in his voice. The Cheruscan's face was bland, however.

'I would. Tullus too,' answered Varus. 'Tubero will lead you. It'll be an opportunity for him to learn from both of you how things are done.'

IX

When Arminius heard about the Usipetes' raiding party, he was furious. Varus could respond in but one manner. Retaliation. Why did Varus have to pick him to be part of it? The Usipetes were his allies, secret or no. If their chieftains heard that their warriors had been slain by Cheruscans and, worse still, that he had been involved, any chance of their cooperation would vanish forever.

If Arminius could have, he would have seen that the raiding party was wiped out. Thanks to Varus' desire for prisoners, though, the raiders' fate had been taken out of his hands. Varus' legionaries would follow their orders. The best Arminius could do was to order *his* men to slay as many of the raiders as they could, and hope that the ones who were captured and interrogated didn't give anything away. Everything felt risky and uncertain, but he had to remain confident that the Usipetes' chieftains would not find out about his involvement.

At least the situation wasn't all bad. Varus' heavy-handed response would fan the flames of resentment towards Rome among other tribes. Those who might have wavered before would now be eager to throw in their lot when he called on them to do so.

The Usipetes *would* remain unaware, Arminius told himself. His ambitious alliance *would* come together. His plan *would* bear fruit.

A day had passed, and Arminius was riding south on the road that led towards Asciburgium. He had been astride his mount long enough for his arse to start aching. Most of his men were ranging ahead of the patrol, but he was at its front, with two turmae; Tullus and the legionaries were marching behind. Arminius had been counting the stone markers at the side of the paved road since they'd left Vetera, but his bad mood meant he'd forgotten how far they had come. The dull pain in his backside, he decided, meant it had to be about ten miles. The countryside was almost flat, as it was throughout the area. The river flowed along to his left, a constant feature, and there were open fields and occasional farmhouses to his right. From this point on, his scouts would be of vital importance, because no one knew where the Usipetes were.

Once they were found, victory was certain. The Roman force – two cohorts and half of Arminius' cavalry unit – would have no difficulty in dealing with the tribal war band. Ensuring that the Usipetes remained ignorant of their allies' participation in the Roman response to their raid was another matter altogether.

Not long after, Tullus rode forward from his position. Arminius had been impressed by Tullus' soldiers, who seemed well drilled, disciplined and responsive to their officers. This was a solid centurion, who like as not led by example. His men would follow him anywhere. In short, he was someone worth befriending – and also keeping a close eye on. Tullus had not understood Maelo's muttered comment during the early stages of the boar hunt, but he hadn't missed the look Arminius and Maelo had shared after the comment about the smell of blood. At some level, Tullus was suspicious of him, thought Arminius, pulling a hearty smile.

'Seen anything?' Tullus asked in a friendly enough tone.

'Not yet, but it's only a matter of time before my men find them. I suggested to the senior tribune that they scour the countryside ahead of us, in individual turmae, to cover more ground.' Arminius was pleased to see Tullus nodding in approval. 'They have orders to withdraw, unseen, at the first sighting of the Usipetes.'

'Where's the tribune?'

'He insisted on going with my men.' It was clear that Tullus didn't much care for Tubero. After what had happened on the patrol to Aliso, Arminius wasn't surprised. He filed the detail away for future use.

They rode on for a time, and then Tullus asked, 'Did the Usipetes' chieftains sanction this raid, d'you think?'

'If they did, they're damn fools,' said Arminius with feeling. 'Such acts will always be answered, in force.'

'Their entire people will suffer because of this.'

'They will.' But if my alliance remains unaffected, I don't care, thought Arminius harshly.

During the silence that fell after, Arminius caught Tullus rubbing at a puckered scar on the fleshy part of his left calf.

'That an old injury?'

'Aye. Nothing's ever the same once it's been thrust through by a blade. If I have regular massages, and remember to stretch it every morning, it doesn't cause me too much trouble. I can't march like I used to, worse luck. After a few miles, it begins to feel as if someone's tightening a vice inside the muscle.'

'Scar tissue,' pronounced Arminius.

'That's what the surgeon said. There's nothing to be done with it, other than keeping it as supple as possible.' Tullus threw him a glance. 'You must have had an injury or two.'

Arminius rapped his ornate helmet. 'I have a nice scar on the top of my head, courtesy of a warrior with a *falx* in Illyricum. Lucky for me, his blade was poor quality, and broke as it smashed my helm.'

'They are fearsome weapons. I've seen soldiers' brains dribbling from their cracked skulls after a strike from one. Your gods must have been smiling on you that day.'

'Donar was,' replied Arminius, thumbing his hammer amulet. 'I was careful afterwards to buy the most expensive helmet that I could afford. Under the braided hair and silverwork, this thing is half a finger of bronze thick.'

'It must be heavy.'

'At the end of a long day, my neck and shoulders know about it,' Arminius admitted. 'But you get used to it.'

'There's no point complaining, because everyone's in the same shitty boat.'

They both chuckled, and Arminius thought: He's starting to like me. Good.

Several hours later, Tubero returned at the head of one of Arminius' turmae. He was in buoyant mood, because they had been first to sight the Usipetes, in a settlement some four miles away. 'I was quick to pull the men back,' he said, 'although I wanted to ride in there and let the savages have it.'

'It was wise not to do so, tribune,' said Arminius.

'We could still attack them today,' cried Tubero, his face alight.

If we do that, thought Arminius, eyeing the sinking sun, some of them are bound to get away in the poor light. And if they've noticed that we Cherusci are involved . . . 'Your eagerness is infectious, tribune.'

Tubero grinned. 'You want to take them too!'

'I do, of course.' Arminius hesitated, and then added, 'I wonder if your plan might work better tomorrow, tribune, at dawn.'

Tubero frowned. 'How so?'

'Some of the Usipetes might still have their wits about them today. Give them a night of drinking whatever beer they find, however, and hit them first thing in the morning, and they won't know what has happened until it's too late. The whole thing will be done inside an hour.'

Tubero rubbed a finger across his lips, thinking. 'What about the villagers?'

'Most of them will already be dead, so the timing of our intervention won't make that much difference. Leaving the assault until tomorrow will also reduce the possibility of casualties. Imagine how pleased Varus would be not just that you succeeded in your mission, but that you lost only a handful of men.'

Tubero nodded.

'Another thing struck me, tribune. The Usipetes must have crossed the river by boat. Taking those craft would remove any chance of the raiding party escaping. If you were to send a century or two along the bank, say . . .'

'I could order them fired at dawn,' cried Tubero. 'When our trumpets sound the attack.'

'An excellent plan, tribune,' declared Arminius.

Tubero smiled, as if the entire idea had been his all along.

Arminius had ridden his horse a short distance off the road, into the middle of a field of young barley. As ever, Maelo was by his right side. Around them in a loose semicircle were all of his mounted warriors. The men's faces were fierce, eager, expectant.

The night-time cool was with them yet, but the sky was cloudless again, auguring the high temperatures of the previous few days. They had ridden from the marching camp with great care, passing the settlement by leading their horses, to reach their position in good time. It wouldn't be long before the trumpeters with Tubero sounded, however. The sun was peeking over the tops of the hazel and crab-apple trees that dotted the riverbank to their right.

Arminius was about to give his men their final orders. And more.

He chewed his lip. This moment had come sooner than he had wished. Even these, the men of his own tribe, might give the game away after he spoke to them – not here, but later. All his work, all his plans, everything he had dreamed of since he was a boy, could be undone by a subsequent unguarded remark to a Roman in Vetera.

Maelo sensed his unease. He leaned forward, rubbing his horse's neck. 'Arminius, they're loyal to you, heart and soul,' he said in a low voice. 'You don't have to tell them everything, just enough so that they understand why the raiders have to die. They won't flinch from the job. It's not as if there's any love lost between we Cherusci and the Usipetes.'

'True.' Arminius straightened his back, throwing back his shoulders. 'There's something I need to tell you.'

Silence fell.

'We Cherusci may serve Rome, but in our hearts, we're free men. Isn't that right?'

'Aye!' came a responsive roar.

Arminius tapped his silvered helmet. 'Despite all the trappings, I have *never* liked serving Rome. Never liked having to do what its *emperor* said, most of all when it had anything to do with our own tribe, or others. I don't want to pay this new tax either. What am I – a faceless labourer in a workshop?'

More voices of agreement.

'There comes a time in a man's life when servitude can no longer be borne.'

They watched him, naked curiosity – and wariness – filling their faces. 'Not every hunting dog loves its master, Arminius, but it still does his bidding,' called one warrior. 'The dog that bites its master can expect to have a knife drawn across its neck.'

'Especially if that hunting dog sleeps by its master's side,' added another.

'You speak true,' said Arminius. 'Auxiliaries – like us – who rebel against Rome are punished in the most severe ways. But if the Romans were to suffer a catastrophic defeat, if they were to lose thousands of soldiers at one stroke, I say that you will die of old age rather than at their hands, on a cross or in an arena. Why? Because afterwards, those Roman whoresons would be too scared to cross the damn river!'

His men liked that, but they still looked uneasy.

'You're talking about rebellion, Arminius,' said the warrior who'd mentioned the hunting dog.

'I am, plain and simple.' He let them suck on the marrow of that, and was pleased to see increasing numbers of men nodding. He raised his voice again. 'I have had enough of the Roman yoke around my neck. I *say* I am free, yet I have to do the Romans' bidding, have to pay their damn tax. I am a leader of the Cherusci, but I serve alongside one of their legions, fighting peoples with whom I have no quarrel. It is time to change these things. Time to become my own master again. Time to stand up and *fight*.' His eyes tracked over his men, slowly. 'Are you with me?'

'I am,' said Maelo, punching a fist in the air.

'And I!' Arminius was delighted to hear the warrior who'd spoken about hunting dogs and their masters. The men around him voiced their accord. It took a few moments, but then, like the rocks that follow the first stone of a landslide, the rest of his warriors joined in.

Arminius raised his hands. 'I am thankful that we are as one on this, but the Usipetes must not hear us, my brothers.'

'Why in Donar's name not? We should wake them so that we can all fight the Romans!' declared one man.

A good number of voices called out in agreement, but they quieted as Arminius began to speak again.

'It would give me great pleasure to act so, but the place to fall upon the Romans is not *here*. It's not *now*. We are too few, and I wish to wipe out not two cohorts, but three legions! The attack today must go ahead. If possible, every Usipetes warrior must be slain.' He continued as his men's faces filled with dismay. 'The truth of it is that the Usipetes' chieftains have already agreed to join our cause. If they find out that we have murdered some of their kin, Roman orders or no, they will tell me to shove it up my arse. That's if I'm lucky!' He was pleased that some warriors laughed. 'It's not just about the Usipetes either. We need several tribes to join us. If the Usipetes pull out, my chances of winning anyone else over will sink into the marsh, never to be seen again.'

Silence.

'I say this with a heavy heart, but we *have* to follow Varus' orders today. We must go even further in fact, to ensure that word of our involvement never crosses the river. If possible, every last one of the raiding party must be slain.' Arminius sat stiff-backed on his horse, his stomach twisting in knots. Ten heartbeats passed. A dozen more skipped by, and still no one spoke. Arminius held his peace, keeping his expression stern.

'Swear that if we act as you ask, you will deliver thousands of the whoresons to us,' demanded the 'hunting dog' warrior. 'Swear that we will wash away the stain of our actions with Roman blood.'

The weight of hundreds of men's stares bore down on Arminius. Donar, help me, he asked. The wrong word, or a slip of the tongue, and he would lose them.

'With Donar as my witness, I, Arminius of the Cherusci, make a solemn oath. With you by my side, I will teach the Romans a lesson that they will never forget. Their blood will flow in rivers; their cries of anguish will rend the heavens. Thousands of them will die, among them Varus himself. We will take their eagle standards as our own, and afterwards sacrifice their senior officers to the thunder god. In Rome, the *emperor* will tremble at the news of what we have done. Never again will his legions march through our lands! Never again will they trample our people!'

'I want to see that day,' declared Maelo, loyal as ever. 'I will follow you.'

'So will I, by all the gods,' said the 'hunting dog' warrior.

And like that, as if a god had passed his hand over them, his men's mood changed from wary and unsure to fierce and blood-hungry. 'I will do as you say, Arminius!' 'And I!' 'I'm with you!'

A moment later, the sound of trumpets rang out from the north.

Arminius smiled. He had won them over in the nick of time.

X

Tullus was standing at the head of his cohort in a mixed field of emmer and millet. To the legionaries' left, spelt was growing; to their right, lentils. The settlement lay to their north, about a quarter of a mile away. Dozens of thatched houses were visible past the crops. A fox trotted along the cart track which separated their field from the next, casting wary glances at the interlopers to its territory.

They had reached their position without incident, leading Tullus to think that the Usipetes had killed the inhabitants' dogs. Even at this distance, it was normal for visitors to attract a hysterical chorus of barking, yet their only greeting had been the crowing of a solitary cock.

There were no spirals of smoke rising from the roofs, so no women were up, preparing barley porridge or baking flatbread. Small boys weren't herding cattle to pasture, or sneaking in twos and threes to the river on fishing expeditions. Tullus felt even more certain that everyone was dead, and that the Usipetes were sleeping off the beer and mead they had drunk. He put the inhabitants' fate from his mind. Their misfortune, and the Usipetes' lack of foresight, would see the entire matter resolved fast.

His men had already spread out six centuries wide, with gaps of thirty paces between each unit. The other centurions were experienced men – but Tullus still made one last pass along the front of the cohort, checking that the legionaries were ready to advance, that they knew prisoners had to be taken. Some looked nervous. Many were praying. That was normal. Most wore fixed, determined expressions and the tense nods they gave Tullus was reassurance that they would do their job. He hadn't long resumed his own place, at the very right of the front rank of his century, when the unmistakeable blare of trumpets carried from beyond the settlement to the north. Tubero and Bolanus, the other cohort commander, were ready. Arminius and his men would be too. Regardless of his ambivalence towards the Cheruscan, Tullus knew the man would play his part.

His stomach knotted now, as it always did before a fight. He offered up his usual prayer, a calming ritual. Great Mars, hold your shield over me and my men. I swear to offer a sacrifice in your honour if most of us make it through. He had learned long ago not to ask that all his soldiers survived. 'Now,' he said to the two musicians by his side. As their instruments added their noise to Bolanus' trumpets, Tullus heard Arminius' horns sound to the south. 'Draw swords! Advance, at the double!' he shouted.

The charge began. The half-grown crop of emmer and millet, never to be harvested, was trampled into the earth by hundreds of studded sandals. They crossed a narrow cart track and entered a field of bitter vetch, flattening that too. A lone pig, one that must have escaped the Usipetes, ran off, squealing. Still there was no movement from the settlement. Tullus kept an eye on the other centuries' positions, but he made no attempt to keep his front rank parallel with the next unit along. There was no point.

This would not be a set-piece battle, when the legionaries halted a short distance from the enemy to hurl their javelins. Because of the village's irregular but typical layout – a centre point of a raised, palisaded mound with buildings and workshops of varying size arranged in large, irregular rectangles around it – any sense of formation would be lost as they arrived. From that point, Tullus would lose control of all but the eight or ten nearest men. The trumpeters would provide him with the wherewithal to issue basic orders to the rest of the cohort if needs be.

A hundred paces out from the first buildings, they came across the first body, of a man, lying on his front. Judging by his muddied sandals and worn tunic, he'd been a farmer. As they ran by, a cloud of flies rose, disturbed, from the red stain between his shoulder blades. The corpses came thick and fast after that. Men, women, children. The old, the lame, even the animals had not been spared. Beside a dead boy of about four, Tullus saw a pup that had had its skull crushed. He turned away in disgust, but the dreadful sights were everywhere, too many to block out. What had been done to the village women was the hardest thing to stomach. It hadn't mattered to the Usipetes whether they were toothless grandmothers or girls too young to have a monthly bleed. They had all been raped before being murdered. Upturned dresses hid the terror that must have distorted their faces, but the corpses' terrible wounds and their blood-smeared thighs were enough to bring bile rushing up Tullus' throat.

'Kill!' he shouted, unleashing the beast. 'Kill!'

'KILL!' his soldiers roared back. 'KILL!'

They were almost on top of the houses before the first Usipetes warrior emerged, tousle-headed and bleary-eyed, from a doorway. With an animal roar, Tullus outstripped his men. The warrior was still gaping in disbelief when Tullus' gladius rammed into his belly so hard that its tip emerged from his back. Tullus' ears filled with his victim's screams and he wrenched the sword free. Thrusts that powerful often caused a blade to wedge in a man's backbone, he thought. That could have meant a stupid death for him. It was fortunate, therefore, that the three other Usipetes inside the house were as drink-fuddled as their dying friend.

Tullus stormed through the doorway, kicking one warrior in the face and smashing the iron rim of his shield on the head of another even as he tried to rise. One of Tullus' legionaries was hot on his heels; he dispatched the third warrior as Tullus spun back to kill the men he'd stunned with precise thrusts to the chest. In-out. Blood everywhere. In-out. More crimson sprayed. Tullus was about to dispatch his first moaning victim when he caught sight, through the door, of the boy and the dead pup. With a curl of his lip, he stepped over the wounded man. 'Leave the filth to die,' he ordered.

Eight soldiers were waiting outside; the others had splintered off as he'd expected. Around them, chaos reigned. By a bonfire that yet smouldered, a score or more of dazed-looking Usipetes had been surrounded by several times their number of legionaries. They died still reaching for their spears. Others who had fallen asleep nearby met the same fate. Wood splintered as door after door was kicked in. Screams of panic followed as warriors woke to the sharp end of Roman swords.

A number of the houses were raised off the ground, standing on four thick wooden legs. When some of the legionaries discovered axes in a workshop, they sought out a building with Usipetes inside and instructed their laughing comrades to prevent any from leaving. As the structure began to wobble beneath their blades, the warriors within tried to climb down the ladder by the door. Two died before the rest retreated inside. Ten heartbeats later, the chosen leg collapsed. The entire structure followed, and as the warriors who yet lived tried to extricate themselves from the wreckage, they were finished off by the cheering legionaries.

The tactic was such a success that it was copied on other raised houses. It was a cruel way to die, but Tullus didn't intervene. What he'd seen had so revolted him that he didn't care how the Usipetes were slain. What counted was that their own casualties were few, and that they captured a number of prisoners. How many, Tullus hadn't yet decided. His men could bathe their swords in Usipetes blood for a time longer.

Not all the raiders proved so easy to kill, however. When spirals of smoke rising from the direction of the river announced the destruction of the Usipetes' boats, groups of warriors began to band together, even to try and break out of the settlement. While their desperate efforts were contained, it didn't end there. A short while later, Tullus' optio Fenestela came pounding over. There was blood spattered all over his face, which made him uglier than ever. He was unhurt, though, which relieved Tullus more than he liked to admit. 'What is it?'

'Tubero ordered us to herd as many of the Usipetes into the palisaded compound as we could, sir. It was a good place to trap them, he said. Trouble is, they weren't all as panicked as we might have liked. Some of them shut the gate. We've already lost five or six men trying to get inside.'

Tullus cursed. 'How many are in there, do you think?'

'Fifty, maybe more, sir.'

'Have you seen Bolanus or Arminius?'

'Bolanus' men are clearing out the rectangle to our left, sir. Arminius was talking to Tubero, last I saw.'

He should have told Tubero they'd turn the palisade into a defensive position, thought Tullus angrily. 'How many men have you gathered up?'

'Fifteen from our century, sir. They're watching the gate.'

'Take these legionaries, and one of the trumpeters. Encircle the palisade as best you can. I'll assemble a couple of centuries and come to join you.'

Fenestela's face grew concerned. 'Will you be all right with only a trumpeter, sir?'

Tullus threw Fenestela a sour glance. 'Piss off.'

'Very good, sir.' Fenestela eyed Tullus' nine soldiers. 'You heard the centurion, you foot-dragging pieces of shit! Follow!' He ran back the way he'd come, the men hard on his heels.

Tullus had his trumpeter sound the recall once, and not too loud. He didn't want panic to spread among the soldiers further away. It wasn't long before he had two centurions, several junior officers and more than a hundred legionaries standing before him in rough order. Tullus bawled out the reason that he'd ordered them to his side, and they replied with gusto.

Perhaps two centuries were with Tubero at the palisade. Success had eluded him thus far, Tullus saw. A decent number of legionaries lay in and around the gate, and Tullus asked that none of his men be among the dead. The Usipetes were giving no sign that they were ready to surrender.

Ordering his soldiers to form up beside Tubero's, Tullus went to see what was going on.

Tubero was lecturing Bolanus – who seemed most unhappy. There was no sign of Arminius. 'You've brought more troops,' said Tubero. 'Good.'

'Aye, sir, nearly two centuries.'

'We'll take the gate with the next attack, then. There are five ladders on the ground up there. If we fetch another half-dozen, that will be enough.'

'You had the men attack already, sir?' Tullus let his eyes wander to the bodies by the entrance.

'I ordered an immediate charge when I arrived, yes,' replied Tubero, bridling.

The number of dead had already told Tullus that the assault had been a resounding failure, and Bolanus' expression confirmed it. 'It didn't succeed, sir?'

Tubero's lips thinned further. 'No.'

'The Usipetes defended the palisade savagely,' said Bolanus. 'Eight legionaries were killed and a good number wounded. I mentioned sending to the camp for the bolt-throwers—'

'To Hades with the bolt-throwers!' cried Tubero. 'It would take half the day to transport them here. The men will attack again *now*. We outnumber the dogs four, five to one. They'll never hold.'

Tullus took a deep breath and said, 'It could be that you're right, sir, but they've seen the smoke from the boats, and our greater numbers. Every one of them knows he's going to die, which is why they're screaming blue murder, rousing themselves into battle frenzy. We'll lose a lot of men.'

'Your point is, *centurion*?' Tubero laid heavy emphasis on the last word.

'There's no need to suffer so many casualties, sir.'

'I am in charge here! I—'

Tullus' frustration bubbled over. 'Governor Varus sent me on this mission because of my experience, sir. A frontal assault isn't our only option.'

'Are you trying to tell me how to do my job, centurion?' cried Tubero.

'No, sir,' said Tullus, clenching his jaw.

'Good.'

'Maybe we should do as—' began Bolanus, but Tubero cut him off.

'The Usipetes haven't got enough men to defend the entire perimeter,' he said, as if no one else would have seen this. 'Take a group of soldiers around to the far side, Tullus. Scale the palisade, hit the bastards in the rear, and open the gate.'

He's seen sense, thought Tullus, guessing from what Bolanus had started to say that the original idea had belonged to Arminius. 'Very good, sir.'

Then came the sting in the tail. 'You can have twenty men.'

Twenty? thought Tullus in alarm. Arminius wouldn't have said to use that few. Would he? 'Forty would be better, sir.'

'Are your men are not up to the task?' needled Tubero.

'I'm not saying that, sir,' Tullus began to protest.

'Fine. Twenty it is then.'

'That's not enough, sir,' said Bolanus.

'If I want *your* opinion, Bolanus, I will ask for it.' Tubero's eyes were like chips of flint as he regarded Tullus. 'Be quick, centurion. I don't want to wait around all day.'

'Sir.' You spoilt, arrogant brat. Fuck you, Tullus thought, saluting. 'You'll attack when you hear the fighting begin?'

'Of course.'

Tullus strode off, lamenting his inability to keep his temper under control. Thanks to Tubero, it was possible that he had just opened a swift route to Hades for himself and twenty men.

Despite his fury, Tullus did not rush his soldiers into position. They were veterans, whose lives were too valuable to waste because of a new tribune's pique. If they had to die, he would ensure that they did so armed with everything that might help their cause. To scale the palisade fast, without men injuring themselves, ladders would be vital. Tullus gave thanks for the locals' raised houses. It was a simple matter to remove four ladders from buildings that hadn't been hacked down. Thus equipped, he, Fenestela and twenty legionaries from his century took a circuitous route out of the settlement – now also lined with Usipetes' corpses – and back through the fields they'd traversed a short time before. He could but hope that the warriors within the compound weren't keeping watch, or that his party was far enough away to remain unseen.

Fenestela hadn't queried their orders before Tubero or the men, but he'd served with Tullus long enough to do so in private. In low tones, Tullus explained what had happened. 'I was trying to stop lives being thrown away without need. The prick wouldn't listen. No doubt his head's full of the glory that this "stunning" victory will earn him. The quicker it's done, the better it will sound in his report to Varus.' He sighed. 'I lost it for a moment, Fenestela. I made it clear that it wasn't he who was in charge, but I. That's why we're on this fucking suicide mission.'

'I would have done the same, sir,' said Fenestela, spitting. 'He's a cunning bastard. Even if we fail, those tribesmen won't be able to hold out for long, so whatever happens, Tubero comes out smelling of roses. We'll just have to do the job without getting killed, eh? That's the best way of pissing him off.'

'You're incorrigible, Fenestela,' said Tullus, taking heart.

'I've no idea what that means, sir, but I'll take it as a compliment.'

Tullus laughed. 'It means, Fenestela, that there's no one else I'd rather have with me.'

Fenestela's grin made him uglier than ever. 'Likewise, sir.'

Tullus was pleased to find a small copse of beech and hornbeam northwest of the settlement. Whether it held a sacred purpose, he wasn't sure, but it ran quite close to part of the palisaded compound. He couldn't have asked for a better way to conceal his men. Leaving them in the depths of the trees, he and Fenestela crept to the copse's edge, where they took refuge behind a towering beech. They waited in silence, scanning the top of the palisade. There was still a considerable clamour going on, but it appeared to be coming from over by the gate.

'If there are any sentries, they're not doing a good job,' Tullus said after a time.

'Why don't I have a look, sir?' Fenestela indicated the branches above. 'I was a dab hand at climbing trees when I was a lad.'

'That was neither today nor yesterday,' said Tullus, watching with some amusement as Fenestela shed his belts and shucked off his mail shirt and the padded *subarmalis* below.

'Gods, but that feels good,' said Fenestela, raising and lowering his arms to let air waft under his sweat-sodden wool tunic.

'Get up there,' growled Tullus, linking his two hands.

Boosted to the first branch, Fenestela had soon scrambled above that to the second and then the third. Tullus' nerves jangled as he watched. If any of the Usipetes spied Fenestela, any chance of a surprise attack would vanish. To his relief, no shouts rose from within – close by at least – but he didn't relax until Fenestela leaped down to rejoin him. 'Well?' he demanded.

'There are a couple of warriors patrolling the walkway. They'll pass by soon.'

'We wait, then, until after they've gone.' Tullus clapped Fenestela on the arm. 'Keep an eye out as you get your kit on. I'll fetch the men.'

When Tullus returned, Fenestela reported that the sentries had gone by, oblivious to his presence. 'Fifty heartbeats ago, sir.'

'We move now.' Tullus didn't waste any time encouraging his soldiers. They knew what needed to be done – he'd already made that clear. Urging the men with the ladders out of the trees first, Tullus felt his pulse racing as if he were facing an enemy charge. Fortuna, give me two sixes now, he prayed.

They tramped through the greenery to the base of the palisade, which was about one and a half times a man's height. Muttered curses rose from the soldiers in the lead as brambles tore at their hands. Tullus glanced to the left and right, along the top of the palisade, but could see nothing. 'Up, up as fast as you can,' he said to the assembled legionaries. 'We'll regroup on the other side, and then head for the gate as if Cerberus was about to tear chunks out of our arses. Clear?'

'Aye, sir.' It was pleasing that, despite the danger, most of his men grinned.

Four ladders. Four men to lead the way. Four men to risk their lives first. Tullus was one, Fenestela another. The two others were legionaries who'd volunteered before Tullus had asked. The rest took their places behind the climbers, in little lines. Tullus' guts churned. They were few, so few. Fucking Tubero, he thought, you'd better order the attack when the fighting starts. He began to ascend. Beside him, the others did the same. One rung. Two. Three, and Tullus' head was almost over the spiked edge of the wooden rampart. It was then he realised that the red horsehair crest of his helmet would already be visible. Other than shouting, there was no better way to advertise his presence. Heart pounding like a smith's hammer on a white-hot blade, he placed his feet on the last rung, gripped the timbers with both hands and threw himself over the top of the palisade without checking if there were any warriors close by.

The air drove from his lungs as he landed on a narrow walkway; his nostrils filled with the tang of untreated timber. Tullus' flesh crawled; he was as helpless as a newborn that had fallen from the cot. He struggled to his knees and stood, finding to his relief that he could see no tribesmen, nearby at least. The compound was dominated by a large, grassy mound. Past it, he made out the gate and, around it, scores of warriors. They were too far away – three hundred paces or more – for him to estimate their exact number, but they outnumbered his force several times over. Loud thuds announced the arrival of Fenestela and the two legionaries. Tullus leaned out over the edge and beckoned at the rest. 'Move it! Move!'

By the time that the last of his men were atop the palisade, Tullus, Fenestela and the others had clambered down to the inside of the compound. Crazy though it was, they had still not been seen. Unslinging their shields, they waited for the final soldiers to join them. To calm his jangling nerves, Tullus studied the large space. It was typical of local villages, a gathering point for the entire community, where religious ceremonies, weddings and festivals could be held. The only structure was a large stone altar that stood in front of the earth mound. Tullus' jaw clenched. They would have no shelter as they made for the gate.

'Gather round,' he ordered. 'Our task is simple. We sprint to the gate like runners at an Olympic games. They'll notice us long before we get there, but we keep moving at all costs. Once we reach the gate, we open the bastard and let our brothers in.' They wouldn't get that far of course, but sounding confident was vital.

'Will our boys attack when they hear the fighting, sir?' asked a soldier.

'They will,' replied Tullus, thinking: I wouldn't trust Tubero as far as I could throw him, the miserable whoreson. 'But we don't need any help, do we?'

'No, sir!' said Fenestela. 'We'll shit on those Usipetes bastards from a height!'

Not every soldier's face registered the same certainty as Fenestela's. Some looked plain scared, but Tullus had no time to indulge them. 'Form up. Five wide, four deep. I'll take my usual place. Optio, stand in the rear rank, on the left.' The unspoken part of Fenestela's job would be to ensure that no one tried to retreat. Cynicism filled Tullus. Not that there was any point, here. 'Draw swords. Follow!'

He broke into a run, and twenty-one soldiers chased after. Tullus counted his steps, as he had since his first battle. It made the stomach-churning job of charging towards men who would kill him if they could a little easier.

A little.

Ten paces. Twenty. Thirty, forty, fifty. There had been no cries of alarm yet, no shouts from the Usipetes by the gate, or from the sentries on the walkway. Where in Hades were they anyway? Tullus didn't look, didn't move his eyes even a fraction from the main body of warriors. His mouth was dry, but sweat was running from under his felt arming cap. He swept it away with his right arm. Sixty paces. Seventy. Gods, are they blind and deaf? he wondered. Despite himself, he began to hope. Maybe the racket from without the palisade was concealing the noise of their approach?

At ninety-one paces, Tullus heard a cracked shout, then another. They'd been seen. He risked a look to the left, and to the right. One of the sentries was dancing up and down like a cat thrown on to still-hot embers, and yelling at the top of his voice. Tullus' eyes slid back to the gate, and the men defending it. Heads were turning, incredulity was registering, but no one had moved yet.

'DO NOT SLOW DOWN!' he ordered.

Content that a good number of the Usipetes were holed up in the palisade, Arminius had taken Maelo and a dozen of his best warriors to ride through the settlement and see how the rest of the raiders were faring. The one-sided nature of most of the fighting was most gratifying. So too was the lack of prisoners. The red mist of combat was affecting the legionaries as well as his own men, thought Arminius with satisfaction, which was just what he'd hoped for. Apart from at the palisade, it wouldn't be long before the battle ended. With luck, there would be almost no captives. It was time to seek out Tubero once more, to see that the same happened there.

Bolanus saw him approaching, and gave him a friendly look, but when Tubero noticed, he got only a haughty nod. What a prick, thought Arminius. But a useful one, potentially.

'Arminius,' said Bolanus. 'Is all well?'

'It is. Any remaining resistance will soon be crushed.'

Tubero glanced at the warriors atop the palisade. 'These ones won't hold out for long either.'

Arminius noted legionaries' bodies before the entrance that had not been there when he'd left. It seemed the boy still wasn't using his brain. 'Have you sent for the bolt-throwers, tribune?'

'For the love of Jupiter! You asked before. Tullus said the same thing,' Tubero snapped. 'No, I have not. I want to finish this before sundown. Tullus and twenty legionaries are going to scale the other side of the palisade and open the gate.'

'That's not very many men, tribune.'

'It is if I order an attack the moment fighting begins within,' retorted Tubero with a sniff.

Arminius set aside Tubero's annoying self-importance and the fact that

Tullus and his men stood a good chance of being killed. The palisade *would* be taken soon, one way or another. Hundreds of legionaries were on hand now, and he could do nothing about the prisoners who might be taken from this point on. What concerned him as much was the chance of raiders escaping over the palisade's unguarded back wall. He had to intervene, because success was within his grasp. Arminius lowered his voice so that the others present couldn't hear – the better to protect Tubero's fragile ego. 'It's clear that the gate must be taken, tribune, but I wonder if a multi-pronged attack would work better.'

Tubero scowled, but he didn't protest as Arminius explained how his men could split up and stand on their horses' backs to climb the palisade – in different places. 'The mission will be an unqualified success whatever happens, tribune, but fewer legionaries might die if you thought my advice worthwhile. The loss of a senior centurion would be a grievous loss. Varus—'

'All right, I see what you're driving at,' Tubero admitted, his colour rising. 'Order your men into position. They're to attack when the trumpets sound.'

'A fine plan, tribune.' Arminius inclined his head, feigning respect. 'You heard, Maelo. See that it's done.' Maelo muttered his agreement and Arminius added, in German, 'I want none of the Usipetes to escape, d'you understand?'

'Aye.' Maelo dragged his horse's head around and rode off.

'What did you just say?' demanded Tubero.

'I told him that you were relying on our men, that they must not fail,' he lied.

Even with an approving nod, Tubero could convey disdain.

Arminius didn't care. It wouldn't be long before almost every Usipetes warrior was dead. What few captives were taken could be dealt with back at Vetera. His secret *would* be safe. If Tubero's arrogance was the price he had to suffer to achieve that end, so be it.

XI

A hundred paces, Tullus counted. A hundred and five. A hundred and ten, and the old injury in his left calf began to register its unhappiness. He ignored the darts of pain it sent up his leg, and the slight tightness in his chest. By the time he'd counted to a hundred and thirty, the warriors by the gate had begun to charge. They came in a great, disorganised mob, chanting and waving their spears. The distance between the two groups narrowed fast. Tullus kept up his fierce pace; so did his men.

At a hundred and sixty, however, he was forced to admit that the gate was too far away. He could not reach it before the warriors got to them. Shit, Tullus thought. Shit. The legionaries were keeping pace, and he knew in his gut that they, much younger than he, could maintain this speed right to the end. But he couldn't. The pain from his left calf was agonising, and there was a burning sensation filling his lungs. He would have to live with the consequences of covering less ground. Or, more likely, die with them.

'Slow down,' Tullus croaked. He dragged in a breath, let it out, took another, spat a great string of phlegm on the ground. He had lost count, but it didn't matter. The Usipetes were fifty paces away, and closing fast. They were spreading out as they came, in a widening circle that would soon envelop Tullus' small band. The gate was at least eighty paces beyond them. It might as well have been in Judaea, he thought. If Tubero hadn't been out for his blood, *this* was the moment to send his troops surging to the attack, but Tullus still couldn't hear anything from the other side of the palisade. They were on their own.

'HALT!'

Tullus took a look to his left. Four legionaries. Over his left shoulder, three ranks were resuming their shape. Between the helmets and red faces, he made out Fenestela, still in position. Gods, but he was proud of them. Many troops would have refused to charge towards certain death. His had done it, and in good order. 'We can still make the damn gate,' he cried. 'Form square! Five men wide, four deep, two within. Fenestela, take the opposite corner to me.' He let his men decide who would face the enemy first, and who would act as the reserve. Used to assuming this shape in training, they'd obeyed in a few heartbeats. 'Forward. To the gate, at a walk,' he shouted. 'Now!'

Although his soldiers did not have javelins, Tullus saw that most of the warriors were in the same boat. The surprise attack had meant that most had grabbed only one spear when they woke, rather than the two or three per man that was normal. The missile storm that presaged face-to-face combat would be far lighter, and they would lose fewer shields to lodged spears. At thirty paces, perfect range, it came. 'Shields up!' he bellowed. 'Walk!'

Thunk. Thunk. Tullus felt a surge of relief. His shield hadn't been hit.

Thunk. A gurgling cry of pain from behind him, a dead weight hitting him in the back.

One down, thought Tullus. 'Keep walking,' he ordered.

Again his soldiers retained their discipline. They covered another ten paces, leaving behind the body of the legionary who'd been struck in the neck by a spear. Twenty-one of them, with twenty shields. A second volley from much closer saw those numbers reduced to twenty, and eighteen. They were surrounded now, yelling tribesmen edging towards them over the flat ground, spears ready to thrust. Tullus' heart, which had slowed after their run, began hammering off the inside of his ribs again. 'Halt! Close order!'

He shifted position, withdrawing a step and half turning to the right, so that the corner of the square became rounded, and gave his right side more protection than if he stayed facing forward. Feeling a spreading numbness in his sword hand, he relaxed his grip on the weapon's hilt. Stay calm, he thought. Stay focused. 'You know how to play this, brothers. Keep tight. Watch for their spears. Take 'em in the belly when you can.'

The nearest warriors were ten steps away. Three were bearing down on Tullus: a nervous-looking youth not old enough to shave; a thin, black-bearded man so similar in appearance to the boy that he had to be his father; and a shaggy-haired brute who looked to have the brains of a senile mongrel. Tullus could have taken the first two together, and the big one on his own, but all three was a different matter. Acid filled the back of his throat.

Perhaps wanting to prove his courage, the youth attacked first, driving his spear overhand at Tullus' face.

'Spear!' Tullus roared, ducking down to peer around the side of his shield, and praying that the soldier behind heard his warning. The weapon hissed overhead, the youth's body following with the effort of his thrust. It was a simple matter for Tullus to stab him through the abdomen. Not too deep, just enough to slice his opponent's guts to ribbons, and out again. Down went the youth, bleeding everywhere, bawling like a kicked child. His spear dropped from nerveless fingers, and Tullus eyed Blackbeard with contempt. 'Your son's going to die screaming at your feet! How do you like that?' he cried in German.

Enraged, Blackbeard shoved forward, past the brute. He drove his hexagonal shield at Tullus' *scutum* while trying to stab him with his spear. It was a crude move, one Tullus had seen before. He outweighed Blackbeard by some margin, so he bent his knees and braced himself behind his shield. The impact didn't push him backward, but he hadn't expected Blackbeard's spear blade to snag in the mount for his horsehair crest. Tullus' head was wrenched backwards. Waves of agony shot through his neck. His experience, and the bitter knowledge that he would die if he let go of his shield grip, kept his arm high.

Blackbeard cursed and tugged, tugged and cursed, pulling Tullus' head to and fro and sending stabs of intense pain down into his chest. Without warning, the spear blade came free. Blackbeard cried out in triumph and drew back his arm to strike again. Sucking in a breath, Tullus somehow found the strength to slide his left foot forward a step and launch a counter-punch with his scutum. Blackbeard stumbled. With a quick lunge, Tullus stabbed him in the foot. He withdrew to the square, leaving his opponent to stagger away, bleeding and shouting.

Tullus prepared to face the brute, but the warrior had taken several steps backwards. So too had the men to either side of him. Tullus' gaze shot left to right, and back again, over his shoulder. There were wounded, dead and dying Usipetes all around the square. The remainder were pulling back, out of sword range. They weren't beaten: this was the tribesmen's way. Attack, retreat. Attack, retreat. It was an opportunity for his men to advance.

'Towards the gate, at the walk. NOW!'

Leaving four legionaries on the ground – Tullus didn't check to see if they were dead or alive – they tramped on. Like a shoal of fish threatened by a predator, the nearest tribesmen retreated, without breaking formation. A number of them broke into song again, chanting the *barritus*, the sonorous war chant for which all Germans were famed. Damn them, but they're brave, thought Tullus. Not one of them has armour, yet they'll still fight us. 'Keep moving!'

Ten paces. Fifteen. Twenty. The gate was close enough to see the giant locking bar that had been dropped into place behind the two doors. It would take at least six men to shift the damn thing. Six men who wouldn't be able to fight as they lifted it. What did it matter? thought Tullus as the Usipetes' leader, a broad-shouldered chieftain in a red-patterned cloak, bellowed orders and his warriors surged forward once more. We'll never get there. 'For Rome, brothers! FOR ROME!'

'ROME!'

The roar slowed their enemies a little, but no more than that. Scenting victory, for they yet outnumbered the legionaries by at least three to one, they darted forward, long spears at the ready. The shaggy-haired brute came for Tullus again, leering, uttering dire threats in his own language. His arms were thick as decent-sized tree branches and Tullus' mouth felt even drier. One decent spear thrust anywhere – to his shield, or his body – and he'd be finished. 'Did your mother fuck a bear?' he cried in German, hoping he'd used the right words. 'Or were both your parents animals?'

The brute's face twisted with rage and he charged straight at Tullus, who leaned forward into his shield, left leg bent at the knee. Head below his shield rim, glancing around the side of it, he stabbed his opponent a heartbeat before they collided. There was a grunt of pain – Tullus shoved his blade forward with all his might – but the impact with the brute was still sufficient to send him stumbling backwards. He felt his enemy collapsing on top of him rather than saw it, fell down on to his arse and then his back. The dead weight pressing him into the earth prevented Tullus from moving much, other than his right arm. He had his sword yet, so he stabbed the brute again for good measure. Warm fluid sprayed over his hand. There was a groan and Tullus repeated the action over and over, until his fingers could no longer grip the ivory hilt. Unsure if the brute was dead, but prevented from rising by the body on his shield, he sagged back on to the earth and closed his eyes. His ears filled with the noise of battle: men's shouts, heavy *thunks* as shields met shields, cries of pain.

The dice in his mind's eye spun slower and slower, and came to a stop.

'I think the centurion's still alive,' a voice shouted.

To his surprise, Tullus felt the brute being rolled away. Fenestela's ugly mug peered down at him. 'Having a rest, sir?'

Tullus could not think of a comeback. 'I was.'

'Are you hurt, sir?'

'Winded, that's all.' Tullus let the optio pull him to his feet, realising that the Usipetes had retreated again. There were nine legionaries who could fight, and Fenestela, and he. It wasn't enough. There was still no noise of an assault on the palisade. Despite their heavy casualties, more than two score warriors surrounded them, and the gate was thirty paces away.

Fenestela's face was bitter as he jerked his head at it. 'So near, and yet so far, eh?'

A devilment, a madness born of desperation, took flame in Tullus' heart. 'I say we can reach it. They won't stand before a wedge, if we do it fast.'

Fenestela's expression said that he didn't believe Tullus' words any more than Tullus did himself, but instead of arguing, he bared his teeth. 'What do you say, brothers? Shall we show these savages how real soldiers can fight?'

Tullus' heart filled as the legionaries rumbled their agreement. They also knew that forming the wedge was nothing more than choosing a way to die. 'You're good lads,' he said. 'Form up!'

Tullus was bone-weary, but he took position at the point of the wedge. It was the most dangerous position, and he was the centurion.

Tullus didn't hear the shout from the top of the palisade. His soldiers had come in behind him. Fenestela was at his right shoulder, hurling insults at the Usipetes. A gap-toothed legionary who'd been in his century for ten years was at his left, muttering under his breath what he was going to do to the next warrior who came within reach of his blade. Without looking, Tullus knew that the rest were also there, a mass of sweaty, tired, blood-spattered figures who would follow him until they were dead. 'Now!' he shouted, and broke into a shambling run.

He fixed his gaze on a warrior with long braids of hair and an oval, blue-painted shield. Kill him first and drive on, he thought. Don't think about anything else.

At last Tullus registered the shouting. Or more, he noted the alarm in the voices. His pace slowed a fraction; his eyes flickered up to the walkway over the gate, where two Usipetes were screaming and pointing. Tullus couldn't make out their words, but he felt a flare of hope. When he saw a figure clambering over the rampart – one of Arminius' tribesmen – and then another, his heart soared. He had no idea why the auxiliaries rather than legionaries were attacking, but he didn't care. 'Halt!'

His soldiers obeyed, but he could sense their confusion. 'Why, sir?' Fenestela's breath was hot in Tullus' ear.

Tullus pointed with his sword. Dismayed cries rose from the Usipetes by the gate as they too noticed the Cheruscans swarming over the top of the palisade. Five, eight, a dozen. There were warriors appearing all along the rampart. Confused – how were so many of them getting up? – Tullus laughed as he realised. The clever bastards were scrambling up from their horses' backs. He studied the faces of the Usipetes who blocked their path, and let the panic seep in for a few more heartbeats, let them see the Cheruscans dispatching their sentries and leaping down into the compound. 'Charge now, and they'll break,' he said.

'Give us the word, sir,' Fenestela replied.

Tullus shouted the order, and they moved forward. To his delight, the warriors melted away like morning mist before the sun. Three of the bravest stood their ground, backs to the gate, but Tullus and his reenergised soldiers cut them down in a frenzy of blows. Setting down shields and sheathing blades, they heaved and wrenched at the great, square length of timber that barred the entrance. Tullus could hear sword hilts being hammered on the planking from the outside. Fortuna hadn't given up on him just yet, he thought as they lifted the locking bar to one side and pulled wide the doors. He was almost knocked over by the tide of Cheruscans who came barrelling in. Content that they would finish off the Usipetes, Tullus leaned against the wall and closed his eyes as they charged past. Gods, but he was tired.

'You're still alive then.'

Tullus looked up at the sound of Arminius' voice. 'Just. I wouldn't be if it hadn't been for your men.' It was odd to feel grateful towards a man he wasn't sure he trusted, but there it was.

Arminius dipped his chin in recognition. 'I was surprised he gave you so few men, but it was even odder how he watched and listened like a fox outside a coop full of hens as you began your attack. I'm not sure when he would have sent his men forward.'

A dull anger pulsed behind Tullus' eyeballs. The whoreson Tubero had hoped he would die.

'Sir!' Fenestela appeared by Tullus' side. 'The Cheruscans are killing all of the Usipetes, sir.' He glanced at Arminius, who gave a casual shrug and said:

'Their blood's up, like yours.'

Tullus rubbed a hand across eyes that had gone gritty and painful. Did Arminius want every warrior dead? In that weary moment, he didn't care. 'The pieces of shit were for carving us new arseholes, Fenestela, in case you'd forgotten.'

'Aye, screw them,' said Fenestela. 'It doesn't really matter, does it?'

'No,' said Tullus, glad to be alive. 'It doesn't.'

Neither man saw the flicker of satisfaction in Arminius' eyes.

When the patrol got back to Vetera, Tullus' soldiers were dismissed to their barracks. After they'd dumped their kit, many of the tired legionaries headed straight for the baths. Afer and the rest of the contubernium decided to do the same, but Piso hung back. 'I want to check on Vitellius, see that he's settling into the hospital.'

'It was only a flesh wound that he took,' said one of his comrades. 'Visit him later, after you've had a good soak.'

'I'll go and see him now,' demurred Piso.

'Tell him to get his arse back here,' Afer threw in. 'I'm already missing his sarcasm.'

'I'll tell him.' Piso felt bad for Vitellius, who had not long recovered from the beating inflicted by Aius and his friends, and then been selected by Tullus to enter the stockade as part of the surprise attack ordered by Tubero. Piso felt a little guilty too, that Vitellius might not have been injured if he'd been fighting fit, so he stopped at the quartermaster's long enough to buy some wine. It was illegal for army wine to be sold privately, but it could always be had if a man was prepared to pay. Armed with a covered jug of what was reputed to be some of Sicily's finest, he made straight for the *valetudinarium*.

The camp hospital was a large, square building facing on to the *via principalis* and adjacent to the northern gate. It was typical of *valetudinaria*, consisting of a large entrance hall and two concentric sets of rooms set around a central courtyard, with a circulating corridor that ran between them. The passageway enabled staff and patients alike to move about without being exposed to the weather. Survival rates within for many diseases and ailments were good, but it wasn't a place men liked to visit unless they had to. Piso had been twice for minor problems: conjunctivitis the first time, and a sprained wrist the next. He'd never before had occasion to visit a comrade, in particular one who had been injured in combat.

The unmistakeable tang of *acetum*, the disinfectant used by surgeons, hit his nostrils as he stepped inside the doorway. Piso quite liked it. The reception area was jammed with the casualties from the patrol. Groans rose from some of the worst cases, while others lay as if already dead. Poor bastards, thought Piso. Only the soldiers with minor injuries seemed pleased to have reached the place. Stretchers had been laid out in preparation, ready to carry the men within; the wounded were being assessed by teams of surgeons and orderlies. He cast his gaze over the room, but couldn't see Vitellius anywhere. He watched, fascinated, as a surgeon he recognised stopped by a legionary with a thick bandage wrapped around one thigh. 'You were with the patrol, soldier?' asked the surgeon.

'Aye, sir.'

'What happened to you?'

'A German spear, sir. I got knocked over by a warrior, and he ripped my shield to one side. I stuck him as he did. Even though he was dying, the dog still managed to stab me.' The legionary winced as the surgeon probed at the bandage. 'It bled like a bastard – sorry, sir – really badly. I was lucky that a comrade whipped a strip of leather around my leg, and tightened it with a piece of wood.'

'What colour was the blood?'

'Bright red, sir. It was pumping out.'

The surgeon's face grew wary. 'The artery must have been severed. When did the leather come off?'

'Our medical orderly undid it after the fighting had ended, sir, to see if the bleeding started again. It did, damn quick, so he reapplied it. Every hour or so, he let the pressure off, to keep the leg from going dead, he said. It kept bleeding until that evening, but it's been all right since.'

'Any pain?' The legionary pulled a face, and the surgeon rephrased his question, peering beneath the edges of the bandage, top and bottom. 'Does it throb, like an infected finger might?'

'No, sir.'

'Good. There's no discoloration of the skin that I can see. Best to leave the bandage on until tomorrow.' The surgeon glanced at the orderly. 'Have him carried to one of the minor-wounds wards. He's to have poppy juice if he wishes, five drops, twice daily. Put him on the examinations list for the morning.'

'Yes, sir.'

The surgeon moved on to the next case, and Piso clutched at the orderly's arm as he passed. 'A comrade of mine was taken here just now.'

'Half the world has a mate in here,' retorted the orderly, but he paused. 'What kind of injury had he?'

'A flesh wound, in the forearm.'

'He's lucky then. If you can't spy him, wait until the stretcher-bearers pick up this man here, and follow them.' He indicated the soldier whom the surgeon had just examined. 'There are two wards for minor wounds. Like as not, you'll find him in one of those.'

'My thanks.' When the stretcher-bearers arrived, Piso trailed his way after, along the hospital's central corridor, down the building's long side and around to the short side. Offices, storerooms and bedrooms for the medical staff lined the first section of the passageway, and were followed by two operating theatres, and wards for the most severe cases. If the cries of pain and the surgeon's terse instructions to 'Give him more poppy juice!' and 'Pass me the damn clamp, quickly!' were anything to go by, dramatic, risky surgery was under way. His nostrils full of the smell of blood and piss, and images of the dead at the settlement, Piso didn't linger.

The legionary with the leg wound was carried into the first minor-wounds ward, so Piso stuck his head into the second, a small dark chamber almost identical to a barrack room for eight men. All the bunks were occupied, but there was no sign of Vitellius, so he returned to the first chamber. He found his friend watching with a scowl as the leg-wound soldier was shifted on to a lower bunk – which, from the kit that lay on the floor beside it, looked to have been Vitellius' until that moment.

'There you are,' said Piso, grinning.

'I'd just got comfortable,' replied Vitellius in a sour tone. 'Trust me to choose the bed that someone else needs more than I do.'

'You might have a bad arm,' butted in one of the stretcher-bearers, 'but this man has a wound that could start bleeding at any time. Do you want him exsanguinating over you from the top berth?'

'Of course not,' snapped Vitellius.

'Gratitude, brother,' said the leg-wound soldier, looking a little embarrassed.

Vitellius brushed it off with a wave of his good hand. He eyed Piso. 'Come to check up on me?'

'Aye, to see how you were.' He raised the wine. 'And to bring you this.'

Vitellius' face cheered. 'You're a true comrade. We'll have a drop right now.'

Piso scouted around for a cup, but could see none. He took a slug, and made a face. 'Finest Sicilian, it is not. Never mind.' He passed it to Vitellius, who poured a long draught down his neck without swallowing. 'How's the wound?' asked Piso.

Vitellius lifted his injured right arm, which had a fresh linen bandage on it. 'The surgeon said it must have been a damn sharp blade. Went straight in, straight out. It seems clean enough. He sluiced it with acetum twice – gods, but that stung like a bastard – and had it dressed. Two or three days, I'll be here, he reckons, long enough to make sure it stays uncontaminated. After that, I can come back every few days to have it dressed. Not too bad, I guess.'

'Aye, you were lucky.' Piso thanked the gods again that he had not been part of the attack.

'Where are the rest?'

'In the baths.'

'I could have guessed,' said Vitellius, scowling. 'I'm not to go there until my wound has healed, the surgeon says.'

'A wise idea. Sweat, dirt, blood and massage oil aren't the things to get in to a cut,' Piso agreed, remembering a surgeon giving his father similar advice.

'That's not taking into account the bastards who piss in the baths!' added the leg-wound soldier. 'There's always one of those.'

'I can remember the day one of my tent mates shat in the *caldarium*,' chipped in a legionary from another bunk. 'Said he'd eaten some meat that had turned, but that didn't stop us giving him a good kicking.'

Everyone laughed.

'There's quite a party air in here,' boomed Tubero, sweeping in, a staff officer and a servant on his heels.

'Sir!' Everyone who could stand shot to attention. The leg-wound soldier and another saluted from their beds. 'Sorry, sir, it's difficult to get up,' said one.

'At ease, at ease. Injured men are allowed some leeway.' Despite Tubero's jocular manner, no one forgot his rank. They watched him with nervous eyes and fixed smiles as he paced to and fro, glancing at them. 'Were any of you in the patrol that wiped out the Usipetes?'

It wasn't surprising that a tribune didn't recognise the men he'd just commanded, thought Piso, but it rankled just the same.

'I was, sir,' said Vitellius.

'Me too, sir,' added the leg-wound legionary.

'I was there as well, sir,' said Piso as Tubero's eyes fell on him and his jug of wine.

'You've come with refreshment for your comrades, I see. I like that.' Tubero held out his hand, and the servant passed over a small amphora. 'This fine vintage, from my own supplies, is also for you brave men wounded in the empire's service. You fought well at the settlement. Rome is proud of you.'

A chorus of 'Thank you, sir' echoed from every corner of the room as Vitellius accepted the gift.

'I'll expect you all back on duty soon. There's to be no shirking!' said Tubero. With that, he was gone.

Pompous little prick, thought Piso. He could see the same opinion mirrored in Vitellius' eyes, but neither of them knew the others well enough to risk saying so out loud.

'He's the one who went wild on that mission to Aliso, isn't he?' asked a middle-aged soldier with a bandaged head.

Piso and Vitellius exchanged another look. 'He is,' said Piso.

'I heard that if it hadn't been for him, the Usipetes would never have raided over the river. He and his officers killed four warriors for no reason, or so they say.'

Piso threw caution to the wind. 'That's about right.'

'Aye,' muttered Vitellius.

'So what was he like on the patrol you've just come back from?' asked Bandage Head.

Piso shifted beneath the weight of seven men's gaze. 'A little reckless, perhaps.'

'Bollocks to that. He's a glory-hunter, pure and simple,' said Vitellius. 'He threw us into an ill-prepared attack against a fortified position. Plenty of men died before he realised his mistake, or more like before our centurion intervened and told him how to do it better. Even then, he didn't listen. Twenty of us got sent to take the enemy in the rear, when it should have been a half-century or more. We two' – he indicated the leg-wound soldier – 'and another seven of our comrades are lucky to be here.'

Men pulled faces, and asked the gods that they never had to serve under Tubero.

Vitellius read Piso's wariness. 'I was only speaking the truth. Besides, we're all comrades here. Now, are you just going to stand there holding that jug, or pour some for our friends?'

Telling himself that there was no need to be concerned about gossiping, Piso offered the wine around.

'What about the good stuff?' asked Bandage Head with a sly grin.

Vitellius made an obscene gesture at him. 'You heard the tribune. That's just for us three, who risked our lives for Rome.'

XII

Varus leaned back in his chair, admiring the gilded candelabra over his head and thinking about what Tubero had told him. The patrol had returned to Vetera not long before, and the tribune had been quick to come to his office in Legate Vala's house. He would have Tullus and Bolanus report to him later, but the tribune's account of his mission seemed straightforward. There was little doubt in Varus' mind that it would be corroborated by the two centurions. Tubero wasn't just an arrogant, smooth-cheeked pup from Rome: he *did* have some ability. His task hadn't been that difficult, but he had completed it with some style. 'Burning the boats was clever,' Varus said.

Tubero's face went pink. 'Thank you, sir. As it happened, the measure proved unnecessary, but at the time it seemed the best thing to do.'

'What were your casualties?'

'Thirty-one legionaries, sir, and ten auxiliaries. Half that number of wounded. I've just been to the hospital to check on them; the surgeons say most will—'

'Those numbers are higher than I would have expected,' said Varus, frowning for the first time.

Tubero's colour deepened. 'More than a third of the legionaries who died were lost by Centurion Tullus in his attempt to take the compound gate from the inside.'

'A pity. His soldiers are veterans. Hard men to replace.' Admiring the candelabra again – Vala really *did* have good taste – Varus missed Tubero's look of relief. So too did Aristides, who was tidying away documents in the background.

'Yes, sir.'

'And you say that there are a dozen or so Usipetes prisoners?'

'Correct, sir. It's unfortunate, but none appear to be men of rank.'

'That's to be expected. Tribal leaders are like centurions. First to put themselves into danger, leading by example – you know how it is.'

'Yes, sir.' Tubero stood a fraction taller.

'Did the troops perform as they should have? And Arminius' Cherusci?'

'Our men did, sir. The Cherusci were . . .' Tubero hesitated before saying: '. . . a little undisciplined. More prisoners might have been taken if it hadn't been for them. Arminius apologised to me afterwards; he said that they had lost the run of themselves.'

'That's unsurprising,' said Varus with a shrug. 'I hesitate to call Arminius' people "savages" – they are our allies, and much of the time they're an agreeable lot. But they are not Roman. Arminius is more civilised; he won't have been at fault. I doubt that there's a leader alive who could rein his people in during a fight. It's something to bear in mind when you meet the German tribes in battle. They lack self-control, but they have the courage of lions.'

'I'll remember, sir.'

'The interrogations have started, I presume?'

'Yes, sir. Nothing interesting so far. The captives are all saying the same thing – that their chieftains had nothing to do with the raid.'

'Have any died yet?' asked Varus.

'I don't think so, sir.'

'Time for that to change. See to it that two – at least two – die under questioning. In brutal fashion. It's important that the other prisoners witness it.'

Tubero blinked. 'Yes, sir.' Behind Varus, Aristides made a faint sound of disapproval.

Their distaste amused Varus. 'Unpleasant it may be, tribune, but the method is tried and tested. Men are quick to reveal all they know when their comrades' guts have been spilled on the floor before them.'

Tubero's chin firmed. 'I'll see that it's done, sir. Any new information will be brought to you at once.'

'You may go.' Tubero was at the office door when Varus said, 'Tribune.'

'Yes, sir?'

'Well done.'

Tubero's cheeks turned crimson. 'Thank you, sir.'

Varus felt satisfaction as the senior tribune left the room. Scant praise worked best, he had always found. He sensed Aristides behind him. 'You disapprove of torture.'

There was a sniff. 'I don't like it, master, no.'

'Is it acceptable if the information obtained saves Roman lives?' There was no reply, and Varus said, 'I too find the practice repulsive, but a lifetime's experience of power has taught me that nothing is ever black or white. Instead, things tend to be a dull shade of grey, which means that when it comes to obtaining useful intelligence, torture can be acceptable.'

'I am grateful to be spared the need ever to make such decisions, master.'

For once, Varus was envious of his slave's position. He shoved away the uncomfortable feeling. 'There must be paperwork that needs signing while I wait for Tullus and Bolanus to arrive.' He chuckled. 'Don't answer, just bring it to me.'

'Of course, master,' replied Aristides with a faint tone of smugness.

While he scrawled his signature over and over, Varus considered Tubero's performance since his arrival. It wasn't uncommon for tribunes to be haughty, spoiled brats who needed constant monitoring for the first period of their service. After the incident with the cattle-herding Usipetes, Varus had been convinced that Tubero would fall into that category – and was perhaps even an extreme example thereof. This concern had for the most part been laid to rest by the mission to wipe out the raiding party. Tubero still had much to learn, but he had done a good job. With the right guidance, he would develop into a fine leader. When that quality became clear, it would reflect well on *him* with Augustus, Varus mused, and that could only ever be a good thing. Until this appointment, he had spent years in the political wilderness. It wasn't impossible that the same could happen to him again. Better to mentor Tubero, rather than put him down.

There was a knock. One of the sentries entered and announced the centurions' arrival.

'Send them in,' ordered Varus.

Without being told, Aristides cleared away the letters and returned to his position at the back of the room, where he had a small desk of his own.

Varus stood as the two crossed the threshold, showing them his regard. He had always had time for centurions, the backbone of the army throughout the empire. They were the salt of the earth, he thought, in particular this pair. 'Tullus. Bolanus. Welcome.'

They both saluted. 'Governor.'

'At ease, at ease. We're not on the parade ground.' Varus picked up a graceful blue glass jug from the table by his desk. 'Wine?'

The two glanced at one another.

'I'm having some,' said Varus, to put them at ease.

'My thanks, sir. I will if you will,' said Tullus.

'I don't want to be the odd one out, sir,' added Bolanus. 'Thank you.'

'Excellent.' Varus poured a healthy measure into three glasses and handed them out. He raised his high. 'To the emperor. May his reign continue for many years.'

'To the emperor,' Tullus and Bolanus repeated, and they all drank.

'To a fruitful mission,' said Varus, toasting them. 'Well done.'

'Thank you, sir,' they replied. 'We weren't in charge of course,' said Tullus.

'I know, Tubero was. But a senior tribune needs experienced officers around him, in particular with his first taste of combat. Your success leads me to assume that he performed well. Would I be correct?' Tullus and Bolanus exchanged another look, one that told Varus they had talked beforehand about what they would say. Although it didn't surprise him, he felt a flicker of irritation. 'Come now, we are friends here. You can speak your minds, with no fear of retribution.'

'Tubero commanded well, sir,' said Bolanus. 'I have no major complaints.'

'And minor ones?' Bolanus grew a little awkward. 'Tell me!' Varus ordered.

'During the fighting, some of the Usipetes managed to barricade themselves inside the village compound, sir. Tubero's response was hasty. Instead of assaulting the compound in a number of places, and overwhelming the defenders, he ordered a direct attack on the front gate. It didn't succeed, and eight legionaries died.' Another word – 'unnecessarily' – hung in the air.

It could have been worse, thought Varus. 'And at that point, Tubero ordered you, Tullus, to scale the far side of the palisade?'

'That was my suggestion, sir,' replied Tullus.

'Not the tribune's?'

'No, sir.'

Varus registered Bolanus' nod of agreement. He felt annoyed that Tubero had neglected to mention this detail, but wasn't altogether surprised. At the same stage in his career, he might not have either. 'I see. And it was during your attack that many of the casualties were lost?' Again Tullus and Bolanus glanced at one another, and Varus began to wonder if the mission had not been as straightforward as Tubero had made out. 'Well?'

'That's correct, sir,' said Tullus.

'What happened?'

'I had only twenty men and an optio with me, sir. There were upwards of sixty warriors within the compound.'

'But the legionaries outside must have been attacking the palisade at the same time, splitting the defences?'

'They didn't do so immediately, sir,' said Tullus.

'Was there some kind of miscommunication?' demanded Varus.

'I suppose so, sir.'

'You had no trumpeter with you?'

'No, sir.'

That was an oversight on Tubero's part, thought Varus. 'Bolanus, you were outside the compound. What was going on?'

'I think the tribune didn't quite realise the importance of diverting the defenders' attention from Tullus and his force, sir. It was fortunate that Arminius was on hand to advise Tubero. He sent our men to the attack after that. Tullus opened the gate, and the remaining warriors were soon overwhelmed.'

Tubero must have been distracted, Varus decided, or, as Bolanus had said, he had misjudged the 'perfect' moment to order the attack. It was fortunate indeed that he'd sent Arminius on the patrol. 'I am glad that you survived, Tullus. Your death would have been a sore loss to your legion, and to the empire.'

'Thank you, sir,' said Tullus, raising his glass.

Varus was about to move the conversation on to the preparations for the summer campaign when Tullus let out a meaningful cough. 'What is it?' asked Varus.

'I was unhappy with how few prisoners were taken, sir. The warriors inside the stockade were our best hope, but Arminius' men reaped them as if they were ripe stalks of wheat.'

It was curious that Tubero had also mentioned this, thought Varus. 'They lost the run of themselves,' he said, deciding again that the simplest answer was the correct one.

Another cough. 'I wondered if Arminius had ordered his men to act as they did, sir.'

'Why would he do such a thing?' demanded Varus, frowning.

'I don't know, sir,' Tullus admitted, looking awkward. 'But I thought that perhaps they went about killing the Usipetes with more zeal than was necessary.'

'"Perhaps?" So you're not sure? You have no evidence to back up your theory?'

'No, sir.'

'Unless you have some kind of proof for me, centurion,' said Varus in a reproving tone, 'I suggest you stitch your lip.'

'Yes, sir.'

'Now, back to the preparations for the march east,' declared Varus. The centurions warmed to the topic, which pleased him. He wasn't the only one looking forward to getting out of the damn camp. When they had drunk a second glass of wine, he thanked both again and dismissed them.

'They were being opaque about what happened with Tubero, Aristides, or I'm no judge,' Varus said when the sound of their sandals had died away.

'I agree, master.'

So I wasn't imagining it, thought Varus. 'They were covering for him.'

'I wouldn't know, master,' said Aristides, ever the diplomat.

It was best to be pragmatic, Varus decided again. The desired result – the destruction of the raiding party, and the taking of prisoners – had been achieved. He had enough on his plate without having to worry about Arminius, or to dig around to discover the mission's every detail. It seemed definite that Arminius' men had lost their self-control, and that Tubero had been overeager in his approach to the attack on the compound, forgetting the basics of planned assaults. These were both things that were easy to remedy. He could speak to Arminius the next time they met. 'Fetch me the manual on siege tactics,' he ordered. 'Write a note to Tubero, recommending that he read it. I'll sign it. Have both sent to his quarters.'

'Yes, master.'

That was one problem dealt with, thought Varus. His satisfaction lasted as long as it took Aristides to come into his line of vision with an armful of documents. Varus gave them a baleful glare. For every one issue that he resolved, there were always six more to sort out.

Jupiter, let the day that we march out of here come soon, he prayed.

Knock.

Varus, who was still at his desk, eyed the door to his office with something akin to resignation. 'Enter.'

In came the sentry. 'Arminius is here to see you, sir.'

'For once, a visitor I am happy to receive. Send him in.'

'Governor,' said Arminius, saluting.

'It's good to see you, Arminius.' Varus came around his desk to shake the Cheruscan's hand. 'You'll have some wine.'

'I never say no to wine,' replied Arminius with a broad smile.

'A man after my own heart. Aristides, do the necessary, will you?' Varus offered his guest a chair. 'I must thank you for what you did on the patrol.'

Arminius looked a little surprised. 'I did my duty, that's all.'

'I meant the advice you gave Tubero, during the attack on the palisade.'

'Ah, that. Anyone would have done the same.'

'Maybe so, but it saved Tullus' life, and the lives of a good number of legionaries.' Varus raised the glass that Aristides had just handed him. 'My thanks.'

With a gracious nod, Arminius accepted the toast. 'I am grateful to you for sending me on the mission.'

'It's a pity that we have so few captives.'

Arminius' face grew concerned. 'If you're referring to my men's actions inside the stockade—'

'I am,' said Varus in a cold voice. 'Tullus tells me that more prisoners could have been taken.'

'True enough. My warriors did run amok,' Arminius admitted with an apologetic look. 'One of my best men had been cut down in the village, you see. The number of slain legionaries outside the gate didn't help either. Nonetheless, I can only apologise, governor. They failed you. *I* failed you,' he said, wringing his hands now.

It had been a genuine mistake, Varus decided again. Arminius wasn't lying, that was clear. 'See that it doesn't happen again.'

'You have my word on that.'

Varus smiled to show that the matter was closed. 'Now, if you've come to tempt me out of here with a day's hunting, I will have to turn you down. My conscience, or should I say Aristides, would not permit it.'

Arminius eyed Aristides. 'It's you who keeps the governor on the straight and narrow, eh?'

'He doesn't need me to do that, sir,' demurred Aristides. 'I'm only a poor slave.'

'You're indispensable, that's what you are,' said Varus.

Muttering his thanks, Aristides bowed and retreated to his desk.

'You're busy then,' said Arminius.

Varus indicated the piles of documents before him. 'I have twice as much to do as normal. It's because we'll be leaving soon, of course, which means it can't be ignored.'

'I don't know how you do it, governor,' said Arminius. 'I loathe officialdom and the mountain of paperwork that goes with it. Thank Donar that I too have a scribe. If it weren't for him, the quartermaster would be bending your ear about me every other day. Why does everything have to be filled out in triplicate?'

'That's the army for you,' said Varus, chuckling. 'All the empire's property and resources have to be accounted for. It's how it has been since Augustus became emperor.'

'Which means we have to accept it,' said Arminius, raising another toast. 'To Augustus.'

Varus echoed Arminius' words, and then set down his glass. 'Something makes me doubt that you came here to discuss the intricacies of military paperwork.'

'Ha! You know me well, governor. I was wondering if you had given any thought to punishing the Usipetes for the raiding party?' He laughed. 'I'll rephrase that, because you will have done. Have you decided what the tribe's punishment will be?'

'After a fashion. The prisoners didn't yield much information, but every last one maintained that they had left their villages without their chieftains' knowledge.'

'And you believe them?'

'They were treated in a most unpleasant fashion. I do.'

'I see.'

'With this in mind, I concluded that the most punitive type of response – burning settlements and killing the inhabitants, you know the drill – would be counterproductive. We are trying to pacify Germania, not set it alight. The raid can't go unanswered, however. The Usipetes' leaders may not have known what those warriors would do, but they should have. They have a responsibility to Rome to prevent their people acting in such an unlawful and barbarous manner.'

'Taxes, then?'

'Indeed. A heavy tax. I haven't decided the exact amount, but it will be determined by the number of dead in the settlement, as well as the number of soldiers, Roman and auxiliary, who were lost in the action.' Varus cocked his head. 'Why do you ask?'

'I wondered if you would allow me to be among those who delivered the message to the Usipetes – either with a sword, or a letter demanding more tax.'

'You are ever the empire's servant, Arminius,' said Varus, looking pleased. 'Very well. You shall be in charge of the patrol.'

'I am grateful, governor. How strong a force will it be?'

'Strong. Although their villages will be spared, the Usipetes need to see – and fear – Rome's might. Take your entire command; I will also send three cohorts of legionaries. Tullus, whom you know, will be your second-in-command.'

'Tullus is a fine centurion,' said Arminius. 'What about Tubero?'

Varus studied Arminius' face for signs of sarcasm, but finding none, relaxed. 'This is a delicate mission. I want veterans in charge.'

'Understood. When shall we leave?'

'The message should be delivered as soon as possible. Tomorrow, or the next day at the latest.'

XIII

The following evening, the sun set in a blaze of glory, staining the western sky many beautiful shades of pinks and reds. Arminius and Maelo were sitting by Arminius' tent, and at their feet, a small pile of burning logs glowed. Around them, their warriors crouched by their own fires – it had been cooler than normal that day – and to the right, beyond their unit's position, hundreds of legionaries were doing the same. An earth bank to Arminius' left marked the southern rampart of the marching camp.

'Let me go in your stead.' Even in the poor light, the unhappiness twisting Maelo's face was clear.

'This is something that only *I* can do,' replied Arminius. 'I am the chieftain, not you.'

'Then I should also come.'

'I go alone.'

The camp's position, less than a quarter of a mile from the main Usipetes settlement, had been chosen by Tullus upon their arrival. No communication had been sent to the tribe's leaders. That would happen in the morning. As Tullus had suggested, and Arminius agreed, they could stew overnight. The centurion was a clever man, thought Arminius. Short of sacking the place, he couldn't think of a more intimidating measure. More importantly, however, it afforded him a chance to talk to the Usipetes' leaders in secret – this very night.

'What if the chieftains are aware of our involvement in the annihilation of the raiding party?' asked Maelo.

'They won't have heard a word.'

'How do you know? They didn't seem too happy when they came out to look at us.'

'Would you react well if two thousand Roman troops appeared outside your village a few days after some of your warriors had broken the imperial peace?'

'I suppose not,' admitted Maelo. 'Yet they might still know what we did.'

Arminius kept his voice level. 'Then, when I go in there, they'll torture and kill me.'

'All the more reason for me to come, as protection.'

'Two spears wouldn't be enough, Maelo, and you know it. You would also die, and there's no point in that. I can't take a decent-sized escort with me either, because I've got to get over the rampart unseen. The Romans must not find out that I'm leaving the camp. Even if I managed to sneak a few men out, it would make the Usipetes suspicious.'

'I don't like this plan, Arminius.'

'I *must* meet the Usipetes' chieftains, and before tomorrow, when Tullus reveals the penalty for their warriors' crimes. They are more liable to accept the punishment taxes if they understand that Varus still trusts me, that everything is in place for the ambush to work. They won't have to wait long for revenge, in other words.' Maelo continued to look unhappy, and Arminius said, 'What would you have me do? When we ride east with Varus, opportunities to win over other tribes could be few and far between. This is a perfect opportunity to cement the Usipetes into our alliance. If not now, then when?'

'You're right,' replied Maelo, using a branch to give the fire a savage poke.

They watched the resulting stream of sparks rise, pinpricks of light that winked out one by one.

'The Romans' lives will be snuffed out like those sparks,' said Arminius, thinking of his aunt and cousins. 'Think on that while I'm gone.'

'Donar protect you.'

'It is in his name that I do this.' Arminius remembered the sacrifices he'd seen as a boy, and took strength from the memories. 'Got the rope?'

'I have it here.'

'It's dark enough. Time to move.'

They had already discussed where Arminius should go over the earthen rampart of the rectangular marching camp, which had been thrown up when they'd arrived. The four gateways – in the middle of each side – and the corners were manned at all times. At regular intervals, sentries patrolled the ramparts between these points. Arminius, Maelo and three warriors crept into position midway between a corner and a gate. Arminius could feel his heart thumping a protest. It was one thing to *talk* about getting out of the camp unseen, and another to *do* it. If he were caught, there would be hell to pay. No, he thought, it would be worse than that. Tullus would suspect him – correctly – of treachery.

Move, he told himself, before your courage leaves you.

'Ready?' he asked the trio of warriors.

'Aye,' they whispered back. 'The gods guide you, Arminius,' said one.

'You must play your part too. Be convincing. Go.'

He and Maelo watched as the three staggered out from the shadows cast by the rampart. Talking in loud voices, they wove their way towards the nearest corner of the defences, from where the sentry that guarded this section would soon appear. It wasn't long before a voice challenged them. Arminius waited until their conversation with the sentry was well under way before he gave Maelo the nod. His friend gave him a lift at once, up on to the walkway. Guts wrenching with nerves in case he should be seen, Arminius knelt and heaved Maelo up beside him. There was no cry of alarm then, nor was there as Maelo unravelled the rope tied around his waist and threw it over the rampart.

'It will be too risky to try and get back in,' hissed Arminius. 'Send out a turma at dawn, when the gates open. I'll meet them half a mile away, among the trees that border the road west. If Tullus asks where I am, tell him I had to pray to our gods.' Arminius had to believe that that would be enough to allay Tullus' suspicion of him, which had been made more evident by his comment to Varus about the killing of the raiding party.

Maelo nodded to show he'd understood, and braced a foot against the battlement. Without hesitation, Arminius climbed over the edge. Once he'd worked his way between the spiked branches, he lowered himself hand over hand into the ditch beyond. At the bottom, he gave the rope a sharp tug. Without waiting for Maelo to pull it back up – they were both on their own now – he clambered out of the trench and crawled on his hands and knees for some distance. Hidden in the blackness, he listened for the count of a score of heartbeats and more. To his intense relief, he heard nothing. Neither he nor Maelo had been spotted.

The first part of his mission had been successful.

That meant the real danger was about to begin.

Asking Donar for his continuing protection, Arminius strode towards the Usipetes' settlement. A challenge rang out some distance from the first longhouse, and fresh sweat slicked down his back. 'I am a friend,' he called out in a low tone. 'Arminius of the Cherusci is my name.'

'It's an odd fucking hour to come calling,' said the sentry, looming out of the darkness with a levelled spear. He peered at Arminius' face, took in his well-cut clothing and grunted. 'Especially considering the company you keep. I saw you earlier, with your warriors, among the damn Romans.'

'I am a friend of the Usipetes.'

'I don't know many who would agree with that statement.' His lip curled. 'You're unarmed. Did you think that would stop me from gutting you right here?'

'I left my sword behind because I didn't want it tripping me up as I climbed out of the Roman camp. They don't know I'm here,' said Arminius. 'I must speak with your chiefs. *At once*.'

The sentry, who stood an impressive two hands taller than Arminius, grunted again, but his spear remained where it was. 'They'll all be abed.'

'Wake them up then.'

'You're not Usipetes. You don't get to order me about,' snapped the guard, but Arminius had noted the faint tone of uncertainty in his voice.

'Would you rather be the warrior who wakes his leaders for a night-time meeting, unwelcome as that might be, or someone who killed a visitor come with an important message?' he demanded. 'Make your choice, but do it fast.'

With a curse, the guard directed a companion who'd been dozing against the wall of the nearest house to take his place. 'Know that I'll cut your balls off if you're lying,' he said to Arminius.

'Just take me to your chieftain.'

Grumbling under his breath, the guard led Arminius deep into the settlement, a jumble of longhouses and workshops interspersed with vegetable patches. Dogs barked warnings as they passed, and Arminius saw armed warriors standing by the entrance to more than one longhouse. This alone revealed the depth of the Usipetes' unhappiness at the Romans' presence. Much good it would do them if an attack proved necessary. His force outnumbered the tribesmen by some margin.

They came to a halt by a longhouse which faced on to a square area of beaten earth. A meeting place, so the dwelling of a leader. It seemed that Arminius *had* convinced the sentry, who took no nonsense from the warrior outside the door. A muttered conversation and some choice curses saw the sentry disappear inside. A few moments later, the building's owner emerged, clutching a new-kindled torch. Arminius gave silent thanks as he recognised the red-haired chieftain who had translated for his fellows at Vetera. This one was no rash fool.

Red Head lifted his torch towards Arminius and the tall guard. Surprise filled his face. 'It *is* you, Arminius. I thought the sentry was raving.'

'He was not.' Arminius took a step forward into the arc of light.

'You have a nerve showing up here, after what has happened.'

Uncertainty stole up on Arminius. Did Red Head know of his involvement in the killing of the raiders? 'I am a friend to the Usipetes, and hope always to be,' he said, raising his hands, palms showing.

'Tell that to the warriors who lie dead on the other side of the river,' spat Red Head. 'Seize him.'

Gods, he *does* know, thought Arminius, fighting panic. He did not resist as the two guards grabbed him by the arms, but he wasn't ready for Red Head's quick punch, straight into his solar plexus. The air shot from his lungs, and a ball of pain exploded in his middle. Arminius' legs buckled, and if it hadn't been for the hands holding him, he would have dropped to his knees. Stars floated across his vision, and nausea tickled the back of his throat.

'Four hundred of our warriors, dead. The cream of the tribe, our future, gone.' Red Head lifted Arminius' head by the hair. 'I'm going to enjoy listening to you scream your way to hell. We'll make your journey there slow.'

Arminius tried to speak, but retched instead. The pain in his belly was as severe as that he'd felt when he took the falx blow to his head.

'Take him inside,' ordered Red Head. 'Bind him. Gag him as well. The less poison that comes from his snake's tongue, the better.'

Arminius retched again and again, until dribbles of spit hung from his lips. When he looked up, Red Head was gone. The tall guard, who had released his arm, was eyeing him with a disappointed expression. 'I knew you were trouble.'

Arminius opened his mouth to protest, but the guard stepped in and wrapped a strip of dirty cloth around his face, knotting it at the back and preventing him from speaking. Next his hands were bound behind his back, so tight that he groaned. Without further ceremony, he was bundled inside the longhouse and thrown to the floor by the central fireplace. At once the blackness which had threatened to take Arminius loomed.

It was a relief to let it take him.

A foot nudged Arminius in the belly, where the punch had landed. The pain brought him to his senses again. He opened weary eyes to find the tall guard stooped over him.

'You're still with us. Good.' The guard levered him up into a sitting position. A half-circle of men stood around Arminius, keeping him close to the fire. He recognised most of them as chieftains who had come to petition Varus after Tubero's misguided attack on the cattle-herding youths. Every face was angry, closed, hard. They were the faces of men who knew of his treachery. Fresh, cold fear uncoiled itself in Arminius' bruised stomach; it caressed his spine and chilled his heart. No one looked inclined to let him speak. If they didn't, he would die. All his efforts would have been in vain. It was that last realisation which galled him the most.

'Let me speak, please,' he tried to say, but it came out as 'Ehhh gneee eeeek, heeeese'.

A rumble of laughter spread around the assembled chieftains.

'The viper cannot hiss when its mouth is sealed shut,' said Red Head.

'He'll try again when this is buried in his flesh,' one man declared, lifting a poker and placing it in the embers of the fire.

'A fine idea,' said another. 'I'll cut him a new arsehole after that.'

'Not here,' said Red Head. 'My family is asleep a few paces away. The priest says we can take him to the forest.'

'Aye, the sacred grove.' 'Good idea.' 'That's the place to send him to hell.'

Once he was in the trees, with a priest at hand, Arminius knew he would have even less chance. The devotees of Donar liked their blood sacrifices too much to worry about talking to their victims. The chieftains' level of fury meant that they thought Tullus was going to attack in the morning, Arminius decided. They had nothing to lose by killing him. He stared at Red Head, willing the man to glance his way. I came to offer you a chance for revenge, he said with his eyes. Remove the gag.

Red Head didn't look at him.

I am your faithful servant, Donar, as I always have been, Arminius prayed. Allow me to do you great honour by ambushing the Romans in your forest.

His hopes fell as the tall guard and another warrior began to steer him towards the door.

'Wait,' ordered Red Head.

The two men holding Arminius stopped, and he prayed even harder.

'Perhaps things aren't as simple as they seem,' said Red Head.

There were scornful cries at this. 'It's as plain as day!' snapped one man. 'Arminius promised us revenge on the Romans, but he did nothing to stop them massacring our warriors. Then he rides up with the troops who've been sent to do Donar knows what to us. The man's a liar, and as rotten as a badly cured ham.'

Did nothing to *stop* the Romans, Arminius repeated to himself, feeling hope for the first time. They *don't* know that I took part in the killing!

'I'm more than prepared to kill Arminius still,' said Red Head, 'but there's no harm in talking to him first.'

'Why waste our time?' snarled one chieftain. 'The whoreson has always had a silver tongue. He'll just try and convince us that there was nothing he could do.'

'You may be right,' said Red Head. 'But answer me this. Why would he bother coming unarmed into our settlement, in the dead of night, if not to tell us something important? He's no fool.'

There was no immediate answer.

'Aye, let him speak then,' said a chieftain with thick bushy eyebrows. 'We can replace the gag quick enough if we don't like what he says.'

Arminius' fear eased a little as Red Head stepped in and untied the strip of cloth that had bound his mouth. 'My thanks,' he muttered through dry lips.

Red Head made no acknowledgement. 'What is it you wish to tell us?'

'First, the Romans are not here to attack the settlement.' Arminius heard instant sighs of relief, and knew that *that* had been the right thing to say first. 'They come with word of punitive taxes imposed by Varus.'

'You swear this?' demanded Bushy Eyebrows.

'On my life, and that of my father, and his father before him. As Donar is my witness, the Romans are only here in numbers to intimidate you. Varus does not wish to inflame the situation any more than it already is.' This seemed to satisfy, so he went on, 'But the taxes he is to impose are heavy indeed. Some of your people may not be able to pay.'

'And if they cannot?' demanded Red Head.

'The Romans are practical if nothing else. They will settle for things other than silver. Cattle, grain, slaves: they do not care.' Angry comments rained down on Arminius, but he raised his voice. 'Know also that the annual taxes due in three months will still be payable.'

The Usipetes' fury rekindled further, and this time Red Head had to restore order. When silence had fallen, he regarded Arminius with cold eyes. 'We would have heard this unwelcome information in the morning. Spit out the real reason for your visit.'

'What I have to say is for chieftains' ears only.' Arminius glanced at the tall guard and the warrior who'd been at the door.

Red Head jerked his head, and the two retreated outside.

'While I understand your young men's reasons for raiding across the river, what they did was most rash.' Arminius could see that some of the chieftains agreed with him, which was a start. 'The Romans will never tolerate such incursions. To do so would make them appear weak. I was grateful not to be chosen by Varus to search for the raiding party. It grieved me to learn afterwards of the warriors' fate. It's a mark of their bravery that so few prisoners were taken.' This was the real test of how much they knew. If even one chieftain denounced him as a liar, the priest's knife would soon be carving open his chest. Heart thudding, Arminius studied the watching faces.

'I presume that they tortured the captives?' asked Red Head, and Arminius breathed again.

'Yes.'

'Bastard Romans. What did they say?'

'All of them swore blind that you chieftains had had no knowledge of their raid.' Arminius saw that that had been true. To a man, the chiefs looked relieved. 'It's unfortunate that their answers were only one side of a double-edged sword. If Varus believed that you had ordered the raid, you would already be lying dead while the settlement burned around you. Instead he thinks that you were unaware, and his punishment for that will be the taxes I have mentioned.'

'Damned for knowing, damned for not knowing,' snarled Bushy Eyebrows.

'Dead if we'd known, beggared because we did not,' corrected Red Head, his tone acid. 'The difference, though small, is worth noting.'

'Remember the annual taxes, which will also be due soon,' said Arminius. He saw the hopelessness rising in the chieftains' eyes. Their anger towards him had been eclipsed. This was the moment to strike. 'Do not lose faith,' he urged. 'All is not lost. Some time past, you will remember that I came to you with a plan. A plan to attack Varus and his legions while they are on the march this summer. With Donar's help, I intend to wipe them from the face of the earth.' He paused, studying their expressions, and took heart. No one had told him to shut up, and at least two men were nodding in agreement. Not Red Head, though.

'You may also recall that the Bructeri stand with the Cherusci on this. The Chatti are soon to join us. Taking part will grant you Usipetes a chance to avenge not just your dead warriors, but to redress the great injustices that will be laid upon you tomorrow. You will not have to wait long for vengeance. Varus' army will march east inside the next month. I know this and more because he regards me as a trusted ally, a man in whom he can confide. A friend.' Varus' acceptance that his men had merely been over-eager in their killing of the Usipetes was proof of that.

Now Arminius judged that he might have about half of them, but not more. He flailed around inside his head, worrying that, even at this point, the chieftains would give up. Bend the knee to Rome. Pay Varus' taxes although that would mean bleeding themselves dry. I've killed and lied to get this far, he thought. What's another lie? 'In recent days, I have had word from the Marsi and Angrivarii. They too will fight with us! Six tribes will field a mighty force that will crush the Romans like men step on ants. With the Usipetes by our side, we will be invincible.' Arminius knew he couldn't sound desperate, so he let his words settle among the chieftains. He prayed that they took root.

No one spoke. Each dragging moment seemed to last an eternity.

'How many soldiers will Varus lead over the river?' asked Red Head at last.

'Three legions, and a number of auxiliary units. None are full strength – they never are – so all told there will be about fifteen thousand men.'

'And you expect to field?'

Arminius couldn't blame Red Head. When a man was about to risk his life, and those of his people, he had every right to know such important details. He was asking, though, and *that* was good. 'By my reckoning, close to twenty thousand warriors.'

'On an open battlefield, that superiority will not be enough,' said Red Head, and a few heads nodded.

Arminius was ready. 'You speak true, but it was never my intention to fight the Romans face-to-face. Your warriors' strengths, and mine, are those of courage, speed and agility. Ambush Varus, and we can utilise all those qualities at once. Imagine your warriors like the clouds of midges that plague our peoples every summer, but far more deadly. They will dart in from the forest and attack the Romans. Before the enemy can react, they will escape not above, as midges do, but to the safety of the trees. Together with the other tribes, they will do it again and again and again, until none of the Romans are left alive.'

'I like the sound of that,' growled Bushy Eyebrows.

'And I!' 'And I!' 'I am with you, Arminius!'

Arminius nodded as if their reaction had been what he'd expected from the start.

Red Head did not join in, but nor did he try to stop the chieftains' loud cries. He waited until his fellows had fallen silent.

Arminius' fear resurged. If Red Head spoke against him, the others' opinions would change like a gust of autumn wind. 'Well?' he asked in his most confident tone. 'Are you with us?'

By way of answer, Red Head slit his bonds with a dagger. 'I will fight with you,' he said with an evil smile. 'And so will every Usipetes warrior.'

XIV

Tullus was in his tent, making his last preparations before leading his troops towards the Usipetes' settlement. He eased a little more of his mail shirt up here and there, so that it hung over his gilded belt. Doing this made him look less impressive – the pulled-out shirt gave him a slight paunch – but the belt helped to transfer some of the mail's dead weight on to his hips. If he didn't do it, his knees would be screaming by the end of the day. His belt was on, his sword too. The metalwork of the scabbard and his helmet had been polished, and his mail scrubbed. Tullus had suffered no one else to do it. Today was a day to impress. To send home the message to the Usipetes that Rome's soldiers were to be feared. To make them understand that if the emperor wished it, their people could be crushed underfoot.

He peered with a critical eye at the bracelets on his wrists, and the multiple *phalerae* suspended on his chest by a leather harness. They shone back at him, gold, silver, bronze, each one the acknowledgement of an action that had been judged valiant. On at least half of the occasions, Tullus reckoned he had done no more than any soldier would, but he was the one who'd been spotted by a tribune or legate. Thrice, he'd only been trying to reduce the number of casualties suffered by his men. Perhaps two of them had been won justly, Tullus had once declared to Fenestela and besides, it was becoming unfashionable to wear them. He'd been shocked by the vehemence of his optio's reaction. 'That's bullshit, sir, plain and simple,' Fenestela had said. 'I've lost count of the times when you have thrown yourself into places that most soldiers would run a mile from. That takes balls, sir. Real balls. So you be fucking proud of those medallions. Sir.' Fenestela had blushed then, and the memory of that made Tullus smile.

He ran a comb through the horsehair crest of his helmet, and wished that he'd had it redyed before leaving Vetera. It would do, he decided, putting it on. The savages will be too busy listening to me shout to notice it.

'Sir?' It was Fenestela's voice, from outside the tent.

'Coming.' Picking up his vitis, Tullus joined his optio, whose equipment and helmet had been burnished as much as his own. 'You look the part.'

Fenestela grinned. 'So do you, sir.'

'Are the men ready?'

'Yes, sir. The three cohorts have assembled on the *intervallum* as per your orders. The cavalry as well.'

'Has Arminius returned?' At the officers' meeting earlier, Maelo had reported that his superior had gone to pray to his gods in a nearby grove. Tullus had been irritated – by rights Arminius should have told him – but not that surprised. The Cheruscan was the force's commander, so he couldn't protest, and it hadn't occurred to him to question the sentries about when Arminius had left the camp.

'Yes, sir.'

'Good. Walk with me,' directed Tullus, heading for the intervallum. 'I suggested to Arminius that the plan stays the same. We advance to within a hundred paces of the settlement, and then deploy in a line one cohort deep, with the horses on the flanks. I'll have the trumpets sound, and we will wait to see what they do.'

Fenestela's chuckle was unpleasant. 'Not very much they can do, is there, sir?'

'Take nothing for granted, optio.'

'I won't. But they'd have to be fucking mad to do anything other than roll over and show us their throats, like submissive dogs.'

'That's what I think they will do too,' said Tullus, 'but we stay on our guard nonetheless. A beaten dog can still bite.'

It didn't take long for the Romans to form up outside the settlement. The cohorts arrayed themselves in good order, three centuries wide, and two deep. A twenty-pace gap separated each unit. Arminius' horsemen spread out in a long line on either flank, curving around like the encircling wings of a bird of prey. Tullus' century had a place of honour, in the front rank of the middle cohort. Although Arminius was the force's commander, his place was with the cavalry, he'd said, and so it was Tullus who would deliver Varus' ultimatum.

Tullus sat astride his horse to the right of his men, with a standard-bearer and trumpeter close by. Plenty of eyes must have watched from within the settlement as they had taken up their positions, but apart from a couple of boys who had wandered a short distance from the houses to peer in awe, few people had been seen. An occasional figure had scurried from one house to another, or peered around the corner of a house, but that had been it. Trickles of smoke rose from the roofs, proving that the settlement had not been abandoned.

Tullus saw little fear in his troops' faces when he'd ridden along the front of the formation, delivering a rousing speech similar to that he used before battle. They were here to serve the emperor, and to serve Rome. They were here to ensure that Germania remained at peace. They were here for each other. They were all brave men, who would do their duty, who would fight valiantly if it came to it. 'Not that I think the savages will attack,' he had said. 'They'll shit their breeches at all of our finery, and do what they're told.' That had raised a laugh, and they had cheered themselves hoarse when Tullus had promised every man extra measures of meat and wine that night. He scrutinised the settlement, but could see no indication that any resistance was planned. The calm was unsettling, but it arose from the Usipetes' fear, Tullus decided, which worked to their advantage.

'Ready?' he asked.

The trumpeter nodded.

'Sound, as loud as you can.' Tullus had told the trumpeter beforehand to play the set of notes used to announce the arrival of a general on a parade ground. The Usipetes wouldn't know its real meaning, but he had little doubt it would tell them that they were being summoned.

The blaring noise died away.

There was no immediate response. Tullus studied the point where the road led into the settlement, but his eyes also roamed from left to right over the houses, searching again for signs of treachery. He saw nothing.

At a count of perhaps thirty heartbeats, the Usipetes' leaders had still not appeared. Irritated, Tullus had the trumpeter sound again. If they didn't emerge soon, a messenger would have to be sent in.

His anger eased as a party of men emerged into view from between the buildings. Perhaps twenty in number, there weren't enough to pose a threat. Nonetheless, the tension among the legionaries became palpable as the tribesmen approached. 'Steady,' Tullus ordered. He rode out a short way to meet them – alone, straight-backed, confident – showing the Usipetes that Rome's soldiers were scared of no one. In reality, his mouth was dry and his heart pounding. They wouldn't dare harm me, Tullus told himself. To do so would guarantee the deaths of everyone in the settlement, and they know it.

He recognised many of the chieftains who had come to Vetera to petition Varus, among them Red Head. Half a dozen of the group were warriors, an honour guard no doubt, and a few appeared to be slaves, carrying extra spears for their masters. To a man, the Usipetes looked aggrieved. Good enough for them, thought Tullus, picturing the villagers murdered by the raiding party. We wouldn't be here if they hadn't turned a blind eye to their young warriors. He didn't think about Tubero, whose stupidity was the root cause of it all.

'That's close enough,' he cried when the Usipetes were fifteen paces away.

The chieftains shuffled to a resentful halt.

Tullus did not speak, letting them stew, letting them see close up how many soldiers he had.

Red Head broke the quiet. 'Have you come to destroy our settlement?'

Tullus didn't reply at once, and was glad to see fear replace the resentment in many of the chieftains' eyes. His last doubts that they might spring an ambush, or fight, vanished. They would pay Varus' taxes. 'Thanks to the governor's clemency, not today,' he said, and let the silence build once more.

Red Head shifted from foot to foot as he listened to the other chieftains' muttered questions. 'Why are you here?' he asked at length.

'You know why.'

'Because of what our warriors did,' admitted Red Head.

'That's right. Governor Varus has sent me to deliver a message,' said Tullus in his best German. Keen to reduce the chance of misinterpretation, he reverted back to Latin, speaking slowly so that Red Head could translate. 'You will have heard that the raiding party was all but wiped out, and the survivors sold into slavery. The matter does not end there, however. Violations of the imperial peace will *not* be tolerated by the emperor. Will *never* be tolerated. A suitable punishment has to be visited upon your entire tribe, and Varus has decided it will take the form of taxes. Heavy taxes.' Red Head's shoulders bowed a little as his words sank in. Good, thought Tullus. This will teach the dogs not to break the peace in future. 'Do you understand?'

Red Head interpreted. When he had done so in Vetera, there had been uproar. This time, there were weary nods and shrugs. A few hate-filled glances were thrown in Tullus' direction, but that was to be expected. If there had been none, he would have been suspicious.

'We understand,' said Red Head, sounding like an old man. 'How much will the taxes be?'

'Forty-one Roman soldiers and auxiliaries died in the clash with your warriors. Twenty were wounded. Altogether, four hundred and eighty-seven villagers were murdered. Varus has set the death price at three hundred denarii per soldier, and half that amount for each wounded man. You will pay a hundred denarii for each slain villager. I believe that the total comes to . . .' Tullus paused before delivering the hammer blow. '. . . sixty-four thousand denarii.'

There was pandemonium as Red Head translated his words. No one made a threatening move towards Tullus, however. He watched, cold-faced, until a modicum of calm had been restored.

'You have to understand, centurion, that our people do not use money the way that you Romans do,' said Red Head. 'We are not rich. This tax will beggar us.'

'That is none of my concern,' barked Tullus. 'You should have thought of the possible consequences before you let the raiding party leave.'

'We didn't know what they were going to do!' cried Red Head.

Tullus' smile was pitiless. 'Governor Varus will take payment in currencies other than coin. Cattle, slaves, furs, even women's hair is acceptable. Take them to Vetera, and a state official will value what's presented.' Tullus could see distaste mixed with the impotent anger writ on Red Head's face, and the same emotion mirrored in his companions' expressions. It was perhaps stooping low to mention their women's hair, he thought, but the demand for the stuff in Rome, where it was used to manufacture wigs, was massive. A lot of money could be raised in this manner.

Red Head conferred with the other chieftains. 'How long do we have to pay the tax?'

'Varus wants half the amount paid within seven days – that's thirty-two thousand denarii. You have until the end of harvest to find the rest, as well as the annual tax. Just over three months.'

Red Hair winced. 'And if we have not come up with the full amount by then?'

'Soldiers will return to take payment – by force.' He didn't need to add that as many of the settlement's inhabitants as were required to make up the shortfall would be enslaved.

Red Head explained to his companions what he'd said. Tullus was satisfied to see dull acceptance instead of burning anger in the chieftains' posture. 'We accept Varus' tax,' said Red Head a moment later.

'A wise decision,' Tullus declared. 'I want seventy sheep delivered to my camp within the hour as well.'

Red Head's mouth opened in protest, and closed again. 'I'll see it's done.'

Tullus was about to pull his horse's head around when an altercation at the back of the group of Usipetes caught his eye. One of the chieftains, purple-faced with anger, was jabbing a slave in the chest with his forefinger, and saying the same words over and over. It was not Tullus' business, and he would have turned away, but the slave reminded him strongly of a wounded legionary whom he'd had to leave behind once, in Illyricum. Ambushed on patrol by a superior force of enemy tribesmen, Tullus and his troops had had to execute a fighting withdrawal. It had been a snap decision to abandon the legionary, a man whom he'd known for years. Tullus had acted thus because of the barrage of rocks being heaved on them from above, inflicting serious and mounting casualties among his soldiers. It had been the right choice to make, but the legionary's anguished cries haunted Tullus' dreams on occasion. He still hoped that the man had died under a boulder rather than at the hands of the enemy, but there was no way of knowing.

Tullus watched as the chieftain began raining blows on the slave's head and chest with his clenched fists. At last the slave defended himself, throwing a punch at his master, but his ankle fetters soon caused him to fall to the ground. Roaring abuse, his owner kicked him. Next, he drew his sword. Tullus' conscience burned, as it had on that bloody day in Illyricum.

Without thinking, he urged his horse forwards. Red Head and the rest gaped as he rode past, right up to the furious chieftain, a large-framed man with tattooed biceps. He glared at Tullus while the slave looked on in confusion. What the chieftain muttered next was unclear, but it was far from complimentary. Tullus' anger boiled over, and he moved his horse forward, separating the chieftain from his minion. 'Your slave is coming with me,' he said in Latin, and then in what he thought was the German equivalent.

'The dog is my property, not yours!' snarled the chieftain, stepping close to Tullus. 'I do with him what I want.'

Tullus placed the hobnailed sole of his boot against the man's chest and shoved him backwards. 'Consider him part of Governor Varus' tax.' He glanced down at the slave. 'Speak any Latin?'

A blank stare.

'Come with me,' Tullus ordered in German. 'You're mine now.'

The slave's eyes registered surprise and something else – gratitude, perhaps; it wasn't clear – but he got to his feet with alacrity and moved to Tullus' side.

Helped by those around him, his owner had regained his balance. At once he took a step towards Tullus, his sword raised. The other chieftains tensed.

Tullus' guts twisted. It had been rash to act as he had. A single wrong move now, and the Usipetes would be on him like a pack of stray dogs savaging a bone. He took a quick look at the slave. The fear in the man's eyes – and the livid weals marking every exposed part of his flesh – hardened Tullus' resolve. The slave was clearly mistreated on a regular basis. 'Lay a hand on me, or this man,' he cried in Latin, 'and, as the gods are my witnesses, I will order my men to attack your settlement.' He shot a look at Red Head. 'Tell him!'

Red Head gabbled a couple of sentences, and the big chieftain scowled. With great care, he hawked a great gob of phlegm through the air; it landed at the slave's feet.

'Fuck you too,' said Tullus. He knew how to say that in German.

The chieftain snarled something back and again lifted his blade.

'Go on, you prick,' said Tullus, his temper starting to gain the upper hand once more.

Red Head gestured at the chieftain, speaking in a low voice. Tullus caught the words 'too great a risk'. With a face as black as thunder, the chieftain retreated a few paces.

'You treat him with great dishonour,' said Red Head. 'Slaves are the property of their owner, to do with as they wish.'

'It is the same among my people,' said Tullus.

'Why are you stealing this slave then?'

'Because I felt like it,' replied Tullus in an icy tone. He had no inclination to explain his real motive.

'Such is Rome's way too,' said Red Head, his face bitter.

'That's rich coming from a chieftain whose warriors butchered innocent villagers on the other side of the Rhenus,' retorted Tullus.

'They acted so because . . .' Red Head hesitated, then added, 'There's no point arguing with you.'

'No, there isn't. Pay the tax, or suffer the consequences,' snapped Tullus. He glanced at the slave. 'Follow me.' Wheeling his horse, he rode back towards his soldiers. The slave trotted after, his chains clinking.

After conferring with Arminius, Tullus waited an hour – extra intimidation – before marching his troops and the seventy sheep back towards Vetera. Varus had received them the moment they'd returned, and was pleased with their news. 'They'll think twice before letting anything like that happen again,' he said. 'A job well done, Arminius, centurion. There shouldn't be any unrest at our backs now when we march east.' He saw Tullus' enquiring look. 'I want us on the move by the ides of the month. See to it that your cohort is ready. Your men too, Arminius.'

The preparations could begin tomorrow, thought Tullus, leaning against the door of the kitchen, a clay cup of wine in his hand, watching his new slave light the fire under the cooking grate. Evening had fallen, and he was in his quarters. The slave's resemblance to the legionary that Tullus had abandoned didn't end at his face or his black hair. He was also young, short and wiry, and well muscled. Once his fetters had been struck off at the legion's forge – Tullus wasn't prepared to keep a slave like that, regardless of the risk of flight – he had ordered him to cook his dinner. It was a gamble whether the man knew how to prepare decent food, but it gave him something to do. Tullus couldn't decide what to do with him. He already had a servant, a cantankerous old Gaul called Ambiorix, who'd been his slave since the start of his time at Vetera. However, Ambiorix was in bed with a fever, and had been for two days. When he returned to duty, he would resent the newcomer.

'What's your name?' Tullus asked in German.

The slave placed another twig on to the burning pile of tinder. 'Degmar,' he said without turning his head.

Instead of feeling angry at this disrespect, Tullus was amused to feel a sneaking admiration. The man had balls. 'Degmar. What tribe names its sons so?'

Now Degmar looked at Tullus, his face a mask. 'Marsi.'

The Marsi lived to the east of the Usipetes, between the rivers Lupia and Rura. They had a history of being hostile towards Rome, but at this moment, were at peace. 'How did you come to be a slave?'

A scowl. 'It was during a cattle raid that went wrong, two years ago. We didn't find all the Usipetes' sentries as we crept into the settlement. The alarm was raised. Every warrior in the place woke, and we fled. I tripped and fell, like a child. Thanks to my clumsiness, I was captured.'

'That was ill fortune,' said Tullus.

'It was my fault, and no one else's.' Degmar's shrug was bitter.

Two years in captivity would have been hard, thought Tullus. Poor bastard.

'You had no reason to intervene earlier, yet you did . . . master. I owe you my thanks.'

A little discomfited, Tullus waved a dismissive hand.

'Can I ask why you did it?'

'You look like a good soldier of mine.' The man's screams rang in Tullus' ears, but he blocked them out. 'He died.'

Degmar's eyes regarded Tullus, unblinking, for a moment, and then he went back to tending the fire. 'I am grateful to resemble him. Being your slave can only be better than what I endured among the Usipetes.'

Tullus didn't want a second slave, and Ambiorix would give him grief about it, of that he had no doubt. He thought of the chieftain who'd owned Degmar, and wondered if it would gall him further to know that his former property was a free man. 'Did you leave a wife among your people? Children?'

'A wife.' A flicker of emotion passed over Degmar's face, and was gone. 'She was pregnant for the first time when I went on the raid. Only Donar knows if she survived the birth. If she did, she has remarried, like as not. She's a good-looking woman.'

That made up Tullus' mind. 'Why don't you seek her out?'

Degmar's forehead creased. 'You are my master, but I ask you not to mock me. I am *your* slave now.'

'I do not jest. Cook me a decent plate of food, and you can have your freedom. I'll draw up the paperwork so you can get past the checkpoints at the bridge. After that, you can skirt the Usipetes' territory before you head south, to Marsi territory.'

Degmar's expression grew incredulous. 'Why would you do this – for a meal?'

Again Tullus remembered the legionary he'd left behind to die. 'I'm in a good mood, that's why.' He wagged a finger. 'It does depend on what you produce for my dinner, mind!'

Degmar chuckled. It was the first time he'd let down his guard in any way, and Tullus' heart warmed.

'Your offer is generous indeed, but I cannot accept it,' said Degmar.

'Is your cooking that bad?' asked Tullus, smiling.

'I owe you my life.' Degmar saw Tullus' confusion. 'My owner was threatening to kill me.'

'Why?'

'He had a terrible temper.' Degmar lifted his tunic, exposing his belly.

Tullus winced at the mass of scars, old and new. Some looked to be healing burns. 'Why would he slay you, though?'

'I do not make a good slave. My mouth runs away with me.' Degmar's lips quirked. 'I had just muttered something about the Usipetes being spineless worms for submitting to your tax.'

Tullus snorted in amusement, surprised that Degmar would repeat such a thing to a Roman who yet had the power of life and death over him. 'Your people would not have bent their knees to me?'

'In the face of such a force, I think they would have. They hold little love for Rome, but they're no fools,' admitted Degmar. 'I wasn't going to tell *him* that, though, was I?'

Now Tullus laughed. 'You're one of a kind, Degmar of the Marsi. If you won't accept my offer of freedom, what would you do?'

'I will be your servant, and bodyguard, if you'll have me. I know you have soldiers who serve you, but I will be your hound. Sleep outside your door. Watch your back, protect you against treachery.'

'Despite the fact that I am Roman?'

A wry shrug. 'Roman or not, you saved my skin.'

Tullus felt his respect for Degmar grow. 'How long do you propose to serve me so?'

'Until I have repaid my debt to you.'

Tullus had never really wanted such protection, but Degmar's desire to pay him back rang loud and clear from his words. The Marsi warrior was an honourable man, Tullus decided, and to refuse his offer would be disrespectful. I'm getting old, he thought. Sentimental. 'I accept your offer.'

'My thanks.' Degmar bent his head a fraction.

It was the most acknowledgement he would get, thought Tullus, amused once more. German tribesmen could be so different to Romans. Despite the manner in which they had been thrown together, despite Tullus' senior status and Degmar's lowly one, the warrior addressed him – almost – as an equal. It was a surprise to Tullus that he didn't altogether care.

He watched as Degmar got on with preparing the fresh-caught bream that had been a gift from another centurion in the cohort. Tullus still had no idea if he could cook – he would find out before long – but the man looked well able to handle himself in a fight. It was then that an image of Tubero popped into Tullus' head.

With such a venomous and high-placed enemy, thought Tullus, there was nothing wrong with having a man like Degmar around.

PART TWO

Summer, AD 9

The Roman Camp of Porta Westfalica,
Deep in Germania

XV

Falling from the narrow gap between door and doorframe, a thin beam of sunlight on Varus' face woke him up. He stirred, aware that he'd been too hot under the blanket. Curse it, he thought, refusing to open his eyes and admit that another day had begun. What paperwork will Aristides have to torture me with? What officers and chieftains will come whinging to my office? It would be the same shit; just another day, as it always was.

A faint, dusty smell – the odour of not just his bedchamber, but his entire quarters – reminded him that he had woken in Porta Westfalica, not Vetera. Varus' burgeoning sour mood vanished in a heartbeat. He opened his eyes, and sat up with a smile. He was in Porta Westfalica! Here his duties were far lighter. The room's faded grandeur and its dark red-painted walls, the latest fashion in Rome five or more years before, were of no concern. He didn't mind that the absence of regular occupants and, as a consequence, lack of heating during the winter meant that patches of mould had bloomed in the corners. They had been cleaned off, but the smell remained. This and the numerous cracks in the plaster were badges of his summer sojourn, to be relished.

Opening the door, Varus exhilarated in the warm sunlight that swept in, lighting up the room. Even the temperature seemed warmer than in Vetera. He took a step outside, acknowledging the sentry's salute with a cordial nod. Along with other chambers, a dining room and the kitchen, his bedroom faced on to a large, colonnaded courtyard, the centre of which was occupied by a herb garden, apple trees and a selection of statues. All of it had seen better days. Although it was the commandant's quarters, the entire place had a shabby air, like a holiday villa at Capri that hadn't been used for several summers.

Other than the principia, few other permanent buildings had been constructed here. Porta Westfalica was only occupied during the summer, so there was little point in erecting barracks and suchlike until the place became a fixed camp. The large house had been Varus' home since their arrival a month before, and would remain so until their departure. He had the slaves burn fires daily in every room with a fireplace, and the place was being scrubbed from top to bottom. It wouldn't be long before the building was as good as new, he thought.

Freed of his wife, who had refused – again – to accompany him, he was free to behave as he wished within these walls. Sleep all day, drink all night, if he wanted to. Varus smiled. He didn't want to act like a carefree, single tribune again, but it was nice to know that he could do so without being nagged. Outside, he was also master – governor of the whole region, come to monitor the tribes, to see that Rome's laws were being followed and its taxes being paid. Vetera lay just over a hundred miles to the west. The distance gave Varus immense satisfaction. Only a fraction of the official messages and letters that were the bane of his life in Vetera managed to reach this island of refuge. It wasn't a coincidence. The important ones did get to Porta Westfalica, but the rest were dealt with on the spot – Varus had delegated the camp commander at Vetera to open every last letter – relieving him, for the summer at least, of a considerable amount of arse-ache.

He took a deep breath of the dawn-crisp air. Gods, but he felt five years younger.

Footsteps behind made him turn. 'Morning, Aristides.'

'Good morning, master.' Aristides was already dressed, and his hair oiled.

Varus couldn't resist poking fun. His slave didn't like his room here, or his bed, or much else, as far as Varus could tell. Even the baths – in particular the baths – weren't up to standard. 'Did you sleep well?'

Aristides made a face. 'My rest was tolerable, master, thank you. And you?'

'I slept like a babe. Now, I'm ravenous.' Varus clapped his hands and a moment later, a slave emerged from the kitchen. 'I want a table and chairs out here,' he said, pointing at a sunny spot in the centre of the courtyard. 'And food. Lots of it.'

'At once, master.' The slave hurried from view.

'Enjoy your meal, master,' said Aristides.

Varus cast a look at his scribe, who was also heading for the kitchen. It was Aristides' habit to breakfast with the other slaves, a situation Varus knew he hated. It wasn't surprising. The domestic slaves were of several different races, uneducated types who looked down on the learned Greek. Feeling a little sympathy – he wouldn't want to break bread with most ordinary soldiers – Varus toyed with the idea of inviting Aristides to join him, before dismissing it. His manumission might be impending, but there was no point giving Aristides ideas above his station, something that sharing his master's table was sure to do. Just because he's been with me for half a lifetime doesn't make him my friend, thought Varus.

After a busy morning receiving visitors, Varus had an agreeable meal with Vala, his deputy, a thoughtful, middle-aged man with a shiny bald pate. One cup of wine with the food – fresh-roasted venison in plum sauce – had turned into two, and then three. Varus had had the wherewithal to call a halt at that stage, but there was no denying the warm glow that encased him as he and Vala rode out of the vast camp towards the local settlement. Aristides' disapproving expression and protestations about unfinished paperwork had not been enough to deter Varus from taking a look at the site of the proposed forum.

'It will wait,' he'd said to Aristides. 'I'll be back within the hour.' Lips pursed, Aristides had retreated to Varus' office in silent protest.

A century of legionaries followed on behind Varus and Vala, protection and a mark of the governor's status rolled into one. Vala was pontificating about something or other to do with the relationship between Tiberius and Augustus. Varus' attention began to wander, helped by the wine and Porta Westfalica's surroundings, which fascinated him. The camp's location was unusual. It had not been built in a strong site – a hilltop, or with good views all around. Instead it had been erected on the bank of the River Lupia. The reasoning for this was sound: equipment, food and supplies could be transported from Vetera to this point, so it needed to be well defended.

Varus was pleased to catch sight of a fleet of sizeable barges approaching from the west. Like as not, their cargo would include large quantities of grain, enough to feed the legionaries for a few days, or half a month, perhaps more. That would keep the quartermasters off his back at least.

'What do you think, sir?' asked Vala.

Varus realised that he didn't have a clue what Vala had been saying. 'About what?' he said, without meeting his subordinate's eye.

There was a short silence, during which Vala must have been wondering where his superior's head had been, and then he replied, 'Whether the rift between Tiberius and Augustus has been resolved for good, sir.'

'I have no idea, Vala,' replied Varus, a little irritated by this, one of the favourite topics for gossip among officers. 'I'm not in Rome. Even if I were, I wouldn't be party to such information. Most of what we hear is gossip, remember, stories that have travelled all the way from the capital, being twisted and distorted with each telling. They're about as reliable as the ramblings of a drunk who props up a bar. Interesting, often. Funny, sometimes. But not to be believed.'

They had reached the outskirts of the settlement, which lay a short distance to the east of Porta Westfalica. The usual sprawl of premises lined each side of the dirt road. Carpenters and blacksmiths plied their trade alongside potters and cobblers. There were vendors selling olives and wine from Italy and Hispania, pottery and ceramics from Gaul, and furs taken from animals trapped locally. If the sellers of tinctures and potions were to be believed, there were cures on sale – at 'the best prices' – for blisters, aching muscles, sore backs, bladder infections and every venereal disease under the sun. The off-duty legionaries who were talking to a purveyor of the last were careful not to meet Varus' eye as he rode by. Their efforts didn't work with the soldiers accompanying Varus. A chorus of jeers and catcalls rained upon their comrades, who were too embarrassed to retaliate. Grinning, the officers in charge of Varus' security detail did not intervene.

Varus pretended not to notice what was going on. Prostitutes and the infections that they were prone to carry had been around since the dawn of time, and so too had their customers. Trying to stamp out the practice would be as pointless as pushing water up a hill. Besides, it was up to lower-ranking officers to ensure that their soldiers were healthy enough to complete their duties, not him.

A little further on, his attention was drawn to the selection of amber laid out by a trader who was loudly declaiming that the woman bought such a gift would love her man for evermore. Varus admired the largest piece on the counter, an orange-gold lump the size of his clenched fist, and wondered whether his wife would like it. He rode on without stopping. It was beneath his station to haggle with a mere trader, never mind the fact that the man would quadruple the price the instant he realised who Varus was. Perhaps he'd send Aristides out to take a look, and see if he could purchase it for a reasonable sum. If it could be worked into a necklace, earrings and a set of bracelets, so much the better.

Gift ideas for his wife receded as the settlement's centre drew near. 'They've been busy,' he said, pointing at several fine, stone-built houses. With their open fronts, which were filled by a smarter class of trader, and their staircases at the side which ran up to the floor above, they stood in stark contrast to the wooden shacks used by the shopkeepers they had passed. 'These weren't here last summer, I don't think.'

'I believe you're right, sir. Give it a few more years, and this will be a proper little garrison town.'

'Have you visited Pons Laugona? It's impressive.' Official duties had taken Varus to the civilian settlement a number of times. It lay on the River Laugona, some fifty miles to the east of the camp at Confluentes.

'I haven't yet had the chance to, sir.'

'It's like a town anywhere in the empire, really. There are blocks of apartments, factories producing pottery, statues and metalwork. An aqueduct has been built. Only the centre of the settlement has piped water so far, but that will change. But it's the forum and in particular the municipal building that are the most inspiring. It's fifty paces by forty-five, with a central courtyard, and annexes that are respectable in size. There's a massive gilt statue of Augustus too, which wouldn't look out of place in Rome.'

'The locals are trying hard then,' said Vala.

'Aye,' replied Varus. They were nearing the open space that would form the proposed forum. Catching sight of a group of the town's leaders whom he'd already met – among them the unctuous ones he had disliked – he told himself that their enthusiasm was to be embraced, not spurned. Their energy would see what had happened at Pons Laugona replicated here. It was for the good of the empire. Perhaps it was because of the wine he'd consumed, perhaps the ease with which he could become the politician, but Varus felt his annoyance fade. He raised a hand, pulling a broad smile. 'Greetings!'

The dignitaries, chieftains of one rank or another, approached together. Their salutations filled the air. 'Governor, you honour us with your presence!' 'Welcome to our humble settlement, Governor Varus.' 'May Donar bless you, governor.'

'Governor, what a delight.' Aelwird, the portly man who'd got up Varus' nose the most, stepped to the front and bowed. His long, greasy hair fell around the sides of his face. A whiff of ripe body odour reached Varus' nostrils a moment later, and he had to work hard not to recoil in disgust. Aelwird might have taken to wearing a Roman tunic and sandals, but he didn't yet appreciate that regular bathing was both good for the soul and one's social interactions.

'Aelwird. Have you met Legate Vala, my second-in-command?'

'I have not yet had that pleasure.' Aelwird bent at the waist again, as much as a fat man could. 'I am overjoyed to make your acquaintance, Legate Vala.'

'Greetings, Aelwird,' replied Vala, inclining his head. His eyes flickered to Varus, who muttered under his breath:

'A sycophant of the first order.'

Vala's lips quirked.

'These are my fellow council members.' Aelwird, who hadn't noticed the exchange, indicated his companions, and reeled off a list of Germanic names. As he said each one, a man bowed.

Varus made little effort to remember who the tribesmen were. They recognised him and Vala, and that's what mattered.

With Aelwird by his right side, and Vala on his left, and the remainder of the council behind, they walked to where most of the activity was taking place.

'I've been telling Vala about Pons Laugona,' said Varus. 'No doubt you want to emulate what's been erected there, or even better it.'

Aelwird grinned like an urchin who'd been handed a coin. 'I haven't seen the forum at Pons Laugona, but two of my colleagues have. Of course we want to outdo what their council has had built, governor.'

Mutters rose from the others, and Varus was sure he heard the words 'Filthy Tencteri'. He'd forgotten. These men were Bructeri, with a smattering of Cherusci, if he remembered aright. 'Would tribal rivalry have anything to do with it?' he asked, smiling.

Aelwird chuckled. 'Perhaps a little, governor, but do not fear. Our primary desire comes from wishing our home to become the easternmost Roman town in Germania. When it is built, we want news to reach the emperor's ears of his loyal subjects here, so far from the capital.'

Varus and Vala were walking back to where they had left their horses when Varus' gaze chanced upon a group of men standing off to his left, close to the workers digging the municipal building's foundation. The newcomers – they hadn't been there a few moments before, Varus was sure of it – stood in sharp contrast to Aelwird and his fellows in their Roman clothing. Every last one was clad in traditional tribal dress. Some were bare-chested, but what alarmed Varus was that they were all armed. The dwellings near Porta Westfalica didn't quite constitute a town yet, and therefore didn't have the law that prohibited weapons inside the settlement limits, yet few residents carried more than a knife. No doubt they had spears and so on in their houses, but they weren't evident on the street, like this. 'D'you see that lot?' he asked Vala.

'Just spotted them, sir,' Vala replied, his eyes narrowed. 'I was wondering whether to summon your escort.'

'Don't. It would give the wrong impression. We get to our horses, and then pretend to take our time adjusting saddlecloths and reins.' Varus glanced back at the council. 'Aelwird? Another word.'

Aelwird hurried over. 'Yes, governor?'

'Those tribesmen. The ones staring at us,' said Varus, without looking. 'Do you know them?'

Aelwird's eyes moved to the group. 'They're Cherusci. I know a few of them, governor, yes.' He scowled, hesitated, but said nothing more.

'What is it?' demanded Varus.

'It's idle gossip, governor, nothing for you to be concerned with.'

'I'll be the judge of that. Tell me.'

'The group is visiting the town to trade. They've been camping nearby, and drinking in the taverns each night. A few of them have been boasting about how . . .' There was a slight pause before Aelwird went on. '. . . how they're going to ambush your legions.' He cast an unhappy look at Varus and then Vala. 'I would have mentioned it, except I didn't think it worth troubling you with, governor. Their boasts are nothing more than what you might hear in any inn, or around a campfire, on any night of the year. You know how it is when men have drunk too much.'

Could anyone fawn so much and not be genuine? Varus wondered. He threw another glance at the tribesmen. 'Are any of them of rank?'

'Not a one, from what I've been told. They're young warriors, out to impress. Full of piss and wind, if you'll excuse the expression.'

Varus stared for longer than he had before, seeing that most of the warriors were smooth-cheeked. He glanced at Vala, who shrugged. 'They don't seem dangerous, sir,' he muttered.

The warriors were the exception rather than the rule, thought Varus. The majority of the locals were content with being Romanised – he only had to look at the construction going on to see that. 'It's the way of all youths,' he said to Aelwird. 'I was no different, on a day. No doubt you were the same, Vala?'

Vala grinned. 'I won't argue with you there, sir.'

Aelwird looked relieved. 'If I had drink taken, I was known to exaggerate when I was younger, yes – even to lie about what I had done.' He leaned a little closer to Varus. 'If you wish, I could have a few of them rounded up and questioned. A thorough beating and we'd know one way or another if there was any truth to their story.'

Varus toyed with the option before he shook his head. 'That won't be necessary. Arminius – you know him?' Aelwird nodded, and Varus went on, 'He's an ally of Rome, but he's also Cheruscan. According to him, there hasn't been as much as a whisper of discontent among his people towards the empire these past months.'

'I've heard much the same from other auxiliaries,' said Vala.

Aelwird beamed. 'That's certainly the feeling amongst my tribe. With Augustus' rule comes peace and prosperity. Yes, we will all have to pay taxes to the imperial treasury, but the benefits of becoming part of the empire far outweigh those costs.'

If there had been any doubt left in Varus' mind about the need to question the group of warriors, Aelwird's last comment saw it vanish. Those who said that the Germans were complete savages had closed minds, he thought. Within a generation, the whole region would be but another prosperous part of the empire, like Hispania or Gallia. He swung himself up on to his horse. 'My thanks again for the tour, and commendations on your plans for the town. Submit your application to form a council before the harvest is taken in, and I'll see that it's approved in the shortest time possible.'

'You have my undying gratitude, governor.' Aelwird all but kissed Varus' boot.

Varus waved a benevolent farewell as he rode away. By the time they had reached his escort, the group of tribesmen had disappeared down a side street. It was proof to Varus that there was no cause for concern. If one century puts the fear of the gods into them, what would three legions do? he wondered.

XVI

'Where in Donar's name are they?'

It was the morning after Varus' trip to see the site of the new forum in Porta Westfalica, and Arminius was in a foul mood. He had just returned to the camp after two days away. Was that too long to expect that things might proceed as planned? He paced the small sun-dappled clearing, over and back, around its perimeter, across it again. A dozen of his men stood well back among the beech trees, out of his way, watching in silence. It wasn't far to the town, but the group was deep enough in the woods to mean they couldn't be spotted from the road that led southwest, towards Pons Laugona and other Roman settlements. Their horses were tethered nearby, also out of sight.

He glared at Osbert, who was nearest.

'I don't know,' replied Osbert in a calm voice.

'It's been too long. Go and look for them,' ordered Arminius. 'No! Stay where you are,' he snapped a heartbeat later. 'I don't want a Roman officer wondering what one auxiliary is doing on the road on his own.'

Osbert hadn't moved. 'Aye. The less reason to arouse suspicion, the better.'

'Something forgotten by the young Cheruscan fools who've been flapping their lips in Porta Westfalica's inns. Word of what they've been saying reached Varus' ears, you know that?'

'Aye, you said.' Again Osbert kept his voice level.

'It was pure luck that Varus chose to regard them as loud-mouthed drunkards and nothing more. If he'd taken them in and interrogated them – if my prick of a brother Flavus had heard anything of this—'

'Except Varus didn't. And Flavus is none the wiser,' said Osbert. 'Calm down.'

Arminius took a step towards him. 'What did you say?'

The air grew tense, yet none of the others interfered. It was a warrior's right to challenge his chieftain at any time, but few lived who dared to cross Arminius.

'You heard me, Arminius,' said Osbert. 'Losing your head now won't achieve anything.'

'I wouldn't take that from most men.' Arminius' voice was light, but there was an ice-cold timbre to it.

'I'm not most men,' replied Osbert, sticking out his chest.

A heartbeat, two heartbeats' pause, and then Arminius said, 'You're not, and in this case, you happen to be right. If there was ever a time for self-control, it's now. I want to cut the fools' balls off when they arrive, *and* make them eat the whole bloody lot, but I won't.'

Men laughed, and the atmosphere eased. 'Maybe they're not coming,' Arminius continued. 'It'll be obvious enough that I know – or suspect – that they let their mouths run away with them, and that that's the reason I've summoned them to a meeting.'

'If they go to the Romans—' Osbert began.

'If that happens, we might have to leave the camp in a hurry. But I doubt that it will. They're youngsters, less steady than you or I. Maelo will have put the fear of the gods into them. Knowing that you'll be hunted down and put to death with a wicker hurdle convinces most men to obey.' Arminius cocked his head. 'Listen! They're here.' As silence fell, he put a hand to his ear. The unmistakeable sound of riders and horses reverberated from the direction of the road. Although they could not be seen, everyone tensed, laying a hand to his weapon.

When Maelo emerged alone into the clearing, there was a uniform exhalation of breath. He raised a hand in salute to Arminius, who was already stalking to his side. 'Well?'

'They're with me,' said Maelo. 'I had to lay it down in no uncertain terms, but they came.'

'All of them?'

'No.' Maelo pursed his lips and spat. 'Three were on the piss in the settlement. We searched the inns and brothels, but had no luck finding them. Useless pieces of shit.'

'Have they run to the Romans?' demanded Arminius.

'The ringleader thinks not. He reckons they're in some shithole we didn't find, sleeping off a drunk.'

Arminius buried his anger. 'Fetch the rest.'

Maelo vanished the way he'd come, returning soon after with another dozen of Arminius' men and, in their midst, five dishevelled-looking, unarmed warriors. Red-eyed, hair standing on end, wearing stained tunics, they were obviously hungover. Their flushed complexions paled, however, as they recognised Arminius. They did not resist as Maelo and his companions herded them across the clearing with brandished spears.

'Greetings,' said Arminius in a pleasant tone.

There was a muttered chorus of replies, but no one met his eye.

'Any idea why you're here?' he asked.

'Aye,' replied one warrior, a young man of perhaps twenty with shaggy brown hair. 'Because our mouths ran away with us in Porta Westfalica.'

'That's a good start,' said Arminius. 'I like a man who's honest. Tell me what it was that you said. What your comrades said. Do not leave out a *single* detail.'

'We had come to the settlement to see the size of the Roman camp,' the warrior started. 'Everyone in the villages is talking about your ambush, of what a war leader you are, and of the glory that will be won by those who take part in it.'

It was good that expectations were running high, thought Arminius.

The priest Segimundus was playing his part. 'So you want to be there at the ambush?' he probed.

'Upon my life, I do! I can think of nothing better.'

Arminius studied the warrior's companions' faces as they echoed his fervent vow. It was hard to tell if they were telling the truth – all that was plain was their fear – but it wasn't surprising that such a group would come to spy out the forces that they might soon be fighting. 'Once you had seen the camp, why didn't you leave?'

The warrior's flush returned. 'We had come this far. We thought that a few drinks wouldn't do us any harm. To toast what we would do, when it – the ambush – happened.'

'I can picture the scene. One cup of wine was followed by a second, and a third, and before you knew it, you'd had more than you can remember. Am I right?' Arminius' question was laden with sarcasm.

'Aye, it was something like that. I can't remember who mentioned the ambush first. It seemed funny at the time, to be talking about such a thing so close to a Roman camp.'

'Were there any legionaries in the tavern?'

'No. I made sure of that much before we started drinking.'

Arminius' eyes pinned the warrior's, but he did not look away. 'Go on,' ordered Arminius.

'I can't remember everything that was said. I was quite drunk by that stage, you see. The talk was all to do with how surprised the Romans would be, and of how many legionaries each of us would kill, and how much booty we would take.' Ashamed, the warrior dropped his gaze. 'It was a rash thing to do.'

'Young warriors like you have always been full of bravado, and always will be. There's nothing wrong with that. What was stupid beyond belief was the fact that you mentioned such things, drunk, in a tavern adjacent to the very force we want to destroy.' Arminius sighed, imagining how Tullus might have reacted if he'd overheard the youths. 'Your comments could have endangered the whole enterprise, could have ended something that I have planned to do for many years – before it had even started. Have you any idea how angry that makes me?' This last was delivered in a furious hiss.

The warrior's shoulders drooped further. His companions shuffled their feet. Around them, Maelo and Arminius' men stood ready. It would take but a word, and the youths would go down under a flurry of blows.

I have a number of choices now, thought Arminius. We could kill them, and send a message to their villages that the same fate would meet anyone else as foolish. The second option was to slay just one or two, and to free the others, letting them carry word far and wide of his punishment. A third possibility was for his men to beat the warriors black and blue, and send them away with a warning.

Roughing them up would not be effective enough, Arminius decided. Killing a few would be, however. He was reminded of the rare Roman practice of decimation, which he had once witnessed: the condemned legionaries had broken and run during a battle.

As soon as it had arrived, his certainty about executing some of the youths faded. How had he become so Roman? Arminius wondered. German warriors who fled from an enemy had to live with the shame of their actions, and remained outcasts from their tribe until they proved their bravery again. Not only was this form of punishment effective, but it was far less savage than men having to murder their comrades with clubs or their fists.

The youths' crime was nowhere near as severe as those who had shown cowardice during a battle. Their loose talk *could* have had disastrous consequences, but it appeared from Varus' decision to do nothing that they – and he – had got away with it. What *was* his best course of action? Arminius wondered.

'Shall we kill them?' This from Maelo.

Several of the young warriors began to pray aloud.

'They deserve it,' replied Arminius in an iron tone. *Let them think that that's their fate.*

'Give us the word,' said Maelo, picking at his nails with a long dagger.

The blade gave Arminius an idea – a perfect one. Drawing his own knife, he approached the prisoners. Unhappy glances shot between them as he drew near.

The ringleader was one of the few not to back away. He squared his shoulders as the blade moved towards his face.

'I have every right to slay you for what you did,' said Arminius.

'You do.' The warrior met Arminius' gaze. 'Maelo knows my family. I ask that they be told I died well.'

Arminius let the dagger point come to rest on the warrior's cheekbone, just under his eye. There were horrified looks from the other youths. At first, his victim only flinched a little, but Arminius left it there until tiny beads of sweat had broken out on his forehead. 'Rather than remove your eye before I kill you, maybe I should take your tongue,' he said, dragging the blade lower, to the warrior's lips. 'That would stop you talking out of turn, even in the underworld.'

The youth's face was dripping with perspiration now, but he did not retreat. 'Kill me and have done,' he muttered.

This one *was* a warrior, thought Arminius. One of his companions looked as if he might be too. The rest, well, they too would fight for him after what he was about to do. Lifting his dagger a fraction, he opened the warrior's cheek with a quick flick of his wrist. Not a deep wound, or a long one, but enough to leave a permanent scar. The warrior let out a gasp of pain, but held his position, ready for whatever else Arminius might have planned.

'Each of you will receive this mark,' Arminius announced, moving to the next warrior. Realising that perhaps he wasn't to die, the man straightened his back and prepared himself.

Flick. Arminius opened his cheek. Another gasp.

'You will receive it not only as punishment, but to mark you out as men who are to fight in my ambush,' said Arminius. He saw their surprise, and smiled. 'You still want to take part, I assume? Still want to redden your spears with Roman blood?'

'Aye!' cried the ringleader; his comrades quickly joined in.

'Excellent,' said Arminius, cutting another man's face. He sliced the fourth warrior's cheek, and then the fifth. Despite their pain, their relief was palpable. Then Arminius caught one of the men smirking. He cursed inside. The wounding would *not* be enough. Without hesitation, he confronted the one who'd smirked. 'You think this is funny?'

Panic flared in the warrior's eyes. 'No, I—'

He couldn't say any more, because Arminius' dagger was buried in his chest. Arminius twisted the blade to and fro, making sure. When he tugged it out, gouts of warm blood spattered his hand and tunic. The warrior dropped at his feet like a bag of wheat. He kicked once and was still. Blood began to pool around him. His companions looked on in horror.

Arminius let them think that there would be nothing more for a dozen heartbeats. He stepped back, his bloodied dagger by his side, moved his harsh gaze across the remaining warriors. 'Does anyone else think this situation is amusing?'

No one answered.

'Know that you will be among the first warriors to attack the Romans.'

His words fell like lead slingshot bullets from the sky. The command was as good as a death sentence, and the young warriors knew it, but an end in battle was preferable to a blade between the ribs in this glade.

'Before that, though, some of my men will take you to the ambush site,' said Arminius. 'You will help to erect the earthworks that will hide us from the Romans. Work parties from other tribes will be there too. I command you to go among them, explaining what happened here, and why you have been marked so.' This was the sting in the tail. If any of the warriors did not comply, they would be forever known – because of their scars – as cowards. The only other option would be to abandon their tribe and become outcasts, friends to none. That in itself would be a death sentence to most men.

The ringleader was first to respond. He stepped forward, chin held high, blood yet trickling down his cheek. 'Before mighty Donar, bringer of thunder, I swear to follow your every command. May the god strike me down if I fail you.'

Arminius bent his head a fraction.

One by one, the warrior's companions swore similar oaths.

When they were done, Arminius dismissed them. 'Word will reach you of the time to meet. It will be soon after the harvest. Keep your spears sharp.'

Arminius' mind was made up by the time he'd reached the huge camp outside Porta Westfalica. Not only would he call in on Varus, but he would issue the governor with an invitation to go deer hunting. With Varus to himself for a day, there'd be plenty of opportunities to discover if he had any reason to be concerned.

Wrapped up in his thoughts, he didn't spot the woman squatting by the roadside until the last moment. Her woollen shawl was cast over her head, and from beneath it came the sound of weeping. The sight was unusual enough to make Arminius rein in. Maelo and his men did the same. Arminius glanced at the nearest sentries, a pair of legionaries who were slouched over their shields. 'You there! What's going on?' he demanded in Latin.

Realising his rank, the soldiers straightened with alacrity. 'The stupid bitch came to the gate two hours ago, sir. Wanted to speak to the governor himself,' said the older, a man with a heavily stubbled jaw. His companion, who was short and thin, snorted. 'Goes without saying, we didn't let her in,' the stubbled legionary went on. 'She wouldn't take "No" for an answer, though. Eventually the officer in charge of the guard came out and had a word. She was screaming that her daughter had been raped by one of our boys, that something had to be done, that he had to be found and punished.'

Arminius glanced at the woman, whose sobbing continued unabated. If she was play-acting, she was putting on a fine performance. 'What did the officer do?'

There was a contemptuous sniff. 'He asked a few questions, sir, about what had happened. Whether any coin had changed hands, what the man's name was, what century he served in and so on. She grew angry, shouting that her daughter was no whore. How could anyone know what the bastard's name or unit was, when he hadn't said? "I demand to speak to Publius Quinctilius Varus," she repeated over and over.'

'Did he agree to take it any further?' asked Arminius, knowing what the answer would be.

The sentry gave him an incredulous look. 'No, sir. He tossed her a few coins and told her to clear off.'

'That's more than I'd have offered her, sir,' commented the second legionary. 'She's giving me a damn headache.' He spat in the woman's direction. 'Leave, before we make you,' he said in poor German.

The soldiers' offhand cruelty incensed Arminius. Throwing his reins to Maelo, he dismounted and crouched by the woman's side. 'Tell me what happened,' he murmured in German. There was no response, and he touched her shoulder. With a wail, she recoiled. 'I mean you no harm,' he said. 'I am of the tribes, like you.'

The shawl moved a fraction, revealing a pair of terrified eyes. 'Who are you?'

'I am Arminius, a chieftain of the Cherusci. You also look to be Cheruscan.'

A slight nod. Suspicion had replaced the fear. 'You serve the Romans?'

'I do, but that does not mean I will see injustice unanswered.'

The shawl fell away. Lines of worry, old and new, scored the woman's tear-stained face, and her straggling hair was more grey than blonde. There were red scratches on her cheeks, the marks of her fingernails, yet she was still striking. Strip the care and the years away, thought Arminius, and she'd be a real looker. Like as not, her daughter was too, which would explain much.

Arminius paid no heed to the sound of an approaching horse – riders passed by all the time in a spot such as this – until it stopped a little distance behind him. 'Out of my way!' barked a familiar voice: Tubero's. Anger kindled in Arminius' belly, but he didn't look up.

'Greetings, tribune,' said Maelo.

'Ah, Maelo. I didn't recognise you.' The aggression vanished from Tubero's voice – almost.

'Off the road. Let the tribune past,' ordered Maelo in German.

Arminius decided to stand as Tubero and his escort began to ride past. Surprise creased Tubero's face as he recognised Arminius, and took in the woman behind him. His lip curled a fraction, but he made no comment. 'Arminius,' he said with a civil nod.

'Tribune.' Arminius watched Tubero go by, thinking: You piece of shit. Arrogant Roman bastards like you are proof that I am doing the right thing.

'Ignore that worthless dog,' he muttered, returning to the woman's side. 'Reared at the top, but he still acts as if he was born on a dungheap.'

The woman threw him a pathetic smile.

Arminius set aside his fury and spoke in a calm, gentle tone. 'Tell me what happened to your daughter.'

'We-we came here yesterday. With the wool from our sheep, to sell. It was late by the time we had sold it, so I found us a room in an inn. It was a rough place, but the landlord swore no harm would come to us. All the same, we retired straight after some food, to avoid any trouble. One of the soldiers who was drinking there must have seen my daughter, though. We hadn't been asleep for long when he shouldered the door open.' She wiped away fresh tears. 'I screamed, but one of his friends was outside to stop anyone helping. He held a knife to my daughter's throat while he, while he . . .' A cracked sob left her lips.

Arminius ground his teeth. Crimes such as this were common in and around Roman camps. More often than not, the perpetrators got away with it, because senior officers were out to protect their own rather than see justice done. Yet again, Arminius thought, one rule applied to the rulers, and another to the subjects. The response from the guard officer, and in particular the coins he'd thrown, was more than the woman could have expected.

'I am sorry for the harm done to your daughter,' he said at length.

'Will you help?' For the first time, there was hope in her expression.

Arminius struggled to meet her gaze. 'Finding the soldier who did it – well, it would be nigh-on impossible without a name, or a unit.'

'Gaius. I'm sure that his friend called him Gaius,' she said at once.

'That's one of the most common Roman names,' he countered.

'His face was covered in pox scars.'

'Plenty of men have been so marked.'

It was as if she sensed him wavering. 'My daughter – she's fifteen years old! She's still bleeding from what the brute did to her. You must be able to do something. Please, I beg you!'

A red mist blurred Arminius' vision as he remembered his aunt, who must have suffered a similar fate before she had to watch her son being tortured to death. Before she herself was slain. He squeezed the woman's arm until she gazed into his eyes. 'The man who raped your daughter *will* pay for what he did. Trust me. I swear by almighty Donar that vengeance will be yours.'

'When?' she asked in a whisper.

'Soon. I cannot say any more.'

'I will wait,' said the woman, palming the tears from her face. 'How shall I know that he has been punished?'

'You can speak to no one about this, do you understand? No one,' ordered Arminius in a low tone.

'I won't. I swear it, on my daughter's life.'

'As I live and breathe, as my name is Arminius of the Cherusci, you will *know* that the whoreson has seen justice.'

Her eyes widened.

Arminius longed to tell her that soon the rapist – and all his comrades – would be food for the crows, but to say anything might endanger his plan. '*Everyone* will know,' he said.

XVII

It had been a long, hot day – a twenty-mile patrol to the east, at the head of his cohort – but it was over, thought Tullus with some satisfaction. He had seen nothing untoward – far from it. The legionaries had been received well in the villages they had passed. The welcome had been tepid, it was true, but it was degrees warmer than when they had arrived, two months earlier. The whole process was a marked improvement from their reception in previous years. It was progress, Tullus decided, a sign that the tribes were growing used to Roman rule. Even his cynical optio Fenestela had commented on the locals' more amenable attitude.

The cohort returned to Porta Westfalica in baking afternoon heat. Every field of grain beside the road had been full of tribesmen and women taking in the harvest, both sexes stripped to the waist under the sun's blinding orb. Tullus' soldiers had loved the sight of so many bare breasts, and they filled the air with whistles and catcalls. The tribesmen shouted back insults, but Tullus didn't try to silence his soldiers' barrage. If a woman went about half naked, she could expect but one response.

Reaching the camp, Tullus had dismissed the cohort. He'd overseen his own century as they stripped off their equipment, taking the time to praise the men who'd led the pace, or who had impressed with their well-presented kit. That done, he had made for his own tent, where Ambiorix and Degmar had been waiting. It was amusing, but the feud he'd seen coming between his two servants had never materialised. Gaul and German, old man and young, they had formed an odd friendship that revolved around a sharing of duties. Ambiorix lit the fire. He did the cooking too – that was one of his favourite tasks. The rest, however – the clothes-washing, cleaning of weapons and armour and sleeping by the tent entrance – he was happy to relinquish to Degmar.

Once Tullus had washed, using the bucket of river water carried up by Degmar, he parked himself outside his tent on an old stool. It had been with him on campaign many times; he liked to sit on it, cup of wine in hand, and observe his soldiers with a benevolent but watchful eye. On this occasion, however, he found his attention drawn by Ambiorix and Degmar. More often by Degmar, who looked to be in a foul humour.

Assuming that they had quarrelled, Tullus began to listen in. Ambiorix was busy preparing the evening meal. From the smell emanating from the pot that hung over the fire, Tullus reckoned it was fish stew of some kind. Degmar was sitting cross-legged alongside, Tullus' phalerae in his lap, and was using a strip of cloth to polish the individual decorations.

'Want a taste?' Ambiorix was proffering a wooden spoon. 'I think it needs a little salt.'

Degmar grunted something that might have been 'No' or 'Yes'.

Ambiorix frowned. 'What was that?'

'Decide for yourself. I don't care,' Degmar muttered in his poor Latin.

'Don't take out your bad mood on me! We agreed that you're the one who has to clean his kit.'

'It's not about that,' said Degmar, scowling.

'What's wrong then?' demanded Ambiorix.

Degmar didn't answer; he redoubled his efforts with one of the phalerae, polishing away until Tullus thought he would wear the thing down to a nub.

Tullus forgot about Degmar for a time as Fenestela came to report on a legionary who'd gone lame during the march. 'I sent him to see the surgeon. Piso isn't the best soldier, but he's no shirker,' said Fenestela.

Tullus chuckled. 'It was Piso? I should have known.'

'He's coming on, as you said he would,' opined Fenestela. 'Slow progress, but steady.'

'Wine?' Tullus raised the jug.

'Why not?'

'Degmar, another cup,' called Tullus.

Degmar sloped over with a vessel for Fenestela, who raised his eyebrows at his set, angry face.

I'm not imagining it, thought Tullus. 'What has you in a temper?'

Degmar's mouth turned down further. 'It's nothing of any import.' He glanced down, to either side, anywhere but at Tullus.

Tullus' curiosity grew. Apart from Ambiorix and Fenestela, there was no one within earshot. 'It is odd for you to be in such a foul mood, and even more for you not to want anyone to know you're talking to me. Spit it out.'

Degmar squatted down on his haunches, close enough that he could mutter. Fenestela looked surprised by this familiarity, but Tullus didn't comment. It continued to amuse him that Degmar didn't call him 'master', yet served him like a faithful hunting dog. If it ever came to it, Tullus was gut-sure that Degmar would die in his defence. 'Tell me,' he ordered in German.

'I was over by the auxiliary lines earlier,' Degmar began.

In itself, that wasn't unusual. 'Swapping boastful stories, were you?'

Degmar's lips twitched. 'Something like that. I drank a skin of wine with some of the Cherusci I know. When I took my leave, I stopped by their horse pens. They have some fine mounts. A little time passed. I was leaning over the enclosing rail; the Cherusci must have thought I'd gone. They started talking among themselves.' He cast another furtive glance around.

Tullus had never seen Degmar look so agitated. 'What did you hear?'

'I couldn't catch everything they were saying – they were too far away – but there was something about a gathering of the tribes, and an ambush. That was mentioned several times. So was Arminius' name.'

Having seen little to nothing of the Cheruscan leader since their arrival in Porta Westfalica, Tullus' suspicions had lain dormant. Now, they tolled a loud alarm in his head. 'Is that all?'

'Aye.'

'They could have been talking about the Dolgubnii, or another hostile tribe, even something in the past,' said Tullus, forcing himself to be logical. He studied Degmar's face. 'You don't agree.'

'No.' Degmar's tone was vehement.

'Why?'

'There was something . . .' Degmar struggled to express what he meant, before saying several words in his own tongue.

Tullus thought he recognised one of them. 'Furtive?'

'Yes, furtive. That's how they were acting. It was most noticeable when a warrior came over to the pens by chance a moment later, and was shocked to see me. He was angry too, although he tried to hide it. "Been eavesdropping?" he asked. I clutched one of my ears, and told him that I've been deaf in it since childhood. I had been admiring their horses, nothing else. He seemed to believe me, but I caught him watching as I walked away.'

'That's not much to go on. Have you nothing else?'

With a scowl, Degmar shook his head.

Tullus would have laughed off such a story from many men, but this was such a departure from Degmar's normal behaviour that it demanded attention. 'What are your thoughts?'

'My head says it was nothing more than idle gossip, bragging about how they might like to act, or what other tribes might want to do.'

'And your belly?'

Degmar met Tullus' gaze. 'It's telling me that Arminius will betray Varus' trust. The dog is planning something. An ambush, perhaps, maybe in alliance with other tribes.'

Tullus wondered again if the odd feeling he'd had about Arminius might have its basis in fact. It was almost too shocking to be true. 'My thanks for telling me.'

'You don't believe it,' said Degmar with a scowl.

'I didn't say that,' Tullus replied, unwilling to speak his mind to a servant.

Degmar dropped his gaze. 'I should have kept my mouth shut.'

He was looking out for me, thought Tullus, feeling bad. 'Stay friendly with those Cherusci,' he suggested. 'See if you can learn any more.'

Degmar shrugged and stood. 'They will be suspicious of me, but I'll try.'

Tullus watched as Degmar wandered back to Ambiorix and the fire.

From that point, Degmar's story would not leave him. After a time, Tullus realised that he had overlooked a crucial fact: Degmar didn't give a damn about any Roman but him. An attack on Varus' legions would be as joyful an occasion for him as for a rogue Cheruscan warrior. That meant he had approached Tullus out of fealty alone, so he *was* convinced that an attack of some kind was coming.

Was Arminius capable of such treachery? Tullus wondered. He had fought for Rome for years, and been decorated for his bravery numerous times. Varus' trust in him was implicit. Everyone Tullus could think of considered the Cheruscan to be a solid and reliable individual. As far as he was aware, it was only he who had found Arminius' winning persona a little hard to take, his hearty manner a trifle forced.

The moment from the boar hunt returned to mind, when Maelo had said something to Arminius about the sacred ground they had been on. There had been another soon after, when Arminius had suggested that Varus had no need of his escort. Maybe I did pick up on something then, thought Tullus, and perhaps my concern over the slaughter of the Usipetes at the stockade was well placed.

Yet if he was right, especially about the latter, why in all the gods' names had Arminius done it? Tullus could not come up with a plausible reason – that was, until he reconsidered the possibility that Degmar *had* overheard something important. If Arminius was gathering together an alliance of tribes, it stood to reason that the Usipetes, living close to the Rhenus, might be part of it. Assuming that they were would explain why Arminius wanted the entire raiding party wiped out. If word had reached the tribe's chieftains of his men's involvement, the Usipetes would have withdrawn from the coalition. They would also have informed other tribes of Arminius' treachery, ruining his entire plan.

That was why so few prisoners had been taken, thought Tullus. It all made perfect sense. Astounding though it was, Arminius *had to be* plotting an ambush. His excitement didn't last. Without any proof, convincing his superiors of the Cheruscan's guilt would prove impossible. Even if Tullus managed to convince one of the tribunes, say, Varus would also have to be persuaded, and in *his* mind, Arminius could do no wrong. When Tullus had suggested the killing of the Usipetes in the stockade might have been deliberate, Varus had not wanted to know. There was no one else Tullus could turn to – apart from Fenestela, whose lowly rank meant that he was even more powerless.

The only option left to him, Tullus concluded, was to listen, watch and wait.

It was a bitter realisation.

Every moment of travelling felt like time wasted, so Arminius had ridden hard to the ambush site, which lay some fifteen miles northwest of Porta Westfalica. Some miles from the camp, he had turned off the main road, on to a cattle-droving track, and worked his way cross country so that he wouldn't be seen by the legionaries manning the regular outposts along the main route to Vetera. Now, with his horse sweating from the journey, he had emerged on to the path down which he would lead Varus' legions in the near future. Gods willing, he added inwardly.

No one had given him a second look as he rode out of the Roman camp alone, which was a benefit of his high rank. To the average soldier and lower-ranking officer, an auxiliary prefect was above questioning. Other senior officers, such as legates and camp commanders, might have looked askance at his behaviour, but they weren't around, or even aware of his departure. Varus might have wondered where he was going, but Arminius had been careful of recent days to mention how sick his mother was. When he'd asked permission to visit her, Varus had told him in no uncertain terms to go whenever he wished. 'As long as your official duties are in order, I don't care,' Varus had said. 'We won't be in the area for much longer. Attend to your mother.'

Arminius was to take Varus hunting on the morrow, part of his ploy to keep the governor thinking he was a personal friend, a true ally of Rome. There would be plenty of opportunities then to spin Varus a fine tale of how his mother's fever had broken, leaving her weak but on the road to recovery. He would have 'to go and see her again', of course, which would allow him to continue supervising the building of the earthworks that formed such an integral part of his plan.

Arminius was pleased to note scores and scores of men at work among the trees to the left of the narrow track, evidence that his requests for labour from the various tribes continued to be answered. It seemed that his original desire to remain at the site, encouraging and cajoling the disparate groups, had not been necessary. That was as well, Arminius knew, for he wouldn't have been able to test Varus' friendship – or trust – that far. Maelo could have done the job, but his absence would also have been noted after a day or two. It had been much easier to fabricate the 'need' for an ordinary ranker to spend time away from the camp, and had allowed Arminius to assign the job to another of his men, Osbert. Although not high-ranking, Osbert was tough, unafraid of hard work and fluent in the various tribal dialects. Most important, he was charismatic. Not as much as I am, thought Arminius, allowing his arrogance its head, but not far off.

He'd find Osbert soon, but checking on the earthworks' construction – and letting his face be seen – came first. Once his horse had been watered and tied to a long, pegged rope so that it could graze, Arminius made for the nearest section of fortification. It was set back thirty to forty paces from the track, as per his instructions. Few among the toiling men noticed him approach. Those who did failed to recognise him at a distance, which gave Arminius the chance to study their handiwork.

The organisation he had set in place continued, but it had been refined – and improved. Osbert had been an excellent choice, Arminius decided. The workers' industry was as impressive as that of the legions when they constructed roads. Some groups moved earth, while others built the fortifications, or dug drainage channels to its rear. Among the trees further back, axe-wielding warriors were chopping branches that would be used later to disguise the earthwork. Men had even been designated to fetch drinking water from the nearest stream, Arminius noted with pleasure.

The rampart had none of the straight lines so beloved of the Romans, but that didn't matter. It snaked alongside the track, taller than a big man, uneven but roughly parallel. In its current unfinished state, the earthworks might go unnoticed by an incurious traveller, but anyone who looked closer would see the imposing manmade structure at once. Nonetheless, it *had* been built in the right place, Arminius decided. Any further back, and his warriors would be too far from the Romans to spring an effective ambush.

There was still time for the entire thing to be rendered almost invisible. Once the heavy work was finished, wicker fencing would be arranged before it, and the cut branches set at its top. The plants growing between the fortifications and the track – which had not been disturbed – also had another month of growing.

'Arminius!'

'It's Arminius!'

Heads turned. Mattocks and spades were lowered, fabric-wrapped bundles of cut turves eased to the ground. Men began to gather.

Arminius donned his smile with impressive speed. 'You've been working hard, I see!'

Hours later, he was still working his way along the great earthworks. He'd taken care to spend a period with each tribal grouping, and within those, he had talked to as many warriors as possible. It was natural for the Angrivarii to be here – their territory lay close by – but there were men here from the Usipetes, the Bructeri and even the Chatti, whose lands were more than a hundred miles to the southwest.

If Arminius had needed proof of the different tribes' enthusiasm for his plan, and their willingness to take part in it, this was it. There was no more important time of the year than the harvest, when the food that would carry a man's family through the winter was taken in. Yet here they were, hundreds of them, breaking their backs to build the fortifications that he'd asked them to. Their labour would stand them in good stead, he had told them, to roars of acclaim. The damn Romans would be unaware of their presence until it was far too late.

Arminius was talking with a small group of Chauci – a tribe that had not declared for his cause thus far – when Osbert appeared. Arminius gave Osbert a look to show he'd seen him, and continued to compliment the warriors for their hard work. The earthworks were well built, just the right height and depth. The drainage ditches to the rear were ingenious, he told them; they would prevent flooding if the usual heavy autumn rain fell. The warriors warmed to his tribute, and they cheered when he thanked them for their willingness to act when the rest of their kind would not. 'When you return to your people,' Arminius continued, 'let them know how many tribes are labouring side by side. Be sure to tell them how remarkable the earthworks are, and how well they will hide us. They must hear of the narrowness of the track, and the streams that crisscross it, and of the treacherous bog that lies on its other side. This is the perfect spot to ambush Varus and his legions!'

The Chauci loved that, brandishing their tools as if they were spears, and promising Arminius that they would return with their tribe's full strength. Content, Arminius slipped to Osbert's side. They shook hands, and he gripped Osbert's shoulder. 'Progress has been excellent. I'm in your debt. If it continues in this way, the earthworks could be completed in . . .?'

'Ten days, if all goes well,' Osbert finished for him.

'Ha!' cried Arminius. 'That's better than I could have expected.'

'I would love to take the credit, Arminius, but the talk each night over the fires is never about my persuasiveness. It's about the new tax, and the wrongful punishment visited upon the Usipetes. Warriors speak of *you* as the leader who will strike off the shackles that Augustus wishes us to wear. In their eyes, you are the man to rid this land of the Romans' blight.'

Arminius' spirits lifted further. The hard work he'd put into winning over the tribes had paid off. Nonetheless, he would continue to mingle with the toiling warriors, 'pressing the flesh', so to speak, and recognising their contribution. When the labouring was done, and the warriors returned to their homes before the ambush, they would praise his endeavour to the skies. Arminius could think of no better way to ensure that their tribes honoured their pledge to him.

Within the month, thousands of spears would be at his command.

Here.

XVIII

In Porta Westfalica, Varus was cursing. It had been a mistake to come to the principia. Aristides had promised it would take but an instant to sign off the orders for another consignment of grain before he went hunting, but of course things were never that simple. Officer after officer had appeared, each one with his own urgent request for Varus' ruling. Soldiers in one cohort were demanding 'nail money' for the replacement hobnails they needed as a result of an extended patrol. A settlement ten miles to the east of Porta Westfalica claimed to have no money to pay the imperial taxes that were due. There were allegations of corruption among the boat captains who ferried goods along the river from Vetera – instead of army supplies, they were purported to be transporting quantities of valuable goods such as olive oil for unscrupulous merchants.

These were only the start of the woes filling Varus' ears. Scores of mules were suffering with sweet itch, caused by the midges that hung in clouds over their pens. The senior veterinarian was at a loss. An outbreak of gonorrhoea in two centuries of the Nineteenth had put forty-one soldiers in the camp hospital. Varus had been astonished to hear that the patients all blamed one prostitute, a 'beauty' revelling in the name of Venus. Complaints were coming in from local farmers that legionaries were killing their livestock for meat at every opportunity. A quartermaster's stores had been burgled, and two amphorae of fish sauce stolen.

Plagued by his conscience, Varus had dealt with each of these time-consuming problems in turn. As ever, most could not be resolved on the spot. More information would be required before a decision was possible. The centurions in charge of the men requesting 'nail money' would have to make official reports about the state of their troops' sandals *before* the patrol. The impecunious settlement was to be given half a month to find the monies due before soldiers searched the place, with powers to seize goods in kind. A hearing into the dishonest ships' captains was called for – Varus would have to preside over that one. Every veterinarian in the three legions was to be consulted about better treatments for sweet itch – and so on.

Several times Varus grew close to clearing the line of men before his desk, but then more appeared at its tail. Frustration stung him. The patch of sky visible through the window was brightening fast, and he could feel the warmth radiating from the rays of sun illuminating the floor by his feet. Dawn had gone; morning was here. Arminius, who had returned from visiting his sick mother, had stressed that the earlier they left the camp, the better. 'We will be out all day, and it tends to be as hot as the day you killed that boar,' he'd said. Any chance of tracking down a large stag would soon vanish, thought Varus, because *he* wouldn't be up to slogging through the forest in the sapping heat. He came to a snap decision. 'Aristides.'

The Greek was in his customary place, by his elbow. 'Master?'

'Find out why each of these officers are here. Unless it's a matter of life or death, they can wait until Vala arrives.'

'Of course.'

Varus watched sidelong as Aristides bustled from around the desk, writing tablet and stylus in hand. It amused him how much pleasure his scribe derived from moments like this, when he had a passing but real power over men whose social position towered above his own. A discreet cough from the tribune in front of him – Tubero – brought Varus back to the matter in hand: an outbreak of dysentery in the Eighteenth. 'Tell me again how bad it is.'

Tubero nudged the surgeon he'd brought with him, a balding Greek with a protuberant wart on one cheek. 'It's not too severe yet, governor,' he said. 'Only three men have died, but it will be far more if the affected cohort isn't isolated at once.'

Varus wanted to scream, Why this, now? Dysentery was a serious matter. 'Do so at once, but position their tents close to the camp rampart. Use the healthy men in the cohort to dig the ditch and move the tents.' There wasn't much more he could do, thought Varus, but it might be best if he didn't go hunting. If the disease spread any further . . .

It was as if Tubero had discerned his reluctance to stay. 'I can manage the situation, sir,' he offered. 'I'll oversee everything, and report back to you this evening.'

Varus hesitated. How hard is it to isolate a cohort? he wondered and said with a smile, 'Excellent, tribune. I leave things in your capable hands. We shall speak again later.' He advanced from behind his desk. With confused faces, the officers stood to attention. 'As you were,' he said, sweeping past. 'Aristides will take note of your queries, and Vala will deal with them later.'

'Sir—' protested a senior centurion, but Varus had gone. The last of his guilt evaporated as the officers vanished from sight. He spent his life enslaved to the demands of others. The world wouldn't end if he wasn't there for a day, the dysenteric cohort would not all die, and his legions wouldn't fall apart. He'd be back at his desk tomorrow and, if needs be, he would stay at it until the backlog of administration had been cleared. Even the idea of that living hell wasn't enough to take the spring from Varus' step as he emerged from the principia. The sun wasn't *that* high in the sky, and there was a hint of cloud cover moving in from the east. The day wouldn't get too hot, and Arminius was a man of his word – he'd be waiting for Varus still, by his tent lines.

Varus' high spirits lasted until the headquarters was perhaps fifty paces behind him. 'Governor! Governor Varus!' called a voice. Hunching his shoulders, Varus stopped. The junior officer responsible – an optio, by his appearance – hurried over at once. Varus' hopes that he might yet get away rallied – he'd put a flea in the upstart's ear damn quick – before slumping once more. The brawny, silver-haired chieftain dogging the optio's footsteps was none other than Segestes, leader of part of the Cheruscan tribe. Segestes was a fierce ally of Rome, which made him a valuable asset, but he was also a rambling, loud-mouthed boor with a love of his own voice. Varus despised him.

'Governor!' Segestes called. 'A word, if I could.'

Wishing for the power to make himself invisible, Varus instead pulled on his politician's cloak. The smile, the cordial salute, the warm tone. 'Segestes. What an unexpected pleasure. In ordinary circumstances, I would invite you to share a cup of wine, but I have a pressing engagement—'

'That can wait,' interrupted Segestes.

Varus took a breath of outrage. Ally or no, Roman citizen or no, he would not be spoken to in this manner, in particular by someone who resembled one of his elderly, hirsute house slaves.

'Want us to get rid of him, sir?' asked the lead soldier in his escort. There was a hopeful look in his eyes.

Varus was about to give the order, but Segestes beat him to it. 'My pardon, governor,' he called out. 'I did not mean to cause offence. It's urgent that I speak with you.'

Varus waved a hand at his escort. 'Stand down.'

The optio stepped aside, allowing Segestes past. Close up, the sweat beading his brow was evident. He bent his head towards Varus. 'Governor.'

'Segestes. It has been too long,' lied Varus. 'What has brought you to the camp this fine morning, and in such a hurry?'

Segestes' wild eyes roamed over Varus' escort and the optio. 'We need to talk – alone. There are far too many sets of ears here. How about your headquarters?'

Varus pictured the queue of officers. 'Out of the question.'

Segestes' face grew pained, even frantic. 'What I have to say is for your ears alone, governor. Please.'

Varus was about to refuse, but Segestes' uncharacteristic humility –

and his distress – piqued his interest. 'Wait here,' he ordered his escort. The soldier began to object, and Varus silenced him with a look. 'You too,' he directed the optio. 'Walk with me, Segestes. If we converse in low tones, no one will hear.'

Segestes' disgruntlement eased, and he fell into step with Varus as he paced along the via praetoria. There were incredulous looks from everyone they met. Ordinary soldiers, officers low- and high-ranking: none could believe that the governor of Germania was strolling about the camp with a tribal chieftain. Varus wondered if it had been rash to leave his escort behind, or to leave Segestes with his sword. He discounted the idea in the same breath. Segestes – an old man in poor physical shape – wasn't here to assassinate him.

'I bring you calamitous news,' muttered Segestes.

Unease stirred in Varus' belly. 'Go on.'

'Arminius is a traitor.'

Despite his shock, Varus kept walking. Ignoring a surprised mule-handler, he stared at Segestes. 'A traitor. Arminius.'

'As the gods are my witness, it's true.'

'Arminius is as loyal as you are! He has served the empire since he was a boy, fought with the legions for nigh on a decade. Augustus saw fit to elevate him to the equestrian class.' Varus could reel off Arminius' list of achievements by rote.

'He has done all of those things,' agreed Segestes, 'but he's also a treacherous, scheming whoreson. He plans to attack your legions as they return to Vetera.'

'Have you taken leave of your senses?' Heads turned, and Varus realised that he had raised his voice. He leaned close to Segestes. 'What you're talking about . . . it's insane.'

'It may seem that way, governor, but it's true. Every word.'

'How have you come by this information?'

'A warrior whom I trust, whom I have known my entire life, heard Arminius talking to Inguiomerus, trying to persuade him to join forces. It seems that Arminius has been recruiting chieftains among the tribes for some time. Knowing my loyalty to the empire, the dog didn't approach me. The idea of twenty thousand spears behind his banner might have won over other chiefs, but not I,' Segestes said, his jaw jutting.

Inguiomerus led another faction of the Cherusci tribe. Varus regarded him in the same light as Segestes. Loyal. This unwelcome revelation felt like part of a bad dream. 'Twenty thousand warriors?'

'That's what he said. As well as his portion of the Cherusci, the Chatti and Bructeri are with him, and the Usipetes. The Angrivarii and Marsi too.'

This was the proof that Segestes' source was lying, or that the old man was rambling, thought Varus. 'You expect me to believe that six tribes have united? Arminius is many things, but he's not a worker of magic, to persuade men to set aside vendettas that go back generations.'

'The warrior who told me was *not* lying.'

'I would give more weight to your words if you brought before me someone to corroborate them,' challenged Varus. 'The warrior himself perhaps.'

Segestes' face darkened. 'He would not come.'

'Perhaps that's because you imagined him,' challenged Varus.

'I'm old but no dotard!' protested Segestes. 'It was too dangerous for him to accompany me.'

'I dined with Inguiomerus not seven days since,' said Varus. 'It's hard to imagine a more pleasant evening, or a steadier ally of Rome.'

'Looks deceive, governor. You are in great danger.' Segestes clutched at Varus' arm.

Varus regarded Segestes' hand as if it were a fresh-landed splatter of horse shit. Realising that he had gone too far, Segestes released his grip. 'You must listen to me.'

'I *must* do nothing!' erupted Varus. 'You are no one to command me, old man.'

'The tribes' cohesion will fade away without Arminius. Have the bastard clapped in chains at least,' Segestes pleaded.

The notion of imprisoning Arminius because of one man's testimony, even if that man was an ally, was inconceivable. 'I'll do nothing of the sort. Not only is Arminius loyal to Rome, he's a personal friend of mine.'

Segestes laughed. 'I'd hate to see your enemies.'

Varus stopped dead. 'Enough! Find your own way to the gate.' Beckoning to his escort, he strode back towards the principia. He was going to meet Arminius, and hunt down a fine stag.

Tullus sat on his horse at the edge of the parade ground beyond the camp's perimeter, drilling his cohort. The moves were an age-old routine, performed every three to five days, wherever they were. Just because they had done the same manoeuvres hundreds of times before didn't mean that they didn't need to keep practising, he bawled whenever he heard a soldier grumble. If there was a war on, they might be excused, but there wasn't, so they could shut their damn mouths or feel the weight of his vitis across their backs. Tullus would have been worried if they hadn't complained – that, and his tough response, were part of the ritual.

Shouting by the gate drew his eyes from his toiling legionaries. He squinted, making out a number of tribesmen leaving the camp. There had been no trouble for months, but that didn't mean it couldn't happen now. Tullus was preparing to summon one century of legionaries to his side when the altercation ended. Raining insults down on the sentries, the tribesmen, a party of ten or so, rode away. Tullus studied the group as it drew closer. The leader was a silver-haired, well-built older man – a chieftain – and the rest were his retainers, professional warriors, confident men with good-quality arms and armour. Tullus didn't recognise any of them. The chieftain was busy giving vent to the remnants of the anger that had taken him at the gate. Tullus heard the name 'Varus', and the German for 'idiot', and then the tribesmen had passed by.

Tullus' curiosity was piqued. Telling Bolanus to take charge for a short time, he rode to the main gate. There he found the usual complement of sentries, and a flustered-looking optio. When Tullus reined in rather than pass inside, he didn't quite manage to hide his dismay. He came to attention. 'Sir.'

'Who was it that just rode out?' asked Tullus.

A look of disgust. 'Segestes, sir, a chieftain of the Cherusci.'

Tullus knew the various factions of Arminius' tribe, but had never clapped eyes on Segestes before. 'What was he so pissed off about?'

'I'm not sure, sir. A while back, he rode up to the gate, demanding to speak to Varus. He wouldn't be fobbed off, so in the end I took him to the principia myself, minus his warriors of course. Varus happened to come out of his quarters just as we appeared, and they had a short conversation, which didn't go well. There was a lot of shouting, most of it by Segestes, but at the end, Varus lost his temper and ordered him to leave. Segestes muttered to himself the whole way back, but I could only make out the occasional word. He kept mentioning Arminius, though, I heard that. He's a traitor, Segestes said, a snake that couldn't be trusted.'

The words came to Tullus as if down a long, dark tunnel. 'Say that again.'

The optio blinked. 'He kept saying that Arminius was a treacherous dog, sir, things like that. I have no idea why.'

Tullus' original suspicions mixed with Degmar's story in his head, but he kept his focus. 'And the disturbance at the gate?'

'That wasn't anything much, sir. When Segestes' men realised how angry he was, they threw a few insults at my boys, who gave it back in kind. Segestes got his lot under control quick enough and rode out, still griping about Varus.' The optio stared after Tullus, who had ridden away, into the camp. 'What did I say, sir?'

'Have no fear, optio, you told me everything I needed to know,' Tullus called out. He would seek an audience with Varus. The half-suggestive tale that Degmar had chanced to hear wasn't much in the way of evidence, but Segestes' behaviour confirmed its veracity. He *had* to act.

At the principia, Tullus was infuriated to discover that Varus had already departed, and wouldn't be back until nightfall, perhaps even the next day. Demanding a writing tablet and stylus, he scribbled a short note to the governor about what Degmar had said, and how he'd heard Segestes shouting similar things. He had just sealed it with a lump of wax when, to his surprise and displeasure, Tubero emerged into the courtyard, a surgeon in tow behind. His brow furrowed. 'Centurion Tullus.'

'Tribune.' Tullus snapped off a professional if uncaring salute and, in a casual move, dropped his hands, which were holding the tablet and stylus, to his sides.

'What has you here, away from your men?'

'I've come to see Governor Varus, sir.'

In response, a humourless smile. 'He's not here.'

'So I found out, sir,' said Tullus, trying not to show his irritation.

'The place is empty, apart from a few clerks. When Varus left, everyone went about their tasks for the day. What did you want to see him for?'

'Nothing important, sir,' lied Tullus. 'I'll come back another time.'

Tubero sniffed and walked off, the surgeon scurrying behind.

Prick, thought Tullus, saluting again. He glanced about, and caught the eye of a passing clerk. 'You there.'

The clerk, a scrawny youth, pointed an ink-stained finger at himself. 'Me, sir?'

'Come here.'

With shuffling feet, the clerk obeyed.

'You work for Governor Varus?'

'Yes, sir. Well, Aristides, his scribe. Both.'

'Is Aristides about?'

'No, sir. He's gone for a bath.'

Bloody Greek, thought Tullus. 'Give him this. Say that it's a note for Varus from Centurion Tullus. Understand?'

The clerk looked from the tablet to Tullus and back again.

With a curse, Tullus rummaged in his purse. He flicked a silver coin into the air. 'This, if you see it into Aristides', or Varus', hands.'

'Consider it done, sir.' The coin vanished somewhere into the clerk's tunic. The tablet he gripped against his bony chest.

'About your business then.' With Segestes' accusations backing up Degmar's story, Varus would act at last, thought Tullus. Content that he had done enough, he watched the clerk hurry into a nearby office.

Tullus was most of the way back to the parade ground when Tubero returned to the principia in a foul mood, the surgeon still with him. 'Without Varus' official stamp, the damn quartermaster won't release the medicines and equipment we need,' he barked.

'I could have come back for it, sir,' said the surgeon.

Tubero threw him a contemptuous look. 'I wouldn't trust you with it.' He stormed into Varus' office, past a pair of soldiers who were sweeping the floor and a clerk who was carrying bundles of letters from one room to another. The place was otherwise empty of the usual throng. A second clerk sat at Aristides' desk, transferring figures from one document to another. He jumped up as Tubero entered. 'Sir!'

'Tribune Tubero. I'm looking for Varus' stamp.'

'It's here, sir.' The clerk pulled open a drawer and passed over the stamp, a solid lump of brass. An image of an imperial eagle and the words 'QUINCTILIUS VARUS' were etched into its base.

Tubero took it with a grunt. He had half turned to go when something made him regard the clerk again. 'What's that in your other hand?'

The clerk flushed. 'Nothing, sir.'

Tubero sensed his reluctance with the speed of a predator smelling blood. 'It's a letter.'

'Yes, sir.'

'Who wrote it? Who's it for?'

'A centurion gave it to me, sir. It's for Governor Varus. "Tell him it's from Centurion Tullus," he said.'

The name made Tubero stiffen. 'Give it here.'

The clerk hesitated, then did as he was told.

'I'll give it to Varus with my own hands,' Tubero promised, stowing it in his purse. This had been Tullus' reason for coming here, he thought. Why had the dog lied? He would find out later, when he'd read the letter. After that, Tubero decided, he would throw it away.

Tracking down the stag had taken the entire morning and at least half the afternoon. Despite the partial cloud cover and the protection of the trees, it had been warm and muggy. Hot, sweating, talking little with the other hunters, Varus' mind had been occupied with following the stag's trail and being among the first to take a shot at it if the chance arose.

Maelo had been scouting ahead of the main party, and was the one to spy their quarry as it grazed in a clearing. When Varus clapped eyes on it, he was even more impressed by Maelo's restraint in not taking it down himself. The stag was a king among deer, bull-necked and as tall as a large horse. It had more than ten tines on each of its large, curved antlers, and its mounted skull would be the talk of every dinner party, Varus thought, his heart pounding with excitement. In all his years of hunting, he had never killed such a majestic beast.

It took an age to creep close enough to loose an arrow. Varus was conscious that both Arminius and Maelo, the only ones to accompany him, could have brought down the stag much sooner than he. They had refrained because he was the guest. Determined to repay their generosity with a well-aimed arrow, he was mortified when, fifty paces from the stag, he stepped on a twig. With flared nostrils, the mighty deer glanced to and fro, its gaze fixed in their direction. 'Let us all loose,' Arminius mouthed. 'This is our only chance.'

It was a bitter medicine to swallow. Never the best marksman, Varus was at the limit of his bow range. He took a shot anyway and, within a heartbeat of his arrow hissing into the air, so did the two Cheruscans'. Black streaks, they flew faster than the eye could see. The stag was running by the time the shafts came scudding down, but two struck it, one in the haunches and the other in the chest. The last arrow, which Varus suspected was his, landed short. Their quarry thundered off into the forest at full tilt, for now at least appearing uninjured.

'Hades!' muttered Varus. 'I am sorry, Arminius. I'm not the hunter that either of you are.'

'Rubbish,' Arminius replied. 'And you hit it anyway.'

'You flatter me. Mine was the shaft that didn't have the range.'

'I'm not so sure.'

Varus grimaced in denial. 'Will the arrow in its chest kill?'

'I don't know. It depends how deep the head penetrated. Even if the stag does collapse, it could be miles from here. Fetch the dogs, Maelo.'

Maelo slipped away, following the trail they'd taken. A good distance to their rear, a party of warriors had been keeping the noisy hounds away from their quarry. On this occasion, there were no legionaries accompanying Varus. Vala would have protested. So too would his other senior officers, but none of them knew. It had been a trifle childish, like Varus' desire to escape his duties, but he had decided to hunt with his friend Arminius without an escort. And here they were, deep in the forest, alone. Varus didn't feel concerned in the slightest; he was more annoyed that he'd alerted the stag to their presence. He took a mouthful of watered-down wine from the skin that hung over his shoulder, and handed it to Arminius. 'When the dogs arrive, we follow them, eh?'

'We can do, but there's no certainty of tracking it down before sunset. Our best bet is to leave the job to Maelo and the men with the dogs. You and I will return to Porta Westfalica, to my tent, where an amphora of the best Italian wine awaits us. I was saving it to mark our success in the hunt, but I don't see any problem in opening it early. With a little good fortune, Maelo will bring the stag to bay.' Arminius drank deep and handed back the skin. 'What do you say?'

Varus' pride made him reply, 'I had thought to carry the hunt through to its conclusion.'

'So had I, but there's no pleasure to be had in spending hours sweating through the forest with a pack of noisy dogs. We've played our part, don't you think?'

'Your argument is persuasive,' Varus conceded. 'Let us go back then.'

'I'll wager that Maelo will return with the carcase in time for us to dine like the emperor himself. The head will be yours, of course.' Arminius lifted a hand, stilling Varus' protest. 'I won't have it any other way. None of us can say with any certainty whose arrows struck the beast. In any case, you are my honoured guest, and friend.'

'My thanks.' Varus smiled in acceptance. Any thought he had of mentioning Segestes' rant disappeared from his mind. To bring it up would be insulting to Arminius, the finest of men.

XIX

Bone-weary from supervising the soldiers of the dysentery-affected cohort as they moved their tents, Tubero looked at Tullus' letter that evening. In his wildest dreams, he could not have predicted the contents. If the notion that Arminius was a traitor was shocking, the revelation that he purportedly intended to ambush the army was doubly so. Before he had read the note, Tubero would have laughed at such a preposterous suggestion. Now the notion, however crazy, kept spinning around his head. Tubero hadn't liked Tullus from the start, but the senior centurion was no fool. He wouldn't compose a letter like this without being convinced that Arminius was traitorous.

If Tullus' hunch was correct, thought Tubero with growing glee, by intercepting the letter *he* had just been handed the chance to steal the glory. What more glittering start to his career could there be than foiling such an evil plan? The unfortunate episode with the Sugambri cattle-herders would be forgotten. In Rome, his taskmaster father and even Augustus would hear of his initiative. Everyone would know his name.

It didn't trouble Tubero that he had no German servant who could 'overhear' Arminius' warriors' conversation about the ambush. If Varus demanded to meet Tubero's 'witness', he could employ the Phoenican merchant who sold wine in the camp. The greybeard was a skilled and convincing liar – the day before, Tubero had caught him out when ordering an expensive vintage only because he'd known the going price. For a few gold coins, Tubero suspected, the man would sell his own mother. Getting him to swear that he had eavesdropped on a group of Cherusci would be easy.

Tubero reined in his growing enthusiasm. Tullus' theory was still just that, a theory. There was no proof to be had, just the word of two tribesmen, one a lowlife servant, the other a chieftain who might have reasons to discredit Arminius. If Tullus was wrong, he, Tubero, risked monumental embarrassment by bringing the matter to light. Indeed, his intention to tell Varus could be a career-ending move. Discretion was the key, Tubero decided. He would broach the topic with Varus in an indirect, vague manner. If the governor appeared open-minded, he would proceed. If not, well, the conversation could end before it had started, with Varus none the wiser.

By the following morning, however, Tubero's hopes of glory were in ashes. He had called on Varus early, and been welcomed into the governor's quarters. Varus' good humour had soon changed to irritation in the face of Tubero's suggestion that Arminius *might* be disloyal. As Tubero's ears rang with Varus' praise for Arminius, he had been swift to row back from his initial approach. Cursing inside, he had tried another tack, mentioning camp gossip that he'd heard, about unrest among the tribes.

Varus had poured scorn on that theory too, saying that *his* sources were telling him no such thing. He'd smiled then, and told Tubero not to worry, that the mission to track down the Usipetes' raiding party would not be his only experience of combat during the year of his posting. Deciding that Tullus must be deluded, and discretion was the better part of valour, Tubero had given Varus an apologetic smile, and thanked him for his understanding.

Relieved that he had not been found out, and angry that he had come so near to making a complete fool of himself, Tubero had thrown the letter into the latrine trench nearest his quarters.

Two days had passed, and there had been no response from Varus. Arminius was as visible as ever, drilling his men outside the camp, or leading out patrols, which told its own story. Tullus had no way of knowing whether Varus had received his note, but the coin he'd given the clerk should have ensured that he had. Why then had he done nothing? Tullus was consumed by a gnawing frustration. The least that Varus could have done was to question him about what he knew. Wary of acting above his station, he bided his time, hoping that each successive day would bring with it a messenger summoning him to Varus' presence.

No summons arrived.

In the end, Tullus was spurred into action by a chance encounter with Arminius. A week had gone by, and Tullus was by the camp's main entrance, talking to the centurion in charge of the sentries, an old friend of his. The pair were standing out of sight of those approaching the defences, so Tullus heard Arminius' voice before he saw him. It was clear from the Cheruscan's tone that he was annoyed. For reasons Tullus couldn't explain, he placed a finger to his lips, interrupting his friend, and moved to the entrance. He poked his head around the wall, seeing Arminius riding up with a group of his men. His angry gesticulations confirmed his bad temper. It was frustrating that Tullus wasn't able to make out Arminius' words, but his interest – and suspicion – increased further when the Cheruscan silenced his men as they drew near. Why had he done that? wondered Tullus. Most Romans spoke no more than a smattering of German.

Despite Tullus' suspicion of Arminius, it was illogical to ascribe a malevolent motive to his actions. Even more frustrated, Tullus returned to his friend with a laughing explanation that he thought he'd heard some of his men coming back from patrol and had wanted to hear what they were saying.

Tullus might have done nothing further but Arminius' exaggerated reaction a moment later changed his mind on the spot. Entering the camp, Arminius greeted Tullus like a friend whom he hadn't seen for twenty years. The scowl he'd worn outside had been replaced by a beaming smile. 'It's been too long since we shared a skin of wine. Come to my tent this evening and we'll put that right,' he cried. Tullus had muttered his thanks, and thought: The dog *is* up to something. I *have* to talk to Varus.

Tullus wasn't sure when the best hour to visit Varus was – too early in the morning, and the governor might be angered; too late, and Tullus would have to compete with the host of officers with requests to make of Varus. Arriving at mealtimes could be considered rude, and Varus' afternoons were taken up with more paperwork and other official duties. In the end, Tullus decided that there was no good time. Telling himself that Varus *would* listen to him, he made his way to the praetorium around the usual hour for the midday meal.

Varus was there, which was an excellent start. Once the sentry outside the front gate had carried word of Tullus' presence inside, he was admitted without delay, which was also heartening. Tullus' wait in the atrium wasn't that long either, but that didn't stop his palms sweating or his stomach from churning. He was escorted into Varus' presence by the scribe Aristides, a man whom Tullus knew little, but who seemed a decent type. 'He's in a good mood,' Aristides confided as they entered the central courtyard. 'Cook prepared a venison stew using meat from a stag that Varus helped Arminius to bring down.'

Tullus wanted to pummel his fists against the wall. Arminius would be present at the meeting, even though he wasn't here in person. There was nothing to be done about it, so he squared his shoulders and ran his fingers through his helmet crest, ensuring the feathers were all straight.

'You look good, sir,' whispered Aristides.

Tullus gave him a brittle smile. They were nearing Varus, who was seated at a table strewn with the evidence of a fine meal: platters of bread, vegetables, meat and fish, and jugs of wine. Varus looked up as Aristides announced Tullus. Smiling, he indicated that Tullus should take a seat.

'My thanks, sir.' Tullus' flagging hopes revived. This was an honour indeed.

'Wine?' asked Varus.

'A small cup only, sir. My duties for the day aren't over yet.'

Varus gave him an approving look. 'Aristides, do the necessary.'

After a toast to the emperor, the pair made small talk for a time. Varus asked about Tullus' unit, whether he was happy with how the summer had gone, and if he was ready for the march back to Vetera. Tullus would have been uncomfortable to be in the governor's presence under normal circumstances; in these, he felt most ill at ease, and his answers bordered on monosyllabic. It didn't take long for the conversation to peter out.

'I don't imagine that you came to exchange pleasantries.' Varus' tone was jovial but commanding.

Tullus cleared his throat and did his best to calm his pounding heart. 'No, sir. I came to see you about Arminius.'

Varus looked surprised. 'Arminius? What about him?'

Tullus felt as if he were teetering on the edge of a cliff, but there was no backing away, not unless he made up a story on the spot – something he doubted his blank mind could do right now. 'I've had my suspicions about him for some time, sir.'

'I remember,' said Varus, interrupting. 'You thought his men too bloodthirsty.'

'Yes, sir.' Tullus ploughed on. 'A short while ago, I sent you a letter laying out my concerns.'

'I received no letter.'

Tullus blinked. Fool of a clerk, he thought. Did he really think I wouldn't check up on him? 'That's strange, sir. Let me explain.' Ignoring Varus' disapproving expression as best he could, he continued, 'It hasn't been anything solid, just a look here, or a comment there. In my mind, he's just too genial, sir, too friendly to us Romans. Equestrian he may be, but the man's a tribesman. See him with his warriors, and he's a different beast to the one he is with us.'

Varus held up a hand, stopping him. 'Spit out whatever it is you have to say.'

Dry-mouthed, and concerned that his efforts would be in vain, but determined to make his point, Tullus obeyed. Varus listened in tight-lipped silence.

'Is that it?' he demanded when Tullus had finished.

'Yes, sir.' Tullus held Varus' gaze.

'Your bravado is commendable,' said Varus, his voice icy. 'You stroll in here, accept my hospitality, drink my wine and *then* have the barefaced cheek to make unfounded, wild accusations about a personal friend of mine, a man who is a loyal servant of the emperor. You would have me believe not only that Arminius is a traitor, but that he's planning to annihilate my army!'

'My intent is always to serve the empire, sir, and nothing more,' Tullus protested.

'Arminius' credentials are beyond suspicion. He stands recognised by Augustus himself,' snapped Varus, his colour rising. 'Do you question our emperor's judgement?'

'Of course not, sir,' replied Tullus, realising that coming here had been a complete waste of time.

'If you had even a single shred of evidence, I might feel inclined to listen to you, but you come to me with nothing. Nothing!' Varus pointed, stiff-armed, towards the door. 'Leave, before I lose my temper.'

'Sir.' Resigned, angry, impotent, Tullus rose and snapped off a parade-standard salute. He had almost reached the door when Varus called out:

'Centurion.'

'Sir?'

'Because your service record up to this point has been exemplary, I will pretend that this meeting never happened. In return, you will speak of our conversation, and of Arminius, to no one. *No one.* Understood?'

'Understood, sir.' I *will* find the clerk and kick his arse, thought Tullus.

Varus didn't waste any more words on him, just waved a hand in dismissal.

As Tullus made his way back to his tent, his disappointment was leavened somewhat by the knowledge that there would be no demotion, no punishment for his rash behaviour. This awareness didn't remove the sour taste from his mouth, or the bitter feeling in his heart. Arminius was beyond reproach. Unassailable. Tullus could only watch and wait.

And pray that his gut feeling was wrong.

Tullus was kept busy in the warm, sunny days that followed as preparations got under way to ready the cohort for the hundred-mile journey back to Vetera. The right amount of grain and meat for each man had to be requisitioned, which meant an inevitable clash with the quartermasters, each of whom seemed to have been born with a reluctance ever to release any foodstuffs or goods in their care. Assessments of soldiers who were unwell, or suffering from injuries, went on every day. Places in the baggage wagons for individuals unfit to march were in high demand, for no centurion wanted to have to order soldiers to carry a comrade back to Vetera.

Endless equipment checks were necessary, to ensure that every legionary's kit was in good order. Tullus paid particular attention to his men's sandals, and the iron hobnails that decorated their soles. Soldiers tended not to replace them as often as needs be, because the cost of the hobs came out of their own purses. Wise to this, Tullus inspected his men's footwear every two days before a long march.

He was afforded no chance to track down the scrawny clerk he'd paid to deliver the letter. What was the point? Varus had heard him out, and refused to give any weight to his concerns. Despite his workload, he kept abreast of the news entering the camp, and of Arminius' activities. If Arminius was up to something, he was making a fine job of concealing it. According to the senior centurion in the cohort stationed beside Arminius' tent lines, the Cheruscan's auxiliaries did little apart from perform their routine duties and, like everyone else in the vast camp, prepare for the march to Vetera. Tullus could have ascribed a malign motive to the shunning of Degmar by the Cherusci – the Marsi warrior had failed to uncover more information – but that too could have been down to something mundane, such as Degmar's truculent manner, or the mere fact that he was not Cheruscan.

In any case, Tullus had no time to ponder anything. What had happened to his letter to Varus. Why Varus would hear nothing said against Arminius. Why there had been no unrest. Whether Degmar had overheard idle gossip of no import, and if Segestes had been trying to discredit Arminius. Each night, Tullus dropped on to his blankets, bone-weary, and fell into a deep, dreamless sleep. Woken by the trumpets at dawn, he tackled the mountain of work before him. It was not until the evening before the legions' planned departure from Porta Westfalica – his tasks complete at last – that he had a chance to consider Arminius. Knowing that nothing short of a miracle would stop the army from marching, his worries rekindled with a vengeance. If anything was to happen, it would be in the next few days.

He and Fenestela were sitting by the fire outside Tullus' tent, cloaks over their shoulders to ward off the evening chill, and cups of wine in hand. He had not confided in his optio before because of Fenestela's deep cynicism towards non-Romans, and Germans in particular. Living with his concerns about Arminius had been preferable to having his ear bent about it ten times a day. Now, Tullus decided he had nothing to lose by revealing all.

'Looking forward to getting back to Vetera?' asked Fenestela.

'Aye. You can't beat a decent mattress under you at night, or a pillow to lay your head upon. And when the winter weather arrives, blankets alone won't keep you warm. A brazier in the room, and a sturdy roof overhead, is what you need.'

'Damn right,' said Fenestela. 'We're not getting any younger.'

Nor will we, if Arminius has his way, thought Tullus. 'I've got something to tell you.'

Fenestela's eyes narrowed. Positioning his cloak, he nodded. 'I'm ready.'

Checking again that they were alone, Tullus explained everything to Fenestela, from the uncomfortable feeling that he'd had about Arminius upon meeting him at Vetera, to the looks he'd seen Arminius giving

Maelo, and, later on, Segestes' story. 'You heard what Degmar overheard, of course.'

Fenestela's face had grown angrier by the moment. 'The miserable cocksucker! Pox-ridden goat-fucker!'

Tullus grinned. It felt good to have someone who took him at his word, even if that someone was as jaundiced as Fenestela.

'You told Varus all that, and he didn't believe you?'

'Why should he think there's a real threat? There's not a single piece of solid evidence in what I've said.'

'When you take each thing on its own, maybe,' said Fenestela, 'but place them together and they fit as snug as the tesserae on a nobleman's bath-house floor.'

Tullus sucked on the marrow of that, and didn't like what he tasted. 'It could still be coincidence. You have to admit that.'

'Maybe,' muttered Fenestela. 'Let's hope that it is. Otherwise we could be about to plant ourselves in a big, steaming pile of shit. Could you approach Varus another time?'

'And say what?' challenged Tullus, his frustration spilling over. 'Beg your pardon, governor, but my optio, a trusty veteran, thinks that I'm right about Arminius being a traitor.'

Fenestela's teeth flashed in the gloom. 'He would kick your arse out of his office so fast you wouldn't even know you'd arrived.'

'That would be the least of it. Without proof, I can't go near Varus again.'

Fenestela issued another set of ripe oaths. 'If Arminius *is* up to no good, and we do nothing, many men will lose their lives.'

Bitterness coursed through Tullus' veins. 'That's right.'

'What can we do then?'

'Hope for the best. Ask the gods to prove us wrong for thinking Arminius is a traitor, and, regardless, to watch over our every step on the road home. We must be ready for treachery, right up until the moment we cross the damn bridge over the Rhenus.'

'I will never have been so glad to feel its planking below my feet.'

'You and me both.' Tullus took a sup more wine. They *would* be all right, he thought. Maybe he was mistaken about Arminius.

It was then that he noticed the luminous disc rising above the level of the tents. His skin crawled. At harvest time, the moon was often deep white or yellow in colour, sometimes with shades of orange. It was rare indeed for it to be tinged with crimson. In normal circumstances, Tullus didn't place much store in natural phenomena, but this moon seemed gods-sent. He nudged Fenestela. 'Look. In the sky.'

Fenestela swore. 'That's not a good omen.'

'No. Pass the wine.'

'Here.'

Tullus hefted the near-empty skin and poured what he thought was half into his cup before handing it back. 'Where did you get this stuff? It's not bad.'

'The old Phoenician.'

'The old rogue who was at Aliso?'

'One and the same. Most of what he flogs is worse than bad vinegar, but he has some decent stuff stashed away. I thought it'd be a treat, tonight being our last here at Porta Westfalica.'

Tullus shoved away the idea that this could be their last night anywhere laughing at himself for remembering the crazed soothsayer he had met in Mogontiacum fifteen years before. 'Do you think he's abed? I've a notion to stay up a while yet.'

'So have I,' said Fenestela. 'The Phoenician won't care about being woken up. Sleep is less important than profit to his kind. I'll go.'

Tullus brooded as he waited for Fenestela. Wild possibilities tumbled around his mind, foremost among which was the idea of killing Arminius tonight, ending the matter with a few thrusts of a blade. It would be simple, and not that hard to achieve. There *would* be a significant chance of being slain by Arminius' warriors, of course. Even if he survived, there would be consequences. Varus would have thrown him out of the legions in disgrace, at the very least.

After a time, Tullus abandoned the idea. His career aside, murdering men in the dark wasn't his way. He let out a gusty sigh. Apart from doing nothing, which went against his entire nature, the only option left was to risk Varus' displeasure by approaching him again. It was an even more daunting prospect than before. In the morning, Varus would be wrapped up with the logistics of getting his army on the road. Officers of every rank would be hanging off him, asking for orders and reporting problems of every kind. Tullus' intervention – in public, with a huge audience – would be about as welcome as a flooded sewer on the street down which the emperor was about to pass.

Yet he had to do something.

Fenestela's return soon after was welcome. Tullus had a thirst on him as great as if he'd walked the length of the Syrian desert without a water skin. A hangover might imperil his chances of convincing Varus, but his frustration and anger needed releasing. Getting pissed with Fenestela, his oldest comrade, was the best way Tullus could think of doing that, and the only way of keeping the demons at bay.

If only for a night.

XX

Arminius had slept little. Despite his best efforts, he had spent the night trying to come up with details he might have forgotten, and worrying that Varus would realise what was going on before he and his warriors rode away for the last time. His lack of rest should have left him feeling gritty-eyed and weary, and prone to losing his temper. This was an extraordinary day, however. When the first hint of light entered his tent, Arminius sprang from his bed, his spirits buoyant. Tomorrow, I will fulfil my oath, he thought.

Donar will have his blood offering.

Arminius made his way to the centre of the rectangular space formed by his men's tents, shivering a little from the predawn chill and, if he were honest, nerves. A faint line of red marked the eastern horizon, an indication that sunrise was not long off. The sky, yet glittering with stars, was almost clear of cloud. There was no wind. It would be another glorious autumn day, he thought, like the previous seven days or more. These weren't the best conditions for an ambush – fog or rain was preferable – but it might change later, or by the following day. If fine weather were all he had to complain about, however, he'd be a lucky man. Donar, be good to us, Arminius prayed. Let Varus and his men remain unsuspecting until it is too late.

He wasn't surprised when Maelo appeared. They embraced. 'Couldn't sleep?' asked Arminius.

'Not much. You?'

'The same.'

'We can rest when it's over,' said Maelo with a smile. 'Our plan remains the same?'

'It does. We leave camp at the head of the column, following protocol. It's important that we range far enough ahead that the other auxiliaries don't see us. By mid-morning, having "heard" the "news" of unrest among the Angrivarii from a passing traveller, we ride back and inform Varus.'

'What if he doesn't believe you?' asked Maelo, ever wary.

'He won't be able to resist,' said Arminius with confidence. 'The territory of the Angrivarii is *so* close, and if word reached Augustus that Varus had ridden past a tribal uprising without bothering to investigate, there'd be hell to pay.'

'You're a clever bastard.'

Most of the time, this would have made Arminius smile, but he was feeling a deal more superstitious than normal. 'Call me that in a few days, when we have succeeded. Until then, pray as you've never done before.'

Maelo thumbed his hammer amulet. 'And this afternoon, we find the other tribes?'

'Aye. Varus won't be alarmed that I want to scout a little of the route ahead. By this evening, gods willing, we will have met up with our allies. Varus' legions will continue marching north, further from their roads. We'll fall on them tomorrow.'

A trumpet called from the legions' lines. A second joined it, and then a third. Within a few heartbeats, innumerable others had begun to blare, shredding the once peaceful air with their strident summons.

'It begins,' declared Arminius, squaring his shoulders. 'Let's rouse the men.'

Woolly-headed from the wine he had drunk with Fenestela, Tullus had traced his way to the principia before dawn, which was where he had the bad luck to run into Tubero yet again. The tribune looked as if he were about to go on parade: armour shining, boots buffed, fresh-dyed helmet crest. He frowned at Tullus. 'Drinking last night, centurion?'

'I had a drop, sir, same as you probably did,' replied Tullus, cursing inside his inability to hold back. He and Fenestela were like twins in that respect, each as bad as the other.

'I don't touch wine before an important march,' said Tubero, in a smug tone. 'Whereas you look as if you tried to outdo Bacchus – and lost.'

A passing centurion threw Tullus a disapproving glance. Tullus didn't have the energy to react, or to mention Tubero's drinking when they had been in Aliso. 'I'm fine, sir,' he said, making to walk past.

Tubero blocked his path. 'Where do you think you're going?'

'To speak to Varus, sir.'

'Do you know how busy the governor is at this moment?'

Tullus' temper flared. 'After a lifetime in the army, I've got more of an idea than you do, sir.' He grated out the last word.

The sentries' eyes almost fell out of their heads, and Tubero's face turned crimson. 'How *dare* you be so impertinent?'

'My apologies, sir,' said Tullus, cursing inside.

'We'll have words about this later. Back to your unit! Varus doesn't wish to speak to you.'

The bile welling up at the back of Tullus' throat wasn't because of the wine he'd drunk. Like as not, Varus wouldn't have paid his warning any heed, but now he would never know – and it was all because of *his* big mouth. He longed to enter the principia regardless, but that would give the tribune permission to have him arrested. 'Yes, sir.'

If Tubero hadn't been there, Tullus would have regarded Varus' sallying from the entrance at that very moment as nothing short of divine intervention. As it was, it only added to the shit he was in. Despite the gaggle of staff officers around him, Varus caught sight of Tullus and smiled.

Tullus stepped forward, called out, 'Governor!' but Tubero intervened. 'I'm just getting rid of this centurion, sir! He accosted me with a wild tale of wanting to speak to you, but as you can see, he's much the worse for wear. I've ordered him back to his cohort.'

Varus studied Tullus, frowning. His staff officers did the same. 'You *do* look seedy, centurion,' said Varus. 'That's poor behaviour from a veteran of your standing – particularly today of all days.'

'I'm fine, sir,' protested Tullus.

'You had better be.' Varus' tone was acidic. 'Why are you here?'

Tullus did his best to ignore the line of disapproving faces. This was his final chance. 'It's about Arminius, sir.'

'Not that, again!' snapped Varus. 'You've given me your opinion of him. I do *not* wish to hear it yet another time. Arminius is a tried and trusted Roman ally, and that's an end to it. If I hear of you spreading sedition about him, you can expect to end your career in the ranks. Understand?'

'Yes, sir,' replied Tullus, staring at the ground.

'Get out of my sight,' ordered Varus.

As Tullus walked away, defeated, he could see Tubero smiling from the corner of his eye. His ears were full of the other officers' muttered comments. Cynicism filled him. Why had he even bothered? The army's route was set and, if his hunch was correct, it was a path to Hades.

Arminius and his men had ridden almost eight miles towards Vetera before they reached a crossroads, where a cattle-droving track crossed the road, running in a north-south direction. Arminius reined in, and gazed at the northward-leading section with a pensive eye. This was the spot he had chosen, and which he had visited several times over the previous year. It felt unreal – and exhilarating – to be here with Varus' legions only a couple of hours behind.

There had been no sign of the other auxiliary cavalry, a unit of Gauls, for some time, which was just as he'd wished. The Gauls had shown no inclination to increase their leisurely pace as Arminius' riders left them behind. 'What's the hurry?' some had shouted in poor Latin. 'Vetera isn't going anywhere.' The same relaxed air had been apparent in the whole army before the legions had set out from Porta Westfalica, filling Arminius with a dark joy. Why wouldn't it? he thought. The summer was over, the harvest in, the taxes collected. There had been no trouble among the tribes. It was time to return to their bases on the western bank of the Rhenus, and there enjoy the quieter period of winter.

The same unperturbed attitude was evident among the contubernium – eight legionaries – whose job it was to guard the crossroads. Three were sitting by a fire outside their tent, while the rest stood at the junction, looking bored. They called out greetings to Arminius' men, who responded with friendly salutes. The most senior, a veteran who looked similar in age to Tullus, sauntered over and saluted Arminius. 'Scouting, sir?'

'Aye. I've a mind to head that way.' Arminius pointed north.

The legionary shrugged. 'Few people use that route, sir, just some of the local farmers. I doubt you'll find much of interest.'

'Probably not,' agreed Arminius with a resigned-looking smile. 'But even when there's naught to see, a scout has to keep looking, eh? Just as a sentry has to stand watch, regardless of the fact that nothing will happen.'

'I ain't complaining, sir,' said the legionary, chuckling.

'Nor I,' said Arminius, smiling and thinking: If only you knew the reason I am here. 'See you upon our return.' Aiming his horse towards the track, he signalled that his men should follow.

He reached another junction after two miles, where an even tinier path crossed the one they were on. A band of Marsi warriors was waiting there, which Arminius had been expecting. The Marsi were the last tribe he had won over, not a month since. It was a feat he was proud of, because his people and theirs had a history of bitter feuding. The price had been high: one of the three legions' eagles would go to the Marsi when the slaughter was over. Even this glittering prize had not persuaded all the Marsi, however. From the guarded looks on the waiting warriors' faces, they fell into this undecided category.

Arminius pulled a broad smile and dismounted. 'Well met, brothers!'

Most of the warriors ignored him, or just grunted. Arminius' riders muttered angrily, and one spat. Arminius threw them a furious glare, and they subsided.

A tall, spindly man with twin braids of hair falling on his shoulders stood forth from the grouped Marsi. 'You're Arminius.'

'I am. And you are . . .?'

'Ecco.' He stared at Arminius' hand for a moment before he shook it. 'We've been here for hours.'

It was pointless for Ecco to be annoyed, thought Arminius, fighting irritation. He'd had no way of predicting the exact timing of his arrival, and the Marsi warrior would have known that. 'I am grateful that you came,' he said, dipping his head. 'Your chieftains knew the path I had chosen, but I wanted there to be no chance for error when the time came. Many thousands of warriors have answered my call, but your spears will still be needed.'

Ecco made a non-committal noise. He glanced up and down the narrow track, then gave Arminius a disbelieving look. 'You're going to lead the legions down this?'

Arminius could feel Ecco's companions' eyes on him, as heavy as the lead weights that drag a fishing net into the depths. He struck a confident pose, and threw his voice so that all could hear. 'I am. This very day.'

Ecco curled his lip. 'Why would they even consider it?'

'Your misgivings are understandable, my friend.' Arminius waved at the beech and hornbeam trees that pressed in on each side. 'This is not a good route for an army to take. There's no space for the legionaries to march in their normal formation. Their cavalry won't be able to deploy – they'll even have to dismount in places. The wagons and the artillery – well, you can imagine how difficult travelling through here will be. And as for what will happen when we reach the first stream . . .!'

'There's marsh up ahead too,' said Ecco.

'Indeed there is,' agreed Arminius, grinning. 'The track winds around a hill after that.'

'These are things that Varus will hear from his scouts. Each one is a good reason for him to keep his army on the road to Vetera. Taken together, well, only a madman or a fool would set out on this path,' declared Ecco, glancing at his companions and receiving their approval.

'Varus is not mad. Nor is he a fool,' declared Arminius. 'Better than either of those, he's my friend. The man trusts me as he would his own flesh and blood. I have built a relationship with him these many months; I have taken him hunting, and shared enough wine with him to launch a warship. In his mind, I am a Roman, a nobleman such as he. Which, to all intents and purposes, I am! Did not Augustus himself, the *emperor*' – Arminius spat the last word – 'grant me equestrian status some years past? The notion that I could be a traitor is anathema to Varus.'

'Even so, why would he agree to leave the main road?'

Arminius threw a friendly arm around Ecco's shoulders, and was pleased when the other did not pull away. 'Because I – his chief scout – will ride back from here with urgent news. I'll mention little about the track. Instead I will tell Varus that the Angrivarii have risen against Rome, in protest against the new tax. The temptation for Varus to crush a small tribe – whose territory lies so close to his army's route – will be as irresistible as an overripe plum to a wasp.'

Doubt lingered in Ecco's eyes. 'Why go to all this trouble? We could just attack Varus' legions on the main road. Rumour has it that almost twenty thousand spears have rallied to your cause. With those numbers, victory is certain.'

'Not certain. Underestimate the Romans at your own peril.' Arminius' tone was light, to avoid giving offence. 'Let the legions take this narrow path, however, where they will have to march out of formation, their cavalry and artillery useless, with no way of turning back or striking out to either side, and victory becomes ever more likely.' He gave Ecco a conspiratorial wink. 'Have you seen the earthworks?'

Ecco shook his head.

'Some miles further on, the other tribes have been constructing fortifications along one side of the track. They're hundreds of paces in length, taller than a man, and hidden by the trees. Thousands of warriors can conceal themselves behind them. When the signal's given, they will fall upon the unsuspecting Romans with the speed and force of a landslide.' Arminius glanced at Maelo for confirmation.

'He speaks the truth, as Donar is my witness,' said Maelo. 'They're an impressive sight, Ecco. The Romans won't realise a thing until it's far too late.'

'The weather is changing too.' Arminius lifted his gaze. The section of sky visible above the trees was a threatening shade of grey-black. 'There's rain on the way. It won't take the legions long to turn the place into a complete quagmire. Have I convinced you yet, Ecco?'

Morning was passing by the time Arminius and his men had returned to the vanguard, comprised that day of the Nineteenth Legion. Ordering his followers to travel at the army's head as before, he went on, accompanied by Maelo. The marching legionaries took up the entire width of the road, meaning the pair had to ride on the narrow strip of ground on one side. Moving against the general flow attracted curious glances aplenty from the tramping soldiers, and shouted questions from centurions and *optiones*. Continuing to play his affable role despite his rising desire to do the opposite, Arminius bestowed broad smiles aplenty and repeated, 'My news is for the governor, and he alone.'

He was encouraged by the large numbers of civilians throughout the column. Mobile vendors of food and drink, who'd been supplying the army through the summer months, walked up and down alongside the files of legionaries, selling watered-down wine, bread and sausages. There were women too – soldiers' common-law wives, or whores – carrying bundles of clothing and pots, and packs of shrieking children running along, playing chase. Here and there, in the breaks between cohorts, were wagons laden down with baggage, injured men and what looked like more than one officer's personal belongings. Arminius even spotted a soothsayer, promising anyone who'd listen that he could read the future from the way a scatter of crows was flying overhead, or the pattern of clouds in the sky. His spirits rose further. Everything he was seeing was against military regulations. Non-combatants – women, children, merchants and the rest of the raggletaggle that followed an army – were banned from walking with the legionaries, in particular the vanguard. All vehicles were supposed to travel with the baggage train, much further down the column.

By rights, the next section of troops in the column should have been ten soldiers from every century in the three legions, eighteen hundred men, carrying the tools necessary to dig out a marching camp. There was no sign of them. Their absence was understandable, thought Arminius with grim satisfaction, because Varus and his legates were expecting the army to utilise the temporary earthworks built close to the road in previous years, and later on, parts of the permanent camps such as Aliso. Once he had delivered his calamitous 'news', and the legions began travelling in a different direction, a marching camp would be required that night. Work parties would have to be separated out from each legion, and sent forward. Even if this were done the moment he'd spoken to Varus, the site would not be ready when the main body of the army arrived. It was a small thing, thought Arminius, but it would begin to unsettle the Roman troops.

The engineers, who should have come after the camp-builders, were nowhere to be seen either. This was not unreasonable: the army was travelling along a paved road, straight back to Vetera. Once the column headed off this route, however, things would change. The first deep stream would bring the army's progress to a standstill until the engineers and their equipment had been brought forward.

The ox-drawn wagons carrying Varus' and the most senior officers' baggage were in the correct place at least. Escorted front and back by half a cohort of legionaries, they were a score or more of heavy-laden vehicles with creaking axles, sweating drivers and passengers who'd cadged a free ride. Arminius spotted Aristides in the back of one wagon, his face screwed up with discontent. He had a rolled-up document in each hand, and was vainly attempting to keep away the clouds of flies that hung overhead.

'Enjoying the ride?' Arminius called out. Surprised to see him, Aristides shook his head in vehement denial.

'I'm being eaten alive.'

'The biting flies are attracted by the cattle. Get out and march with the legionaries,' Arminius suggested, knowing full well that the scribe wouldn't be up to walking twenty miles a day.

Aristides gave him a dark look. 'I'll stay where I am.'

'As you please,' said Arminius as Maelo chortled.

They rode on, soon catching sight of the First Cohort of the Nineteenth Legion, Varus' designated protection for the march back to Vetera. Everything about these troops stood in contrast to the soldiers who'd gone before. Sunlight flashed off their standards, polished armour and helmets, and their ranks were as neat and straight as if drawn by a carpenter's rule. The measured tread of their hobnailed sandals added a deep cadence to the general clamour. They were an impressive sight, and reminded Arminius again why he would always try to avoid direct confrontation with the legions. German warriors were stout-hearted fighters and unafraid of dying, but standing toe-to-toe with legionaries in battle was a poor idea.

The more vigilant manner of Varus' escort was borne out when a challenge rang out as the pair drew near. 'Halt! Identify yourselves,' bellowed a centurion from the front rank.

Arminius raised a hand in a peaceful gesture. 'I am Arminius of the Cherusci, commander of the ala attached to the Seventeenth. I bring urgent news for Governor Varus.'

A few words saw Arminius and Maelo waved on, past the marching legionaries. A large party of horsemen followed on the soldiers' heels. Despite his confidence, Arminius' stomach did a neat roll as he spotted Varus in the midst of his staff officers. If his story was in any way unconvincing, his entire plan could unravel.

He glanced at Maelo, and alarm filled him. Sweat was rolling down his second-in-command's face. There was a wild look to his eyes too, such as a sheep has, seized by the slaughterman, a moment before its throat is slit.

'What in Donar's name is wrong with you?' hissed Arminius.

'He'll know. Varus will know what we're up to.'

'*He fucking won't!*' Arminius smiled and waved at Varus, who had seen him. 'In his mind, we are trusted and proven allies. For us to commit treachery would be unthinkable.' Maelo swallowed, nodded, but looked no less panicked. Twenty paces away, Varus was beckoning. 'Control yourself, Maelo, or I swear I'll cut your balls off, and shove them down your damn throat.'

Maelo swept an arm across his face and forced a grin.

'Arminius!' called Varus.

'Greetings, governor,' said Arminius, adopting a sombre tone.

Varus' smile vanished. 'Is something wrong?'

Donar, help me now, Arminius asked, turning his horse so that he was on Varus' right side and moving in the direction of travel. Head down, Maelo copied him. The army stopped for no man. 'In a manner of speaking, yes,' said Arminius. 'We encountered a merchant fleeing south while scouting. He reported that the Angrivarii have risen in numbers against Rome.'

Varus scowled. 'In Jupiter's name, why?'

'The new tax, it seems.'

'Taxes are sent to plague us all! One might as well fight the rain as resist them,' said Varus in a weary voice.

'If everyone realised that, the world would be a simpler place,' agreed Arminius.

'The Angrivarii live to the north of here – not far, is it?'

'Some thirty to forty miles, no more.' Heart thumping, Arminius kept his mind fixed on the image of an iron fish hook, decorated with a fat worm, sinking delicately below the surface of a river. A short distance below, a fine trout watched it with beady eyes. Take it, thought Arminius. It's there just for you.

'Your second-in-command – Maelo, isn't it – is he all right?' asked Varus. 'He seems unwell.'

Arminius threw a casual glance over his shoulder at Maelo. It was a small consolation that his face was no longer running with sweat, but his complexion was a pasty shade of grey. Arminius made a dismissive gesture. 'The fool ate some fish last night, governor. Fish that was reputed to have come from the sea! He's been paying for his thoughtlessness since dawn. Coming out both ends, it is, regular as anything.'

'Enough, Arminius,' ordered Varus, looking pained. 'I have more to be concerned about than Maelo's insides. Tell me every word that this traveller said.'

Relief flooded through Arminius. He was careful not to add many specifics to his fictitious report. An innocent bystander would not be someone to note warrior numbers and suchlike. 'The man was terrified,' he concluded. 'He lingered long enough only to tell me his tale before riding south.'

'How strong a tribe are the Angrivarii?' asked Varus.

'They're not numerous. If every stripling and greybeard among them took up a spear, I'd wager they could field three and a half thousand warriors. Maybe four,' replied Arminius.

'Did the traveller say anything about neighbouring tribes?'

Varus was no fool, thought Arminius. He didn't want to lead his soldiers towards a widespread uprising. 'No, nothing.'

Varus rode on without replying, and Arminius' stomach churned. In the bright sunlight, his story seemed as thin as old gruel. He wanted to keep talking, to ensure that Varus was persuaded to act, but feared to say too much. Remaining silent was as hard, however.

His heart beat out an unhappy score. To his rear, he heard Maelo retch. Arminius clutched at the sound like an ill-fed beggar seizes a thrown crust. 'I told you not to eat that fish,' he said. 'The sea lies more than a hundred miles to the north. That should be enough to put any man off.'

'I know,' Maelo replied, groaning.

'The timing of this uprising is inauspicious,' declared Varus. 'What do they hope to achieve this late in the season?'

Arminius felt a line of sweat trickle down his back. The usual time to go raiding, or to start a war, was at the end of spring, or in early summer, when there were months of campaigning available. 'If I know the Angrivarii aright, reason will have had little to do with it,' he said in a confiding tone. 'Hot hearts are wont to overpower cold minds, they say among the tribes. Even now, it would be my instinct to react in the manner the Angrivarii have. It's my Roman training that allows me to hold back, to think before I act.'

Varus regarded him with a smile. 'Whatever the reason, their treachery cannot be overlooked. It's fortunate that word reached us so soon, before they have had a chance to rally other tribes to their cause. Imagine also how difficult – and unpopular – it would have been to turn the army around close to Vetera. All we have to do now is, what – take a route to the north?'

It took a mighty effort for Arminius not to cheer. Instead, he said in a calm voice, 'Correct, governor. We can follow the track upon which my men and I met the traveller.'

'Good.' Varus was already calling for his staff officers, and ordering that the engineers, and as much of their equipment as was feasible, be brought forward to their usual position. His legates were to be summoned, that they might discuss the best strategies to take against the Angrivarii. Word was to be passed along the entire column of the change in route, and the reasons why. Although contact with the enemy was not anticipated for a day or more, security was to be raised. 'I want every man on the alert,' commanded Varus. He turned back to Arminius. 'Once again, I am in your debt.'

Arminius made an awkward gesture. 'I was only doing my duty.'

'As ever, you did it well. Now, though, you'd best return to your men. Leave some to ensure that the vanguard chooses the right path north, but I must ask you to take the rest ranging ahead – to see what you can find. For all we know, the Angrivarii could have sent raiding parties south.'

'A wise decision,' said Arminius. 'I will also need to send riders to fetch the few men who missed our departure this morning.'

'Do what you must, Arminius,' replied Varus, waving him away. 'Send any urgent news to me at once. Otherwise, report to me tonight, in camp.'

'Very good,' said Arminius. The next time I see you, I'll plant a blade in your throat, he thought. 'Come on, Maelo.'

'Arminius!' called Varus when they had ridden only a dozen paces.

Beside him, Arminius sensed Maelo stiffen. He turned, pulling a confident smile. 'Yes?'

Varus raised a hand. 'You didn't say farewell.'

'Pardon my haste. I wished only to begin my patrol. Farewell.' Thank you, great Donar, Arminius thought, feeling a tide of relief as they rode on. 'Gods above, I'm glad that's over.'

'You're not the only one,' muttered Maelo.

'I should have left you with the men. You're a warrior, not a spy.' Arminius' grin was half serious, half joking. 'I still would have cut your balls off if you'd given the game away, mind.'

'I'd have deserved it,' Maelo admitted.

Easing their horses into a trot, they made their way towards the vanguard. Although no one questioned their passage, Arminius did not relax. It was yet possible that things could go wrong. Varus could develop doubts, and send a messenger to recall him. He had no idea where Tullus was, but if the centurion saw them, he might do something. So might that prick Tubero, if he appeared. It wasn't likely that Flavus would catch sight of him either, riding as he was at the rear of the column, but Arminius kept a wary eye out for his brother too.

At length, they had left the legionaries of the vanguard behind, and the Gaulish cavalry too, and reached the safety of the open road. Only then did the events of the previous hour begin to seem real.

After so many years, the time for retribution was at hand.

XXI

It wasn't long after dawn, and Varus was sitting in one of the partitioned rooms in his large tent, comfortable stool beneath him, thick carpets underfoot, oil lamps on gilded stands illuminating the chamber. The sound of orders, and grunts as furniture was lifted, came from all around him – the entire structure was being dismantled, ready for the day's march – but where he was remained a little island of calm. The forest that had surrounded them since their departure from the main road the previous day was invisible yet, which was a pleasure. Varus had already seen enough trees to last him a lifetime.

'Some bread, sir?' asked Varus' cook, a dour veteran who had been with him since he took up his governor's post.

Varus, who hadn't slept well, gave an irritable shake of his head. Already he was preoccupied with the impending day's march, along the narrow path that Arminius had specified. The previous afternoon's journey had been difficult and unpleasant. A night's rain would have worsened the conditions further. It was as well, Varus thought, that the legions didn't have to travel far.

Wise to his master's mood, the cook retreated in silence with the plate of fresh-baked flatbreads.

'Aristides,' said Varus.

The Greek hurried over from his desk, and the mounds of documents that he'd been poring over. 'Master?'

'Has there been any sign of Arminius?'

Aristides knew that his master was well aware there hadn't – they had had no visitors other than the cook since the last time Varus had asked. He scratched at one of the multitude of bites that decorated his face and arms and, after a moment, ventured, 'No, master. Should I go outside and ask the guards?'

'Yes. Have a soldier sent to the main gate as well, in case he's arrived there. Have the auxiliary lines checked too, for the few of his riders who stayed behind yesterday.'

'Master.'

Varus glared at Aristides' retreating back. How one word could reveal that the Greek didn't understand – or appreciate – his concern about Arminius' absence, Varus wasn't sure, but it did. All he has to be worried about is his damn bites, thought Varus, feeling jealous. I have a whole army to think of, and a tribe of damn Germans to find and subjugate.

The smell of hot wine dragged his mind back to the present. His cook had reappeared, unasked, this time with a silver goblet, from which wisps of steam were rising. 'I thought you might like some wine instead, sir,' he said. 'It's your favourite vintage, heated up and diluted a little. I've laced it with honey as well.'

Varus felt a smile break out. 'Good man.' Taking a sip, he toasted the cook. 'It's perfect.'

'If you need another, sir, just call. I'll keep my brazier hot until the last moment.' The cook retreated towards the back of the tent, where his kitchen was situated.

Good mood restored, Varus decided that Arminius had been delayed by something – like as not being unable to track down some of his men – but he would appear sometime during the day. Even when Aristides returned to report that there had been no sign of the Cheruscan, and that his last riders had left before dawn to scout out the route ahead, Varus remained ebullient. When had Arminius ever let him down? A second, smaller goblet of wine fortified his spirits further. He put on his full general's uniform: bronze, muscled breastplate, red sash, baldric, fine sword and crested helmet. Donning his crimson cloak last, Varus sallied from his tent, head held high. Mud squelched beneath his boots. It had rained even more than he'd realised overnight, which was annoying, for it would slow their progress on the narrow track.

His legates, Numonius Vala among them, and Lucius Eggius and Ceionius, his camp commanders, were waiting outside. They greeted him with smiles and salutes. 'It's a fine morning for hunting rebel tribesmen, sir,' declared Vala.

Varus cast an eye upwards. Most of the clouds that had deluged the land a few hours before had gone. A watery sun was climbing above the treetops to the east. It was no guarantee that the weather would remain dry, but Varus had long found it best to remain positive. 'Indeed it is. Make your reports.'

The Eighteenth Legion had been selected to form the vanguard that day, Varus was told. The Gaulish cavalry would precede it. To avoid the problems of the previous day, the engineers would march behind the first two cohorts of the Eighteenth, the better to be able to swing into action when their services were needed, as they would be.

'As you're aware, sir, some of the non-combatants and wagons have been travelling together with the soldiers,' said Vala. 'Do you wish them separated as if we were on campaign?'

All eyes swivelled to Varus, who smiled in dismissal. 'The Angrivarii are a small tribe, who live more than thirty miles away. I see no reason to travel as if we are afraid. Besides, there may be points at which soldiers are needed to help move wagons over streams and so on. Is there anything else? No? To your positions, then.'

By late morning, Varus' good humour was again wearing thin. Not long after the army had left camp, the wind had picked up, bringing with it banks of dark clouds that had emptied themselves over the forest and the slow-moving column. Although there had been breaks in the downpour, they had been scant. The wind continued to gain in strength, delivering more clouds – and rain – from the north. While the trees to either side afforded more protection than if they had been on a plain, there was no escaping the sheets of precipitation which hammered down from above. All a man could do was to hunch his shoulders and ride – or walk – on.

Varus could have summoned a covered wagon – there was even an official litter somewhere in the baggage train – but he didn't wish to be perceived as a 'soft' general, who could not endure what his soldiers had to. Leading by example was important. He wasn't going to be above calling for a new, dry cloak when the time came, however. Wool that had been soaked in lanolin could keep out the rain for a decent period, yet it became waterlogged in the end. Varus pitied his legionaries, each of whom possessed but one cloak. By the day's end, they would be like bedraggled rats. And the smell in their tents – Varus wrinkled his nose at the mere thought. The odour of men who'd marched twenty miles carrying heavy kit was ripe at the best of times, but the confines of a tent, and wet wool – which stank – increased it manyfold.

The constant downpour, and the passage of so many feet, both animals and men, had turned the forest track into a quagmire. Mud had splattered up to Varus' horse's fetlocks. The legionaries in his escort had dirty cloak hems, and brown legs from the knee down. The group of slaves following Varus and his staff officers, most of whom wore no protection against the rain, were muddy, and drenched to the skin. However bad it was here, near the vanguard, he brooded, things would be worse further along the column. Like as not, the wagons carrying the artillery were getting bogged down, even stuck.

Varus felt his temper – and frustration – rise, but there was nothing he could do other than to keep his forces moving forward. Dealing with the threat of the Angrivarii was a necessity, and there was no way of turning around. His army was like a large wagon which had gone down a narrow alleyway. How long the alley was, Varus had no idea. Arminius would know, but there was no sign of *him*. For the umpteenth time that morning, Varus wondered where he was, and what he was up to. Ordering a messenger to the vanguard, Varus commanded word be brought from his remaining cavalry, the Gauls, about the ground to the north. 'I want to know when the damn forest ends,' he called after the rider. 'As soon as possible!'

He received the information he'd requested from an unexpected source soon after, not from the messenger, but a bedraggled-looking Tubero, who sought him out. 'The Gauls have ridden five miles and more in front of the vanguard, sir,' he reported. 'There are clearings here and there, and a patch or two of bog, but the forest appears to continue for some distance.'

'I see.' Varus digested this, holding in his urge to rant and roar, to lambast Tubero for not reporting what he wanted to hear. Stay level-headed, he told himself. A day's bad weather isn't going to kill us. Nor is a forest. 'Why were you with the vanguard?'

'I wanted to see what was going on, sir.'

Varus smiled in approval. 'A worthy attitude.'

'It's hard to remain patient when you're stuck back down the line, sir – you know how it is.'

'You've identified one of the most aggravating things about an army on the move. As a commander, you often don't have an idea in Hades what's going on. What did you discover?'

'Not a great deal, sir. The engineers are working as hard as they can. Chopping down trees and widening the track is simple enough, but building bridges takes time. According to their senior centurion, they've constructed two already this morning. They're working on a third as we speak.'

'Are there more watercourses?'

'Four or five, sir, according to the Gauls. All but one are fordable on foot, though. The wagons will get through if they have soldiers to help keep them moving.'

'I suppose that's something,' said Varus. 'But we'll never make twenty miles today.'

'No, sir.' Tubero's voice was emphatic.

'Has anyone seen Arminius?'

'I don't believe so, sir.'

'If he's run into some kind of problem, he should have sent word back,' Varus grumbled. 'Maybe he's clashed with a party of Angrivarii.'

'Do you think it possible that he has abandoned us, sir?' ventured Tubero.

'Arminius has been an ally of Rome for many years. He'll be back soon, you'll see,' replied Varus in a bluff tone.

'As you say, sir,' said Tubero, looking awkward. 'With your permission, then, I'll be off.'

'Yes, yes,' said Varus, remembering how he had dismissed Tubero's vague querying of Arminius' loyalty. Before you go, though . . .'

'Sir?'

'What are you doing with a cavalry helmet?' asked Varus, gesturing.

'This?' Tubero tapped the ornate, silvered helm that was hanging by a loop from his belt. 'It was a gift from my father, sir, before I left Rome. Most likely, I'll never get to wear it in a charge, but I like to imagine that I might, one day.'

It was a little odd for a tribune to carry such a helmet, but it wasn't against regulations, thought Varus. As he watched Tubero ride away, his mood threatened to sink a little further into the mud. His mind was taken from his worries soon after, however, when word came that the engineers had finished their bridge. The way forward was clear for another mile and a half, the messenger reported. Things were improving, thought Varus.

His feeling was buoyed up when the rain eased and stopped a short while later. The cloud broke up, allowing warm sunshine to bathe the forest, and the soaking, mud-covered Romans. Varus took the opportunity to change his cloak, and to eat a hunk of bread and cheese. Drier than he had been for hours, and with his rumbling belly silenced, he decided that he had been unfair to Arminius. The Cheruscan hadn't made the route towards the Angrivarii difficult. He hadn't brought down the rain either, or churned the ground into mud. Morale was still high, as evinced by the bawdy marching song that the nearest legionaries had begun to sing. The engineers would ensure that the army maintained some kind of momentum.

The desired total of twenty miles might not be reached, and it might be late before the marching camp was built, thought Varus, but the day *would* end well.

Piso was a short distance off the track, widening the route of the approaching army along with his comrades and the soldiers of another century. Two of the other centuries under Tullus' command were spread out around them in a loose formation among the trees, watching for signs of the Angrivarii. The rest of Tullus' cohort was with the engineers, who were assessing the next stream, a quarter of a mile to their front. Despite his warnings to stay alert, few men were concerned about being ambushed. The Angrivarii lived many miles away, and the army was three legions strong. Only a fool or a madman would attack such a force. All the same, Piso laid down his equipment close to where he was working. Regulations stated that a man's shield and javelin had to be within five to ten paces when he was working, and the unit's officers enforced this with zeal.

Wet, stinking with sweat, but relieved to have set down his kit, he walked around the beech, deciding where to place his first axe blow. He was grateful that it was a young tree – some of those that lay only a few paces deeper into the forest were as thick as his waist, or even larger. This one, Piso reckoned, was at least twenty years old. It stood the height of five men, and its trunk was about the size of his thigh.

'I can see you, Piso!' bellowed Tullus from the road.

Piso jumped. Where in damnation had *he* come from? he wondered. Tullus was supposed to be with the engineers, making *their* lives hell.

'You're not here to admire the bloody trees, just chop them down,' shouted Tullus. 'Start using that axe, or you'll feel my vitis across your back.'

'Yes, sir,' Piso called out, trying to ignore Vitellius, who was snorting with laughter from his position by another beech. Afer, off to his right, was also chuckling.

'Bastards,' muttered Piso, hoping that Tullus would find fault with them too, so that he got a chance to mock. His luck wasn't in this time. Tullus walked on, bawling encouragement and threats by turn at other soldiers. Piso focused on his beech. If he struck the bark just there, it wouldn't land on anyone when it fell, he decided. He swung around at the hip and let fly. The axe head sank in with a satisfying *thwack*. Piso drew back his arms and hit it again. *Thwack*. This time, the blade landed several fingersbreadth from the spot where his first effort had struck. He cursed, aimed better and struck his first mark. Before long, he had removed a decent wedge, and could not miss. Switching sides when he'd hacked halfway through the trunk, Piso chopped until the muscles in his arms were burning. As the tree fell, he glanced around to see if his efforts had been enough for Tullus, but his centurion was gone.

'It's a trick he has,' called Vitellius. 'He stays long enough to make you think he's still watching, and then he pisses off. Better not relax, though, because he'll be back before you know it.'

Piso couldn't see Tullus up or down the road. Resting the axe head on the ground, he wiped the sweat from his brow. 'How many miles d'you reckon we'll have to do this for?'

Vitellius swung his axe. *Thunk*. 'How would I know? Never been in this godsforsaken spot in my life. We keep doing it as long as Tullus tells us to. It's a break from marching, and that can't be bad.'

'True,' admitted Piso grudgingly. He readied himself to split the trunk, and bring it as close to the ground as he could. That way, marching men could step over it with ease.

'Alarm!' roared a voice off to his left. 'Raise the alarm!'

Piso froze; then he glanced at Vitellius, whose head had turned in the direction of the shout, and to Afer, who had already dropped his axe and grabbed his shield. Piso copied Afer. There was no time to remove the protective leather cover, heavy with absorbed rain. They drew their swords; Piso shuffled to Afer's side, where they were soon joined by Vitellius and the rest of their contubernium. Other legionaries were also bunching together, but without an officer to direct them, no one tried to form a solid line. Piso did his best to stay calm, but there was already a vague sense of panic in the air – every legionary knew the dangers of fighting in open formation. If an enemy came at them fast, now, they would sweep into the gaps like a river through a half-built dam.

Through the trees to their left, it was possible to see the soldiers who'd been standing guard retreating in poor order. 'Alarm!' many of them were yelling. 'Angrivarii!'

Piso felt sick. He glanced behind him, wondering where he'd run if he had to.

'Steady,' growled Afer.

Shamefaced, Piso fixed his gaze on the sentries. With a little luck, they'd be able to group together when they met, but that would depend somewhat on when the enemy hit them.

'Close up! Close up! Form a line!'

Tullus' arrival had a dramatic, calming effect. Men knew what to do; they steadied when a leader took charge. Piso and his comrades shuffled sideways until they met the legionaries of another contubernium. To either side, the rest of their comrades did the same. Tullus shoved himself in between Piso and Vitellius. 'What can you see?' he demanded.

Piso squinted. 'Just our men, sir.'

'I can't make out a damn thing, apart from my soldiers,' said Tullus. 'Vitellius?'

'Nothing, sir.' Vitellius sounded a little embarrassed.

Tullus sounded his whistle to attract attention. 'You there, with the rusty mail!' he roared. 'What's going on? Where are the Angrivarii?'

There was a moment's pause, and then the sentry he'd addressed replied, 'There's no sign of them, sir. It might have been a bear.'

Cries of disbelief – and relief, if Piso's comrades felt anything like him – rose from the defensive line.

'A bear? A FUCKING BEAR?' cried Tullus, as general laughter broke out.

'Yes, sir,' came the sheepish reply. 'I was sure it was a warrior – that's why I raised the alarm – but when everyone started shouting, it thundered off through the undergrowth like a boulder down a hill. It couldn't have been a man, sir.'

'Damn fool,' said Tullus, and more laughter erupted. 'Remain in your positions,' he ordered, and stamped forward to the soldier who'd spotted the bear. They conferred, and then Tullus advanced deeper into the trees, sword and shield at the ready. Despite the likelihood that the Angrivarii had not arrived, Piso didn't relax until Tullus walked back and announced that 'If a tribesman can leave a shit that big and smelly, my name's Alexander of Macedon.'

Amused, relieved looks were exchanged all round.

'The fun's over, you maggots,' warned Tullus. 'Take a drink of water, and then back to work. The vanguard will catch up if you're not careful, and I'm not having my arse roasted by a tribune because you're too damn lazy to finish your task. I want every tree in the vicinity levelled by the time I come back! Those of you on guard, keep your eyes peeled. I want no more false alarms. D'you hear me?'

'Yes, sir,' the legionaries yelled.

'Get to it, you dogs, because there are plenty more trees further along,' announced Tullus, ignoring the chorus of groans that followed him down the track.

Piso reduced the trunk of his first tree to something less than ankle height before he paused for breath. That done, he cast around for Tullus, and saw his crested helmet disappearing to the north. An optio was approaching from the other direction, so there wasn't much chance to talk. 'Who was the fool who raised the alarm?' he called out.

'I think it was Julius Long Nose,' answered Vitellius.

Piso chuckled, relieved yet again that his name was unusual. So many men went by the common first names – Julius, Marcus, Quintus and so on – that individuals had to be differentiated by their second or last names, or a nickname. 'Long Nose,' he yelled. 'We're not going to let you forget that bear!'

Long Nose's sour response was drowned out by a chorus of laughter, whistles and cries of 'Bear! Bear!'

'Nice one, Piso,' said Vitellius.

Piso grinned, relishing the comradeship he now felt. Even when the rain began to fall again later, his spirits didn't falter. It was just water, and he could dry out by the fire in camp that evening. The trees in their path could be cut down, the streams crossed one way or another. In a day or two, they would sort out the Angrivarii and, that done, return to Vetera. Back in barracks, there would be time to have his name inscribed on the bronze fasteners he'd taken from Aius at dice. Between one thing and another, Piso had forgotten to have this done before leaving Porta Westfalica. Although it was unlikely that anyone would see Aius' name etched on the back of the fasteners, and Tullus could vouch for him if needs be, Piso had felt uncomfortable about using them. As a result, they had been sitting in his purse since the night he had beaten Aius. In an odd way, the fasteners had begun to feel like a good-luck talisman, which was why Piso wanted to hold on to them.

He traced their irregular shape through the leather of his purse.

Fortuna, I am your faithful servant. Watch over me, as you always do, he prayed.

XXII

Piso was sick of trees. Beech trees. Hornbeam trees. Oak trees. He'd seen enough of them to last him for the rest of his life. He had lost count of the number he had cut down, or helped to fell that day. His arms ached like they had during his training, and it was a struggle to swing the axe more than a few times before having to rest. And brambles – he was sick of them too. They grew everywhere, in great dense patches. Every exposed part of Piso's skin bore red lines where he had been caught or scratched by their thorns.

Lucky for him, everyone was in the same state, which meant that Tullus recognised it as generalised exhaustion rather than individuals shirking their duty. During the midday meal break, he ordered that the legionaries who'd been on sentry duty would change places with those who had been widening the track for the army. Piso felt a warm rush of gratitude towards his centurion. Watching out for bears and Angrivarii warriors – who everyone said were unlikely to appear – would be easy in comparison to hacking down trees.

The short rest was more welcome than the idea of cold food. Men squatted down on their haunches, or sat on fallen trunks, uncaring of the damp that soaked through their cloaks and tunics. Some even lay down under the trees, where the ground was a little drier. Few talked, and when they did, it was to complain about Varus, who had commanded them to march into this living hell instead of back to Vetera, where they belonged.

'What a man needs on a day like this is soup, or at the least, hot wine,' complained Vitellius, ripping up a chunk of bread and shoving it into his mouth.

There was a loud chorus of agreement from the rest of the contubernium, gathered in a circle around a flattish stone that was serving as a table. Helmets and sodden felt liners, yokes, equipment, javelins and shields covered the ground at their feet.

'That would require a fire,' observed Piso, indicating the sodden earth and dripping trees. 'Even Vulcan would struggle to light one in this shithole.'

That raised a chuckle from some.

Tullus arrived then, as he so often did, out of nowhere. There was no sign of Degmar, his Marsi servant, but that didn't surprise Piso. Like as not, he was off scouting somewhere. The horsehair crest of Tullus' helmet had sagged down to either side, like an old man who combs his hair down the middle, and his cloak was soaked, same as everyone else's, but his confident demeanour remained. 'Men,' he said by way of greeting.

'Sir.' Piso and the rest began to rise, but Tullus waved them back into their positions.

'There's no need to move. You look too comfortable.' The legionaries managed a dutiful laugh, and he smiled. It didn't last, though. Piso felt a tickle of unease as Tullus' expression became grim. 'You're staying alert?'

'Aye, sir.' 'Of course, sir.' 'You can rely on us, sir.'

A stern nod. 'Good. Forget about Long Nose making the mistake with the bear. If you see anything unusual this afternoon, shout! I want the men at the front of the damn column to hear. There'll be no reprimand if it's a false alarm, I promise you. I'd rather know about something I don't need to worry about than the other way round, if you get my drift.'

Piso wondered forever afterwards how Tullus could have timed his advice better.

Without warning, a shoal of spears flew out of the trees to their left, whipping into Piso's vision as a blur of long, black streaks. A heartbeat later, a similar cloud was hurled from the right. Next came a succession of loud cracks, which was followed by a rain of slingstones, whizzing towards the Romans like so many angry bees. Caught unprepared, without their shields, legionaries were struck down in their dozens. Two of Piso's contubernium slumped dead into the mud, without even the chance to cry out. A spear slammed into the tree behind him; another thumped into the ground by Afer's feet. Behind Tullus, a legionary uttered a surprised 'Ohhhh' as his forehead was smashed by a stone; he dropped like a discarded child's puppet. Piso and his comrades gaped, not believing what they were seeing.

Not far off, a mule brayed. It wasn't the normal, complaining sound, but a deep, distressed cry. Another mule joined in, and then another, mixing with the screams and cries of men that filled the air around them.

Piso felt numb, nauseous, paralysed.

Tullus was on his feet, gesturing. 'Up, you maggots, if you want to live! Grab your fucking shields!'

Guts churning with fear, expecting a spear between the shoulder blades, Piso scrambled towards his scutum. Uncaring that he had no time to take off the leather cover, he lifted it and faced to his left. Fresh fear coursed through him as another volley of spears hummed in from behind, from the trees on the other side. Fresh slingshots poured in as well, from the left, from the right, from above. Ten paces away, a legionary went down, roaring for his mother.

'Pair up with another man,' bawled Tullus, who was standing, shieldless, in the middle of the track. 'Stand back to back – protect one another. Keep your heads down! MOVE!'

Piso shoved himself up against Afer, while Vitellius and Long Nose did the same alongside. Just doing that was respite of a kind, although they still weren't wearing their helmets. Piso watched, amazed, as Tullus stalked up and down, ordering men to join them and form a line. He seemed oblivious to the spears raining down around him, and his calmness transferred in some measure at least to those he confronted. Little by little, man by man, the line began to take shape. As the storm of spears and stones eased, it became a solid file, perhaps thirty paired legionaries, facing both ways towards the once gloomy, now deadly forest.

Another scatter of spears flew out of the trees, wounding one soldier and killing an injured man.

There was a loud crack as a slinger released, and a last stone streaked into sight, thunking harmlessly into a tree.

No more followed.

'Steady, brothers,' cried Tullus. 'It's not over.'

The stunned legionaries glanced at their comrades, at the widespread carnage. Bodies were strewn everywhere: face down in the mud, staring blankly at the grey sky, propped against tree trunks, sprawled over each other. The spears that had silenced their banter forever protruded from their flesh at jaunty angles, like so many hedgehog spines. They stuck into the air from the mud and poked out from tree trunks: *frameae*, fearsome weapons that every Roman recognised. Their shafts varied in length from that of a man's arm to one and a half times his height, and their short, sharp iron blades delivered a mortal wound with ease. Of the stones that had hammered down, there was less sign. Most had vanished into the mud, but occasional examples lay by the men they had slain, innocuous-looking shiny lumps of rock no bigger than hen's eggs.

Tullus' voice broke the silence, giving the legionaries something to do. 'Ease forward, careful like. Pick up your helmets and any javelins that you can, then back to where you were.'

As Piso and his comrades started to obey, a fearful humming began. It rose from the mouths of hundreds of hidden warriors on either side, a deep buzzing sound that made the skin crawl.

HUUUUMMMMMMMM! HUUUUMMMMMMMM! On and on it went, until every hair on the back of Piso's neck stood up. The terrifying sound ebbed and flowed, growing louder and louder each time, as the waves of a rising tide smash with growing intensity off a cliff. At length, it became a deep-throated roar, a swelling shout that even threatened to drown out the sounds of the injured legionaries and the mules.

HUUUUMMMMMMMM! HUUUUMMMMMMMM!

Piso grabbed his helmet, and a javelin, and shot back to where he'd been standing. His comrades were close behind him.

The noise continued unabated for what seemed like an eternity. Just when Piso thought it could get no worse, the singing warriors began to clatter their weapons off the iron rims and bosses of their shields. *CLASH! CLASH! CLASH!* The metallic banging melded with their war cry in terrifying unison.

HUUUUMMMMMMMM! HUUUUMMMMMMMM! CLASH! CLASH! CLASH!

Piso felt an overwhelming need to shit, and he clenched his buttocks tight. Beside him, he heard a man vomit. The tang of fresh piss reached his nostrils a moment later. Wails of fear were rising from elsewhere, and the line of legionaries began to waver.

'If we break, we're fucked,' hissed Afer. 'Stay where you are.'

Grateful to be told what to do, Piso obeyed. The legionary three men along hadn't heard, however, or was too scared to listen. He stepped out of line, naked terror contorting his face. 'They'll kill us all!'

Tullus was on him like a snake coming up out of a burrow on an unsuspecting mouse. *Crack!* His vitis struck the soldier in a flurry of blows – against his helmet, twice, on his chest, over his shoulders. For good measure, Tullus delivered a whack across the face that raised a massive red weal on the man's cheek. 'GET BACK, YOU FUCKING MAGGOT!' he roared. 'INTO LINE, BEFORE I GUT YOU MYSELF!'

Cowed, shame-faced, the legionary retreated. Tullus gave him a withering look before his eyes, stony cold, raked the rest of the soldiers. Few dared meet his gaze. As if the enemy wanted to listen to Tullus, the chanting and hammering of weapons died away. 'That was their war cry, you useless shower of limp-pricks!' yelled Tullus. 'It's called the barritus, in case you didn't know. Yes, it's bloodcurdling. Yes, it's terrifying. Yes, you think you're going to die when you hear it.' Tullus stalked fast along the line, eyeballing them in turn. 'SO FUCKING WHAT? YOU ARE SOLDIERS OF ROME! OF FUCKING ROME! WHAT DO YOU

CARE FOR THE SCREECHING OF A HORDE OF STINKING BARBARIANS? EH? EH?'

'Nothing, sir,' shouted Afer.

Tullus bounded back to stand in front of Afer. 'What's that? I can't hear you!'

'NOTHING, SIR. I DON'T GIVE A SHIT, SIR.'

A pitiless smile split Tullus' face. 'That's right. We don't give a SHIT about them and their fucking war cry, do we? DO WE?'

'NO, SIR!' Piso and the rest roared at him.

Tullus had a shield in one fist now, and a sword in the other. With fierce intensity, he began to beat the blade off the iron rim. At the same time, he chanted, 'ROMA! ROMA! ROMA!'

The legionaries copied him. A little further down the line, Piso heard Fenestela take up the cry, and encourage his men to do the same. Every time the sound was repeated, the soldiers' fear leached away a little, to be replaced if not by courage, then by resolve. When Tullus was content that they had steadied, he ceased his hammering. Piso and his comrades did the same, muttering encouragements to each other, things like, 'We'll show the bastards what for.' 'Let them come!' 'Dirty savages!'

'Ready, my brothers,' said Tullus, from his new position in the centre of the line, facing to the right of the road. 'They might still charge.'

They waited.

And waited.

And waited.

Nothing happened. There was no barrage of spears and stones. The Germans' barritus was not sung again, nor were their shields battered with weapons. The legionaries began to share uncertain looks. If their attackers had not vanished, what in Hades were they doing?

Again Tullus stepped into the breach. 'This is all part of the whoresons' plan. They've gone, for now. Starting with you' – and he pointed at the first legionary in the line – 'every second man is to remain in position. Every other man is to break rank, and see to the injured. Move!'

Piso left the defensive formation with reluctance, but his attention was soon taken up by his injured comrades, many of whom were in urgent need of care. The luckier ones, with bruised ribs and limbs from slingshots, or flesh wounds from spears that had struck glancing blows, were able to look after themselves. Supervised by a prowling Tullus, and directed by a lone orderly who'd appeared, Piso and his comrades made the casualties as comfortable as was possible in the wet, dirty conditions. It was clear that some men would not make it, and Piso grew used to seeing the orderly giving them long pulls from his flask of poppy juice. His mind was quick to turn from the fate of the wounded to his own, and his comrades'. Their attackers, whoever they were, had gone, but they might well return. The army was yet at a standstill. Fresh fear licked at Piso's spine. They were like a shoal of fish, left by the ebbing tide in a tiny rock pool: easy prey.

'What are we going to do, sir?' he asked the next time Tullus came striding by.

'We're waiting for orders,' replied Tullus. A shadow flickered across his face. 'We'll be told to get moving, and find a place to camp. Making plans about what to do will be easier behind fortifications.'

Afer joined in. 'Was it the Angrivarii who attacked us, sir?'

The darkness passed again over Tullus' face, but Piso still had no idea what was going through his centurion's mind. 'That's what many will say,' said Tullus. He walked off. 'Be ready to move at a moment's notice.'

Piso eyed Afer. 'What's up with him?'

'No bloody idea. What matters is that he's here, eh?'

'Aye,' replied Piso with feeling. Rumours had reached them from down the column of heavy casualties among other units, of dead centurions, foundered wagons and widespread panic among the non-combatants. Whatever they had suffered here was mild by comparison, and it was attributable in the main to Tullus. 'May the gods keep him safe.'

'I'll second that,' said Vitellius, raising his eyes to the grey, cloud-covered heavens.

If the gods heard their prayers, they were not interested. Heavy rain began to fall once more, pouring down on their upturned faces in torrents and increasing the already deep gloom. Lightning flashed deep within the clouds, once, twice, thrice. A few heartbeats later, there was an ominous rumble of thunder.

It was hard not to think that Jupiter was angry with them, thought Piso, seeing his own unspoken disquiet mirrored in his friends' faces.

Piso had not thought his dislike of the forest could escalate, but in the sodden, bloody hours that followed, he grew to loathe it with every fibre of his being. It became the limits of the Romans' world. Dense, green, dripping with moisture, it appeared to go on forever, mile upon mile of beeches, hornbeams, oaks and trees Piso didn't even recognise. Tall ones, shorter ones, thick-trunked and thin-, gnarled, diseased, aged and saplings, they stood side by side, in disapproving legions of their own, sentinels at the entrance to another world. At times, it seemed to Piso that they were watching the sweating, tired legionaries. *That* was a most uncomfortable feeling, inviting thoughts of malign forest spirits, druids and blood sacrifice.

Rare breaks in the endless treeline included areas of bog and the damnable streams and rivers that had to be forded. The dangers posed by the former were played out in grisly detail when a mule that had broken away from its handler charged headlong into the middle of a patch, where it sank at once to its hocks. Braying with indignation, it struggled to get free, succeeding only in burying itself to its belly. Further frantic efforts saw it end up chest deep in the mud. Its plight attracted the attention of everyone within sight, but nobody moved to help it. Grateful that they were not the ones trapped, many soldiers hurled insults at the unfortunate beast. Piso considered throwing a javelin at it, to try and end its misery before it endured a slow death by drowning, but his aim wasn't good enough, and if Tullus or Fenestela saw him 'wasting' a weapon, there'd be hell to pay. And as Afer reminded him, it was a damn mule, not a man.

The watercourses were less perilous than the bog, but there was still ample opportunity to trip and fall thanks to the moss-covered, slimy rocks lining their banks, and the difficulty in negotiating them carrying shield, javelins and unwieldy yoke. A legionary in the contubernium ahead of Piso and his comrades slipped and broke a leg, and others sprained ankles or bloodied their kneecaps. As the cursing soldiers reminded one another, they were fortunate not to be in charge of any vehicles. 'The poor bastards with the artillery must be cursing Fortuna high and low. Imagine trying to heave a fucking wagon with a *ballista* on the back of it through this,' said Vitellius during the crossing of the deepest stream yet.

Their relative 'good luck' did nothing for Piso's flagging spirits. They had covered perhaps a mile in the previous hour.

Without warning, their attackers reappeared, like invisible wraiths. Once again, the first indication of trouble was when volleys of spears and sling bullets began landing among the legionaries. Curses mixed with cries of pain. Unperturbed, Tullus ordered an immediate volley of javelins to one side of the track, and then the other. Not every soldier had two *pila* remaining – many had been discarded or lost at the site of the previous ambush – and their ragged effort lacked its usual power, but the screams that rose when the missiles landed was proof that they had at last inflicted casualties on the enemy.

A ragged cheer went up, but Piso wasn't alone in being relieved when Tullus ordered them to continue marching rather than standing their ground. 'There's no fucking point in waiting to be killed,' he bellowed. 'We keep moving. Somewhere, there'll be a spot where we can build a camp.'

No one argued. Leaving the three dead soldiers where they had fallen, and hauling the handful of wounded along as best they could, the legionaries trudged on. The men on either side used their shields to protect those in the middle. Frameae and stones were still able to come in from above, but that was a danger that had to be borne. Their waterlogged *scuta* were so heavy that walking with them raised beyond head level was impossible for more than twenty paces.

It didn't take the enemy long to exploit this weakness. Raising the barritus again, they threw their spears up in steep-angled arcs, which sent them scudding down into the midst of the bunched Romans, where they could not miss. Two such volleys had half a dozen legionaries down, dead or injured. Cursing, Tullus ordered the men in the centre to discard their yokes and raise their shields in defence. He kept them walking, but their progress on the narrow track slowed down to snail's pace thanks to the weight of their scuta, and the number of casualties that they were supporting or carrying.

HUUUUMMMMMMMM! HUUUUMMMMMMMM! HUUUUMM MMMMMM! A heartbeat's pause, then: *CLASH! CLASH! CLASH!* It was repeated over and over.

Piso wished he could block his ears to the chilling sounds, wished he could confront the men who were killing them. At least then they could fight back. All he could see, however, were shadowy figures deep within the trees. Pursuing them would be suicide.

'Keep moving, you stupid fucking bastards!' shouted Tullus at the soldiers in front, who had halted again.

'Our centurion's been hit, sir,' shouted a legionary in their midst.

'Keep your shields up,' Tullus ordered his men. 'I'll be back soon.'

Piso and his comrades watched in disbelief as Tullus walked, casual as a man taking a stroll through the forum, around the side of the unit before them. The instant that their attackers saw his horsehair-crested helmet, they began hurling spears and stones.

Piso couldn't watch. He closed his eyes and prayed: Mars, protect him, please.

To his astonishment, Tullus sauntered back not long after. A few paces from his men's shield wall, he even paused to make obscene gestures at the forest, and their hidden attackers. 'Fuck you,' he shouted in German. 'And your pox-ridden mothers!'

His legionaries let out a loud cheer.

Angry cries rose from the trees, and a fresh shower of stones and spears were thrown. There was a loud *clang* as a sling bullet struck Tullus in the back, on his mail shirt. Piso heard the centurion let out a short grunt, but Tullus swaggered back into his position at the front of their formation. The legionaries closed ranks with him at once.

'You all right, sir?' asked Afer, his face creased with concern.

'Aye,' said Tullus, wincing now that he was out of sight of their enemies. 'I'll have a fine bruise, but that's it.' The soldiers in front began to move, and Tullus cried, 'Ready, brothers? Forward, march!'

Despite the showers of enemy missiles and stones, and the unremitting downpour from the clouds above, they managed to make decent progress from that point on. Their march was made easier in no small part by the track, which began to run straight as a Roman road. There were no more large streams either, just shallow affairs that could be splashed through.

After a time, the warriors attacking Tullus and the rest of the vanguard withdrew again. One moment, they were there, and the next, they had disappeared. There was no way of knowing if this ploy applied to the rest of the column. For all Piso and his comrades knew, it was still under attack – communication with other parts of the army bordered on non-existent. It didn't appear to concern Tullus – 'We've been ordered to locate a campsite,' he said, as if they were on a training exercise near Vetera. 'And that's what we'll do.' His calm manner and bloody-minded determination rubbed off on his men, including Piso. They began singing a bawdy marching tune, which Tullus encouraged by joining in lustily with the chorus.

Morale rose further when a low hill appeared close to the track, on the left-hand side. After a brief meeting, Tullus and the other centurions decided that this would be the spot to build the camp. Work began at once, in the traditional fashion, with half the available legionaries providing a protective screen around the remainder, who began felling trees and digging the position's defensive ditch.

Their respite was brief. Their enemies reappeared soon after the construction had begun, emerging from the forest in a great, chanting horde. It was the first time that the Romans had had a proper glimpse of their foes. They were an intimidating sight, hundreds of burly tribesmen in brightly coloured tunics and trousers, with painted shields and spears, who advanced while singing the barritus. Their slingers walked behind, laying down volleys of stones far in front as the warriors moved forward.

Despite the Germans' ferocity, and the losses they'd inflicted on the Romans up to that point, seeing them steadied the legionaries. A face-to-face confrontation with the assailants who'd plagued them for hours was a relief. They weren't forest spirits or demons. They were men, like themselves, who sweated, and bled if they were stuck with a blade. Few had any armour, and most had only spears to fight with. They could be defeated – had been defeated, many times, by the legions. And, as Tullus and other centurions roared at their soldiers, there was no reason that they couldn't be beaten again.

The assault was short and vicious, but the legionaries threw back the warriors, inflicting heavy losses. Undeterred, the Germans rallied and attacked again, but more and more Roman troops – from the column – were arriving on the scene. Their officers flung their soldiers into combat, driving back the warriors for a second time. A third effort also failed. The tribesmen withdrew into the trees and were gone.

Piso did not share in the widespread jubilation that broke out as this happened. He too was pleased by the Romans' success, but he'd listened in on Tullus as he talked with Fenestela not long before. What he'd heard was most unsettling. Tullus didn't think that they'd been ambushed solely by Angrivarii. In his opinion, there were thousands more warriors out there in the forest, ready to fall upon them. His final words to Fenestela rang in Piso's head over and over. 'The tribes have joined forces. Only one man could have done this – and that is someone who knows the legions inside out. From now on, it's about survival, pure and simple. What's important is to get as many of our brothers out as we can.'

That implied that Tullus thought more men would die, thought Piso, his belly clenching tight with fear.

Many more men.

XXIII

By nightfall, the vast majority of Varus' troops were safe behind the unfinished defences of the vast camp on the hillside. The tribesmen were no fools, Varus decided, leaving his command tent. They had withdrawn not long since, unprepared to lose more casualties in open battle. Secure in the knowledge that his soldiers would have a night's respite, he had decided to walk around the camp. The calamity that had befallen his army that day, and the casualties it had suffered, had stunned his soldiers. He had seen the proof of that in the haggard faces as he'd entered the camp some time before. Showing his face might raise morale.

The savagery of the day's attacks had ensured that their problems would continue overnight. Thanks to the number of abandoned wagons and mules that had gone missing, a good number of Varus' men didn't have tents to sleep in that night or dry wood to use in cooking fires. The rain that was still falling wouldn't kill them, nor would the cooling temperatures, but the added privations would be further blows to their confidence.

Ordering a wagon loaded with his entire personal supply of wine, Varus began walking the avenues of the camp, with a reluctant Aristides and a score of soldiers from the First Cohort as company. At every turn, there was evidence that the disorder and chaos affecting his army that day continued. The main streets, the via principalis and the via praetoria, had not been measured and set by an engineer with a groma. Their usual right angles to one another were absent, and there was a noticeable crookedness in the way they ran to the entrances. There were tree stumps everywhere, the remnants of the forest that had covered the hill until a short time before. They varied in size from a lethal tripping-over ankle height to easier-to-spot waist-high affairs. The positions occupied by each unit had been preserved, Varus was pleased to see, but there were far too few tents, and less than half the expected number of mules.

Those legionaries who'd been fortunate enough to locate their heavier gear were safe inside their tents, but other groups of men crouched in miserable huddles in the spots where theirs should have been. Some were using their propped-up scuta and draped-over cloaks as makeshift protection against the rain. Several *contubernia* had even built mini *testudos*, utilising the slope of the hill as a backdrop. Chopped branches held up their shields, and on top they had laid blankets and spare garments. Varus took the time to commend them on this ingenious solution to their lack of shelter. It was heart-warming to note how many centurions were ordering men under the leather porticos of their own capacious tents, and even into them.

Before long, Varus decided to start doling out the wine. Picking a spot at random, he called out, 'Wine ration!' It amused him that the soldiers' response was more rapid, more dramatic, than if he'd followed more normal procedure and had his presence announced. They charged over, uncaring of the mud. At first, no one recognised Varus, clad in an ordinary soldier's cloak, without his helmet. They swarmed around him, smiling, jostling and demanding to know which blessed officer had sanctioned the wine. No one paid any attention to Aristides' disapproving face and muttered comments about their overfamiliarity.

'I did,' said Varus. 'This is my own supply.'

Incomprehension played across the sweaty, dirt-caked faces around him for a heartbeat. Then there was shock, and surprise, and fear. Soldiers who had pressed close to Varus in their eagerness to get some wine shoved backwards against the crowd, while trying to salute and tell their comrades who had appeared in their midst.

'Governor Varus! You honour us with your presence,' cried a legionary with more wherewithal than most.

'It's the governor!' 'Jupiter, it's Varus!' 'Varus has brought his own wine to share with us!' went the incredulous remarks.

A cheer went up, and then another.

Smiling, Varus raised his hands for silence. 'It's been a hard day for every one of us. You've done well, all of you. I am proud of you. Rome is proud of you!'

They cheered again then. 'ROMA! ROMA! ROMA!' It was a hoarse, defiant sound that rose into the darkening sky until it was lost in the clouds.

'Tomorrow will be tough too, I can promise you that,' said Varus, when they had quietened. 'But the going will be easier. We will abandon the baggage train, and leave the forest. The Angrivarii can be dealt with another time. Our destination will be the forts on the Lupia River. Two to three days' march should see us to safety there.'

They liked that, thought Varus, pleased to see the life returning to men's eyes. When he ordered that each soldier was to receive a second, brimming cup of wine, they roared louder and longer than before. 'I'd give you more,' said Varus, 'but I have a whole army to see to.' Laughter broke out now, and by the time he'd signalled the wagon to start moving again, the legionaries were even joking with one another.

Varus had had little idea how successful the wine-delivering mission would prove to be. He was received everywhere by a rapturous audience of soldiers. It seemed that the distribution of free wine by the governor himself was worth a great deal more than a few missing tents. What was supposed to have taken an hour or so soon became something that would occupy much of the evening. At length, Varus reined in his enthusiasm. The meeting with his officers was also vital. 'Aristides, you're to finish this,' he ordered.

Aristides' face registered many kinds of unhappiness, but somehow he restricted it to a plaintive, 'Me, master?'

Varus found his heart hardening, even though Aristides looked exhausted.

The Greek had trudged the last five miles on foot, after the wagon he'd been riding on lost a wheel. Yet he wasn't dead, or injured. 'Yes, damn it,' said Varus. 'You can't fight, but you *can* make yourself useful. To get to Vetera, you need these soldiers' protection. Keeping their spirits up is therefore vital – can't you see that?'

'Yes, master,' replied Aristides, humbled.

'When you're done, requisition the legates' wine too. I want every soldier in the damn army to have had a cup of wine before the second watch sounds. This is my direct order. Anyone who hinders you does so at their own peril.'

The delegation of power made Aristides' chin lift. 'I will see that it's done, master.'

Varus found his senior officers waiting for him in his tent, more than forty of them. They were legates, camp commanders, tribunes, senior centurions and auxiliary commanders. If every senior centurion had been present, there would have been in excess of fifty men. The absence of more than ten spoke volumes about the army's losses that day. Invigorated by the reception he'd had from the soldiers, Varus thrust these grievous casualties from his mind. He stalked through the gathering to his desk, which had been set up with his favourite chair and the lampstands he always took on campaign.

Realising he had arrived, the officers cut short their conversations, smiled and saluted, greeting Varus. Inside a dozen heartbeats, he felt their unspoken hopes, expectations and fears as a physical weight, pressing down on his shoulders like a full sack of grain. With an effort, he threw that off too. 'I thank you for coming.' Calling for a servant, he ordered wine be brought before remembering that he'd given it away. With a smile, he recounted the tale of what he'd done. His story met with what appeared to be unforced approval, which pleased him. Varus had long since learned that his high office tended to guarantee men's support, whether they meant it or not. In this case, however, it mattered to him that they thought his move a good idea. They were all in the same boat. 'First, I want a rough idea of our losses. Vala?'

With a grim nod, Vala began to speak. When he'd finished, his fellow legates made their reports, followed by the auxiliary commanders. Varus listened in silence, feeling a rising sense of fury that his scouts had not been able to prevent the ambush. Where in Hades were you, Arminius? he wondered as the last officer finished his report. 'It's to be expected that losses varied from unit to unit, and legion to legion, and that the cavalry suffered the most, because of the easy targets their horses made for enemy spears. What's heartening is that our casualties were not more severe.' Varus glanced at the centurions, whom everyone knew were the backbone of the army. When it came to fractured, close-quarters fighting, they were crucial. 'I'm grateful for your leadership today, and that of your fellow officers. Your comrades who died or were wounded today will not be forgotten, nor will those ordinary soldiers who lost their lives.'

To a man, the centurions looked pleased.

'I calculate that our overall strength has been reduced by a tenth, perhaps a little more,' Varus continued. 'These casualties are regrettable, but in the light of the element of surprise, the poor weather, and our inability to fight back, they're acceptable. What's vital is that they are not repeated. The best way of ensuring that is to get out of the damn forest, into the open. The savages won't dare to attack us there, where our legionaries' superior armour and weapons can be brought to bear.'

Loud rumbles of agreement followed, but Ceionius, a skinny officer whose uniform always seemed too large for him, cleared his throat. 'You mentioned the baggage, sir. Do you mean to leave it behind? With it, we won't be able to fight as you've described.'

'That's my exact intention, Ceionius. The baggage train is to be abandoned in the morning. The only equipment to be carried is what the men can carry on their backs, and the wounded, of course. Some of the wagons' planking can be utilised to make litters for them, I would imagine.'

'And the artillery, sir?' asked one of the senior tribunes. 'We don't want the savages laying their hands on that.'

'Indeed not. The ballistae and any weaponry left behind – including spare pila heads, sword blades and so on – must be broken or damaged so that it's unusable. Burn the wagons. Despoil any grain that's not being taken. The mules need to be killed too – the men can eat the meat tonight. Use the olive oil to start the cooking fires.' Varus glanced at the assembled faces. 'Equipment and mules can be replaced, but dead men can't be brought back to life. Does anyone disagree?'

There was a chorus of 'No, sir'.

'What about the civilians, sir, and the hangers-on?' asked Eggius, a block-headed officer with stubbly grey hair.

Everyone's eyes focused on Varus, who might have been discomfited if he hadn't prepared for this. Like as not, some of the officers had women following the army, but that wasn't his concern. 'The legions are to march in battle order,' he said in an iron-hard voice. 'All non-combatants are to take their proper place, at the rear of the column. They must keep up as best they can.'

The silence that fell was awkward. No one wanted to imagine the fate of those who fell into the Germans' hands. Varus maintained his stony expression, and nobody dared question him. 'We will strike out for the Lupia, and the forts along the road west. I'm told that it is open countryside for the most part. There's some bog, and small areas of forest, but it's nothing like what we travelled through today. Within two days, three at the most, we'll be back in Vetera.'

'That sounds good, sir,' said Eggius with a grim smile, to a chorus of agreement.

Varus' mind was already roving past their safe return. If he didn't take decisive action soon after this setback, Augustus could relieve him of his governorship early. At his age, and after such an error, there would be little chance of redemption. It was repugnant to think of a slow decline in a seaside villa, his wife's nagging voice in his ear, while the world went about its business without him. He steeled his resolve.

'The weather won't worsen much for a month or more, which affords us time to deal with this rebellion before winter. The moment we have regrouped on the west bank of the Rhenus, therefore, I intend to seek out these accursed Angrivarii and wipe them from the face of the earth.'

His officers liked that, and Varus prayed that Augustus would too.

'Do you think Arminius is lost, sir?' This was Tubero.

Varus noticed Tullus studying him with an intense expression. Tullus had been concerned about Arminius' loyalties before, and had been courageous enough to raise this with him. Perhaps he'd been right all along? Nonsense, you're thinking nonsense, Varus told himself. Arminius will turn up in the end, or we'll hear news of his death in battle against the Angrivarii. At dawn, they would march out of this dreary, rain-soaked forest, and escape their attackers. Within a few days, this mess would be nothing more than an unpleasant memory. 'Yes, I do,' he snapped. 'Something must have befallen him and his men, or he would have returned by now.'

It was easier for Varus to ignore Tullus' stony expression than to challenge it. He took a deep breath and let it out, slowly. Calmer, he said, 'The auxiliary cavalry and infantry are to stay closer to the vanguard than normal tomorrow – I want no units caught out on their own should the enemy attack. As custom dictates, a different legion will lead the army tomorrow. I nominate the Seventeenth. Every other unit will take its usual place in the column, with the exception of the baggage, obviously. Ten riders from each legion's cavalry are to be used as messengers, to ensure that all of us know what's going on.' Varus was pleased at the determination he saw rising in his officers' eyes. 'If we keep our heads, and do not stop marching, we will be through the worst of it by tomorrow evening. A few thousand tribesmen aren't going to stop three Roman legions, are they?'

The answering roar proved to Varus, as his mission to distribute the wine, that those who followed him were not even close to being beaten.

Tomorrow would be different, he decided. A better day for them all.

Arminius hadn't wanted to be absent during the first part of the ambush, but it had been unavoidable. He'd had to coordinate the tribes as they rallied at the agreed point, some miles to the east of the Roman column, greeting their chieftains like conquering heroes, ensuring that old tribal enmities weren't restarted and making certain that they dispersed to the areas that he had decided upon. He had broken the back of his tasks by mid-afternoon, at which point he led his four thousand Cheruscan warriors, eager-faced and armed to the teeth, westward, towards the foe. There would be time that evening to meet all of the chieftains together.

The heavy rain and driving wind did nothing to lower their spirits. To Arminius' followers, the severe weather was physical proof that Donar approved of their ambush. Arminius himself felt blessed. Despite a number of near escapes – Tullus' suspicion, which he'd been aware of, the risks posed by the drunk young warriors, and Segestes' warning, which he had heard about afterwards – he had succeeded in keeping his plan secret until the end. With flashes of lightning searing his eyeballs and thunder battering his eardrums, it was hard even for him to feel sceptical about the divine backing for his plan.

They came upon the camp of the Usipetes and Sugambri first, a sprawling affair of lean-tos made from branches and leaves, small tents and animal hides tacked up between close-growing trees. Judging by the whoops and cheers that met their arrival, things had gone well thus far.

'Welcome, Arminius,' cried a massive warrior, brandishing a cohort standard in the air. 'Our spears are well blooded, but we left plenty of Romans for you and your men.'

'My warriors will thank you for that,' replied Arminius, noting the plentiful signs of a victorious clash with Varus' soldiers. There were many men wearing Roman-issue helmets, and over there, he saw a pair play-threatening each other with *gladii.*

At that point, he was spied by Red Head, who was in the midst of a group of warriors standing around a makeshift firepit covered by an ox skin. He came striding over. 'Well met, Arminius.'

Arminius dismounted, and embraced Red Head. 'It went as we'd hoped, I take it?' he asked.

Red Head threw back his head and laughed, uncaring of the rain that spattered his face. 'It was as if the gods had come down to earth and fought with us! The filthy Romans had no idea that we were there until the first spears and stones landed among them. You should have heard their wails – they were like swine in a slaughterman's pens. Their cries grew even more pathetic when they heard the barritus. They died in their hundreds, while not a single warrior fell. We withdrew and let them march on awhile before attacking them again, with almost the same results. Give them credit, the bastards kept moving forward, and at the hill where they chose to camp, they gave a good account of themselves. We lost more men than we should have there, because some of our warriors had grown cocky with the ambush's success, and tried to take the enemy head-on.'

Angry at this departure from his plan, Arminius began to interrupt, but Red Head was having none of it. 'I see you shaking your head,' he said, his voice rising, 'but remember how four hundred of our young men died not three months since.' Arminius made an apologetic gesture, and Red Head's frown eased. 'It's easy for *you* to remember how disciplined the Romans are. You've fought alongside them for many years. Our chieftains managed to regain control of the warriors soon enough when a couple of charges had come to naught. So did the Sugambri's leaders. We left the Romans to lick their wounds and wonder what in the name of all the gods had happened to them.'

'You did well,' said Arminius in a hearty tone, aware that nothing held his alliance together other than a mutual hatred of the Romans. If he tried to exert more than a subtle authority over the other tribes, they would fade away like stars in a brightening sky. A few dozen dead warriors would make no difference to the size of his army. 'How many men are watching their camp?'

'Two score. They're hidden close to every entrance. Not even a rat can leave the place without us knowing.'

'Fine work,' cried Arminius, throwing an arm over Red Head's shoulders.

'Many thousands of the Romans remain living,' said Red Head. 'Did the other tribes honour their pledge?'

'I am also the bearer of good – nay – excellent tidings,' replied Arminius, smiling. 'Four thousand Cheruscan warriors marched here with me. The Marsi are nearby, with all of their strength. So too are the Angrivarii, Bructeri and some of the Chauci. The Chatti have also sworn to help, although they might not arrive before we have massacred every last Roman in Varus' army. Without taking their strength into consideration, there are still more than eighteen thousand warriors within three miles of here.'

Red Head's eyes were full of respect. 'Never did I think to hear of so many tribes united with one purpose. Truly, the gods blessed you with a silver tongue, Arminius of the Cherusci. To think I came close to killing you.'

If you had even an inkling of my men's role in the slaying of your young warriors, thought Arminius, you still would. 'I thank Donar every day that you had the wisdom to let me speak. My success is in great part thanks to men like you – and so will the final result, when we annihilate Varus' legions and drive Rome from our lands forever.'

If Red Head had had a tail, he would have wagged it then. 'This calls for a drink! Come, there is beer by my fire. The other chieftains will want to hear your news, and to question you about tomorrow.'

Arminius allowed Red Head to lead him towards the group of warriors. His heart was singing. Donar had been patient with him for many years, but tomorrow he would fulfil his vow at last.

Tomorrow.

XXIV

The following morning Tullus rose when it was still dark. Leaving his tent, he found the world cloaked in a damp, cold mist. He ordered the unit's dead fires to be rekindled at once. Some of the oil that had to be destroyed was at hand, making it easy to ignite the damp wood. By the time the trumpets sounded, a reasonable amount of mule flesh had been cooked for his men.

Soldiers with full bellies marched better than hungry ones, he thought with satisfaction as he patrolled the lines, noting the pleasure with which the meat was being consumed. Exhorting each man to do his best that day, he ordered every third legionary to retain his trenching tool. This was against Varus' command, which was to leave behind everything that wasn't a weapon, but Tullus didn't care. It was one thing to discard their heavy leather tents and excess equipment, but it was foolish to divest themselves of all of the tools with which to dig defences.

Following Varus' orders, the Seventeenth was in the vanguard. It was standard procedure for the first legion to change, but Tullus was most unhappy. Stuck in the middle of the miles-long column, surrounded on both sides by interminable trees or marshy fenland, he and his soldiers had not the slightest clue what was happening. Worse, they were helpless to do anything but follow in the quagmire left by those who had gone before. In the depths of Tullus' mind, barely admitted, there was also the niggling concern that if things went really wrong, he and his men would be trapped. He buried the worry as best he could: resignation would get him nowhere. Today was about marching. Surviving. Protecting his troops.

Despite his unease, things went well at first. Everyone was keen to vacate the temporary camp, and the legions got moving with a minimum of delay. The soldiers with common-law wives and families grumbled and bitched, yet they had to follow their orders, like everyone else. Leaving those who could not travel fast – even their injured comrades in the few wagons that had been retained – was easy for the rest. Nevertheless, Tullus was glad when he could no longer hear the wails of distressed babies, the laments of their overburdened mothers and the moans of men who knew that they were, to all intents and purposes, being abandoned. As the legions left the hill, palls of smoke from the burning wagons streaked the sky, and the air was rich with the smell of the olive oil used to set them alight.

There was universal relief when the tribesmen who had plagued them the previous day did not appear. Spirits rose further as the trees were replaced by an area of scrubby grass, not unlike the lands around Porta Westfalica. The open ground meant that the marching pace could pick up, and soon the speed was approaching half of what could be made on a decent Roman road. This was a vast improvement compared to their pitiful progress the day before, and men began to sing. By the time they had bawled their way through three old favourites, Tullus was starting to enjoy himself. He'd heard each of the chants a thousand times before, but when sung loud enough, they still had the power to bring him back to his youth, and the campaigns he had made as a wide-eyed low-ranker.

It was then that the army ground to a halt.

Tullus' soldiers continued to sing, but he waved them into silence. There was no apparent cause for the stop, no sounds of combat, no officers shouting orders. No tribesmen were visible on either side of the cohort's position. It could have been a river or stream that had blocked their passage, but Tullus had a nasty feeling that somewhere up ahead, another ambush had been sprung.

He had his soldiers stand to arms. A sombre air fell as they waited, shields up, javelins at the ready. Nothing happened for a hundred heartbeats. Two hundred. Tullus roared out a question to the legionaries in front, the First Cohort. Beyond them were the legates and tribunes, who were the most likely to know what was going on. After a short delay, he was told that 'You have as much idea as we do', which did nothing for his darkening mood.

The enemy did not appear. Time ground by in a succession of gusty squalls and heavy showers, and an occasional view from behind the ever-present clouds of a beleaguered, pale yellow sun. At length, Tullus ordered his men to ground their shields. They seemed if not happy, then satisfied, drinking from their water bags and talking in low voices amongst themselves. Scanning the landscape, Tullus could see no cause for alarm. That didn't stop his gut from knotting as if he had a bad case of the shits. He'd have liked to confer with Degmar, but there had been no sign of him since the previous day, when he had gone off scouting. Tullus hoped he was still alive.

Fenestela came to find him, his face sour with suspicion. 'What do you think, sir?'

'I think the savages have fucking well sprung another ambush up ahead. All we can do is wait until the vanguard fights its way through.'

Fenestela spat by way of agreement. 'Filthy animal-humping savages.'

Tullus came to an abrupt decision. 'Might as well keep busy. It will stop the men worrying. Have an inventory made of the javelins that are left. The men are to check their equipment.' Tullus began to say more, but chuckled instead at Fenestela's know-it-all expression. 'You're aware of the drill.'

'Aye,' replied Fenestela, smirking. 'You could say that.'

'Go on, piss off. Report to me when you're done,' Tullus ordered with a smile, and thinking that whatever happened, Fenestela had to be among those who survived.

Some time passed – without a visible sun, it was impossible to say how long, but Tullus judged it less than an hour – before a messenger appeared.

Tullus, who was talking again to Fenestela, beckoned as the legionary approached from the direction of the First Cohort. The man's pulpy-looking nose, the recipient of many a punch, stirred his memory, but it wasn't until the soldier reached him that Tullus recalled where they had met. It had been in Vetera, the night that Piso had won too many games of dice.

'Centurion.' Broken Nose saluted, giving no indication that he knew Tullus. 'Are you in charge of the cohort?'

'I am. What news?'

'The vanguard ran into trouble a while back, sir. There was another section of forest, where the savages were lying in wait. Thousands of them, it seems, far more than yesterday.'

If Varus had been present, Tullus would have struggled not to gut him in that moment. Arminius is behind this devilry, he thought. He *has* to be. Fenestela's scowl proved the same thought was in his mind. 'Go on,' Tullus commanded.

'There was heavy fighting, sir. The Gaulish cavalry's horses were panicked by the volleys of spears and stones. The Gauls pulled back, and got tangled up with the auxiliary cohorts, which allowed the enemy to attack at will. It sounds as if they've been almost wiped out. The Seventeenth lost quite a few men too, but they forced a way through eventually. The savages have pulled back now, and the column is moving again.'

'Is there a battle plan?' asked Tullus, knowing there wouldn't – in this grimmest of situations, couldn't – be.

Broken Nose looked uncomfortable. 'Governor Varus has ordered that we continue to advance, at all costs. That's what I was told to tell you, sir.'

'Very well.'

Broken Nose saluted and made to go, but Tullus raised a hand. 'Wait.'

'Sir?'

'What's your name?'

'Marcus Aius, sir,' Broken Nose replied.

It *is* him, thought Tullus. 'Fabricius is your centurion?' He enjoyed the confusion playing across Aius' face that he should know this. 'Well?'

'Yes, sir, he is.'

'You lost a pair of bronze fasteners at dice a little while back, didn't you? The ones for the shoulders of a mail shirt.' Tullus noted the delayed recognition, and then fear, that flared in Aius' eyes.

'I did, sir.'

'If I hear a *single* word about how the soldiers of the First Cohort didn't fight as they should have today, or even how they ran away, I will come looking for *you*,' warned Tullus. 'It won't be fasteners that I shove up your nostril this time either. Understand, you cocksucker?'

Aius nodded.

'Fuck off then, and report to whoever else you're supposed to.'

Tullus felt Fenestela's gaze on him as Aius retreated. He muttered a quick explanation.

'I'd give anything to be in the middle of a bar fight rather than what we're heading into,' Fenestela commented as trumpets ahead of them sounded the advance.

'Aye, that'd be better.' Tullus threw a grim glance at the sky, which was blacker than ever. More rain was coming. Thunder and lightning too. In this dark moment, it was difficult even for a hardened cynic not to think that the gods were unhappy with them, that the tribesmen's deities, powerful in their own heartland, might pose a real threat to the lives of every man in Varus' army.

Jupiter, Greatest and Best, Tullus asked, I beseech you to watch over us now, in our hour of need. Let your thunder terrify our enemies, and your lightning bolts strike them down – Arminius most of all.

Step by muddy step, Tullus and his cohort trudged forward. Their pace was no better than a slow walk, which frustrated and increased tension among his men. Tullus was not immune to the feelings either. When combat threatened, men hated to linger at its edges, waging a losing battle against nausea and the constant need to empty one's bowels or bladder. Yet here in this Stygian gloom, where the only illumination was from lightning flashes, and rolling thunder made it hard to hear a man's voice more than five paces away, it was hard to find the will to fight.

Their slow progress, in a line, reminded Tullus of the way a miller poured wheat into a grindstone. Once the stream of grains fell, there was no way back, just a descent into the hole in the stone's centre, a brief, encompassing blackness, and then oblivion as the top stone moved over the bottom and ground everything to flour. The image made Tullus feel queasy. He ignored the feeling as best he could and concentrated instead on his soldiers, on their readiness, on their morale. His responsibility towards them was a heavy burden, but it was a sharp way of focusing his mind. 'Hold steady, brothers,' he called out at regular intervals as he paced alongside his century. 'There's hot wine waiting for you in Vetera! I'll pay for the first round myself, for the whole damn cohort. Hold on to that happy thought as you march!'

Tullus worried that he was filling the air with useless words, but it seemed to give his men some solace. Their eyes were wary, fearful, and many were praying out loud or rubbing their phallus amulets. Nonetheless, they gave him nods, or shakes of their heads, as if to say, 'We're not done yet.'

At length, the trees in which the latest ambush had been sprung drew near. The sound of fighting – shouts, cries, the clash of arms – had been audible for a little while, even with the thunder. All eyes were fixed towards their front. To everyone's frustration, most of what they could see was the back of the First Cohort. The only men with a wider range of vision were those to the far left and right; they shouted descriptions of what could be seen constantly in response to their comrades' questions. Tullus did nothing to stop this. Information, even a little, was power of a kind. It gave men who felt helpless the idea that they had some degree of control over what was going on.

When he wasn't issuing orders, Tullus also stared into the distance, where running figures were now visible to either side of the column. They were tribesmen attacking and retreating, he assumed. Bring them within reach of my sword soon, he prayed. Let this damn waiting be over!

Two hundred paces from the trees, Tullus was as shocked as anyone else when another ambush was sprung – on them. With loud shouts, scores of warriors rose up from the vegetation to either side of his soldiers. The bastards have lain there, letting thousands of us walk by, thought Tullus in alarm. They were close, dangerously close. Perhaps thirty paces separated their hiding places – nothing more than the bracken, cotton grass and bog rosemary that grew there – from the track, and the Roman column. Bearded, clad in dark colours, waving shields and spears, they charged forward in a muddy, disorganised mass. The barritus rose from their midst, like the wail of demons from the underworld.

HUUUUMMMMMMMM! HUUUUMMMMMMMM!

The chant didn't have the volume of the previous day – there weren't enough of them – but the effect was the same. With the memory of what had happened to their comrades bright in their minds, Tullus' soldiers quailed at this unexpected assault. Fear oozed from them like pus from a lanced abscess, and their formation wavered.

Time fractured for Tullus. His eyes shot from left to right, behind him, took in a succession of random images. The terror in a nearby legionary's face. Another man who had dropped his shield. A third had fallen to his knees and appeared to be praying to the gods for mercy. Fenestela was raining blows on soldiers' backs with the flat of his blade, roaring at them to form a line to either side. One fool had broken ranks and was running towards the Germans, weaponless. It was moments such as this in which battles were won or lost. If his legionaries didn't stand now, they'd be butchered.

Rage filled Tullus. I'm not going to fucking die here, he thought. Not here. Not now. Not today. 'FACE LEFT! FACE RIGHT! SHIELDS UP!' he roared. 'CLOSE ORDER!'

He wheeled right, shoved in against the next man, prayed that the legionaries behind him were doing the same, or he'd end up with a spear in his back. The tribesmen were closer, only twenty paces away. Tullus could see their bared teeth, the sweat beading their brows, the sharp points of their frameae. It was risky, but: 'PILA! NOW!'

Not all the soldiers with javelins heard his order, or responded in time, but some did. A light shower of shafts shot out from the Romans' ranks. At such close range, every one hit something. A man, a shield, it didn't matter, thought Tullus. The volley checked the warriors' charge a fraction, which was vital. Their barritus caught for a heartbeat and, into that silence, Tullus screamed, 'DRAW SWORDS, AND HOLD!'

The tribesmen were no fools. They came on with speed, and maintaining their cohesion. Less than a dozen paces out, they separated at last, the barritus replaced by screams of hatred. Four of them made for Tullus, no doubt because of his crested helmet – or perhaps because he was the last man in the line. A trace of panic entered his mind. If they snaked around him and drove in between the two ranks, it was all over. 'IS THERE ANYONE BEHIND ME?' he shouted.

The answering 'Ayes' had never been more welcome. There were still some spare men, those who had been in the middle of the six-wide column. 'FACE FORWARD! CLOSE THE GAP!' Tullus bawled without looking to see if they obeyed.

Back to his enemies. Two men in the prime of life, shoulder to shoulder, both with spears, one with a hexagonal, blue and red painted shield, the other with a distinctive tribal hair knot at the side of his head. A pox-scarred youth, rough-spun tunic, carrying only a club. And the most dangerous of the lot, a wiry man, similar in age to Tullus, armed with an iron-rimmed shield and a nasty-looking sword. 'Take the one with the club,' he ordered the legionary to his right.

'Yes, sir!' The soldier roared insults at the youngster, getting his attention.

Tullus ducked his head until his eyes were level with the top of his scutum. The pair with the spears would reach him first, he saw, while the older man hung back, waiting for his chance. Roaring like angry bulls, the two warriors closed in. Stab! Stab! Their spears thrust forward in unison. Tullus bent his knees, heard one whistle overhead, felt the second drive into his shield. The impact rocked him back; if it hadn't been for the soldier behind, bracing him with his scutum, he might have fallen. Using the muscles in his thighs, Tullus drove up, looked, and shoved his gladius into the belly of the warrior whose spear had caught in his shield. His actions were exact, precise. In, no more than a handspan, twist a little, out. The man went down, blood blossoming on his tunic, crying like a baby taken off the tit too soon.

The spear hanging from Tullus' scutum made it unwieldy and nigh-on impossible to hold. Yet he had to, because the second spear-wielding warrior was driving his weapon at Tullus' head. The older man had joined him, sword jabbing back and forth, searching for a gap in Tullus' defences. Arm muscles screaming, desperate, Tullus lobbed his shield straight at the spearman. Doing what he always told new recruits never to do, he broke ranks and leaped forward at the warriors, making use of their confusion. Trying to shove away Tullus' shield, the man with the spear didn't even see him coming. Tullus smashed his left shoulder into the man's chest, sending him flying backwards. Tullus also lunged at the older warrior's midriff from the side. *He* hadn't been expecting Tullus' attack either, but still managed to twist away, avoiding a death wound. Instead the gladius ripped open the back of his tunic, drawing only a line of blood across his flank and an outraged hiss of pain.

Tullus spun back to the man he'd barged, managed to stab him through the lower leg, and then he was retreating, fast as he could, still facing the enemy. The older warrior followed him, like a cat on a mouse, and Tullus thought: I'm done. My own fault. They feinted at each other, sparred and then, to Tullus' immense relief, the legionary who'd been on his right shuffled forward a couple of steps, roaring abuse, forcing the tribesman to withdraw.

Tullus resumed his place in the line, called for a shield and was handed one from behind. He had no time to thank the legionary who'd saved him, no time to assess how the rest of his soldiers were doing, because the tribesmen were attacking again. A third less in number than they had been, but advancing nonetheless. The older warrior whom Tullus had injured was among them. In a testament to his bravery, so too was the man he'd wounded in the leg.

'ROMA!' Tullus yelled. 'ROMA!'

It was heartening that the response from his soldiers was loud, and came from plenty of throats.

Tullus put down the man with the leg wound with his first thrust, but the older warrior was killing the legionary on his right as he did. With an animal cry, the warrior leaped into the gap left by the dying soldier. Several tribesmen followed him. Tullus was fortunate to have no one before him, or he'd have been slain as he half turned, exposing his left side, and pushed his sword into the first body he saw – a warrior wearing a dark blue tunic. A frantic look to his left – no one there still – and he killed a second tribesman.

Pounding feet forced him to face front again, to take on first another club-wielding warrior, and then a stripling youth as skinny as his own *framea*. Expecting to be hacked down from behind by the enemies who'd broken the Roman line, Tullus pushed himself to his limit. He took down the club-carrying warrior with a savage thrust to the belly, and then tackled the stripling – who fell for the age-old ruse of a feint to the face with the shield, never anticipating the precise stab to the throat of Tullus' gladius. With both opponents dead or dying, Tullus had a moment, a heartbeat to recover. He was suddenly intensely aware of the bands of pain wrapping his chest, the breath ragged in his throat, the sheer relief that he was alive, not dead.

There were no more warriors in front of him. The rest appeared to be pulling back. Tullus looked over his shoulder, could see no tribesmen, just sweaty, bloody, grinning legionaries' faces. 'Are they all dead?'

'Aye, sir,' replied a veteran who'd been with Tullus almost as long as

Fenestela. 'Or going that way.' His head disappeared from sight, there was a grunt, a moan cut short, and he popped up again. 'That was the last one, sir.'

'Good work.' Tullus cast a look to his left, where the First Cohort was still advancing. Urgency filled him. They had to keep moving if they weren't to be left behind. He glanced to his right, along the line. Pride swelled his heart. He had no idea how many of his soldiers were down, but they had held. They had fucking held!

'Should we go after them, sir?' asked a voice.

Tullus regarded the remaining tribesmen, who were loping off towards the forest. In other circumstances, other battles, he might have agreed, but not today. Among the trees, there would be more warriors waiting, of that he had no doubt, and they were the ones with the advantage in such confined, awkward places. 'Let the cocksuckers go. Check the wounded; treat them if you can. Strip the dead of any equipment you need, and do it fast. We move now.'

Tullus stalked down the line, repeating his orders, assessing his losses and his soldiers' mood. They were bloodied and battered. Six of them would never leave this place, and nearly a dozen more sported wounds of varying severity. These were grievous losses for one clash in an ongoing battle, thought Tullus, especially if they were being repeated throughout the army. His rising sense of concern was countered, however, by the fierce grins his men gave him, and the promises that they'd be ready to march as soon as the injured had been looked at.

They'd make it through – one way or another, he decided.

Nonetheless, Tullus couldn't quite shake off his unease as they resumed their advance. Scores of dead legionaries – the casualties suffered by the First Cohort – were strewn across their path. Many had been dragged to the side of the road by their comrades, but the unit's officers had been keen to move on. That meant that Tullus and his soldiers had to pick their way past – and in some cases walk on – the mud-spattered, bloodied corpses and, worse still, those who had not yet succumbed to their wounds. Having to behave in such a callous manner dampened the brief elevation in Tullus' men's mood like a bucket of water emptied over a smouldering fire.

Rather than say anything, Tullus saved his breath; they'd need rallying later, when the enemy hit them again. Thoughts of Arminius filled his head: how they had first met, how he had charmed everyone, in particular Varus. He was a clever man, a battle-hardened warrior, and a leader of men. He would not attack a force of three legions, even from ambush, unless he had an army at his command. It was feasible, even likely, that the warriors who'd attacked thus far were but a small part of Arminius' host. The rest were in the forest ahead of them.

Where they *had* to go.

Curse Arminius for a treacherous dog, thought Tullus, wishing that he was back in Vetera, dry, warm – and safe.

In that moment, it seemed as far away as the moon.

XXV

Tullus wasn't happy. The ground had begun to climb, and although the gradient wasn't steep, and the path didn't lead straight up the hill, it opened his men up to potential attacks from above. Sure enough, fresh volleys of stones and frameae were soon raining down on them. His cohort and the First – the only unit that appeared to be with them by this stage – now had to fight off a strong assault by hundreds of fresh warriors. Their shields bore different patterns to those borne by their previous assailants, telling Tullus that they were from another tribe, which cemented his conviction that Arminius had rallied more than just his own people.

It didn't take long for Tullus to lose three soldiers in the clash, with almost twice that number injured – losses that were roughly replicated throughout the cohort. Once the enemy had pulled back – there was no point pursuing them – the Romans' march had continued. The slain had been left where they had fallen, the luckiest among them with a coin in their mouths placed there in haste by a comrade. Grim-faced but resolute, Tullus and his men slogged on through the mud, the wind and the constant downpour.

Only the gods knew what time of day it was – the morning had to have passed, but with storm clouds reducing their world to a rain-soaked, grey twilight, it was impossible to be more specific. They had covered perhaps a mile, and the forest began to die away to their right. At first it was only a few gaps in the trees, but after another half-mile, during which they had not come under further attack, the woodland came to an end. Tullus felt like cheering – the open ground meant that they would be safe from attack on one side at least.

His hopes were soon dashed.

'It's fucking bog,' he said to Fenestela, who'd come to report on the wounded. 'That prick Arminius is even cleverer than I thought, choosing to fight us here.'

They both looked, hoping Tullus was wrong, but there could be no mistaking it. Two to three hundred paces of scrubby grass and a few bushes further on, the land's profile changed. Patches of heather and bracken nestled alongside one another; they continued as far as the eye could see. Between them were countless nodding heads of water avens and the unmistakeable yellow flowers of goatweed. These were plants fond of damp, marshy ground. As if to prove the point, the resentful, rattling cry of a grouse rose to meet them.

The significance of what they were seeing sank home faster than a stone dropped down a well. Where there were trees, there was solid ground. A bad place to fight, but it could be done. Men could run away into the forest, if it came to it. But bog?

Fenestela cleared his throat and spat a juicy chunk of phlegm into the mud. 'That for you, Fortuna, you treacherous old whore.'

On another day, Tullus – cynic though he was – might have counselled against such blasphemy. Now, though, he added his contribution to Fenestela's with an energetic hawk and spit. 'The raddled crone is in an evil mood with us – of that there's no fucking doubt.'

Fenestela lowered his voice further, so the soldiers marching alongside – most of whom, locked in their own worlds of misery, did not appear to have noticed the marshy ground – couldn't hear. 'What can we do?'

Tullus cast a jaundiced look at his optio. 'You know the answer to that as well as I do.'

When the thunder came, it was even louder than before – right above their heads.

The heavens opened, releasing fresh deluges of water, and it truly felt as if the gods were laughing at them. Groans – of weariness, resignation, despair – rippled down the line of marching soldiers. A man could only get so wet, thought Tullus, but his spirits could be dragged lower and lower, until they were in the actual mud. In that moment, he felt his own slide several notches downward.

It was impossible to pick the thing he hated most. The gnawing worry that they were about to be attacked, that he might lose all of his men, that he might die himself. The notion that the mad-eyed soothsayer in Mogontiacum so many years before had been right all along. The brown sludge squelching between his toes with each step, and how the grit within it worked its way further and further into his open-toed boots. The twinging ache in his lower back, and the constant stabbing pain from the old injury in his calf. The strength-sapping feeling of cold, soaking wool against his skin, made degrees worse by the biting wind. The apparent ever-growing weight of his armour. The fact that his shield, combat-ready in his left fist rather than slung from his back, appeared to have been magicked into a single piece of lead. The way his sword hilt pinched the skin on the inside of his elbow with each swing of his arm. The infuriating path that rain took from the rim of his helmet on to his forehead, and onward into his sweat-stung eyes.

Fuck it, thought Tullus. Fuck this wet, dreary shithole. Fuck its savage people, and their barbaric ways. Fuck the weather. Fuck the forest. Fuck the stinking mud. Fuck Varus for being a blind fool. And most of all, fuck Arminius for being a traitorous whore's get.

The internal rant took his mind from their miserable situation for all of a couple of hundred paces. Then it was back to the numbing grind. Place one foot before the other; keep up a decent speed so that they remained close to the First. Wipe the rain from his face. Shift the hilt of his sword – again. Grip the edge of his shield with his right hand for twenty steps, to ease the load on his left shoulder. Study the trees to their left with great care for signs of the enemy, and then his men, with equal intensity, to monitor their spirits. Growl encouragement at the laggards; shout back to Fenestela, so that he knew what was going on behind him.

Repeat the whole procedure again and again and again. And again.

Tullus dragged his cohort thus another mile.

The next attack was a hammer blow, far worse than any of the previous assaults.

Wily veteran though he was, Tullus was caught by surprise. So too were his soldiers. Who could have predicted that the tribesmen would have constructed huge earthworks, protected by wicker fencing and cut branches, behind which they could hide in their thousands? Yet that is exactly what they had done – what Arminius, the genius, had had them do.

One moment Tullus was trudging along, half counting his steps, half listening to the filthy joke being told in the rank behind, and the next the world filled again with that damnable sound, the barritus. Before his disbelieving eyes, scores of warriors burst into sight from his left, charging straight at his astonished soldiers. More followed, and more, until there were hundreds of the enemy, emerging from gaps in what Tullus realised – far too late – was a manmade embankment thirty to forty paces back into the trees.

There was nothing to their right – even though it was bog, Tullus checked again – which was something. 'HALT! FACE LEFT! CLOSE ORDER!' he roared, his voice cracking with effort. He was already shoving his way forward so that he could stand on the right of the first rank. 'PLACE THE WOUNDED BEHIND. QUICKLY!'

This time, reduced numbers notwithstanding, they were able to form a decent line *and* throw their pila before the enemy came within gladius range. The paltry number of javelins remaining to them meant that the volley had little effect on the massed assault. Perhaps a dozen tribesmen were punched backward into their fellows, but the rest came on without pause, weapons raised and shouting their hatred. In the lead were five naked warriors, their bodies streaked with daubs of white and blue paint. An alarm sounded in Tullus' head. He had faced berserkers before, and knew how dangerous they could be. Their manic expressions, large physical size and complete lack of fear, not to mention clothing, shouted that these specimens were to be feared. They weren't going to hit the line anywhere near him either, worse luck.

Tullus was moving before he let himself think. With a shove, he forced the legionary behind him into his place; then he wheeled around the back of the formation. It was gut-wrenching that his soldiers only stood two deep now, because of their losses. The wounded who could not fight – almost a score of them – made a more pathetic sight. The ones who could sit upright were propped up against one another, daggers and swords in their hands, but the rest lay in the mud, piss-soaked, wounds bleeding and groaning in pain.

Ignoring this bitter reality, Tullus forced his weary legs into a trot. 'HOLD THE BASTARDS!' he shouted over and over. 'STEADY!' As he made his way towards the centre, he kept peering over his men's shoulders, searching for the berserkers.

Acid filled his mouth as he realised he wouldn't reach the point where they struck the line in time. Fortuna wasn't finished with him yet, Tullus thought, imagining the goddess's pitiless smile as her dice landed to reveal a pair of unbeatable sixes. If the berserkers smashed through, the battle would turn to a slaughter. Already demoralised, facing more warriors than ever before, his soldiers would break and run – into the bog, where they would be cut down to a man, or drown. Tullus set his jaw, managed to increase his pace a fraction, then a little more. The next few moments would cost him his life, but that was a fair price if he could prevent a wholescale rout.

Fierce cries went up, and then there was an almighty crash. The berserkers had hit the waiting legionaries. Their comrades, a short distance behind, yelled their approval. Tullus, still at the rear, and ten paces from the point of impact, had a perfect view of what happened. The force with which the naked warriors struck pushed *both* Roman ranks back a couple of steps. Shouts of anger and terror, and pain, competed with the sound of iron on iron and men's screams. The coppery smell of blood filled the air; mixed with it were its inevitable companions – piss and shit. Tullus heard a man vomiting. His sense of urgency multiplied. All the signs were there. Within a dozen heartbeats, his worst fears would be confirmed. That was how fast the balance of a fight could tip one way or the other.

Instinct and battle experience told Tullus not to try and shove his way into what was left of his soldiers' formation. There lay only madness, panic, men jammed so close to each other that it was impossible to wield a sword. It was a ruthless decision: some of his soldiers would die because of it, but he could think of nothing else. Preparing himself, asking Mars for his help, Tullus stepped away from the swaying ranks a little, and raised his sword and shield.

A cry of agony, a despairing shout from a comrade, and a legionary sprawled backwards out of the line and on to his back. Blood spurted from the deep wound to his neck, turning the plates of his armour crimson. There was a triumphant shout, and the berserker who'd killed him leaped forward to stand over his victim, spear aimed down to deliver another blow.

Tullus had stuck him through and through before the man had even realised there was someone there. Quick as he could, Tullus tugged his blade free, twisting his head so that the blood sprays didn't hit him in the face. He shuffled back a short way, and waited.

Another legionary died in similar fashion within a few heartbeats. So too did his killer, at Tullus' hands. He repeated the simple manoeuvre on a third berserker as well, and was beginning to think he might do the impossible, but the last two crashed through his men together. Tullus managed to wound the nearest berserker in the arm, but it was the man's left, not the one wielding his spear. The berserker turned on him like a rabid dog, baring his teeth and shrieking his pain – or was it contempt at Tullus' effort? – and shoving his spear towards Tullus' face and shield, shield and face. Tullus retreated, head as low as possible behind his scutum, noticing with alarm that the berserker's companion was darting around to his rear. Resignation swamped him. He'd done well, for an old man, but to die with a wound in his back was a shitty way to go.

Thump. Tullus had to forget about his second enemy as he was shoved back a step by the first berserker's spear driving into his shield. Even one-handed, the man had the strength of a boar. The sharp iron point sliced through the layered wood to strike Tullus' mail under his sternum. He staggered, but managed to keep a tight hold on the shield grip. When the berserker tried to free his spear, Tullus countered by pushing forward – hard. The warrior's face was a picture of surprise as he was twisted sideways by Tullus' momentum. The move brought Tullus close enough to slide his sword deep into the side of the berserker's chest. Iron grated off rib bone, then the resistance vanished as the blade sliced everything beyond that into ribbons.

The berserker was a dead man standing, yet he somehow found the strength to let go of his spear and punch Tullus in the head. The blow struck his helmet and despite the felt liner that cushioned his skull, stars flashed across his vision. 'Fucking die!' he shouted, running his sword in until the hilt touched the berserker's flesh. With a shuddering gasp, and a dribble of pink froth from his lips, the man did as he asked. He fell off Tullus' blade as he went down.

Remembering the second berserker, Tullus flinched. Why wasn't he dead? The warrior had had more than enough time to kill him. He twisted his head, could see no one for a heartbeat. Turning, he was astonished to find the final berserker lying face down, chest heaving, almost at his feet. He'd been hamstrung in one leg, and slashed by a sword in the other. Behind him, two of the wounded legionaries were grinning like idiots at Tullus, who took in their bloodied gladii, and laughed with a combination of relief and pride. 'My thanks,' he said.

Tullus left them to finish the berserker off. Seizing a discarded shield, he went to fill the gap in his soldiers' line. His men had almost managed to close it, but not quite. Tullus' arrival came none too soon, and he took delight in the alarm that his appearance, crested helmet on, roaring like a madman, caused among their attackers. One moment they'd been shoving forward into a hole caused by their berserker brethren, and the next, it had been plugged by a centurion who appeared to be insane.

'HOLD, BROTHERS!' yelled Tullus. 'STAY CLOSE!'

From that point, Tullus' world became a tunnel. He lost all concept of weather, location, how much his body hurt, anything other than the man to either side, and the handful of warriors before him. It was galling that despite the berserkers' deaths, the tribesmen continued to attack. Their morale *had* to have been affected, Tullus reasoned, forcing his screaming muscles to continue working.

Keep the scutum up, he thought. Pick a target. Let him come. Duck down, take the blow on the shield front, or its rim. Thrust forward, often without looking. Drive the blade in, sense the victim squirm away in vain, hear his screams. Blade out, feel the blood sheet over his forearm, peer over the shield to see his opponent fall. Glance to either side, check that his companions are alive, still fighting. Shuffle closer to one or the other. Yell at his men to hold, to stay close. Bellow his defiance at the tribesmen, throw whatever insults came to him in both German and Latin. Blink away the sweat that was running into his eyes.

In this fashion, Tullus slew two warriors and shared another kill with the soldier to his right, who had stabbed his opponent at the same time. By this stage, it was agony to breathe, and his every muscle was trembling with exhaustion. It was pathetic how grateful he felt when, without any warning, the warriors withdrew. He watched, panting and offering up silent prayers of thanks to Mars, as they loped back into the trees and their embankment, which had hidden them so well. Their wounded and dying were left behind: a decent covering, Tullus was pleased to see. Worry gnawed at him nonetheless. *His* losses, and those suffered by the cohort and the army in general, were far more pressing. They could not keep haemorrhaging men like this.

For now, though, they had won some space to recover. Tullus lowered his sword, let his shield sag to the ground. Felt the rain, softer now, drifting down on to his face in welcome drops. Breathing deep, he closed his eyes for a count of five. Ten. Crazy as it was in that blood-spattered place of death, sleep beckoned. Tullus rallied what was left of his energy and forced his gummy eyelids open. 'Injured?' he demanded of the soldiers to either side. One was fine; the other had a gaping wound to his left cheek, but averred that he could fight on. With constant glances towards the trees, Tullus marched to the end of his century, assessing his casualties. To his intense relief, they weren't as bad as they *could* have been. Five – only five! – legionaries were dead or dying, and two would follow them within hours. Six more men had minor wounds. Heavy though these losses were, the berserkers' charge could have ended everything. He was overjoyed to find Fenestela still alive: covered in other men's blood, with a gash to his neck, but otherwise unharmed. Tullus grabbed him in a bear hug.

'I heard what you did to those naked fuckers, sir,' said Fenestela when they had separated, smiling. Respect shone from his eyes. 'Few men could have done that.'

'I was full sure I was dead. That helped, like as not,' Tullus said, shrugging. 'Mars was kind to me. So too were a couple of the wounded lads, who hamstrung the last whoreson. If it hadn't been for them, I wouldn't be here.' His vision blurred for a moment, and he swayed.

'You all right, sir?' asked Fenestela, steadying him.

Tullus straightened his spine, grimaced and shook off Fenestela's hand. 'Aye. I have to be. Is there anything to drink? I'm fucking parched.'

Fenestela called for a wine skin.

Reinvigorated a little by several mouthfuls of undiluted wine – Campanian, it tasted like – Tullus sent word to the other centuries in the cohort that they were to treat the injured fast, and to be ready to march. When the messenger returned, he wasn't carrying good news. Three of Tullus' centurions reported that they were down to half their usual strength. A fourth centurion was dead, and the last would not live another hour. Cursing at the delay dealing with this would cause – and with the First Cohort already on the move in front – Tullus ordered the depleted centuries to unite, forming two that were full strength, and for them to do it with all haste.

For a time after that, Fortuna appeared to have cast her capricious gaze elsewhere, leaving Mars to hold his shield over Tullus and his soldiers. The thunder stopped, and the rain eased to a gentle drizzle. There was even a hint of sunshine through a few breaks in the cloud. A rainbow formed overhead, its beauty a stark contrast to the bloodbath taking place at ground level. From somewhere on the moorland beyond the bog came the lonely, warbling cries of curlews. With no sign of the tribesmen other than heads peering over the earthen rampart, Tullus' soldiers regrouped and got moving.

When they caught up with the First Cohort, it was travelling at a snail's pace. Before long, it ground to a complete halt. The unit had come under attack again. Hundreds of warriors rushed out from behind the German earthworks, threatening to overwhelm the First through sheer weight of numbers. With worry gnawing at his guts, Tullus ordered his tired soldiers forward to its aid. They managed to fight their way to the unit's rear after a time, with the loss of two men. If Tullus had thought things would prove easier having another cohort to one side, he was mistaken. It might have worked if the First hadn't lost so many junior officers and centurions – but it had. From his position at the far right of his soldiers, abutting the First, he could see the unit's legionaries weakening like an undercut riverbank hit by a winter flood.

It was unusual to mix troops from two different cohorts, but desperate times called for desperate measures. During a brief respite, Tullus had Fenestela take his place in the front rank. Then, leading half his own century, he made his way behind the First for a short distance, and forward, into the middle of its disrupted formation. The grey-faced, stoop-shouldered legionaries met their arrival with varying degrees of disbelief – and pathetic gratitude. Their spines stiffened too, however, which was what Tullus needed. He interspersed his soldiers between those of the First, all along a section of line eighty men wide, and placed himself in the middle. When the next wave of warriors came charging in, the legionaries stood solid, and threw the enemy back.

They did the same thing on a second occasion, wreaking fearful casualties on the tribesmen. During the short breaks between attacks, Tullus was able to ascertain that his cohort was also holding its own. The rest of the First – to his right – was a different matter altogether. Parts of it were standing their ground, but from the sounds and looks of it – loud cheering from the enemy, and an increase in the force of their assault – other sections were crumbling or had even broken. He began to wonder whether his move to strengthen the First had been wise – if the situation deteriorated much further, the soldiers around him would also crack. If that happened, he and his men would die. Even worse, so too would Fenestela and the rest of his beleaguered century – possibly even his entire cohort.

It was with a sense of real relief, therefore, that Tullus watched the enemy tribesmen pulling back a short time later. They hadn't been beaten – too many of them were sauntering for that to be the case, and hurling insults over their shoulders at the Romans – but they were withdrawing. For a rest, like as not, he thought, feeling a great need for the same. The horns of an unpleasant dilemma now faced him. Another enemy assault would begin soon. Should he stay put, or return to his men? Or even, Tullus wondered, should he push on past these beaten legionaries, away from his allotted position, to where the legion's eagle was? It was vital that the golden standard not be lost – and his men might make the difference in retaining it. That bitter realisation drove Tullus to throw caution – and army regulations – to the wind.

Ordering the First's soldiers to do their best, he rallied his men – three fewer than he'd led in – and took them back to their own unit. Fenestela greeted him with unbridled relief. 'We didn't break, sir, but it was close. We won't be able to hold on for much longer.'

'If we stay here, we'll be raven food by sunset,' agreed Tullus. He pointed. 'Look over there.' He'd spotted an area of dry ground to their right, parallel to the track, increasing the distance between them and the boggy area. Fenestela took one look and also saw the chance it granted. Without further ado, Tullus led his soldiers on to it, around the still unmoving First Cohort. There were unhappy glances from its legionaries, and even a shout from an optio that they shouldn't be changing formation without direct orders from Varus, but Tullus paid not a blind bit of notice.

Judging where the First's centre was proved to be difficult, as the cohort had lost its usual formation. Approximating as best he could, Tullus returned to the path after a few hundred paces. The niggle of unease he'd felt about the eagle now became open disquiet. The casualties here had been horrendous. Legionaries were sprawled everywhere, dead, wounded, somewhere in between. The unit's ranks were so full of gaps that they resembled an old fishing net that had never been repaired.

Not every centurion had been killed, however, and there were also standard-bearers dotted throughout the unit's soldiers. What worried Tullus was that they were *signiferi*, the men who carried centuries' standards. There was no sign – anywhere – of the *aquilifer*, and the eagle he carried.

'Where's the eagle?' Tullus roared at an optio who was tending to the wounded.

The optio looked up. The grief and shame on his face, and the streaks that tears had left on his cheeks, revealed everything. 'It's gone, sir. Lost.'

'*What?*' Tullus seized the optio's arm, shoved his face into the other man's. '*How?*'

'There were too many of them, sir. They went straight for the eagle – twenty berserkers, at least. Our centurions did their best, they shoved us forward, sideways, every way they could to protect it. Three of them died, maybe more, defending it. Scores of ordinary soldiers too. I'm one of the only *optiones* left.' The man hung his head. 'I should have died – would have done, if I hadn't been knocked out for a time.'

Numb, reeling, Tullus left the optio to his misery. Ordering his own cohort to regroup, he went in search of a more senior officer, hoping against hope that they would rebut what the optio had told him. The eagle's loss was almost incomprehensible. Men would do anything – die, take a disabling wound, lose a limb – to prevent such an iconic symbol falling into enemy hands. Tullus would have done the same. He couldn't remember the last time a legion had lost an eagle. The optio had been mistaken, he told himself.

Ignoring the nearby legionaries' dejected, beaten expressions, his fantasy lasted until he came across Centurion Fabricius, of the Second Century – whom he knew – an officious type at the best of times. Now, though, Fabricius looked like a man whose family has just been butchered before him: dead-eyed, with a sickly grey complexion. He gave Tullus a puzzled look. 'You're not with the First.'

'No. I'm Tullus. Senior centurion, Second Cohort.'

'Ah.' Fabricius' disinterested gaze fell, and he picked at the hilt of his sword with bloodied fingernails.

'Is it true?' demanded Tullus. 'Has the eagle been lost?'

There was no reply.

'Answer me!' shouted Tullus, uncaring that Fabricius outranked him.

'Aye. It's true,' muttered Fabricius, unable to meet his eyes.

'I brought my men forward as fast as I could. We would have – I meant to—' Tullus stopped. Empty words and hollow promises would not magic the eagle back. He glanced at the earthworks, and the clamouring warriors atop it. 'They took it back there?'

'Yes.'

'How long ago?'

'I-I don't know. Not long since.'

Tullus' mind raced. If he gathered all of his men, and the soldiers around him, could they sweep forward and cross the enemy fortifications? Could they recover the eagle? He studied the nearest legionaries, and his hopes burned to a white ash. Everyone he could see looked exhausted. His own troops weren't in a much better state. Such men couldn't storm a higher position – against superior numbers – and expect to win, let alone take back a prize that would be defended to the bitter end. You bastard, Arminius, he thought. You filthy, scheming bastard.

Tullus had never felt so bitter. Never been so ashamed. It was immaterial that he had not been present when the eagle had been seized: it belonged to the Eighteenth. His legion – the unit to which he had given fifteen years of his life. Their humiliation was all the greater because the Seventeenth and the Nineteenth still retained theirs. If they escaped this living hell, it would be the death of the Eighteenth. Legions without eagles were disbanded.

In that moment, Tullus' despair threatened to overwhelm him. He longed to lie down in the mud and let the world fall to ruin.

One thing prevented him. His men.

He could not go to Hades knowing that he'd abandoned them. He had to keep his cohort moving. To stay was to die.

'The gods be with you,' he said to Fabricius.

Disbelief flitted across Fabricius' face – then it was anger. 'Where are you going?'

'Back to my cohort.'

'What about the eagle?' demanded Fabricius. 'It has to be recaptured!'

Shame scourged Tullus anew, not least because there was nothing to be done. 'It's thanks to the incompetence of you and your fellow officers that it was lost in the first place,' he snarled.

Fabricius spat into the mud. 'Varus will hear of this.'

'I'll tell him what I did myself,' Tullus retorted. 'He can be the judge of who did the right thing. It won't be you, you fool. Mark my words: stay here, and you will *all* die. We can't fight these whoresons, at least not the way we'd want. Our best chance – our only chance – is to keep marching.'

He walked away, ignoring Fabricius' orders to stand his ground. Gods grant that he comes to his senses before it's too late, Tullus thought, putting the fate of the First – and the eagle – from his mind. In this calamitous situation, his cohort came first, and everyone and everything else came a distant second. Including Varus. Especially Varus. I told him, Tullus remembered, a throbbing fury pulsing behind his eyes. If only he'd listened. But Varus hadn't, and here they were, with hundreds of men dead and an eagle lost – and that was just among the ranks of the Eighteenth. Who knew what was happening to the rest of the army?

A short distance along the path, Tullus was presented in gory fashion with the fate of the senior officers and their escort. Whether it was because the enemy had noticed the number of officers together – legates, tribunes and auxiliary prefects – or the fact that they were only protected by a single cohort, he didn't know, but the attack here appeared to have been made with even more force than that directed against his soldiers. In the carnage upwards of two hundred legionaries lay slaughtered, and among *them* Tullus counted four tribunes, two prefects and a number of centurions. It was a relief to see no legates among the dead, and to note that the senior officers who had survived had not lingered.

He eyed the enemy's earthworks with renewed respect.

It was as if the tribesmen saw him looking. A rendition of the barritus began, and a number of warriors emerged from the nearest gaps in the fortification to hurl abuse towards the path. Some even dropped their trousers in order to wave their genitalia at the Romans. On another day, Tullus would have found a wisecrack to shout back. Instead, he watched the taunting men in grim silence. With their confidence running this high, it wouldn't be long before they attacked again.

How Tullus wished that he had the legion's artillery to call on. Behind the earthworks, the enemy would be packed as tight as a shoal of fish in a net. A sustained barrage from ballistae would cause heavy casualties, and force them out from their defences, whereupon the legionaries would be able to slaughter them. Arminius had foreseen this, however, by tricking the legions on to this narrow, godsforsaken path upon which wagons and artillery could not travel. The result meant that, despite being less than fifty paces away, the tribesmen were invulnerable.

Tullus hadn't trudged much further when cheering broke out among the enemy. He peered, making out a familiar broad-shouldered figure in fine armour, surrounded by a group of excited warriors. It was Arminius,

Tullus felt sure of it. Hearing Arminius' voice a few heartbeats later was the final proof that his suspicions all along had been correct. That sour realisation, although expected, was hard to take.

It was far worse, however, to see his legion's eagle being brandished aloft beside Arminius. It glinted in the weak rays of afternoon sunshine, mocking the Eighteenth's failure. Tullus' fury was such that his vision blurred for a moment. When it cleared, the eagle had been taken behind the enemy fortification, driving the reality of the loss even further home.

Tullus took a silent oath on the spot.

One day, my men and I will return and reclaim what belongs to us – what belongs to the Eighteenth. The eagle will be ours again. By everything that is sacred, I swear it. We will be back.

For now, though, he had to focus on survival.

XXVI

Arminius couldn't take his eyes from the eagle. He'd been near one, and had been impressed by its beauty, but he'd never before laid hands on one, never been able to study one close up. It was typical of a legion's standard, with the golden eagle positioned lying forward, on its chest, wings upraised behind. Staring eyes and an open beak gave the eagle a fierce, imperious expression, which impressed and amused Arminius by turn. You're mine now, he thought, tipping over the wooden staff to feel the eagle's weight. Cast from gold, it was impressively heavy.

The eagle had been brought to him as soon as it had reached their earthworks, borne by the same warrior who'd snatched it from the dying aquilifer: Osbert. Arminius had been delighted that the glory belonged to one of his own. A jostling mob of cheering warriors had accompanied Osbert, but he had suffered no one else to touch the eagle until it had been presented to Arminius.

Arminius had at once repaid the gesture by asking him to stay by his side, so that every man in their host might see who had seized such an illustrious prize. Osbert was still grinning from ear to ear, and seemed oblivious to the small bleeding cuts that marked his arms and chest.

Having taunted the battered legionaries with the eagle, Arminius traced his way along the earthworks for half a mile or more. The standard had a rapturous reception from the warriors assembled behind the defences. There were spontaneous renditions of the barritus, repeated chants of

Arminius' name and shouted oaths that the remaining eagles would soon be taken.

Its appearance before the soldiers of a different Roman cohort – who until that point had had no knowledge of its loss – also had a dramatic effect. Emerging from a gap in the fortifications, Osbert and his companions roared and shouted to get their enemies' attention. Arminius watched as the legionaries – no longer in recognisable ranks or files – pointed and cried out in dismay. Their ragged lines even wavered, *away* from the triumphant warriors.

It was an incredible spectacle, thought Arminius with delight, to see the arrogant Romans brought so low. Their marching speed was pathetic, their usual impressive formation absent. Their mud-spattered cloaks were rain-sodden, their armour dulled and rusting. Few of them had javelins, and even fewer carried any equipment. Many sported crimson-spotted bandages, or were limping. Those with more severe injuries were being helped along by their comrades. At regular intervals, dying men, or those who could not keep up, were being abandoned by the side of the track.

Arminius noted that the Roman officers – what few there were – looked no better than their men. This was telling. The centurions, optiones and other officers were the backbone of every century, every cohort and every legion. It was usual for them to lead by example, and if that leadership were absent, the legionaries would soon give up.

Arminius studied the Romans again with care, and decided that that had in fact already happened. To all intents and purposes, the Eighteenth was spent as a fighting force. Once the Seventeenth and Nineteenth had been as well battered, victory would be his.

He could taste it.

Tullus trudged on. A brown-green wall taller than a man – the enemy earthworks – ran alongside the track without end, sometimes as close as twenty paces from the marching legionaries. Behind it were apparently inexhaustible reserves of warriors, every one of whom thirsted for Roman blood. When the bastards weren't attacking, they were singing their infernal barritus, or showering the legionaries with volleys of frameae from atop the rampart.

Tullus' men had long since used up their pila, and had grown accustomed to picking up the enemy missiles and lobbing them at their owners when given the order. To begin with, their efforts – thrown at a foe above them, by arms that were already tired – caused few casualties compared to those they were suffering. Incensed, Tullus gave his soldiers a dressing-down during a rest break snatched when they weren't under attack. 'You all fucking know how to throw a spear! Ground your shield. Pick a target. Don't loose the damn things until I give the order! Do that, and you'll *kill* men. Throw them like panicked children chucking rocks at a feral dog, and you'll miss!'

His telling-off worked. The next time Tullus directed his men to throw, more than half a dozen warriors were punched back off the top of the earthwork into their fellows. That put an end to the tribesmen standing on the rampart to better use their spears, which reduced Tullus' losses by some degree – at least when hand-to-hand fighting wasn't going on, but that wasn't much of the time.

Three more savage attacks he and his men battled through that terrible afternoon, two of which were in heavy rain, with yet more thunder and lightning. Another six soldiers from his century died, and more were injured. The already muddy track was transformed into a swamp in which a man's leg could sink to mid-calf, making combat twice as treacherous. Bodies of the fallen – most Roman, but a good number of tribesmen – lay on it, *in* it, among the trees, slumped over bushes. Thanks to the volumes of blood being shed, the mud was often dark red in colour rather than brown. In a sarcastic moment, his face planted in it after he'd tripped over a body, Tullus thought it similar in hue to a good Sicilian wine.

Mules, cavalry horses and men's corpses weren't the only things to break an ankle over. Weapons – pila, frameae, swords – were everywhere. So too were shields, pickaxes, pots, pans, blankets and more. Not all the civilians had been weeded out of the army's ranks, as their bodies and belongings proved. Here lay a soothsayer, a startled look on his face, still clutching his *lituus*, or rod of office. There sprawled a merchant, his smashed, empty money box close by. A dead-eyed woman sat on a tree stump, a lifeless infant in her lap and a bawling toddler cradled in her arms. The child's wails mixed with the piteous whining of a tiny mongrel pup, which had stayed by its dead master, a pedlar. Despite his own dreadful situation, Tullus' conscience was pricked by the woman *and* the little dog. He hardened his heart and walked by both. His responsibility was to look after his century, and his cohort. No one else.

When the light began – at last – to dim so much that it was difficult to see his hand in front of his face, Tullus wanted to cry out with relief. His throat was far too dry, however, and his voice spent from shouting orders. The gloom was yet sufficient to see the tribesmen withdrawing from their earthwork in some numbers, and to receive word that a site had been picked for the night's camp by what remained of the vanguard. The quarter-mile it took to reach the spot felt to Tullus like a full day's march. His body hurt as if someone had taken a hammer to every part of him. His bones ached, his muscles shuddered with exhaustion and the old injury in his calf needled at him like the probing in a wound by a drunk, incompetent surgeon. Yet the end – of the day, and their torment, for the hours of darkness – was in sight. The one thing he had to do was to keep his legs moving, to call out a few more encouraging words to his men. This he managed.

Tullus also found the strength to direct his cohort to the centre of what would be the camp – nothing more than an open area of ground by the track – and to have his soldiers prepare what shelters they could. Only when this had been done did he unlock his knees and sit down, propping his back against a boulder. It would have been a good idea to do some stretches, to drink some wine, or water, to eat whatever food there was, but Tullus was too tired. Never had he felt so drained. The instant his eyes closed, he was asleep.

He dreamed not of his soldiers who'd died, but of the woman and her children, one dead, one living, and the whining pup.

Tullus jerked awake, instinct making him reach for his sword. Realising he was among his own, in their 'camp', he relaxed. Night had not entirely fallen, so he couldn't have been dozing for long. As the light from the sky disappeared, the only illumination came from the fires that had been lit. Thanks to the lack of dry wood, there weren't many. The air resounded with the moans of the wounded, dulling the soldiers' muted conversation.

'Damn it all to Hades,' Tullus muttered, unable to put the woman from his mind. How far down the track had she been?

'You're awake.' Fenestela loomed over him, his face concerned. He proffered a wine skin.

'Aye.' Tullus took it and slugged back a couple of mouthfuls. Despite the wine's acidity, he'd have had more, but the skin was light, and it wasn't his. He handed it back with a grateful nod.

'I'd hoped you'd rest a while longer. You were like a beast today. It must have taken it out of you.'

'It had to be done,' said Tullus, worried that he would be unable to repeat the supreme physical effort again. 'How many men left uninjured – in the century?'

Fenestela's chuckle was bitter. 'There are five with *no* injuries. Just over twenty with minor wounds, or wounds that they tell me won't stop them from fighting. Nearly a dozen injured worse than that – a lot of whom won't survive the night. The rest of the cohort is in the same situation, or worse.'

Clenching his jaw, Tullus absorbed this shocking news as best he could. His entire unit was down to less than half strength. These were savage losses – and if they had been repeated throughout the army, which was probable – they were losses that threatened the survival of every man in Varus' command. For some reason, the woman and her child came to his mind again. If they were still alive, they were out there in the dark. Cold, wet, hungry, alone. Tullus cursed. Cursed, and heaved himself upright, cursing again at the pain that radiated from each part of his body. He had every reason in the world not to act, but he couldn't. He *couldn't*. Doing nothing would make him as bad as that whoreson Arminius. 'I'm going back down the track.'

Fenestela looked at him as if he'd taken leave of his senses. 'Why, sir?'

Tullus smiled. When they were alone, Fenestela tended to call him 'sir' only when he disapproved of what Tullus was doing. 'There's a woman back there, with a child. And a pup.'

Fenestela goggled. 'That's sad, sir, but . . . er, it's really none of our concern.'

'I'm making it my fucking concern, all right? Come with me if you wish. Tell the men I want five volunteers. Volunteers only. We leave at once.'

With a roll of his eyes, Fenestela turned on his heel. 'You mad fuck,' he threw over his shoulder.

Tullus let the insult slide, in the main because Fenestela was right. But he was going to do it anyway. If he could save her it would in some small way compensate for the staggering losses suffered by his cohort. So many had died. His heart bled. Fortuna, you're a miserable old cunt, he thought. And what the fuck were you doing today, Mars? Having your flute played by Minerva? You didn't look after us at all. Best do a better job tomorrow, or I'll never sacrifice to you again. Startled by the vehemence of his thoughts, and uneasy that the gods might read his mind, Tullus concentrated on stretching his weary, cramping muscles.

Before long, Fenestela had returned with five legionaries. Three were injured, Tullus noted, his throat closing with emotion. 'More would have come, sir, but I told them you only wanted five,' said Fenestela, making him feel even prouder.

'The optio's told you what we're going to do?' Tullus' eyes moved over the soldiers, who all gave him resolute nods. 'I'd wager that the enemy have long since withdrawn to their tents and their fires. They'll be as hungry and bone-weary as we are. It's a simple job – nothing more than a short walk in the dark.'

They managed a laugh, but he could tell it was forced. They were here, and that was what mattered, thought Tullus. He couldn't also expect them to be happy about it. 'Do we take torches, sir?' asked one legionary.

Tullus hadn't come to a decision on that yet. Without light, they wouldn't be able to see a damn thing, but if they carried torches, they would attract the attention of any tribesmen who might still be around, and *that* would end with only one result. Fuck it, he thought. They'll have gone back to their camps. I'm not skulking down the path like a scared child. 'We do. One at the front, for me, and one at the back, with the last man. That's all. If we hear anything, we can douse them swift enough.' He glanced at Fenestela. 'You coming?'

'You know me, sir. I'm always game for a fool's errand.' Fenestela raised an arm, revealing a pair of wooden torches.

Tullus gave his optio a tight smile. 'Come on.'

The sentries at the camp's edge gave them incredulous looks when Tullus announced where he was going, but they knew better than to question a mad senior centurion. The path along which they had come wasn't hard to follow, littered as it was with weapons and corpses. The latter were challenging to pick their way past, and over, not least because some of them were yet living. When they realised that their own kind had come among them, the poor creatures sent up a lament, pleading to be saved, to be carried to safety, or to have an end to their suffering. Aware that this would happen, Tullus had already instructed his men to say that they'd help those they could on the way back. Despite their best efforts to quieten the wounded, the noise of their cries was considerable. As Fenestela observed drily, only a deaf man would have missed their passage.

Whether Arminius' tribesmen had gone, or thought they were ghosts, Tullus had no idea, but there was no sign of them. He walked on, peering at every tree and bush for signs of the woman and her children. Try as he might, he could not remember the point where he'd seen her. In the darkness, each dripping plant, each lowering tree, looked the same as the next. Judging time was impossible, so he counted his steps. At one thousand – the point at which he'd told himself they would turn back – there had been no sign, or sound, of his quarry.

They had to return, Tullus thought, weariness blurring his vision. Sooner or later, a fucking warrior who'd come to pillage the dead would hear them. He would fetch his friends, and then . . .

An image of the woman cradling her living child while her other one's corpse cooled beside them filled Tullus' mind. If they survived the night, the tribesmen would find them the next day. Slavery, or worse, would be their fate. 'Gods damn it,' he whispered to himself, and then, over his shoulder at Fenestela, 'Two hundred and fifty paces more.'

Three hundred paces later, Tullus came to a reluctant halt. To continue was madness. It was a miracle that they'd come this far without any problems. Fuck you, Fortuna! he thought. I'm never offering to you again, you heartless bitch. He turned. 'Back to the camp,' he said to Fenestela.

Fenestela didn't obey, which rankled Tullus. 'Back, I said.'

'Listen, sir.' Fenestela leaned forward. 'I hear something.'

Tullus pricked his ears, held his breath. For ten heartbeats, he discerned nothing other than the moaning of some poor bastard nearby, but then – beyond belief – he heard the whimper of a child, quickly hushed. It was coming from under the trees, a short distance away. Tullus' spirits rose, but he had to be careful. If the woman took fright, she might run off into the forest, where they'd never find her. 'There's nothing to fear,' he called out in Latin. 'I am a senior centurion of the Roman army. I seek a woman and child.'

There was no reply. Indicating to Fenestela that he and the rest stay put, Tullus walked towards where he thought the sound had come from. After fifteen paces, he stopped and repeated what he'd said. Still there was no response, but nor was there a panicked departure into the dark. Either he had misheard the noise, or the woman wasn't moving. Ten steps more, and he tried again to get her to answer.

This time there was a sob, which was stifled at once, but it gave Tullus heart. He extended his arm, letting his torch shine deeper into the gloom before him. Then he saw her, a huddled figure under a fallen trunk, a natural place to seek shelter. It was the woman he'd seen, and in her arms was a little shape, her child. To Tullus' delight, the pup was there too, curled up at the woman's feet. 'My name is Lucius Cominius Tullus,' he said in a low, reassuring voice. 'I saw you earlier. Come. You'll be safe with me.'

She rose and stumbled towards him, the sleepy pup following. 'My other child, he—' Her voice broke.

'I know,' said Tullus. 'Where is he?'

'I buried him as best I could before dark, just here.'

There was a small grave at Tullus' feet, which he hadn't spotted. The woman had covered it with rocks, which would be enough, he thought. The wolves and other predators would have more than they could eat for days to come. 'Had you a coin to place in his mouth?'

She nodded.

'Let us commend his soul to the gods, and go.' Now that he'd found her, Tullus' unease was taking control. This grim forest, among the dead and, quite possibly, the enemy, was no place for the living. He scooped up the pup, which tried to lick his face. 'Is your child unharmed?'

'She is, thank the gods. The poor mite has been asleep for hours.'

'We'll find her a blanket in the camp, and you.' He made to go, but she caught his arm.

'I-I had given up all hope. You came to save us. Thank you.'

'Aye, well,' said Tullus, feeling pleased *and* awkward. 'Best get back to the camp before we get too excited.' He led the way back to his men. He was still bone-jarringly tired, and grieving for the soldiers he'd lost, and unsure what terrors the next day would hold. Yet finding this still-unnamed woman and her child, and the pup, felt good.

Maybe the gods hadn't abandoned him altogether.

XXVII

Varus sat in his tent, brooding. The dim light cast by a handful of small oil lights on the floor couldn't conceal the fact that it was a tent meant for a contubernium of legionaries. It might have held eight men under normal circumstances, but compared to the vast pavilion he was used to on campaign, it seemed tiny. I should feel grateful, he thought, listening to the rain drumming off the oiled leather. Most of the troops – the ones that survive, his conscience needled – don't have any protection against the weather. It's only because I am commander that I have this. Yet he didn't feel a bit appreciative of his good fortune. He raised his hands, studied the dirt under his fingernails, and the mud splatters that covered every exposed part of his flesh. What he felt was dirty. Wet. Hungry.

These feelings paled before his humiliation, however. Never in his life had he been so degraded. Varus now agreed with Tullus, which made the revelation of Arminius' treachery all the more terrible. Tullus and perhaps Tubero aside, Arminius had tricked every one of them – and him in particular – the way a duplicitous adult cons a small child of its sweets. I am a fool, thought Varus, letting his hands fall into his lap. A complete fool. He had had *no* idea that his army was about to be ambushed when it had turned off the main road to hunt for the Angrivarii.

Varus had no excuses for his ignorance either: he had been alerted, not just once, but several times. Instead of listening to Segestes and later to Tullus, he had laughed off their warnings, or reprimanded them, or both.

Yet they were the ones who'd been correct, and *he* was the one who'd been a blind idiot. What the emperor would make of it, Varus dreaded to think. Whether he would ever have to explain himself to Augustus was another matter, of course, one he didn't like to linger upon.

Varus would have given every last part of his considerable wealth to have had Arminius in chains before him at that moment. Despite his civilised appearance and gregarious nature, the Cheruscan was a lying, treacherous snake. His intent had always been to break the empire's hold over Germania. The planning must have taken months, thought Varus. To unite the tribes – never fond of each other at the best of times – and then bring them together in one place was a considerable feat, and worthy of respect, however grudging. So too was the manner in which Arminius had kept his strategy secret, and how he had found such a perfect location for the ambush.

Varus pictured the countless trees, which had pressed in on either side of the track, confining his soldiers and preventing them from forming up. All part of Arminius' plan. The narrow track, which Varus had laughed about for slowing his army down, and the hellish mud bath that it had turned into. It had also been of Arminius' design. How the legionaries had had to abandon their baggage and, worse, their artillery. That would have been something Arminius hoped for. The damnable hill, and the earthen embankments, which must have taken at least a month to build. Planned in advance too. The bog on one side, cutting off retreat in that direction. Yet another part of Arminius' devilish enterprise.

A sour smile found its way on to Varus' face. Only the *weather* could be described as being outside Arminius' control. His smile didn't last. Perhaps the Cheruscan's gods – the thunder god Donar being one of them – *had* intervened on the tribesmen's behalf. After the lashing rains, and the thunder and lightning of the previous two days, the case could be argued.

'Master?' It was Aristides' voice, right outside the tent.

'Enter.' Varus had been surprised, and relieved, to find that his servant had somehow made it through the day's slaughter.

Aristides unlaced the flap and ducked inside, balancing a tray in one hand. 'I've brought you some food, master.'

Whatever it was he bore – a stew of some kind? – smelled good. Despite his misery, and his shame, Varus' belly rumbled. 'You're a miracle-worker. Where did you get that?'

'You're the governor, master. If anyone's going to eat, even in a place like this, it will be you.'

Varus reached out for the bowl and spoon. Close up, he could see that Aristides' plump face had changed during the last two days. It bore a perpetual expression of anxiety, and there were deep bags under his eyes, lines that had not been there before. He's not made for this, thought Varus. I should have left him in Vetera. 'You look dreadful. Have you eaten? And found a place to sleep?' Realising the stupidity of what he'd said, he cut off Aristides before his servant could pretend to have done either. 'Have the bread.' He gestured at the half-loaf on the tray.

'No, master, I—'

'Take it, I say,' ordered Varus. 'You will sleep in here, with me.'

Aristides looked as if he might cry with gratitude. 'Thank you, master.' He fell on the bread like a starving man.

When they had finished, Varus handed Aristides a small piece of parchment. The Greek looked at it, and at Varus, and back again. 'What is this, master?'

'Forgive the poor quality of the material. My seal has gone missing too, but the wording is clear. My signature is also plain to see.' Still Aristides' face remained blank, so Varus added in a soft voice, 'It's your manumission. A little earlier than promised, but I wanted you to have it before . . .' His throat closed. It wasn't certain what would happen the next day, but the tribesmen hadn't gone away for good. Their relentless attacks would resume at dawn. A bitterness that had become all too familiar coursed through Varus. If the reports were to be believed, half his army had been slain or wounded in the previous two days. The safety offered by the forts along the River Lupia still lay many miles away. What chance would his demoralised, soaking legionaries have tomorrow, against superior numbers of enemies, men with the taste of victory already in their mouths?

In all probability, the fate of Aristides – old, fat, unable to fight – was even more certain. For that, Varus felt huge guilt. As the Greek stuttered his thanks, Varus replied, 'I wish I could have done more. I advise that you find Centurion Tullus in the morning. Tell him that I sent you. Stick by his side, as if you were a limpet on a rock. If anyone makes it out of this hellhole, it will be him.'

'It's that bad?' Aristides' eyes were wide.

'Aye,' grated Varus. 'You saw what it was like today. More than half the army is dead or injured, Aristides, and we're a long way from the river. Arminius' warriors are like a flock of vultures about to pick the flesh from a corpse. Except that in this case, the corpse hasn't yet died.'

'Could we get away on some of the cavalry's horses?'

It was unfair to say that only a Greek would consider fleeing, thought Varus, yet that had been the first thing to enter his mind. 'No, we couldn't. I ordered Vala to take what riders remained earlier on.' It had seemed a good idea in the middle of the battle, with his cavalry powerless to help in any way. Horsemen were useless in woodland, and on narrow paths, in particular when they were mixed with infantry. 'Word reached me soon after we set up camp that they had been ambushed and killed to a man.'

Fear filled Aristides' eyes. 'We're doomed,' he whispered.

'Find Tullus. He's a survivor,' Varus repeated. And a better man than I, he thought. If I had listened to him, thousands of men would yet be alive, and thousands more would not die tomorrow. The last realisation tasted as bitter as hemlock, and Varus came to a sudden decision.

'What use is this to me if we're going to die?' Aristides' fear had been subsumed by anger, and he was waving his manumission under Varus' nose.

Despite the fact that Aristides had never done such a thing during his entire service, this was an offence that merited severe punishment, thought Varus in a detached way. In this moment, he wasn't angered – if anything,

Aristides' show of spirit amused him. Maybe the Greek would use a sword if he had to. 'Tullus is your man. That is my only advice to you,' he said.

Aristides seemed about to say more, but the arrival of Varus' surviving senior officers put an end to their conversation. With Vala dead and another legate injured, but one legion commander remained. Somehow he and the eight remaining tribunes, the two camp prefects, and one primus pilus squeezed into Varus' tent. Soon the space was warm and snug, and the smell of damp wool, leather and stale sweat overpowering.

Varus bid them a sombre welcome. 'I have no wine to offer you, or food. I apologise too for my quarters, which are a little smaller than usual.'

Three men managed a chuckle, but the rest just stared at him, dull-eyed, unshaven, as mud-covered as he. They looked beaten, thought Varus. With an effort, he rallied his strength. Things were bad, but it had to be possible that they could still smash through the encircling tribesmen. Roman armies had come through situations as dire as this in the past. Think of Julius Caesar at Alesia, he told himself. With an image of that stirring victory against overwhelming odds in his mind, he regarded his assembled officers, trying to appear determined, undefeated. 'How stand my legions tonight?'

One by one, Varus' subordinates made their reports, most of which had to do with their casualty estimates. This was bad enough, but an audible groan greeted the news of the loss of an eagle, that of the Eighteenth. More than half the soldiers in his army had been killed or wounded. The losses among the centurionate had also been fearful, which was a mark of the savagery of the day's fighting. Of the hundred and eighty centurions in the three legions, ninety-five were dead or incapacitated. Although many of the injured had been left behind, there were perhaps two thousand in their camp. A good proportion of these men could march, but not fast, and the majority would need to be carried, or helped to walk. Perhaps six thousand combat-ready legionaries remained, along with about five hundred auxiliaries. These figures were made even starker when spoken out loud. No one mentioned how many warriors they faced, but everyone knew that they were now outnumbered. By some degree.

When the last officer fell silent, Varus pinched the bridge of his nose, trying to banish his exhaustion and fear. He racked his brains.

'What shall we do, sir?' asked Tubero, who was present despite a reddened bandage on his left arm.

His officers' gaze felt like a physical weight – a large one, made of lead – on Varus' shoulders.

'Would Arminius be open to negotiation, sir?' This was Ceionius, who looked scrawnier than ever.

Up to this point, no one had dared to mention Arminius, which needled Varus as much as if they'd all been bandying his name about. They were tiptoeing around him, because *he* was the one who had taken Arminius at his word about the supposed Angrivarii rebellion. Well, the cat was out of the bag now, he thought. 'Arminius is a treacherous son of a pox-ridden whore. He's given us no signs thus far that he's interested in talking. Why do you ask?'

Ceionius hesitated, then blurted, 'We could surrender, sir. Maybe he'd think about ransoming us.'

Several officers hissed with displeasure, but none shouted Ceionius down. Instead, all eyes returned to Varus.

It was odd, but Ceionius' weakness rallied Varus' strength. 'Romans do not capitulate to savages or barbarians! It is beneath us. They are little more than animals. We fight on – to the end if necessary.'

As the rest agreed loudly with Varus, Ceionius hung his head.

'What are your orders, sir?' Lucius Eggius still had some fire in his eyes.

'The wounded who cannot walk are to be given a choice,' said Varus. 'They can die at their comrades' hands, or be left behind in the morning. The rest of the injured will have to keep up, or suffer the same fate. Regroup the most weakened centuries to form complete units, using men from the same legion where possible. I want an inventory made of every sword, spear and shield. Before we march out, every whole-bodied legionary is to be fully equipped.'

'Which way shall we march, sir?' asked Tubero.

'We can't go back, or into the bog, and the savages will prevent us from going up the hill. That leaves us one choice. The same route we took today: south-southwest, towards the Lupia,' said Varus, seeing the disappointment rise in their faces. Fools, he thought. Did they expect me to magic a way for us to escape? Or to bring down the aid of the gods? 'Clear?'

The responses were muted, but they came. 'Yes, sir.' 'Very well, sir.' 'Understood, sir.'

'It's the turn of the Nineteenth to form the vanguard tomorrow, sir,' said the last legate. 'But they took a heavier battering than most. I thought perhaps one of the other legions should take their place instead.'

Varus thought at once of Tullus, whom he had wronged, and the Eighteenth. As far as he knew, Tullus was still alive. The next day's fighting might be heaviest at the front of the column, but the soldiers there would also possess the best chance of breaking away of anyone in the army. If Fortuna or Mars were of a mind, a valiant soldier such as Tullus might survive. There was no other way that Varus could make amends – and no way of knowing if the gesture would even make any difference. 'Fine. The Eighteenth will form the vanguard.'

'As you wish, sir.'

'Back to your tents.' Varus wanted to be alone. Not to sleep, because he knew that would elude him, but to plead with the gods, to make a case that *some* of his soldiers would avoid the slaughter on the morrow. Without their help, he feared that every one of them would be killed.

The bitter taste – of hemlock, it seemed again – returned to his mouth. Not for me the death of Socrates, thought Varus, gripping his sword hilt. If it comes to it, I will depart this life as a soldier.

XXVIII

Piso stood in the dark before dawn, shivering in a dripping wet cloak that now weighed twice what it did when dry. The thousands of men around him were in the same boat, which helped him not to complain. They were *all* soaking, cold, hungry and footsore. Many of them bore wounds, a good number of which would prove fatal if they didn't reach a camp with a hospital soon. Piso was lucky in that regard: he was one of a handful to have escaped being wounded thus far. From the corner of his eye, he watched a nearby legionary with a deep slash on his left foot. It wasn't usual for such an injury to be regarded as serious, but here, where to fall behind was to die, it was as bad as being gut-stuck. The man shifted position over and over. Even with the *pilum* he was using as a crutch, he was unable to take the weight on his bad foot for more than a few heartbeats. Poor bastard, thought Piso. He was a standing corpse.

Misery at his own plight soon overtook him again. He – every last one of them – might well be dead soon, and there was fuck all he could do about it.

They were waiting for Tullus to come back from checking the rest of their depleted cohort. When he returned, and the trumpets sounded – if there were any damn musicians left – they would leave the camp. Piso felt a tickle of bleak humour. With no defensive ditch, no rampart, no proper entrances, no avenues and only a few tents, it couldn't really be called a camp. Small wonder then that the tribesmen had attacked during the night. Luckily for him and the rest of Tullus' troops, they had been sleeping right in the middle of the army. The soldiers who'd been near the points at which the bastard savages had sneaked in hadn't been so fortunate. According to the rumours, more than two hundred men had died or been hurt.

'All right?' Vitellius had nudged him.

'Aye,' replied Piso, glad of the comradeship. 'I'm alive. That's what you said counts.'

'Damn right. We're here, and we're alive, and no fucking tribesman is going to stop us getting back to Vetera.'

A couple of the soldiers nearby muttered in agreement, but most didn't say a word. Despite Tullus' and Fenestela's best efforts, morale was poor. Piso wouldn't admit to it, but if it hadn't been for Vitellius, he would have fallen by the wayside long before. The fears he had nursed since the first, terrible ambush by the tribesmen had come true. Tullus had been right. There *had* been thousands of Germans ready to attack the army, of every tribe in the land it seemed. Over the previous two rainswept days, they had slain legionaries the way farmers reaped wheat at harvest time. Nowhere had the horrific losses been driven home more than around Piso. Of his original contubernium, just he, Vitellius and one other soldier remained.

Piso's grief for four of the men – three dead, and one maimed – was still raw, but it was Afer's death that had made him want to give up. Afer, hairy, round as a barrel and hard as nails, had provided the backbone, and the humour, to the eight-man unit. He'd looked out for Piso from the start. He had done so until the end, dying so that Piso could live. Tears pricked Piso's eyes at the memory. A huge warrior with a club had smashed his shield with one blow. Piso had been helpless, panicked as the warrior swung again, but Afer had leaped in front of him, dying even as he buried his gladius in the brute's unprotected belly. Piso hadn't even been able to thank Afer. By the time there'd been a break in the fighting, Afer was dead, the grey soup of his brains oozing from under his felt liner into the viscous mud.

'Right, you shower of shits!' Tullus was back.

Piso shoved away the horrific image of Afer's crushed skull and stood straighter.

'You might not know it, but the Nineteenth Legion has suffered more losses than us or the Seventeenth. Varus has seen fit, therefore, to allow us the honour of forming the vanguard today.' He flashed a grim smile as heads began to nod. 'You're not as stupid as you look, you maggots. This duty is indeed a blessing in disguise. It might be more dangerous at the front, but it also means that we can lead the way for the rest. Set the pace. Most important of all, reach one of our forts before anyone else.'

At this, the assembled men raised a cry. It had little of their usual vigour, but was better than nothing, thought Piso. He prayed that Tullus *would* get them out of this shithole.

When they had quietened, Tullus began speaking again. This time, his tone was grave. 'Varus has also given the order that any soldiers who cannot march are to be given the option of dying at a comrade's hands, or being left here. Once we're on the move, anyone who cannot keep up is also to be left behind. It grieves me that things have come to this. I did not become a soldier to slay my own men – yet I cannot disagree with the governor's command. You've seen for yourselves what the enemy is capable of. Things will be no different today. Those bastards will come at us in even greater numbers than before, or I'm no judge. Men who cannot stay with us *will* hinder our progress, and we can't let that happen, or we'll *all* fucking die.'

There was an uncomfortable silence, during which men tried not to look at their injured comrades. Piso's gaze wandered to the legionary with the injured foot; receiving a ferocious scowl, he was quick to turn his head away.

'The trumpets will sound any moment,' Tullus went on. 'It doesn't grant much time for a man to make up his mind on such a heavy matter. I'll therefore turn a blind eye to any of the injured who try to march. Keep up, and you will reach safety with the rest of us. Fall behind, and I will finish you myself. It's your choice, brothers.'

Piso didn't look at the lame soldier as the trumpets sounded. 'May the gods be with us,' he said to Vitellius.

'We'll bloody need their help,' muttered Vitellius. 'I've sworn a donation to Mars worth a month's pay if I make it.'

'He can have my entire quarter's pay,' said Piso with feeling. 'You can't take coins to Hades, my father used to say, but for the one they put in your mouth, and that's not much fucking use.'

'Except to the ferryman,' replied Vitellius with a sour chuckle.

With the remnants of the First Cohort leading the way, they began to march.

The barritus was being sung even before they cleared the edge of their temporary camp.

HUUUUMMMMMMMM! HUUUUMMMMMMMM!

Around Piso, soldiers quailed and cursed, and cursed again. Braver individuals spat their contempt on the ground. More prayed, and rubbed their phallic amulets. At least one man started to weep. His comrades soon shut him up, but the crying had an instantaneous effect, dragging their morale further towards the mud that their feet were already sinking into.

HUUUUMMMMMMMM! HUUUUMMMMMMMM!

Piso might have been imagining it, but it seemed that the noise had a keener, hungrier timbre to it than it had before. It wouldn't be surprising if it had, he thought. Savages they might be, but they're damn clever – using sound to intimidate, as Hannibal's Gauls did at Lake Trasimene. The story of how the Gaulish had sounded their carnyxes, or vertical trumpets, in the fog at the start of the battle was renowned. The unearthly sound had panicked the legionaries they'd faced, and helped the Carthaginians to inflict a crushing defeat on Rome.

A thousand paces out, and the soldier with the leg wound was struggling, barritus or no. Grunting with pain, he hobbled out of formation. 'Mars protect you, brothers,' he said, holding his head low. Blessings rained down on him, but no one intervened. No one offered to help him walk. To do so would risk their own lives.

'Have a swift journey, brother,' said Piso, feeling like a coward for not doing *something*.

The soldier made no acknowledgement. 'Centurion!' he shouted. 'A moment of your time.'

It was as if Tullus had been expecting the summons. Wheeling out of position at the front of the century, he came striding down the line. Piso and Vitellius had gone past the lame soldier, so they couldn't see what happened next. They shared a glance full of foreboding, but neither said a word. Tullus came past them again not long after, marching back to his place. He was wiping his sword clean on the hem of his tunic. The friends shared another look, but still neither spoke. There was no damn point.

No one fell out of rank after that, in part because the tribesmen's attack had begun. To constant renditions of the barritus, dense volleys of frameae and stones rained down on the Roman column. The legionaries used their scuta as defence as best they could, but there were still casualties. Stones found the gaps, however small, and frameae injured men, or lodged in shields so that they had to be discarded. Those who tried to pull the spears from their scuta became instant targets for the enemy slingers. It was safer to hide in the middle of the column, and grab a shield from the next man who was slain.

The first assault came soon after. A tide of warriors poured out from behind the earthen ramparts, led by a dozen naked berserkers. Lucky for Piso and Vitellius, the berserkers hit the unit behind them, where they wreaked fearful casualties. It took a charge by Tullus and Fenestela, with all that was left of their century, to kill the berserkers and repulse the attack. It seemed then that a madness had taken their centurion, because he didn't stop when their lines had been secured. With a roar of 'ROMA!' he ran straight after the retreating tribesmen. Fenestela was only a few steps behind him. Piso's bowels turned to water, but he pelted after, screaming at the top of his lungs. So did every legionary who could. It seemed every man knew that if Tullus died, they would *all* end up in the mud. He *had* to be kept alive.

There was a savage beauty in the way that they threw back the enemy in that too-short time. The warriors were hacked down in scores, stabbed from behind as they fought to get away through the gaps in their earthen wall, or hurled down into the space behind when the legionaries stormed the rampart with an energy born of utter desperation. The Romans used their swords for the most part, but Piso saw spears, daggers, trenching tools and even clubs seized from the enemy in his comrades' hands. Euphoric from their tiny victory, they would have remained where they were, roaring abuse at the warriors who were already regrouping deeper into the trees. Tullus it was who took control, dispersing the red battle mist with sharp blasts from his whistle and occasional thwacks of the flat of his sword blade.

Whether it was the killing of the berserkers or the fact that they had won a brief victory, no one knew, but Tullus and his cohort were left alone for a short time. The unit to their rear had fallen behind, so Tullus was quick to order a break so that his soldiers could catch their breaths. This was most welcome, yet the sound of savage fighting coming from back down the track wasn't. To further dampen the rise in their spirits, the rain that had plagued them returned with a vengeance, pouring from the heavens in such quantities that any notion of being dry vanished forever. As drenched as rats in a drain, as weary as oarsmen who've rowed at ramming speed for a mile, as fearful as criminals in the arena before the wild beasts are released, the legionaries were glad when Tullus gave the order to get moving.

The First Cohort appeared to have been blessed with similar success to theirs – the track ahead was empty – which meant that Tullus' cohort's initial progress was good. The centurion stalked up and down the column, his face covered in spatters of blood and mud, haranguing his men in a monologue that never ended. For the most part, as Piso complained to Vitellius, and Vitellius complained to Piso, they kept going only because Tullus was so fucking annoying.

It was too good to last.

At a curve in the track, the noise of combat – from the front – became audible. A ripple of unease, of anticipation passed over the legionaries. Tullus' pace didn't alter.

'The First Cohort's run into trouble again,' said Piso.

'No surprise there,' grumbled Vitellius.

They rounded the bend. A few hundred paces ahead, a dense mass of warriors surrounded the soldiers of the First. Even at a distance, it was clear that their comrades were fighting for their lives. Tullus blew his whistle, the trumpeter sounded the advance, and the weary legionaries forced their legs into the semblance of a trot.

They had covered less than half the ground when, with an ear-splitting *crrreeeeaaakkk*, a mighty beech fell sideways from the left, hitting the track with an almighty thud and separating the two groups of legionaries. There was open ground to the right, but it looked to be boggy. Crowds of warriors spilled at once from the earthen embankment and lined up behind the fallen trunk, facing Tullus and his men. They began to sing the barritus, at the same time clattering their spears off their shields. Dismay filled Piso; he could see the same emotion twisting Vitellius' face. 'We're fucked,' said someone in the rank behind.

'HALT!' Tullus spun around, his expression furious. 'I heard that!' he yelled. 'Think like that, and you *will* go to Hades. Decide that you'll fight until the last breath leaves your body, though, and you could make it out of this stinking shithole. Think of that tree as the low wall of a town. All we've got to do is get over it, and we can keep going. You maggots can scale a little thing like that, surely?'

No one laughed. They groaned back at him, but it was a sound of assent rather than refusal.

'When we reach it, I want the first two ranks – twelve men – to form a small testudo. First rank, lean up against the trunk with your shields over your heads. Second rank, kneel behind them and do the same thing. Third rank, split to either side, and protect the formation's sides. Fourth rank, you'll come with me. On my command, we'll tear up the shields, and straight over the fucking tree. The savages won't know what's hit them! Understand?' Tullus paced to and fro, studying their faces.

'It won't work,' hissed Piso, who was in the fourth rank with Vitellius. Soldiers liked to boast sometimes that an ox and cart could be driven over a testudo, but it was an old wives' tale. Men were far lighter, thought Piso, but even still . . .

'Have you got a better idea?' Vitellius answered.

Piso hadn't, so he stitched his lip.

'When the last men have gone over, the next century will form a new testudo and our first two ranks can climb over. The woman and child come last. Then the rest of the new unit follows, and so on. We do not stop until we've thrown the bastards back, and we can move the tree. Fenestela, you hear that?' Tullus called.

'Yes, sir!'

'Pass it on.' Tullus resumed his position and led them forward, at a walk this time.

If Piso had been scared during the previous days, he felt twice as bad now. Sweat slicked his cold, wet back. Fear roiled in his belly, churned his guts. The desire to have a shit was overwhelming, and to piss. From the foul smells assailing his nostrils, some men had already done both. Piso gathered the last shreds of his self-respect – Tullus had muscled in beside him, and Vitellius was on his other side – and managed not to do the same.

It was about two hundred paces to the hacked-down tree.

Two hundred paces during which Tullus' men had to endure the barritus, repeated over and over. It seemed that every warrior in Arminius' host had climbed atop the earthen rampart to sing, or to hurl abuse at them. They did not attack, however, or throw spears, which magnified Piso's feeling of dread. The bastards were waiting until they were all bunched up in front of the obstacle.

A hundred and fifty paces. The sound of fighting beyond the trunk was loud enough to be heard beneath the barritus now. Piso could make out scores of heads and spear tips on the other side. The gods alone knew how many of the whoresons there were – hundreds, maybe. They could be hurling themselves from the frying pan into the fire – they probably *were*. A hundred and twenty paces.

'We've got one advantage, brothers. They won't be expecting this tactic,' said Tullus. 'Make it count. Make it *fucking* count.'

No one answered him.

A hundred paces.

For the first time, Piso saw the lines of weariness on Tullus' face, and he realised that their centurion was human. Tullus couldn't do it on his own, just as they couldn't succeed without him. Piso rallied his courage. 'We'll do it, sir,' he said.

'You can count on us, sir,' added Vitellius.

A few other men muttered agreement.

Tullus smiled. 'You're good lads.'

At sixty paces, the enemy's spears and stones came hammering down from either side, and from the front. Men gurgled and died as they were struck; others screamed and staggered on. Those who were unhurt cursed and sweated and hunched behind their shields as they closed in. Fifty paces. Forty, thirty. Piso could see the warriors facing him. Bearded, moustached, some so young that they were yet smooth-cheeked. Every face twisted with hate; every mouth open, roaring war cries, insults, the barritus. Each man brandishing a shield, and a spear, club or sword, threatening death in any number of ways. Behind stood rank upon rank of their fellows, also clamouring to get at their enemies, the Romans. Us, thought Piso, his belly clenching.

Twenty paces.

Ten.

'Ready?' shouted Tullus. 'First rank, second rank, third rank, form testudo!'

Piso didn't dare to look to the left, where another wave of attackers waited, or at the warriors behind the trunk, who were leaping up and down. He kept his gaze fixed on the soldiers in front of him, who were in place and raising their shields. Get it over with, gods, get it over with, he thought, his fear bubbling in great torrents.

'Fourth rank, ready? Starting from the left, two at a time! Go!' shouted Tullus.

Dry-mouthed, Piso watched the first pair of soldiers from his rank move forward and place their sandals on the angled shields. The shields wavered, but held, and up the men went, their hobs pounding off the wet leather covers. Reaching the top of the trunk, they jumped down, shouting at the tops of their voices.

Vitellius and Piso were next.

Thunk. The sound of a spear landing was so close that Piso almost soiled his undergarment. Feeling no pain, he exulted. It hadn't hit him. What was probably only two frenzied heartbeats later, but felt like a lifetime, his head turned to the left. Vitellius' eyes were wide, and he had dropped his shield. 'Damn spear got me . . . just below . . . shoulder,' he said, grimacing. And stepping aside.

'No!' yelled Piso, distraught. Anyone who was left behind would die.

'Ready, Piso?' Tullus' breath was hot in his ear. 'We go. Now!'

'Vitellius . . .' Piso began.

'Fucking go!' Vitellius ordered. 'I'll be straight after you.'

A great shove from Tullus' shield, a loud curse, and Piso was charging forward and up, grief and rage tearing at him. Tullus was by his side, step for step. *Crash! Crash! Crash!* went their hobs on his comrades' shields. Both were big men, yet the soldiers below them wavered but a little. In half a dozen steps, they were atop the trunk, its bark giving good grip for their sandals. Only one legionary was still alive, his back against the tree, fighting three warriors, while a horde more tried to reach him. Guilt stabbed at Piso. Had he caused the death of the other soldier by delaying?

'ROMA!' bellowed Tullus, and jumped, smashing the bottom rim of his shield off a warrior's head.

Piso followed, before his fear paralysed him. Trying to take a less risky approach, he still collided with a tribesman's shoulder. The warrior went down under Piso, who landed partly on him and partly on his arse. Lucky for Piso, another legionary was hard on his heels. He landed in front of them both, and was able to take on, for a moment at least, the enemies who were swarming forward. The warrior under Piso reared up his head, and, releasing his shield, Piso managed to punch him hard in the face. Piso scrambled to his feet, aware that if he didn't do so fast, he'd be dead. Stab. From close range, he thrust his blade into the upturned face of the warrior beneath his feet. The blade entered via the left eye socket; there was a little spurt of vitreous fluid and the iron ran on, into the man's brain. He let out a grunt of what might have been surprise and dropped to the mud, floppy-limbed, dead.

Retrieving his scutum, Piso pushed forward to stand beside the legionary who'd just arrived. Shoulder to shoulder, shields as close as they could hold them, they fought like men possessed. To their good fortune, the press of enemy warriors was so great that the majority could not reach them. Some men were squeezed so tight that they couldn't wield their weapons. Piso and his companion went to work with grim determination.

Thrust. Stab. Punch with the shield boss. Stab. Stamp a sandal on a warrior's bare foot. Piso killed or disabled two men, and then three. Four. Five. He even head-butted a warrior who came close enough, smashing his nose with two blows of his helmet rim before running him through the belly. That opponent went down, screaming, and the next warrior hung back. For the first time, Piso had time to breathe, to glance to either side. His heart lifted. There were three legionaries on his left. By some miracle, the first soldier over the trunk was still alive, to his right, and beyond him Piso was overjoyed to see Tullus' helmet, bobbing up and down. The thuds behind told him more soldiers were arriving with every heartbeat.

Punch. Stab. Advance. Punch. Stab. Advance.

Step by bloody step, they pushed on, bowing outward from the trunk in a half-moon shape. The warriors pulled back after a time, giving the legionaries a chance to count their casualties – five dead, the same number injured – and rest. Close combat was exhausting work, and the men sagged on their shields, letting the sweat stream from their faces on to the crimson-soaked mud. Those who had a wine skin drank, and passed it around. More than one man had a piss, and there were loud curses from the unfortunates whose calves got splashed from the result. The woman stood with her back against the tree, eyes closed, rocking her child. The pup, which she had tied up in a sling around her chest, kept silent. Tullus walked among the little group, slapping backs, telling his men they had balls of iron and waving fresh legionaries into the front line.

Rather than relax, Piso left his shield behind and clambered back over the fallen tree. He swore as his purse caught on a jutting twig, and opened. Out fell Aius' bronze fasteners and a few coins. Piso made no effort to retrieve them. Too much was going on. His annoyance at the loss of his possessions vanished on the other side, however, when he found Vitellius alive. His friend was leaning against the great trunk, teeth gritted, shoulder half wrapped in a strip of dirty linen. How he would manage without a shield, Piso didn't know, or care – he was alive. Piso helped Vitellius over the tree, cursing at the soldiers who made comments about leaving the wounded behind.

The respite their fierce attack had earned them was sufficient to get what remained of Tullus' unit over the fallen tree. The next cohort was lining up to cross it, even as they were being attacked by warriors on *their* side. By the enemy's rampart on Piso's side, the warriors were massing again. What concerned Piso even more was the fact that the First Cohort had vanished, and the trunk, which was as thick around as three men, would take time to cut through. Eight legionaries were chopping at it with axes, but the tribesmen would be on them like a pack of wild dogs long before they succeeded, that was certain. The barritus, which had stopped, was being sung again, louder and louder. Three berserkers were running up and down before their fellows, exhorting them to follow. In an attempt to stop himself from panicking, Piso concentrated on getting a decent bandage on Vitellius' arm with strips torn from his own tunic.

He could hear Tullus conferring with Fenestela. 'We'll lose half our men holding this position,' said the optio, grim-faced. 'Or more.'

'If we don't move this damn tree, or hack through it, every cohort will have to fight its way across,' said Tullus.

'Not if each unit holds its place until the next is coming over.'

'What are the chances of that? The fucking First have abandoned us. Other cohorts will be no different.'

'Then why should our lads die for them?' cried Fenestela.

'Because removing the obstacle will save lives,' snapped Tullus.

'So the men should continue cutting the trunk, while the rest of us defend them, *sir*?' demanded Fenestela, laying heavy emphasis on the last word.

'That's right, *optio*.'

'As you say, *sir*.'

'Ready, brothers?' called Tullus. 'The savages are coming again. Close order! Second rank, stand in tight against the men in front. The bastards mustn't break our line. The poor fools coming after are relying on us to clear the path.'

Tullus' words sounded like a death sentence, thought Piso. Hundreds of warriors were charging towards them, and the men with the axes had a lot of work to do yet. Bog lay to their right, and to their rear the track was blocked by thousands of other legionaries. Only to their front did any chance of salvation lie – but they had to stand where they were. We're all dead, he thought. A glance at Vitellius, who had far less chance of surviving, made him feel ashamed.

He took his place in the second rank, and prepared to die.

To Piso's surprise, the tribesmen's advance faltered and slowed right down fifty paces out. Then it stopped altogether. Confused, the legionaries glanced at one another, at Tullus – and at last behind them, where more soldiers were appearing over the top of the trunk. Their leader, a fierce-looking centurion whose crest had been sheared off his helmet, made a beeline for Tullus.

'Well met,' said Tullus, grinning. 'We'll be sure to hold the filth back now.'

'Hold them back?' No Crest let out a wild laugh, and lowered his voice. 'There's no point. The battle is lost.'

Despite No Crest's attempt to speak quietly, a number of Tullus' soldiers had heard him, not least Piso.

'What in Hades are you talking about?' demanded Tullus.

'The last legate is dead – slain. So too is Lucius Eggius. All but two of the tribunes have been killed or taken prisoner. Fucking Ceionius surrendered.'

Piso couldn't believe his ears. Vitellius' face had lost the little colour it had. They stared at one another, aghast, their terror rising.

'And Varus – what about him?' asked Tullus.

'He's wounded,' replied No Crest. There was a short pause, and then he added, 'The rumour is that he's talking about suicide.'

'How sure are you of any of this?' hissed Tullus.

'The casualties are as bad as I say. A mate of mine who was in the senior officers' escort told me. Thousands of the bastards hit them about an hour back, for the second time – targeting them deliberately, it seemed. They were almost wiped out – soldiers and officers alike. About Varus – I'm not certain, but that's what everyone's saying. It's total chaos back there. Discipline's vanished, except where a few centurions have kept their heads. Men are running into the bog, surrendering, killing one another. A second eagle has been taken. It's over, brother. Time to run.' No Crest clapped Tullus on the shoulder, and marshalling his men, led them forward on to the track. A section of the waiting warriors moved off at once and aimed for this breakaway group.

Piso and those who had overheard shifted from foot to foot, their willingness to fight soaking away like piss down a sewer. The rest stared after No Crest and his soldiers, dismayed, not understanding what was going on. 'You heard him,' Piso heard Fenestela say to Tullus.

'Not so loud.'

'We can't stay!' hissed Fenestela.

'It's a rumour,' replied Tullus, but his voice sounded uncertain.

'Are all the men to die while we wait to see if it is or not? It's Varus' bloody fault that we're here in the first place. If he'd listened to you—'

'Enough,' said Tullus. 'Let me think.'

'Do it fast. They're going to hit us soon.'

The moments that followed were the longest of Piso's life. Between his comrades' shoulders and heads, he could see the wave of tribesmen advancing once more. Hundreds of them, with a constant stream of reinforcements following from the gaps in the embankment. The warriors came at a walk first, then a lope, and finally a full charge. The fearsome berserkers were in the lead – Piso could see six of them. One was frothing at the mouth, and another was wielding a club big enough to smash in a man's helmet, or to split his shield in two. The soldier in front of Piso began to cry. 'I want to go home. I want to go home. I want to go home.'

'Shut your mouth!' said Piso, but the harm had been done. Fear poured through the ranks. The men at the front began backing away from the enemy. There was precious little space to move – the trunk was only ten steps behind Piso. Despite his own fear, he shoved back, trying to stop the soldier in front from retreating.

'HOLD, YOU SHOWER OF SHIT-EATING MAGGOTS!'

His men stopped, gaped. Tullus was *in front* of them, with nothing between him and the enemy.

Seeing Tullus, the berserkers increased their speed. Perhaps thirty paces separated them from the Romans. Their fellows thundered after them in a great, death-offering tide.

'We're going down that track, brothers,' said Tullus in a loud but calm voice, even as he sidled back into the front rank. 'First, though, we have to throw back these whoresons. Can you do that for me? CAN YOU?'

Twenty-five paces.

'Yes, sir,' Piso and the rest shouted.

Twenty paces.

'I CAN'T FUCKING HEAR YOU!'

Fifteen.

'YES, SIR!'

Ten.

'ROMA!' Tullus roared.

Five.

And then the tribesmen hit.

XXIX

Varus stood in the middle of a circle of legionaries, holding a ripped piece of tunic to the wound on his thigh, and watching as the last men of his escort fought for their lives. They were in the middle of the track, surrounded by a horde of screaming warriors. Rain sheeted in from overhead, as it had since dawn, drenching Roman and German alike. The ground was long-since sodden, and water was gathering everywhere. Pooling in the ruts and footprints that had been left in the mud. Lying around the bodies. Filling the curve of a dropped shield, an upturned helmet, and dripping into the open mouths of dead men. Most were legionaries, Varus noted, feeling a dull sense of shame. The empire's soldiers. Augustus' soldiers. *His* soldiers.

I should have listened to Tullus, Varus thought for the hundredth time. That bastard Arminius was responsible for it all.

Deafening rumbles of thunder were accompanied by dull white-yellow flashes in the clouds. The light was poor enough to make a man think it was near sunset, but Varus knew it couldn't be much after midday. Gloom or no, he could still make out the damnable bog. It ran along their right side, close by, a brown-green blur of heather, cotton grass, goatweed and bog rosemary. There was nowhere to go in that direction. To their left, there would be no escape either. The earthen rampart appeared to have no beginning or end, and behind it were an endless supply of warriors.

To Varus' rear, most of the legionaries appeared to have given up hope. Many were trying to run, even shoving past his escort. The tribesmen were cutting them down in droves, easy prey for their stabbing, flickering frameae. Other soldiers were slaying their injured comrades, or falling on their own swords. A few clusters still fought on, as did the men around Varus, but they were too few, too isolated. They would die soon, as would the men around him. Had Aristides been slain yet? he wondered. He hoped that whenever the Greek met his end, it was swift. What a pity that he hadn't left him in Vetera. At least his wife was there, safe. Despite her incessant carping, it would have been good to have seen her one last time, and their grown-up children. The thought of his family caused a different type of fear to tear at Varus. His name would be mud for evermore, and it was easy to see the same happening to his loved ones, who were blameless. Gods, let them not be harmed because of my mistakes, he prayed.

'What are your orders, sir?'

The question had been repeated twice more before Varus realised it was being directed at him. He blinked, focused. A bloodied centurion stood before him, sword dripping gore, shield peppered with holes made by enemy spears. Varus didn't recognise him, which was irritating. 'What's your name?'

The centurion frowned. 'Claudius Cornelius Antonius, sir. What should—'

'Which cohort do you serve in, and what legion?'

'Never mind that, sir!' cried Antonius, gesturing at the warriors around them. 'I think we should make a break for it. You, me, and a dozen men. Replace your commander's cloak and helmet with those of an ordinary legionary. We'll get through somehow.'

'Flee, like a coward?' Varus gave him a sad smile. 'The imperial governor of Germania does not run.'

'There aren't too many other options, sir,' said Antonius, failing to keep the exasperation from his voice. 'We're being butchered. These legionaries are brave, but they won't hold for much longer.'

A sense of deep calm eased over Varus. It was pointless that more soldiers should die defending him. 'My time has come,' he said, starting to unbuckle his breastplate. 'Help me take this off.'

Shock rose in the centurion's eyes.

'At least two eagles have been lost. All my senior officers are dead, or taken prisoner, and most of my army is food for the wild animals. It is over,' said Varus. 'I deem it best to die by my own hand rather than be taken or slain by the enemy.'

'Sir, I must protest. You—'

'Enough!' barked Varus. 'When I am gone, do with your soldiers as you see fit. Run, surrender, or die fighting – it's your decision.'

'Very well, sir.' With a resigned look, Antonius began to help Varus unbuckle his armour.

'Burn my body if you can.'

'Yes, sir.' The centurion watched, stony-faced, as Varus dropped his breast- and backplate into the mud and drew his sword.

It was ironic, thought Varus, that his blade was as yet unbloodied. The closest he'd come to killing one of the enemy was the warrior who'd speared his thigh, but an anonymous legionary had slain the man before Varus had had a chance to do so.

He knelt. Rain cooled his sweaty face as he stared at the heavens, offering a brief prayer to Jupiter, and another to Mars. Thunder rumbled, as if to tell him that only the Germans' god, Donar, was listening. Varus tried not to think like that, and pictured his dead father and grandfather, who had both died in this manner. He asked them to ensure he didn't botch the job, as he had with his entire army. Gripping the ivory hilt of his sword with two hands, he reversed the blade so that its tip was sitting under the bottom rib on his left side. Its sharp point dug into his flesh a little, but he welcomed the pain. This was the best place, he had been told, near the heart.

HUUUUMMMMMMMM! HUUUUMMMMMMMM! Fresh screams, the clash of metal on metal, the thud of something heavy – a club? – cracking on to flesh. The bubbling sound of blood filling a man's throat. Antonius cursed, roared at his men to fucking hold! The sounds, and the deaths they signified, came to Varus down a long, dark tunnel. More than anything now, he wanted to go somewhere else. A place where he could forget the infernal mud, the bloodshed, his dead soldiers and, most of all, his failure. He bent at the waist. If his thrust wasn't enough, his body had to slide on to the sword and finish what he had started.

He could taste bile in his mouth now, feel his heart racing, almost as if it was trying to escape his blade. Varus clenched his fists on the ivory and tensed his muscles. With a mighty effort, he wrenched the sword towards himself. A ball of white-hot pain exploded in his core, eclipsing anything he had ever felt. Varus used the last of his strength to pull the iron deeper into his body – and to fall forward.

The mud came up to meet him with sickening speed.

Arminius, he thought.

XXX

Tullus didn't know how he had dragged any of his men away from the tree trunk. If there had been more berserkers, they would have all died there. As it was, half the surviving soldiers in his century had fallen before they'd slain the berserkers and thrown the tribesmen back. Despite this tiny success, their enemies didn't withdraw more than a couple of dozen paces. There was no need. Tullus' men were too exhausted – and outnumbered – even to contemplate a counterattack. The warriors were human too, though. They had also suffered many casualties. When men had survived the storm of iron – again – they needed a few moments to catch ragged breath, to let screaming muscles rest, to piss the few drops that felt like an amphora's worth.

The tribesmen knew that they had the upper hand, of course. Tullus and his soldiers needed reinforcements, but their enemies required only a break before they swept to the attack again. So, ignoring the watching warriors the way a lame deer tries not to see stalking wolves, Tullus had started out along the muddy track once more, step by weary step. There had been no time to treat the wounded, no time to do anything other than order everyone who could to follow. 'If you want to fucking live, come with me,' Tullus said. Fewer than twenty men had broken away with him, the vast majority bearing at least one wound. Fenestela was still there, and the new recruit Piso, and his friend Vitellius, who wasn't even able to hold a shield. Most incredibly, the woman he had rescued and her child had survived. So had the pup. It was far fewer than he'd wanted, but it was better than none, Tullus told himself. Better than none. Bitterness washed over him. How had it come to the point where he could envisage his soldiers being annihilated?

Little groups from the rest of the cohort – sixes, tens, sometimes more soldiers – trailed in their wake, but Tullus didn't stop to rally them. That was up to their centurions and optiones, if they lived. His command had reduced to his century, just his century. It was a brutal choice, but if he tried to save any more men than that, they wouldn't make it. The tree had been the final straw. Such a simple thing to do, but so effective. You whoreson, Arminius, he thought.

After a hundred steps, the warriors hadn't moved. Tullus cast a look over his shoulder at them. Maybe he and his men were in luck at last. Maybe the bastards were going to wait for the next legionaries. They covered another fifty steps, and his hope was borne out. Summoning what remained of his reserves of energy, Tullus drove his men into a speed that approached the double pace. Not long after, he was delighted to see a massive stony outcrop to their left, which had prevented the rampart from being continuous. From the look of it, it went on for some distance. Who knew what lay beyond, but having a guaranteed respite from the enemy's attacks felt like a gods-given gift. Tullus let his tired soldiers slow down, bandaged a man's leg, gave several a hearty clap on the back, smiled at the woman, squeezed Fenestela's arm. He kept moving, however. In this pit of despair, to stop was to die.

The rise in his spirits did not last.

Around the far side of the outcrop, more earthen ramparts loomed. Atop them, a mob of screaming warriors was raining spears down on what had to be what was left of the First Cohort. Heaps of bodies on the track were evidence that the fighting had been going on for some time. Tullus slowed up, stopped, and fought a rising despair. He'd cursed the First for deserting them, but had also hoped they had escaped. Here was a warning sign as to their own probable fate.

It was as if Tullus' body realised how beaten he was feeling. Every part of him began to protest at the same time. His thighs ached; his arms shook with fatigue. The base of his spine throbbed, as if an unhappy smith were beating on it with his heaviest hammer. Darts of pain radiated from the point beneath where the sling bullet had struck his mail shirt. A miserable crone was stabbing needles into the old injury in his calf. His eyes felt as if they were full of sand, his mouth and throat were dry and sore, yet his face ran with sweat. What he wanted – *longed for* – was to lie down, and close his eyes. The fucking soothsayer had been right, he decided. The mud would be the end of them all.

'Don't give up on me, you dog.'

'Eh?' Annoyed that he hadn't noticed Fenestela creep up, shocked by what he'd hissed, Tullus wheeled. His optio was close enough for it to be uncomfortable, eyes understanding, but flint-hard. He sees the fear in me, thought Tullus, feeling like an old man, like a failure.

'If you give up, Tullus, we're fucked. Fucked. All of us,' whispered Fenestela. 'Take a look at the men. One look! They're only marching because you're leading them. *You* are giving them hope. *You.* If you can't find a way out of this shithole, there's no chance that they will. As for the woman and her child – they'll be dead by sundown.'

Fenestela was right, thought Tullus. He had been watching his soldiers sidelong since they had set out that morning, seen their morale being nibbled away, piece by tiny piece, with each successive attack. Like as not, they were doomed, but he owed it to the men not to give up. And the woman. What point would there have been in saving her if he abandoned her now? He took a deep breath, straightened his creaking back. 'I hear you. We keep going.'

Fenestela looked relieved. He jerked his head at the beleaguered legionaries ahead. 'The way I see it, our best chance is to avoid fighting and barrel on past them, heads down, right along the edge of the bog.'

Tullus studied the maelstrom and saw that Fenestela's eyes had been sharp indeed. Fear of the marshy ground had kept both sides away from it, which had left a narrow strip at its border clear of combatants. 'A good plan,' he said. 'Form the men up in single file. We'll take it at a slow pace until I blow my whistle, then double-time it through the fighting. Instruct everyone to focus on the ground, not the enemy.'

'Aye.' Fenestela went to leave, and Tullus reached out to stop him.

'What you said. I-I thank you.'

'You'd do the same for me.'

Tullus' heart clenched. 'I would. See you on the other side.'

'On the other side,' repeated Fenestela, winking. Off he went, repeating Tullus' orders.

'Ready, brothers?' asked Tullus, battening down his fear that Fenestela's flimsy plan would fail.

'Yes, sir,' his soldiers croaked back. 'Aye.' 'Get us out of here, sir.'

With a low blast of his whistle, Tullus led the way.

It wasn't possible to double-time it through the combat area – in places they had to wade through the edge of the bog, sinking to their calves. Yet thanks to the savagery of the battle and the mud that covered them from head to toe, they went unnoticed by tribesmen and legionaries alike. Tullus was reminded of the thieves who had once robbed the largest wine merchant in Rome of his best stock by simply overpowering the workers inside his premises and loading the amphorae into their wagons on the street, before everyone's eyes. Men often go unseen, if they act with purpose, as if they were born to be there.

Perhaps half a mile later, they had left the doomed First behind. Breaks in the German rampart started to appear. To everyone's amazement – and relief – they were unmanned. Tullus took heart. Clever though he was, Arminius wasn't fully able to instil Roman discipline into his allies. Like as not, the warriors who'd been assigned to these positions had grown tired of waiting for legionaries to arrive, and decamped to where the fighting was.

His hunch proved correct. Some distance further on, they came across the corpses of the last auxiliaries, Gauls, sprawled along a section of track only a few hundred paces in length. The Gauls had stayed together, and forced the tribesmen to pay a heavy toll before they had fallen. The mounds of corpses were the only signs of the enemy to be seen, however. Tullus began to hope again. The further they travelled without hindrance, the more likely it was that they had gone beyond the last of Arminius' forces.

The cynic in him thought that it was too good to last, and he was right. A short while later, the only thing that saved them from immediate discovery was a slight bend in the track. Hearing the sound of men coming from beyond it, Tullus forced, shoved, cursed his soldiers off the path, *behind* the enemy rampart. If there had been a single warrior still in position there, they would have been undone, but they were met by nothing more than pools of flood water, a few discarded rinds of cheese and the smell of men's piss. Tullus' men sagged against the banked earth and turf wall as if it were the softest of beds, while he kept a lookout from a gap in the fortifications.

Tullus watched, dry-mouthed, as several hundred tribesmen went by, heading towards the fighting. Not a single one as much as glanced towards their position – until, that was, the girl let out a whimper. Tullus saw a warrior's head turn at the back of the group. Fucking brat, he thought, wheeling around. You'll be the death of us all. The woman had already clamped a hand over her daughter's mouth, and he gestured furiously that she should continue to do so, and that his men should also stay silent. Peering back, his heart sank. The warrior had broken away from the party, and was sauntering their way. A comrade called out; Tullus heard the man reply that he had heard something, which was probably nothing, but he needed a shit. He'd catch up soon.

Tullus looked out of the gap until the risk of being seen was too great. The warrior still appeared to be on his own, which was something. Leaning his sword against the earthen wall, Tullus tugged out his dagger and stepped to the other side of the gap. Fortuna, I've tested your patience more than once, he thought, but be good to me one more time, and I swear I'll offer you the finest bull money can buy. Heart thudding, knife ready, he waited. Listened.

Nothing. Tullus breathed in and out, in and out through his nose. His backache got worse. Still he heard nothing. Had the warrior decided to empty his bowels *in front* of the rampart? Seeing a questioning look on more than one man's face, he pointed outside, squatted in mime, and put a finger to his lips. They might escape discovery yet. It was possible that the warrior wouldn't check behind the fortification.

The unmistakeable sound of a footstep close to the gap put paid to that hope.

Tullus pressed his back against the earth, cursing himself for a fool. He should have got Fenestela or one of the others to wait opposite, so that there would be someone to kill the warrior whichever way he looked upon entering. It was too late, however. Tullus had to hope that the warrior turned his head to the right, or that if he looked in *his* direction, there would be enough time to kill the man before he shouted an alarm.

Sweat coated Tullus' palm, loosened his grip on the dagger. He clenched his fist, pricked his ears. A loud fart from outside almost made him laugh. The sound of a man shitting – diarrhoea, it sounded like – was enough to propel him into action. He wouldn't get a better chance. Tullus stuck his head around the gap a fraction, enough to check that the group of tribesmen had passed out of sight – they had – and then he came round the corner as fast as his legs would carry him. The warrior was crouched against the rampart, breeches down, frown of concentration on his face. Too late he heard Tullus coming, too late his mouth opened in horror.

Stab, stab. Stab, stab. With the urgency of a smith beating a white-hot sword into shape, Tullus hammered the blade into the side of the warrior's neck and chest. Four, five, six times. Blood gouted from the wounds on to Tullus' hand. A choking gurgle left his victim's lips, and Tullus stabbed him twice more for good measure. There was a final, bubbling fart, and the warrior slipped sideways to the ground, his expression still disbelieving.

Tullus gagged, not from the coppery tang of blood, but from the harsh reek of fresh shit. A quick check down the track – he saw no warriors – was enough to make him swear to Fortuna that the bull was hers. If he made it, that was. Remember that, Fortuna, he thought. I have to reach

Vetera to be able to fulfil my vow. It wasn't wise to hold a deity to account, but the slaughter had seen Tullus lose all inhibition in that regard.

If it had been the pup that had made a sound, he might have slit its throat, but it wasn't in Tullus to kill a child, in particular one whom he'd rescued. It was almost as if the woman knew – she gave him a pathetic smile as he urged his men from behind the rampart.

'I'll keep her quiet in future,' she whispered.

'See that you do,' Tullus replied, grim-faced. 'We won't be so fortunate again.'

Aware that their fate yet hung by a thread, Tullus sent ahead Piso, one of the three uninjured men. His instructions were to spy out any tribesmen before the group was seen, a difficult task. Piso set off without a word of protest, however, asking only that someone keep an eye on his friend Vitellius. The battle had turned him into a proper soldier, thought Tullus with a degree of pride.

Piso proved his worth twice in the hours before nightfall, loping back down the path to warn them that warriors were approaching. They hid behind the rampart on the first occasion, but the second time there was nowhere to go but into the bog. Shrinking behind the inadequate cover of heather bushes, worming themselves chest deep into the mud, lying flat behind goatweed plants, the terrified party waited for what seemed an age before the tribesmen, many of whom sounded drunk, had gone on their way.

As it grew dark, Tullus picked a spot to spend the night. It was nothing more than a dense copse of beech, to the left of the track, but at a hundred and fifty paces' distance, it was too far for a tribesman to stray for a piss or shit. The rampart had finished some time before, meaning that they were once more in the forest. Despite his little group's miraculous escape, Tullus felt ill at ease. Bands of warriors would pass their position at some point, and see them. The child or the pup might give them away again. They had no food or blankets. Water could be had from the pools lying about, it was true, but his shattered men needed more than that. It was too dangerous to light a fire, even if they had had dry wood. The list of Tullus' fears was endless, and they gnawed away at his guts, an incessant pain that rivalled any of his other aches.

What concerned him too was that he had spotted a fork in the track. He had no idea which way was the fastest route to the Lupia and a Roman fort. In the morning, he would have to choose, and if he made the wrong decision, their survival that day would have meant nothing.

In spite of all his worries, Tullus fell asleep the moment he closed his eyes.

He dreamed of slaughter.

He was fighting for his life against two berserkers. Just as they had that day, the pair split up, one attacking Tullus from the front while the other circled around to his rear. Struggling to hold his own against the first berserker, he could do nothing about the second. As he clashed with the opponent before him, Tullus felt someone grab him by the left arm. Expecting a blade across his throat next, Tullus twisted, tried to turn, spat a curse. Even if he stopped the second berserker, the first would gut him where he stood.

A hand was placed across his mouth. 'Quiet! It's me, Fenestela!'

Tullus came awake with an unpleasant jolt. There were no berserkers attacking him. He was lying on his side, chilled to the bone, under a tree. Fenestela was crouched by him, covering his mouth. Tullus shook his head to show he understood, and moved Fenestela's fingers away. 'A bad dream. I'm all right,' he whispered. 'What is it?'

'Piso's here, sir. He was on sentry duty. He's got someone with him.'

Fenestela's tone drove the last woolliness from Tullus' brain. He sat up, wincing at the pain that issued from every part of his body. 'Who?'

Fenestela leaned in close. 'That warrior of yours, sir. Degmar.'

Tullus' heart leaped. '*Degmar? Here?*'

'Aye. He's just over there, with Piso.' Fenestela jerked a thumb at the edge of the copse.

Tullus hurried over with Fenestela, stumbling over tree roots and the outstretched bodies of his resting men. He spied Degmar squatting on his haunches, chewing on something. Piso stood behind him, half watching the ground that led down to the track, half watching the Marsi warrior. Degmar rose as Tullus drew near; his teeth flashed white in the dim light. 'Well met,' muttered Tullus, extending a hand. They shook, hard. '*Well met*,' Tullus said again, grinning. 'It's good to see you – alive.'

'No surprise that you're still here,' replied Degmar, his lips turning upward.

'Fortuna has been kind to a few of us at least,' said Tullus, throwing a glance at his soldiers.

Degmar let out a sniff. 'It was *you* who got them here, not Fortuna.'

It was true, thought Tullus. What a pity he had not been able to save more men. 'I thought you were dead.' He hesitated. Degmar chuckled and said:

'Or that I'd run, eh?'

'I did wonder that. It wouldn't have been so surprising.'

'I made an oath to you. Arminius' ambush doesn't change that. Until my debt has been repaid, I follow you.'

Tullus smiled. 'To find me, here, you're better than any scent hound I've ever come across.'

'It was complete chance, to be honest. I couldn't find you after I'd finished scouting, and it was too dangerous for me to join another unit – they'd have killed me. I hid for two more days, and then followed after the army. There was no point checking if you were among the dead – there were too many. I assumed that you'd survived and kept skirting around the fighting. That wasn't hard, given the way I'm dressed.' Degmar indicated his tunic and trousers, which were typical of any German warrior. 'I continued moving when it grew dark today, listening out for anyone speaking Latin. I came across several little groups, but none had any senior officers among them. In the end, I started looking for shelter, and came upon this copse. Your sentry saw me first, and called out a challenge in

Latin. Lucky for me, I was able to answer in the same tongue. I gave him my name – and he told me you were here.' Degmar shrugged. 'You're making for the Lupia, I take it?'

'Aye,' replied Tullus, thinking of the fork in the track. 'Do you know the way?'

'I do.'

Weary or not, Tullus could have done a dance on the spot. 'That's more than I could have hoped for. How far is it to Aliso?'

'Forty-five miles, maybe fifty. Expect a slow journey. Three days, or four. We'll have to take smaller paths through the forest. The main ways will be too dangerous.'

Tullus had been expecting this, but he still felt a fresh stab of fear. 'Arminius' warriors are going to attack the local forts?'

'From what I heard, they're going to set alight every Roman settlement east of the Rhenus. Aliso may well have fallen by the time we reach it,' said Degmar. 'If we reach it,' he added without apparent irony.

'Caedicius is a crafty old bird,' Tullus said, remembering the night he and Tubero had spent with him in the spring, and the wine they had consumed. It seemed a lifetime ago. 'The camp will prove hard to take with him in charge.'

Degmar's grunt was non-committal. 'May the gods grant it be so. The road between Aliso and Vetera will be long indeed if we have to march it on our own.'

XXXI

By the end of the third day, Arminius had been aware of the scale of his victory, but the knowledge didn't really sink in until the following morning, when he went to survey the battlefield alone. The contrast between the riotous, drunken atmosphere in the various tribes' camps and the calm of the woodlands beyond was stark, but neither bore any comparison to the staggering scenes of carnage that greeted him on and around the route taken by the ill-fated Romans. His horse, a combat veteran, was first to protest, shying and jinking along the path. Its reaction wasn't altogether surprising, thought Arminius, his nostrils laden with the odour of blood, shit and the gas that bloats dead men's bellies, his ears full of the buzzing of flies and the harsh cawing of the corpse-feeding ravens and crows.

The vast majority of slain warriors had been carried away by their fellows for honourable burial, but the legionaries' bodies lay everywhere, like household rubbish scattered on a midden. Most had been stripped of their armour and weapons, leaving them the indignity of exiting this world in their tunics or undergarments. Face down in the bog, half submerged in murky pools, on their backs, staring at the sky. Alone, in pairs, in groups, under a speared horse, heaped on top of one another like a pile of toys discarded by a child. Back to back, or in circles, where they had fought and died together, or in lines, cut down one by one as they ran. One unfortunate was still on his knees. Several thrusts of a framea had opened his throat, and Arminius wondered if the legionary had been arranged in the position after he'd died, in mockery of his cowardice.

Crushing the heads of the dead had been popular, for, in the Germans' minds, that prevented a man's soul from leaving his body. Scores of legionaries had had their eyes gouged out, and more had been decapitated, with the severed heads being nailed to trees afterwards, as victory symbols and warnings both. The mutilations didn't stop there. Ears had been bitten off. There were legs missing, and feet, hands, even testicles. Stone altars had been erected in a number of places, and there high-ranking officers had been burned alive. Blackened, twisted shapes were all that remained of their bodies. Arminius' gorge rose at the sight, but he was not sorry that it had happened, nor that the legionaries had died in so many other brutal ways. The innumerable corpses were physical proof of his sacrifice to Donar, the bloody embodiment of his oath, laid out in terms so uncertain that no one could miss their intent. This was Rome's reward for its aggressive role in the region for the past quarter-century: divine justice, delivered by his warriors' spears.

Those in the empire's capital would call what had been done here savagery, Arminius thought, but this was how his people – *his* people – treated their enemies' dead. Even if that hadn't been their tradition, the Romans were the invaders here, the wrongdoers, not he and his fellow tribesmen.

What they had done – what *he* had done – was to wipe out Varus and his wolves, the ruthless enforcers of Augustus' rule. In the days that followed, obeying Arminius' orders, thousands of warriors would sack and burn every settlement east of the Rhenus, cleansing the land of Roman influence. He wondered how fast news of the initial calamity – his ambush – would reach the emperor. It wouldn't be long: in extremis, the imperial messengers could travel extraordinary distances each day. Tremble in your palace, old man, he thought. With a stroke, I have wiped out three legions. One tenth of your army. One tenth!

It was frustrating that amidst such incredible success, only two eagles had been taken by the tribes. A third one was missing, and it was this that had taken Arminius from his blankets. His victory, the defeat inflicted on Rome, could not be complete without the last eagle. The gold birds were the ultimate symbol of Rome's power, the beating heart of every legion, and therefore one of the highest battle honours that a leader could bestow on his allies. Varus' head was another, it was true, but that was to be sent to Maroboduus, leader of the Marcomanni tribe, in an effort to win him over to the war against Rome. Arminius had gifted the Nineteenth's eagle to the Bructeri, who had inflicted huge casualties on the enemy, and that of the Twentieth to the Chauci, a tribe that had arrived late, but with six thousand warriors. Without the last golden standard, he could not give the Marsi the reward he'd promised them. The eagle would do more than cement their alliance, it would recognise the tribe's valiance. Their small numbers had not prevented them from wiping out the senior officers and their escort – a pivotal moment in the ambush, when Roman resistance had crumbled beyond repair.

A wailing cry caught Arminius' attention. It wasn't the first time he'd heard such a sound – the women who followed after his warriors were here already, working their way through the dead, searching for money and other treasures. Anyone they found alive received a swift knife between the ribs. This victim was receiving different treatment, for his protest went on and on, a trailing sound of agony and despair. Curious, Arminius urged his horse towards its point of origin, a clearing in the trees hard by a section of the earthen rampart he'd had built. As he drew nearer, sunlight glinted off something metallic at its base, and he saw the facepiece of a Roman cavalry helmet, sitting upright, as a man's decapitated head might. There was no sign of the main body of the helm, and the valuable silver sheeting had been prised away from the facepiece with a blade. The eyeholes in the blackened piece of iron in the shape of a human face seemed to watch Arminius, and he found himself averting his gaze.

Gods, let that have belonged to Tubero, he thought. Arminius had retained an intense dislike of the tribune. To his frustration, there had been no word of Tubero among the high-rankers who'd been slain or captured. In an odd way, Arminius decided, it would be apt if the young politician-in-waiting had escaped – proving him to be as greasy as he appeared.

The man being tortured – by four warriors – wasn't Tubero. From the look of his armour and helmet, which lay alongside him, he was just an ordinary legionary. What wounds he'd had from the battle, Arminius couldn't tell, but since being discovered, he had had his tongue cut out. Red-lipped, dripping gore from his mouth, emitting a high-pitched, agonised wail, he knelt before his captors, hands raised in supplication.

The warriors were so engrossed that they didn't notice Arminius. They were Usipetes, which didn't surprise him. While other warriors preferred to sleep off their hangovers, they had the youths who'd been in the raiding party to avenge.

'I can't understand you,' said one of the warriors, sniggering.

'I think he wants his tongue back,' declared another, a man with a mane of black hair. He waved a blob of red tissue under the legionary's nose. The soldier recoiled, screaming louder, and Black Hair said, 'At last, you viper, you have ceased to hiss.'

His companions fell about laughing.

Black Hair was first to grow serious. 'Hold him,' he ordered. Two of his fellows seized the legionary by his shoulders, and watched as Black Hair pulled a needle and thread from a pouch by his waist. Frowning with concentration, Black Hair began to sew the legionary's lips together. His victim's cries reached new heights, and he struggled so much that Black Hair cuffed him across the head and threatened, 'Want me to scoop out your eyeballs as well?'

The terrified legionary shook his head in a vehement 'No'.

'Stay still, then!' Black Hair bent and resumed his handiwork. Incredibly, the legionary managed to steady himself, although he could not refrain from making muffled groans. When Black Hair was done, he put away his needle and rubbed his hands together. 'My workmanship is a little crooked, perhaps, but it's not bad, eh?'

'Next time there's a hole in my tunic, I know where to come,' said one of his comrades, grinning.

'Greetings!' Arminius called.

The warriors turned. Recognising Arminius, they hailed him as the conquering hero he was. Arminius dismounted, accepted their shoulder claps and hearty praise. 'Been watching us?' asked Black Hair, jerking a thumb at the legionary, who had slumped to the ground. His eyes were glazed with horror, and great sobs were racking his frame. He'd pissed himself as well.

'Aye,' said Arminius.

'I will take his eyes next.' Black Hair chuckled as the legionary gurgled a protest, and said over his shoulder, 'Promises to a Roman mean nothing, you fool.'

Arminius hid his growing distaste with a broad smile, and a promise to deliver more Romans into the Usipetes' hands. They liked that. 'I'll leave you to it,' said Arminius as they returned their attention to the legionary. The four were so wrapped up that they barely acknowledged his farewell.

A piercing cry shredded the air before Arminius' horse had taken more than a few steps. Unsettled, it skittered to and fro, nickering. Shushing it, Arminius ignored the terrible sound and rode off. The clamour died away at last. Whether it was through distance, or the victim's death, Arminius couldn't tell. He didn't care either way.

Time passed – an hour, perhaps two – without any sign of the elusive third eagle. Arminius found himself studying the faces of the innumerable dead, wondering if Flavus could have survived. Despite his antipathy towards his brother, Arminius half hoped that that *had* been the case. There would be no way of knowing. Arminius could never again cross to the western bank of the Rhenus, and if Flavus lived, the same applied to him in reverse. My brother is dead to me from this day on, he decided, putting Flavus from his mind with grim deliberation.

Arminius found the site where Varus had committed suicide, and the blackened patch of ground where his aides had failed to burn his body. He counted the bodies of no fewer than thirty centurions; none of them was Tullus, which he was grateful for. Part of Arminius hoped that Tullus had been among the handful of survivors he'd heard of. Yet it was the eagle and the fact that it wasn't in his possession that kept niggling at him. The damn thing might even have been carried away by the legionaries who had escaped.

Chewing his cheek, Arminius didn't see the raven rise up from a body right at his horse's hoofs. Its sharp, disapproving *kakakakaka* startled his mount so much that it reared in panic. Down he went, off its back like a child who'd never ridden before. Arse-first in the mud, splattered from head to toe in muck, he watched in disgust as the horse took off at a fine pace. The raven alighted on a nearby branch and watched him with a keen eye. *Krrruk*, it said, as if satisfied. *Krrruk. Krrruk.*

Arminius threw a sardonic glance at the body it had been feeding on, a legionary with – now – only one eyeball. 'Keeping you from your lunch, am I?'

Krrruk, replied the raven.

'It's all yours.' Arminius got to his feet, thinking: Donar is having the last laugh. Ah well, he's entitled to it. His bird, his body, his victory.

It would be a long walk back to the camp and a change of clothing, but that didn't matter, Arminius decided. He would think of other gifts that would honour the Marsi for what they had done. Perhaps a couple of cohort standards and an image of Augustus would do.

Something metallic glinted at the edge of his vision. Arminius turned his head, spotting a body face down in the bog some thirty paces away. It was just another corpse, but then he noticed that under its cloak, it was wearing scale armour. In general, only centurions and standard-bearers wore such mail, and it was unusual for either to run away. His interest piqued, Arminius began to squelch his way towards it. What was a little more mud in his boots?

There was no sign of a helmet near the body – like as not, the man had thrown it away to reduce his visibility to the enemy. There were no visible signs of mutilation either, which made Arminius wonder if the soldier had died of his wounds. This was confirmed when he rolled the corpse over and saw a deep wound in the man's left thigh. He had bled to death, Arminius decided, or maybe the poor bastard had drowned, face down in the mud.

It was still unclear whether the man had been a centurion or standard-bearer, but it didn't matter either way. You're food for the ravens now, thought Arminius, using his boot to flip the body back on to its front. Pain radiated from his toes as they met something more solid than armour and flesh. So surprised that he didn't even curse, he tugged at the man's cloak. It took a moment or two to unwrap the woollen folds, and his heart began thumping as if he were about to go into battle. When the cloak fell away, a golden eagle with upraised wings was revealed. Arminius lifted the standard, savouring the *weight* of it, and the miracle that had delivered it into his hands. When he looked, the raven was still on its branch, watching him.

Arminius shivered. Never had a creature seemed more like a messenger from Donar. Never had he been offered such tangible proof of the thunder god's favour. He gave silent, fervent thanks. Anything seemed possible now. Donar was backing *his* mission to rid the tribal lands of all Roman influence.

What more could a man ask for?

XXXII

Tullus and his men spent four long, wet, tiring days on the march. For that entire time, they were each and every one soaked, chilled to the bone and hungrier than a tied-up dog with an empty food bowl. If it hadn't been for the plentiful supply of blackberries and an occasional rabbit trapped by Degmar, they would have gone without any sustenance. The tough conditions were too much for two of the wounded, who died in their sleep. Tullus was left with fifteen soldiers, the woman, her girl and the pup. It was a pathetic total, but he kept telling himself it was better than none at all. Twelve swords – Vitellius and three others wouldn't be able to fight for a month at least – would be an addition of some sort to Caedicius' garrison.

Their chances of reaching Aliso rested on Degmar's shoulders, and Tullus felt ever more grateful that they had chanced upon each other. Without the Marsi's unerring sense of direction, they would have lost their way. Appearing not to need the sun, which for the most part was hidden behind dense banks of rainclouds, Degmar led them along winding, narrow tracks through the forest. When they came across boglands, he seemed able to find a path through that didn't involve drowning. He skirted past the areas of farmland at dusk or dawn, when the local inhabitants were in bed, without the alarm being raised. His one slip-up came when he took the group on to a larger track that led southwest. A close call with a party of Angrivarii warriors – they were not seen – ended the attempt soon after it had started.

Late on the afternoon of the fourth day, Degmar brought them to the top of a low hill. It was perhaps a mile from Aliso, he told Tullus, pointing to the south. Tullus peered through the drizzle, and cursed. Fenestela spat. Across the tops of the trees, in the direction that Degmar was pointing, rose spirals of smoke. There were so many of them, spread out, that they could not all be coming from the camp. 'It's under attack.'

'As I said it would be.' There was an I-told-you-so look on Degmar's face.

Tullus swore again, long and hard. So did Fenestela.

'Do you want to skirt around it and head for the river, a few miles downstream?' asked Degmar. 'Arminius might have set warriors to watch the road to Vetera, but it's possible that they're just concentrating on Aliso.'

Tullus remembered the sick, guilty feeling he'd had when they had fled from the fallen tree. '*No*. If the garrison is still holding out, and it's possible to find a way in, we do so.'

'You're sure?' Degmar's expression now showed he thought Tullus was insane.

'Aye, I'm fucking sure.'

Degmar shrugged. 'Stay here – I'll take a look.'

'Straight from the frying pan into the fire.' Fenestela's voice was resigned.

'Maybe,' said Tullus. 'We can't leave them there, though, can we?'

'It's damn tempting, but I suppose we can't.'

'No, we can't.' Tullus tried not to consider the fact that Vetera lay less than forty miles to the west. Dying here would seem even more pointless than in the forest. Remember the bull I promised you, Fortuna, he thought. A big bastard he'll be, with fine horns and broad shoulders, and balls so big that they almost touch the ground. That beast is yours when I cross that bridge. Not a moment before.

Degmar returned with the news that the tribesmen's encirclement of Aliso was incomplete. He had also spotted a small gate in the northern wall which appeared to be unwatched. The information was enough to cement Tullus' decision to enter the fort. During the late afternoon, the group crept close to Aliso's northern side and hid themselves in the woods. When it was almost dark, they moved to the edge of the trees. Dots of light marked the fires in the enemy camp, which sprawled in disorder as far as the eye could see. The sound of men talking, laughing, arguing carried through the crisp autumn air. So too did the hunger-accentuating smell of cooking meat.

Tullus would have wished for a good plan of action, but that was impossible. What they were about to do bordered on madness. Even if they sneaked past the enemy camp, they risked being taken for attackers by the garrison. He quelled his disquiet. Taking the road to Vetera instead wouldn't guarantee them a safe passage either. For all he knew, Arminius' warriors were guarding the entire route.

By the time several hours had passed, peace had fallen over the tribesmen's encampment. Most of the fires had gone out. There appeared to be few, if any, sentries. Degmar appeared by Tullus' side. 'Ready?' he whispered.

The knot in Tullus' stomach twisted a little tighter. There was no *good* time, no *right* time, he thought. 'Aye.'

Out they slunk, Degmar leading the file with Tullus next and the legionaries after. The woman and child with the pup followed, and Fenestela took up the rear. Tullus was relying on his soldiers' cloaks to disguise their armour; he'd ordered each man to sling his helmet around his neck, removing another tell-tale sign that they were Roman. More than that he could not do.

They reached the enemy position without difficulty, but from there, things became problematic. Finding the gap between the groupings of warriors' tents and lean-tos that Degmar had spied proved close to impossible in the darkness. Unable to stop for long – that would attract attention – they had to walk *through* part of the camp, aiming for the black shape that was Aliso. It was beyond fortunate that any tribesmen in the vicinity who were still up had congregated around a large bonfire, allowing Tullus' party not just to pass by, but to orientate themselves again.

Respect for the defenders' ballistae meant that more than three hundred paces of empty ground lay between the last enemy tents and the fort's walls. Tullus felt relieved to reach it, but too exposed. Any warrior who saw them from this point onward would be suspicious. An alert Roman sentry might raise the alarm, trapping them in no-man's land. When Degmar glanced at him, therefore, he indicated that they should keep moving. 'Quiet as you can,' he hissed in the ear of the first soldier. 'Pass it on.'

Dry-mouthed, with a thumping heart, Tullus stole after Degmar. Two hundred paces later, he began to dream that they might make it. After another twenty steps, though, a muffled curse from the rear gave the lie to that hope. Tullus halted Degmar, and the lead soldier, and paced down the line, asking, 'Anything wrong?'

Every soldier said he was all right until he reached Fenestela. 'What is it?' demanded Tullus.

'The woman's gone.'

Tullus' head jerked around to the final legionary – he hadn't noticed she was absent. 'Where is she?'

'Her brat let go of the pup, and it ran off. The woman told her to forget the damn thing, but she went after it. The mother took off too,' Fenestela muttered. 'To Hades with both of them.'

Peering back at the enemy camp, Tullus could see nothing. He clenched his jaw. To go after the woman would put all of his men at risk. Bad as he felt, he couldn't do it. 'To the wall,' he ordered.

The last eighty paces felt to Tullus like the final steps of a condemned man walking down the tunnel and into the arena. Yet there was no outcry from atop the rampart, and they were able to cross the defensive ditch over a section that the warriors had filled with turves. It didn't take Degmar long to find the door. Throwing up a prayer, Tullus rapped on it with his fist.

There was no response, so he struck it with the hilt of his sword. The hollow thumping noise was loud, loud enough to carry. Tullus' nerves were stretched as tight as wire as he waited but, to his huge relief, a sentry within responded before any of the enemy. Tullus met his suspicious challenge with a reply – in Latin. Quickly, Tullus said who he was, and to prove that he *had* to be Roman, gave Caedicius' nickname, 'Twenty-miler', after his habit of doling out long punishment marches to soldiers. The dutiful sentry insisted on getting his officer, but the door was opened soon after, and in Tullus' soldiers went.

Tullus hung back, unable to put the woman and child from his mind. Without being asked, Degmar stayed by his side.

Fenestela's teeth flashed in the gloom as he reached the entrance. 'We did it,' he whispered.

'Aye. Stay by the door.'

Fenestela sensed Tullus' purpose at once. 'Leave her!'

'I can't. Imagine what they'll do to her when she's found.'

'That's not your problem.'

Ignoring Fenestela, Tullus stalked back into the darkness with Degmar.

'We'll be lucky to find her,' muttered Degmar.

'Go back if you wish,' retorted Tullus, wondering why he was risking his life yet again.

But Degmar stayed where he was, and together they sneaked back towards the enemy positions. They reached it without incident, madly enough, yet trying to decide where to search was futile. The woman could have been anywhere in the disorganised and ramshackle camp, and her child somewhere else altogether. Tullus wasn't prepared to return without trying, however. Conscious that each passing moment increased the risk of discovery, he crept up and down several rows of tents – without success. Degmar roved around some distance away, returning now and then to report that he'd found no sign of her either.

Tullus had given up hope when, of all things, he heard a dog whine.

He pricked his ears. A dozen heartbeats later, there was a stifled cry – that of a woman – and then a slap as someone struck her. A man cursed, and Tullus thought, it *has* to be them. He'd gone perhaps a dozen steps towards the sound when Degmar appeared, knife already in hand. 'You heard that?' he whispered.

'Aye.' Tullus drew his sword.

The scene they came upon was pathetic. A three-sided lean-to, with a dying fire before it. The girl, crouched down, the pup in her arms. Her mother, on her back, with a warrior's bare arse thrusting up and down between her open legs. Two other warriors watching with smirks on their faces.

The standing men were the greater danger, Tullus reasoned. A quick command to Degmar and they fell on the pair like vengeful ghosts. The two died before they could utter more than short, surprised cries. What Tullus hadn't taken into consideration was that the warrior raping the woman might be holding a blade to her neck. The instant he realised his companions were under attack, he ran the iron across her throat. He died not three heartbeats later, Tullus' sword slicing deep into his back, but it was too late. Tullus could only hope that the woman heard him say, 'Your daughter is safe.' He watched the light fade from her eyes with Degmar hissing in his ear that they had to go.

'Come with me.' Grabbing the sobbing girl's arm, Tullus ran for the fort.

Once again the darkness and the late hour combined to help them reach the walls without harm. Fenestela was waiting as ordered, and the door opened before Tullus had time to knock again. 'The woman?' he asked as they barged in.

Tullus gave a savage shake of his head.

You saved the girl, he thought. That's better than nothing.

The knowledge did little to ease his bitterness.

Late that evening, Tullus was once more a guest of Caedicius in Aliso's rundown praetorium. He had seen his men to their quarters, and delegated Fenestela to look after the traumatised girl. A warm bath had followed, and then he'd donned the clean clothes he'd been given. Now he was in civilised surroundings, being served tasty food and drink. The luxuries, although welcome, did little for his mood. The woman was dead, despite his best efforts, and the thousands of warriors whom they had sneaked past to enter the fort were still outside.

Tullus' disquiet wasn't helped by the presence, alongside Caedicius' two cohort commanders, of Tubero. Wounded, dazed-looking and with a black eye, but Tubero nonetheless. He hadn't as much as acknowledged Tullus' existence thus far, other than to grunt when Caedicius had announced him. That suited Tullus to the ground. It was bad enough seeing the prick alive when so many better men were not, without having to talk to him. If what Tullus had heard was true, Tubero had survived because he'd fallen in with a seasoned optio of the Seventeenth, who had somehow managed to drag him and seven ordinary soldiers to Aliso. Rather than seem grateful for his luck, Tubero kept mentioning the fine helmet he'd lost. At length, Caedicius told him to shut up.

The talk was all of what they should do, and when the next enemy attack would be. Bone-weary, grieving, worried, Tullus took no part in it. Caedicius was watching him, however, and saw his long face. Ordering a servant to top up Tullus' wine, he said, 'Aliso hasn't fallen yet, centurion, nor is it likely to anytime soon. We've thrown back the savages three times now, with heavy losses on each occasion. Our ballistae reaped them like wheat, and will continue to do so. Apart from filling in the ditches with cut turves, the stupid bastards have no idea how to take a fortress, and that won't change.'

'Aye, sir.' Tullus pulled a smile. Caedicius was soon drawn back into conversation by Tubero, and Tullus was content to fall silent again. He threw back a mouthful of wine. It was tasty, reminding him of the night he'd got drunk with the two men a few months back. Yet his pleasure soured as he fell to brooding about the brutal events of the previous few days.

Other stragglers from the battle were still coming in – the tribesmen's cordon around the camp was incomplete in many places, allowing men to approach the walls under the cover of darkness, as they had – but the total stood at fewer than two hundred legionaries, and a couple of score civilians. Two hundred left out of fourteen and a half thousand, Tullus brooded. His legion hadn't been the only one to suffer the dishonour of losing its eagle. All three standards had been taken by the enemy.

These were the most severe losses that Rome had suffered for generations – perhaps since the battle of Carrhae, more than sixty years before. The shame of the defeat – no, massacre – was beginning to sink in at last. And the woman – why couldn't she have survived? Another swallow of wine, and his cup was empty. He raised it in the air, but took scant relief from the way a servant filled it at once. Tullus drank the cup back in two gulps, and held out his arm again.

'Don't get too pissed, centurion.'

He looked up. Tubero was regarding him with clear disapproval. 'I'm not drunk, sir.'

'You're heading that way,' said Tubero, his lip curling. 'We need our wits about us, eh, Caedicius?'

Here we go, thought Tullus. I've survived a visit to fucking Hades, only to be dressed down by this prick.

'Leave him alone,' ordered Caedicius. 'You heard what Tullus has been through. It is beyond belief.'

'I was there too,' cried Tubero.

'Maybe so, but you weren't in charge of a cohort that was wiped off the face of the earth. Many of Tullus' men had served under him for years, and you had been with the Eighteenth for – how many months?'

Tubero coloured. 'Three.'

'Need I say more? Let the man drink,' ordered Caedicius. 'He has many shades to honour. *You* have the loss of a helm to mourn.'

Tubero looked furious. Despite his technical seniority over Caedicius, he didn't have the confidence to challenge the veteran officer.

Tullus saluted Caedicius, uncaring – pleased, even – that this further embarrassed Tubero. 'May each and every one have a swift passage to Elysium, sir.'

'I'll raise my cup to that,' said Caedicius, glancing at his senior centurions, who were quick to emulate him. Tubero, glowering, followed suit last.

When they had drunk, Caedicius eyed Tullus with clear intent. 'The camp's walls are strong. There are good stores of ammunition for the ballistae, and our provisions are plentiful, yet we cannot stay here. I suspect that Arminius will appear before long, or another army sent by him. When that happens, Aliso must fall. You know him better than many, Tullus. What do you say?'

'Arminius is a clever bastard, sir,' said Tullus, regretting yet again his failure to persuade Varus of the Cheruscan's treachery, and that he hadn't been given a chance to slay Arminius during the ambush. 'I think you're right. My servant – the warrior who led us here – heard enemy tribesmen talking about burning the camps east of the Rhenus.'

Everyone looked unhappy at this, but unsurprised. Caedicius nodded. 'In that case, our decision has already been made. We must break out of here and flee to Vetera, as soon as possible. Gods grant that we have rain, or even a storm, in the next few nights. That would provide a diversion.'

'What about the civilians, sir?' asked one of the senior centurions.

Tullus had seen the barracks that had been given over to the inhabitants of the nearby settlement, but he had no idea how many of them had taken refuge in the camp.

'I'm not leaving them to be butchered, or enslaved,' said Caedicius, frowning. 'They come with us.'

Doing this would make their escape that much harder, but no one protested, least of all Tullus, picturing the nameless woman dying before him . . . and her child, who yet lived. They listened to Caedicius' plan, which involved departing in the middle of the night, using the same gate through which Tullus had entered Aliso. The two turmae of cavalry would lead the way, acting as scouts and vanguard both. One cohort would come next, then the injured and the civilians, guarded by the survivors of the battle, with Caedicius and the second cohort taking up the rear. It was a simple plan, and risky in the extreme. A single enemy sentry could be their undoing, and every man knew it. Yet their other option – to remain behind the camp's walls, awaiting further attacks – had an even more inevitable feel to it. They had to try.

'If it's all the same to you, sir, I'd like to march with you, at the back,' said Tullus.

Caedicius studied him for a moment. 'You and your men are exhausted. There's no shame—'

'We need to do this, sir,' said Tullus. 'Please.'

Caedicius sighed. 'Very well.'

'Thank you, sir.' This way, thought Tullus, he and his men might be able to salvage a little pride. Dying was yet a distinct possibility. If it were to happen, he would be facing the enemy.

He would run no longer.

XXXIII

After the wind and rain that had lashed Varus' army, Tullus had never thought he would welcome such weather again. Late the following afternoon, however, he was grateful to see dark clouds massing on the northern horizon, and to feel a rising wind carry them towards Aliso. Their chance to escape was coming, because Fortuna had sweet-talked Jupiter into conjuring up a storm. That meant the goddess still wanted her bull, Tullus hoped, quelling a sneaking fear that any lightning that resulted could give them away as they crept out of Aliso.

The rain came bucketing down a while later. A grinning Caedicius gathered his senior officers and declared that if the severe weather continued, they would leave that night. Tullus spread the word among his men, who, like him, had been enjoying the comforts of being warm and dry inside one of the many unused barracks. They listened to his news in silence, their faces wary and fearful. None protested, though, and when he asked them if they were ready, they managed a cheer. Tullus' pride in them flared bright once more. 'Be sure to have a hot meal,' he advised. 'Stew, or a hearty soup. It'll help to stave off the cold, and give you strength for the march.'

'And the shits too, sir, like as not,' cried Piso, to a chorus of laughter.

Tullus let them enjoy the joke, and the inevitable, good-natured insults – about who was most likely to soil himself – that were flung in its aftermath. 'Make your own decisions, brothers, but it's better to risk ruining your undergarments than to get a bad chill. Muffle your weapons and armour as best you can. The last thing we want is for some fool's scabbard to knock off his mail at the wrong moment. Blacken your faces and hands too – any exposed bits of flesh.'

They seemed to take that in. Tullus was about to leave when his eye was caught by the girl he'd rescued, at the back of the room. She had stayed with his soldiers – where else would she have gone? – and hadn't joined in the hilarity. She crouched on her bunk, looking downright terrified. The pup was there too, oblivious to everyone's concerns, its limbs twitching in a happy dream. Tullus was going to ignore the child – his life would be easier if he did so – yet he found himself walking towards her. He hadn't asked for her mother's name, even less hers, before now. He had never even spoken to her. His reasoning had been harsh but sound. Tullus had expected both to fall by the wayside, and knowing nothing about them would have made things easier when it happened. The girl was still here, though, and in a strange way that proved her worth. He gave her an awkward pat. 'Stay strong. We *will* escape.'

She made a brave face and nodded.

'Get what rest you can, and eat something. I will find you a place with the women and children before we leave. You'll be fine with them.'

'I want to stay with *you*,' she protested. 'You rescued me.'

'You can't.' He stared, hoping to make her look away, but she held his gaze. 'I'm going to be at the rear, with my soldiers,' he said in a harsh tone. 'Nearest the enemy.'

'What will happen if we're pursued? Attacked again?'

Out of the mouth of babes, thought Tullus. If that comes to pass, we men will be dead. You will be a slave of the Germans. Out loud, he said, 'We *will* get away in the storm. By the time the tribesmen notice, we'll be halfway to Vetera.' Tullus wasn't sure if she believed him, but he had few words left. 'Mind the pup.' With what he hoped was a reassuring smile, he left her to her sorrow.

As Tullus watched the light leaching from the sky, his worries grew. He found a degree of solace in gripping the ivory hilt of his sword and sliding it a way out of its sheath. It had taken him an age to clean the blood from the blade, and the base of the pommel was still a faint pink colour. Stain or no, it was sharper than ever – he had seen to that. Whatever happened, he and his men would extract a heavy price from anyone impeding their path to Vetera.

The evening dragged by, however, and Tullus felt more and more on edge. There were only so many times that he could go over his kit and weapons, check on his soldiers, spy on the enemy camp from the fort's rampart and check the weather. Following his own advice, he'd had some food, mutton stew, which had warmed his bones for a couple of hours. His nerve-racked guts had betrayed him then, and Tullus had been grateful that none of his men were in the latrines when it had poured out. In the end, reluctant for anyone to see his disquiet, he paced up and down inside the great hall of the principia like a caged beast before it is sent to its death in the circus. The emptiness of the shrine there, its standards and eagle long since departed, seemed to mock him, but Tullus preferred to stay dry and unhappy than to take his restlessness out into the heavy rain, where he risked catching a chill before they even left.

Perhaps three hours had passed when Fenestela came to find him. 'It's time,' he said. 'Caedicius has given the order.'

Tullus' guts gave a final lurch, but there was nothing left to be voided. 'At last. One more soaking, and we'll reach Vetera. I swear I never want to be wet again.'

Fenestela chuckled. 'Nor I. I'd only just managed to dry out my cloak too.'

'Are the men ready?'

'They are. None of the boys with wounds would travel with the rest of the injured. Said they'd rather take their chances with us.'

Tullus rolled his eyes, but pride rippled through him. 'You told them they'd be left behind if anything happens?'

'Aye. It didn't change their minds.'

Tullus cracked a grim smile. 'So be it.'

* * *

From the moment that the gate opened, and the first men filed out, Tullus' heart began to beat like that of a trapped wild bird. At the back with Caedicius, he could see nothing of what was going on beyond the wall, which raised the tension even higher. On tiptoe, as if that would help his hearing, he listened and waited and held his breath. His expectation was that there would be a shout, or a cry of alarm from the enemy, and the situation would dissolve into total confusion and panic, but there was nothing, nothing other than the pounding rain beating down off their helmets, and the flapping in the wind of loose tiles on the barrack roofs.

Some time later, word came that the cavalry and the First Cohort had passed beyond the enemy tents without discovery, and that the civilians and wounded were on their way. It was good news, and so was the fact that the rain continued to hammer down. Rather than relax, Tullus' nerves were stretched tighter. It was a relief to see that Caedicius – even he – was affected by their wait. Caedicius paced to and fro, watching the gate as if it were the entrance to Hades, and a host of demons was about to emerge from it.

After what seemed like an age, the men before them began to move, treading lightly to prevent their hobs clashing on the ground. At the back came two cavalrymen, leading their horses – messengers, should Caedicius need them. Through the gate the soldiers walked, and over a little pathway that traversed the defensive ditches. Tullus' eyes flickered from side to side, searching for the enemy, but he saw nothing. It meant little, though, for the place was as dark as a cavern. Getting lost was going to be easier than finding their way through the tribesmen's lines.

A bolt of lightning flashed out of the clouds, rendering the area as bright as day, outlining his men's fear-struck faces, the sheeting rain, the mud beneath their feet, and the enemy tents and lean-tos. There were scores, Tullus saw, and they would have to pass gut-wrenchingly close to them. The blackness closed in again, but his spirits had risen a fraction. Like him, the men in the lead would have seen where to go. As long as there was more lightning – and the rumbling thunder seemed to promise that – they ought not to trample over an enemy tent. That didn't mean the sentries wouldn't see them, of course, but it was something.

The time that followed was as nerve-shredding as anything Tullus had experienced. Surreal, even otherworldly, because of the darkness, the crashing thunder, the driving rain and the irregular, blinding flashes of lightning. Difficult thanks to the mud, the proximity of the enemy and of so many other soldiers, each trying not to trip or to bang into his fellows. Fearful because of the insanity of what they were doing, the numbers of the Germans surrounding them, the worry that the storm might ease. At any stage, the horses might be panicked by the thunder and whinny or, worse, stampede. Overriding everything was the stark knowledge that their fates rested on a knife edge. A razor-sharp, hair-thin knife edge.

Step by tentative step, they pressed forward. Past the main body of tents, without glimpsing a single sentry. Past the enemy latrines, obvious because of the stench. On to a track that curved around to the front of the fort, and by yet more lean-tos and tents. The gravelled main road out of Aliso came next. A few hundred paces along it, they came upon what had to be a sentry point – a pair of tents by the roadside, and a stone-ring fireplace in between. The tents *had* to be in use, but there was no sign of their occupants – who were like as not within, sleeping. Tullus' mouth felt as dry as his skin did wet, but they made it past. No sound came from the tents; no call to arms. Nothing.

A little further on, a second set of sentries was also dead to the world, and Tullus began to dream that their audacious escape would go unnoticed.

It was ironic that when they *were* seen, it was not by an alert sentry, but by a warrior who needed a piss. Tullus spotted him first: a stooped figure with a cloak over his head, stumbling from a tent by the side of the road, oblivious to the approaching file of Romans not twenty paces away. Once his bladder was empty, and the man turned, he could *not* fail to spot them. 'Two of you, with me. The rest of you, keep moving,' Tullus hissed at the soldier to his left. 'Pass it on.' Drawing his sword, he skidded down off the road, towards the urinating warrior. Two legionaries pounded after. So did Degmar, lithe as a shadow.

They got there a heartbeat too late. Tullus' quarry had finished, shaken himself and turned. Tullus' blade was ramming straight at his unprotected chest, too swift to prevent his escape, but not fast enough to stop him screaming before he died. There was immediate noise from the nearby tents. Pulse racing, Tullus wondered if there was any chance the four of them could kill all the men within. Any hope he had vanished as first two, then five warriors emerged, weapons in their hands. Before Tullus could react, Degmar was among them like a dancer, cutting down one, two men, gutting a third. A shout from the other side of the road announced the presence of more tribesmen Tullus hadn't been aware of. Three more warriors spilled out of the tents by him. On the road, the last ranks of Caedicius' unit were passing. To stay was to die, thought Tullus. Needlessly. 'Fall back!' he shouted. 'Degmar!'

To his relief the Marsi obeyed. In the short time it took the four to rejoin Caedicius – who was in the rearmost rank – the alarm was being well and truly raised. A number of the sentries had horns, which they were blowing with gusto. 'We killed a few, sir, but there were too many,' Tullus said to Caedicius. 'I'm sorry.'

'What's done is done,' replied Caedicius. 'You did well to spot them before anyone else.'

Despite the wind and rain, Tullus could hear the enemy camp coming awake behind them. Soon thousands of warriors would be on their trail. His weariness, which had eased, returned with crashing force. Tullus shoved it away. He could endure this trial. He *had* to, for so many reasons. His men. The girl. Ridiculous it seemed, but saving her, and the pup, had become important. There was also his burning desire to recover his legion's eagle, and to revenge himself on Arminius. Dead, he could not do any of these things. Alive, there was a chance.

At that point, the sentries who had woken ran on to the road and began hurling their spears. Two legionaries were wounded, one fatally. It was too dangerous to risk having all the men march backwards – they risked breaking their ankles – so Caedicius had only the rearmost soldiers turn to face the enemy. The rest had to march with their shields over their heads for a short time, until the warriors had run out of missiles. Although the tribesmen continued to follow them, jokes about having shelter from the rain at last – from their scuta – broke out, and Tullus' heart warmed. If men began to think that they *might* cheat death, their spirits soon rallied.

Some of the legionaries had been issued with bags of *caltrops*, taken from the stores in the camp. At Caedicius' order, they began to scatter the spiked devices across the road. More jokes were made, this time about the holes they'd make in the warriors' feet. Sure enough, there were howls of pain as the unsuspecting enemy walked into the trap. After a quick volley of javelins, the tribesmen fell back.

The Romans marched on for a time without further pursuit. The rain eased, as if it knew that it was no longer needed to obscure their escape. Tullus returned to his men. Caedicius sent orders ahead that if possible the pace should increase, but that the leading cohort was not to lose contact with the civilians and the wounded. Because of the non-combatants, however, there was little change in their speed thereafter. Tullus felt like a cripple trying to outrun a guard dog that has been released on to his trail a mile down the road. The light-armed, running tribesmen would catch them with ease.

He was pleased to be mistaken. A mile marker passed, and then another. By the third, he fell back from his position to confer with Caedicius. 'Do you think they're looting the camp, sir?'

'A shrewd guess. Preferable to chasing after a thousand legionaries in the dark, eh? There's plenty in Aliso to keep them busy. Wine, food, weapons. Soldiers' savings, if they think to rip up the floorboards in the barracks.'

'Gods, let them drink themselves stupid,' said Tullus, thinking of the enormous barrels he'd seen in one of the storehouses, vessels bound with iron rings, almost as tall as two men, and as broad.

'Some of them will do their best. What man wouldn't, if he got the chance?' Caedicius let out a wicked chuckle.

Their hopes were borne out in the hours that followed, as they marched five miles, and then seven, from Aliso. Tullus' men, even the injured, managed to keep up with the rest. Dawn arrived, and a watery sun emerged from behind the clouds, lifting the general mood. The soldiers broke out whatever food they had, and shared it out. Sodden or not, the bread that Tullus was handed tasted divine. He washed it down with the neat wine that Fenestela had managed to procure.

HUUUUMMMMMMMM! HUUUUMMMMMMMM!

The outbreak of the barritus was far to their rear, yet it set Tullus' skin to tingling. His men's faces changed too. 'Ignore it, my brothers,' he cried. 'Five miles or so, and we'll reach the next camp. Reinforcements will be on their way from Vetera as soon as the cavalry get there. All we'll have to do is hold on!'

'ROMA!' a man – Piso? – yelled. His call was like the spark that falls into dry summer undergrowth and starts a wild fire. 'ROMA! ROMA! ROMA!' Tullus' soldiers roared. Their chant was taken up by Caedicius' legionaries, drowning out the barritus.

Tullus' ploy to rally his men's spirits had worked, but it would only be a temporary measure. The enemy would catch them before the next camp. He had no idea when their small group of cavalry would reach Vetera – Caedicius had ordered that they ride off at daybreak – and how long after that a force would be despatched to their rescue. Even if they reached the marching camp, would they be able to defend it successfully? When Degmar asked if he should drop off the road and spy on the men following, Tullus agreed with alacrity. Knowing the enemy's disposition might prove useful.

Next he went to talk to Caedicius, his worries gnawing at his guts like a dog at a juicy bone.

'Six of my riders remain at the front of the column,' Caedicius told him, grinning like a madman. 'They have trumpets.'

Tullus shook his head, confused, a little frustrated. 'What use are musical instruments, sir?'

HUUUUMMMMMMMM! HUUUUMMMMMMMM! The sound was audible again, even though the legionaries were still chanting. Tullus glanced back along the road, and saw the first figures – berserkers, no doubt – loping ahead of a massed body of warriors. They were perhaps three-quarters of a mile away. Tullus felt more bitter than he had in the midst of the ambush, when his death had seemed inevitable. It had begun to seem possible that he might survive, that one day he might retrieve his legion's eagle. That Arminius might come under his blade.

Vetera was perhaps thirty-five miles away, but it might as well have been Rome.

Stay calm, Tullus thought. He focused again on Caedicius, wondering how in Hades he managed it.

'I'm holding back a rider until the enemy are nice and close,' said Caedicius, indicating the two horsemen alongside their position. 'When he reaches the trumpeters, they will sound' – he winked, and added – 'an advance, at double speed.'

'Ha!' cried Tullus with delight. 'The Germans will think that it is troops marching from Vetera to our rescue.'

'That's what I am hoping. It's a gamble, of course. If there are a few level-headed men among the enemy, who can steady their fellows, we're done for,' said Caedicius, looking sombre. 'On the other hand, most of them could be pissed, thanks to the wine they found inside Aliso.'

HUUUUMMMMMMMM! HUUUUMMMMMMMM!

The legionaries' singing faltered, and died away.

'Keep marching, brothers,' shouted Caedicius. 'I won't let them hit us from behind. Pass it on.'

The order went rolling up the column, and the soldiers maintained their steady pace.

By rights, Tullus was supposed to be with his men, further up the line, but his pride wouldn't let him move. If there was to be a fight, he wanted to be part of it. All he'd done for the last seven days and more was run. Even if it meant his death, he was going to face the enemy.

It was as if Caedicius knew – he didn't say a word.

HUUUUMMMMMMMM! HUUUUMMMMMMMM!

Tullus took a look. The berserkers were about half a mile back, and a good distance ahead of their comrades.

Caedicius barked an order at his last rider, who urged his horse forward.

Soon after, Degmar appeared out of the bushes to the side of the road, his chest heaving from the run. Several thousand warriors were following them, he reported, but a sizeable number *did* appear to be drunk. Clapping Degmar on the shoulder, Tullus relayed the good news to Caedicius, who halted the cohort at once.

'About turn,' Caedicius shouted. 'Rear ten ranks, spread out, twenty wide, three deep. Off the road, if you have to. READY JAVELINS!'

Tullus counted the berserkers. There were a dozen, and his gut twisted. That many naked madmen would smash their formation like hammers striking a pane of glass. Their volley was vital, therefore. '*Pilum*,' he ordered, raising his hand, and one was handed forward from a man in the rank behind.

Caedicius was busy too. He couldn't have stood in the front line of a battle for years, yet he hadn't forgotten the little details that stiffen men's spines. Tullus felt his own resolve firm as Caedicius stalked up and down, telling his soldiers that they were the pride of Rome, the best legionaries in the empire. They would fight for each other, and to avenge their comrades, who had been so foully murdered by the whoresons coming down that road. No quarter was to be given, Caedicius roared, not even if an enemy was crying for mercy. 'I want you to cover your blades in blood. I want you to kill every fucking savage that comes near you! Do you hear me?'

'YES, SIR!'

Caedicius began to clash the head of his javelin off the iron rim of his shield.

Every man joined in.

They kept it up until the berserkers were a hundred paces away. The rest of the warriors were at least three times that distance further behind. Caedicius raised his pilum high, and a gradual silence fell.

'Front two ranks, ready javelins!' called Caedicius. 'On my command, ranks three and four will pass their pila forward.'

Tullus tried not to think about the gaps in their far from ideal formation. On the road, they were only six men wide. Seven soldiers were standing a little lower down to either side, in the ditches that ran alongside, and on the rough, grassy ground that extended beyond that. He took a tighter grip on his pilum shaft, thinking that it would have to do.

Caedicius continued encouraging his men until the berserkers were fifty paces away. They were a fearsome sight, their bodies streaked with white pigment, spears ready, mad war cries leaving their throats. 'Front two ranks, take aim,' he yelled. 'Pick your target. On my order.'

Tullus concentrated on a wiry berserker who was taller than any of his companions.

'READY,' cried Caedicius. 'LOOSE!'

Tullus drew back, and threw.

Caedicius was shouting before the shoal of missiles had even reached the top of their arc. 'RANKS THREE AND FOUR, PASS YOUR JAVELINS FORWARD. QUICKLY!'

Tullus held up his hand, and was given another pilum.

Down came their first effort, forty javelins, striking the berserkers like heavy rain on immature wheat. Many of the warriors fell, but Tullus had no chance to count them. Caedicius had ordered another volley – short this time. Up went two score more pila, and down again, their pyramidal iron points ripping into the unarmoured berserkers like hot knives through cheese.

Tullus stared. Counted. Let out an incredulous laugh. Two berserkers remained standing, and one had a javelin protruding from his left leg, crippling him. The pair were no cowards, however. The uninjured man charged on alone, and his companion hobbled after.

The mass of warriors behind continued to advance, yet the annihilation of the berserkers had silenced their barritus, and seen their pace slow to a walk.

Grabbing a pilum from a soldier behind him, Tullus hurled it from fifteen paces. The throw was as good as any he'd ever made. It hit the lead berserker in the chest, felling him like an ox struck with a hammer and spike.

'Come on, you maggot!' roared Tullus at the last berserker, who had stopped in his tracks. 'Come and die on Roman iron!'

Tan-tara-tara. Tan-tara-tara. Tan-tara-tara. Tan-tara-tara. The sound of Roman trumpets was unmistakeable – and they were sounding the advance, double time.

Tullus' breath caught in his chest.

The wounded berserker cocked his head. He listened for several heartbeats, and then he began shuffling backwards, away from the Romans.

Tan-tara-tara. Tan-tara-tara. Tan-tara-tara. Tan-tara-tara. It was closer this time.

The berserker increased his pace, moaning with the pain it caused him. The front ranks of the warriors wavered a little.

'ROMA! ROMA! ROMA!' roared the legionaries.

Tan-tara-tara. Tan-tara-tara. Tan-tara-tara. Tan-tara-tara.

Like a flock of panicked sheep, the warriors turned tail and ran. They didn't stop. They didn't look back, except in terror.

The soldiers' cheering redoubled. It was a small victory – but one to be savoured.

Tullus breathed again and the air felt sweet in his lungs.

Caedicius' cunning had left the road to Vetera – and safety – open. He,

Tullus, would survive. So would Fenestela and his remaining men. And the girl. Even the pup would make it. He laughed as the clouds parted, spilling golden sunlight over the sodden landscape.

Author's Note

No one can argue that Rome carved an indelible mark on world history, both as republic and empire. During its long and illustrious history, many events stand out, among them the wars against Carthage, the decline of republicanism and the rise to power of Julius Caesar, the lives of various emperors: Augustus, Marcus Aurelius and Constantine. Some of its battles are still remembered: the Caudine Forks, Cannae, Zama, Carrhae, Pharsalus and Adrianapolis – titanic struggles some of which Rome won, others lost. Without doubt, another unforgettable conflict was the battle of the Teutoburg Forest, which took place in north-central Germany in the autumn of AD 9. It was a devastating defeat for the ageing first emperor, Augustus. It's not well known today, but much of Germany as far as the River Elbe had been pacified by Rome in the twenty-five years prior to the Teutoburg. This significant achievement was turned on its head when an ingenious ambush devised by Arminius, a Romanised German, and carried out by thousands of his fellow tribesmen, wiped out one-tenth of the empire's standing army – three legions – in a single, bold stroke.

I have done my best in this book to recreate the events that took place during that fateful summer and autumn, and to stick to the historical details that have survived. I apologise now for any errors that I may have made. Many of the characters in the book were real people; these include Publius Quinctilius Varus, Arminius, Lucius Seius Tubero, Gaius Numonius Vala, Lucius Nonius Asprenas, Lucius Caedicius, Marcus

Caelius, Ceionius, Lucius Eggius, Segimer, Segestes, Maroboduus, Fabricius and Flavus. Even lowly soldiers such as Marcus Aius, Cessorinius Ammausias and Marcus Crassus Fenestela existed. (More of Aius and Ammausias anon.) Centurion Tullus is my invention; so too are Aristides, Maelo, Degmar and the soldiers of Tullus' century.

It's annoying that almost no 'real' tribal names of the time survive. By necessity, I invented Osbert, Degmar and Aelwird. Because I used name stems from the German Dark Age era, I hope they sound authentic. Arminius and Segimundus are clearly Romanised versions of German names. Arminius' real name may have been 'Armin' or 'Ermin' – we are not sure. When I began the book, I chose the latter when he was among his own kind, and 'Arminius' when he was with the Romans. In fact I wrote the entire story in this way. My editor was adamant, however, that to give him two names would confuse the reader. There were several long discussions about it, but in the end, she persuaded me to change his name to Arminius throughout – apart from one mention, in the prologue. I hope this move doesn't make him sound 'too Roman'.

The bloody sacrifice in the book's prologue is fictitious, but the ritual described within it, of human sacrifice by German tribesmen, is not. The Germanic tribes were known to have held Donar, their thunder god, in particular esteem. The sounds made by sacred horses are also recorded as being important to the Germans' priests. The tribes' way of life and social customs are not well known, sadly, but the details of their power structure, houses, weapons and agriculture, and the local fauna and flora that I have described, are accurate according to my research. For example, the German method of execution using a wicker hurdle in the bog is recorded. So too are the broad strokes of Arminius' childhood and early life. The word 'berserker' wasn't used at the time, but it wasn't unusual for some warriors to fight naked, and to lead the fight to the enemy.

The construction of the mighty Roman forts along the River Rhine began in the last two decades of the first century BC. They stood for many years and sometimes centuries. Castra Vetera, in which Tullus was stationed, stood on the Fürstenberg hill, a short distance south of the modern German town of Xanten. It's used as farmland now, but its amphitheatre, still in use as a theatre, can be visited. Nearby is a truly impressive archaeological park that is situated on the site of Colonia Ulpia Traiana, the town that grew up after Vetera. It's by no means certain that the Eighteenth Legion was stationed at Vetera, but it's considered likely thanks to the tombstone of Marcus Caelius, most senior centurion of the unit, which was discovered in the area of Xanten. His is the only known memorial to a soldier lost at the Teutoburg. There were bridges over the Rhine at Vetera, spanning the midstream islands. The inscription I described does exist, but on the still-standing Alcántara Bridge in Spain, erected by the order of the emperor Trajan.

It is possible that Mogontiacum (Mainz) may have been the home of the Nineteenth, but it's unclear where the Seventeenth was based. The location of many Roman forts within Germany is known, but their names are not. The town of Haltern-am-See may have been Aliso, but we can't be sure. The camp called Porta Westfalica (a modern name despite the Latin sound) may have been Varus' summer camp, or – more likely – may not. The town of Waldgirmes is the site of the Roman settlement with the large forum and municipal buildings mentioned in the book, but my name of Pons Laugona is invented (I thought it apt because the local river was known by the Romans as the Laugona).

The priest Segimundus did ally himself with Arminius, who must have been a most charismatic character. We are told that the Romans, and in particular Varus, placed implicit trust in him. However, let's not fall for the age-old perception that Varus was a naïve, easily led man with poor judgement. He had a good political and military track record, and had crushed a widespread rebellion in Judaea just a few years before. Augustus was not in the habit of putting men he did not trust in positions of power, and the governorship of Germany was one of the empire's most important jobs.

Tubero's disastrous attack on the cattle-herding youths and the events that followed are fictitious. Varus' summer campaign into Germany, the main purposes of which being to collect taxes and continue the area's Romanisation, was real. He is known to have ignored Segestes' warning about Arminius. The details of the doomed army's march – from the slaughtering of the Roman soldiers at their roadside watch posts to the imagined rebellion by the Angrivarii and the route chosen by Arminius – are as the ancient texts describe. The tribes mentioned as being involved were not all definitively there – only three were – but for Arminius to have had enough warriors, more tribes must have taken part. The terrible weather may have been an invention by the Roman historians who wrote about the battle, to make the scene more doom-laden, more dramatic, but northern Germany *is* prone to severe storms in the autumn, and the drainage ditches found behind the German earthenworks at the Kalkriese battlefield (more of which anon) lend weight to this description.

If you were curious about the references to Tullus' encounter with a soothsayer fifteen years before the battle, go and read *The Shrine*, my free digital short story, which is available on Amazon and other platforms.

As far as I know, there is no evidence for the use of whistles by Roman officers to relay commands. Trumpets of various types were used instead. However, whistles have been found all over the Empire, including in the vicinity of the legionary fortress at Regensburg, in Germany. It's not too much of a jump to place one in Tullus' hands during a battle. A whistle could have been very useful in getting the attention of those who were only a few steps away.

Most academics maintain that the visored Roman cavalry helmets were only for parade ground use, the main reason being their lack of vision. However, increasing numbers of reenactors who ride and train with replicas of these helmets, say that it *is* possible to charge and fight while wearing them. Think also of medieval knights, and the helmets they wore in battle!

I stayed true to the timeline of the ambush as we know it, and the individual events within it, such as the manner of the tribesmen's attacks, the sounding of the barritus, the ditching of the Romans' equipment, the legions' cataclysmic losses, Vala's failed attempt to escape with the cavalry, Varus' suicide and the loss of one eagle in the bog. The gruesome mutilations of Roman prisoners, including the legionary who had his tongue cut out, are described in the histories. Aliso was besieged, yet some of the survivors of the ambush did make it inside the walls. Caedicius was the commander there, and he bravely led his garrison and some civilians to safety as a night storm raged. His ruse of making the Germans think that reinforcements were advancing from the Rhine is recorded – a stroke of desperate genius if there ever was one.

I've had great fun weaving real-life people into this book as minor characters, and also using Roman artefacts that have been discovered in that part of Germany. I have already mentioned Cessorinius Ammausias – he was an ursarius, not of the Eighteenth Legion but the later Thirtieth, and was stationed at Colonia Ulpia Traiana rather than Vetera. A legionary called Marcus Aius, of Fabricius' century, lost two bronze armour fasteners at the Kalkriese battlefield – they were found some distance apart, as if they had fallen from a running man's purse. It was my invention to have Piso win them at dice. The cavalry helmet carried and lost by Tubero is based on the iconic helmet facepiece that was found at Kalkriese. The spices offered to Piso when he goes in search of wine aren't a result of my crazed imagination: peppercorns and coriander seeds – originating in India – have been found in the sewers of Roman camps in Germany, dating from as early as 11 BC. The large wooden wine barrels mentioned in Aliso are contemporary with ones found in nearby Oberaden. The soldiers' coin hoards mentioned by Caedicius as being left under barracks' floors have their basis in a real example, on display in the Haltern-am-See museum, clay pot and all. You can also see vicious-spiked caltrops there, similar to the ones used by the legionaries as they escaped.

Being a writer of historical fiction is a real privilege, because it means that one of my passions in life – history – is now my day job. Most of the time, my work is an absolute joy, which makes me feel even luckier, but with it comes a somewhat unexpected duty of care – that of being as 'true' to history as I can. This is a feeling that has grown on me since my first few books were published, and I hope it shows in my writing.

It has come about for several reasons, one of which is the amount of time that I've spent wearing the gear of an ancient Roman soldier, while training for and taking part in two long-distance charity walks. (With a little bit of luck, you will soon see *The Road to Rome*, the film of our 2014 #RomaniWalk, narrated by Sir Ian McKellen, on a TV channel near you! Here I must also mention, and thank, the hundreds of people who gave so generously to our campaign. The character of Maelo is loosely based on Gwilym Williams, who won a competition I ran during the fundraising.) By my rough estimate, I have now walked more than 800 kilometres wearing equipment and armour that weighs between 15 and 26 kilograms – the weight depending on stage of training/weather/my mood and energy levels. This experience has informed my writing a great deal, and the details you read about marching are, for the most part, direct experience. For example, I believe (as do many re-enactors) that marching Roman soldiers wore their shields on their backs. It's comfortable to do so, and the shield can be unslung and held ready to fight in less than twenty seconds. I've tried walking with the shield in my right hand – as do the legionaries depicted on Trajan's column and other monuments – and found that it's crippling after only a short distance. Slinging it over one shoulder by a strap doesn't work that well either. I think that the ancient portrayals were an artistic conceit to allow the viewer to better picture the soldiers and their equipment.

Live combat is another matter. Even if I could experience the gut-wrenching fear and the utter savagery, I wouldn't want to do so, but my experiences as a veterinary student in Africa mean that I know how to slaughter a goat with a sharp knife. It can't be that different (even if it's psychologically far worse) to do the same to a human. It's easier than you think to cut a throat and take a blade right to the spinal column.

Cursing: it will not surprise you that the Romans were fond – very fond – of swearing. Some of their favourite oaths revolved around the 'C' word, which is regarded by many as one of the worst curse words around. In previous books, therefore, I tended to use the 'F' word (although less attested, there is a Latin verb, *futuere)*. In this book, I felt it apt to use the 'C' word – albeit sparingly. (In an aside, I also had Tullus use the term 'brother' when talking to his men because it is authentic: there are recorded instances of centurions referring to their soldiers in this way.)

Trying to recreate how life might have been is helped by travelling to the places, or the general areas, where the historical events took place. I have been to most of the locations in my books, and walked the ground there. Doing this is a great help when creating the various scenes in the story. As I write this in November 2014, I have just returned from an eight-day trip to Germany, during which I drove, cycled and walked more than a thousand kilometres along the River Rhine, from Xanten in the north down as far as Mainz. On this journey, I visited many museums, the wonderful archaeological park at Xanten, and the sites of several Roman forts. The rich variety of ancient artefacts in Germany, both military and civilian, is really impressive, and set my mind racing with new ideas.

I cannot recommend enough a visit to the park in Xanten, where you can see accurate reconstructions of a three-storey gate to the town, a sizeable section of its wall, the large amphitheatre, workshops, guesthouse and a tavern and restaurant that are open for business. Not far to the east is one of the best Roman museums I have visited, in the town of Haltern-am-See. Some hundred kilometres further inland is the amazing Kalkriese battlefield, thought for some years to be the actual site of the Teutoburg Forest. In recent years, that theory has fallen away somewhat, thanks to the wealth of coins found there that date to the late first century BC. Regardless of this, the location *did* see a tribal ambush on Roman forces. The reconstructed German fortifications and the wealth of objects in the museum there cannot fail to fire one's imagination about the real battle.

The Roman museums in Cologne, Bonn and Mainz are also excellent, each for their own reasons. I feel the Museum of Ancient Shipbuilding in Mainz deserves a special mention, because of its rare finds of Roman river vessels and the extraordinary reconstructions of two of them. As for the entirely reconstructed second century AD fort at Saalburg, all I can say is, 'Go!' If you're into hiking or cycling, you can visit Saalburg on part of the 560-kilometre track that leads along the German Limes, the border defences that linked the Rhine and the Danube for two centuries.

The ancient texts provide another route to the past. If it weren't for Tacitus, Florus, Velleius Paterculus, Cassius Dio and Pliny, I would have been lost when it came to writing this book. Their words, often rather 'Rome-aggrandising', have to be taken with a pinch of salt, but they are still of great value when it comes to research and 'picturing the past'. Textbooks are also indispensable. A bibliography of those I used while writing *Eagles at War* would run to several pages, so I will only mention the most important, in alphabetical order by author: *Handbook to Legionary Fortresses* by M. C. Bishop; *Roman Military Equipment* by M. C. Bishop and J. C. N. Coulston; *Greece and Rome at War* by Peter Connolly; *The Complete Roman Army* by Adrian Goldsworthy; *Rome's Greatest Defeat: Massacre in the Teutoburg Forest* by Adrian Murdoch; *Eager for Glory: The Untold story of Drusus the Elder*, *Germanicus*, and *Roman Soldier versus Germanic Warrior*, all by Lindsay Powell; *The Varian Disaster* (multiple authors), a special edition of *Ancient Warfare* magazine. I'd like to mention the publishers Osprey and Karwansaray, whose publications are of frequent help, and the ever-useful *Oxford Classical Dictionary*.

Thanks, as always, to the members of www.romanarmy.com, for their rapid answers to my odd questions, and to Paul Harston and the legionaries of Roman Tours UK, for the same, and for agreeing to provide men and materials for the covers of this and the next two volumes in the trilogy. Go, Roland! Paul Karremans of the Gemina Project in the Netherlands deserves a special mention too, and huge thanks, for the generous loan of his re-enactment unit's eagle. *Dank u wel*, Paul. I want to thank Adrian Murdoch and Lindsay Powell, mentioned above, for their patience, knowledge and generosity with their time. Not only did they help me with information during many stages of the writing process, and answer my frequent questions, but they were kind enough to read the manuscript when it was done, and to provide further words of wisdom. You are both true gentlemen. I'm also indebted to Jenny Dolfen, the talented German writer and illustrator, for her help with Germanic names.

I owe gratitude to a legion of people at my publishers, Random House. Selina Walker, my wonderful editor, possesses an eagle eye quite like no other. This book would be a much lesser creature if it weren't for her. Thank you, Selina. Rose Tremlett, Richard Ogle, Aslan Byrne, Nathaniel Alcaraz-Stapleton, Vincent Kelleher and David Parrish, thank you! You all work so hard to ensure that my books do well. Gratitude also to my foreign publishers, in particular to Carol Paris and her team at Ediciones B in Spain, and to Keith Kahla and his colleagues at St. Martin's Press in the United States.

Other people must be named, and thanked: Charlie Viney, my superlative agent. Richenda Todd, my copy editor, a real star. Claire Wheller, the best sports physio in the world. Arthur O'Connor, an old friend, for his criticism of, and improvements to, my stories. Massive thanks also to you, my wonderful readers. It's you who keep me in a job, which makes me more grateful than you could know. Anything not to go back to veterinary medicine! Your emails from around the world, and contacts on Facebook and Twitter, brighten up my days: please keep them coming. Last, but most definitely not least, I want to thank Sair, my wonderful wife, and Ferdia and Pippa, my beautiful children, for the boundless love and joy that they bring into my world.

Ways to contact me:
Email: ben@benkane.net
Twitter: @BenKaneAuthor
Facebook: facebook.com/benkanebooks
Also, my website: www.benkane.net
YouTube (my short documentary-style videos):
https://www.youtube.com/channel/UCorPV-9BUCzfvRT-bVOSYYw

Glossary

acetum: sour wine, the universal beverage served to legionaries. Also the word for vinegar, the most common disinfectant used by Roman surgeons. Vinegar is excellent at killing bacteria, and its widespread use in western medicine continued until late in the nineteenth century.

alae (sing. *ala*): auxiliary cavalry units, which were used as support troops to the legions, and commanded by prefects, equestrian officers. The *alae* were of varying strength, either quingenary (512 riders in 16 *turmae*) or milliary (768 in 32 *turmae*). It's possible that Arminius may have commanded such a unit, and that's how I chose to portray him. (See also the entry for *turma*.)

Alara: the River Aller.

Albis: the River Elbe.

Amisia: the River Ems.

amphora (pl. *amphorae*): a two-handled clay vessel with a narrow neck and tapering base used to store wine, olive oil and other produce. Of many sizes, including vessels that are larger than a man, amphorae were heavily used in long-distance transport.

aquilifer (pl. *aquiliferi*): the standard-bearer for the *aquila*, or eagle, of a legion. The images surviving today show the *aquilifer* bare-headed, leading some to suppose that this was always the case. In combat, however, this would have been too dangerous; it's probable that the *aquilifer did* use a helmet. We do not know either if he wore an animal skin, as the *signifer* (see entry below) did, but it is a common interpretation.

The armour was often scale, and the shield probably a small one, which could be carried without using the hands. During the early empire, the *aquila* was made of gold, and was mounted on a spiked wooden staff, allowing it to be shoved into the ground. Sometimes the staff had arms, which permitted it to be borne more easily. Even when damaged, the *aquila* was not destroyed, but repaired time and again. If lost in battle, the Romans would do almost anything to get the standard back, as you will read in the next book in this series. (See also the entry for legion.)

Ara Ubiorum: Cologne.

Arduenna Silva: the Ardennes Forest.

as (pl. *asses*): a small copper coin, worth a quarter of a *sestertius*, or a sixteenth of a denarius.

Asciburgium: Moers-Asberg.

Augusta Treverorum: Trier.

Augusta Vindelicorum: Augsberg.

auxiliaries (in Latin: *auxilia*): It was common for Rome to employ non-citizens in its armies, both as light infantry and cavalry. By the time of Augustus, the *auxilia* had been turned into a regular, professional force. Roughly cohort- or double-cohort-sized units, they were of three types: infantry, cavalry or mixed. Auxiliary units were commanded by prefects – equestrian officers. At the Teutoburg, Varus' army contained six auxiliary infantry cohorts, and three of auxiliary cavalry.

ballista (pl. *ballistae*): a two-armed Roman catapult that looked like a crossbow on a stand, and which fired either bolts or stones with great accuracy and force.

barritus: the war chant sung by German warriors. My description of it comes straight from the ancient texts.

bireme: an ancient warship, perhaps invented by the Phoenicians, with a square sail and two sets of oars on each side.

Bonna: Bonn.

caldarium: an intensely hot room in Roman bath complexes. Used like a modern-day sauna, most also had a warm plunge pool. The *caldarium* was heated by hot air which flowed through hollow bricks in the walls and under the raised floor. The source of the piped heat was the *hypocaustum*, a furnace constantly tended by slaves.

caltrops: anti-personnel devices used by the Romans and other ancient peoples. They were four-sided spiked devices; when thrown, one spike always projected upwards, while the three others gave a stable base. They were useful not just against cavalry and elephants, but foot soldiers.

Campania: a fertile region of west central Italy.

carnyx (pl. carnyxes): a Gaulish bronze trumpet, which was held vertically and topped by a bell shaped in the form of an animal, often a boar. It provided a fearsome sound alone or in unison with other instruments.

centurion (in Latin, *centurio*): the disciplined career officers who formed the backbone of the Roman army. (See also the entry for legion.)

century: the main sub-unit of a Roman legion. Although its original strength had been one hundred men, by the first century AD it had numbered eighty men for close to half a millennium. The unit was divided into ten sections of eight soldiers, called *contubernia*. (See also the entry for legion.)

Cerberus: the monstrous three-headed hound that guarded the entrance to Hades. It allowed the spirits of the dead to enter, but none to leave.

Civitas Nemetum: Speyer.

cohort: a unit comprising a tenth of a legion's strength. A cohort was made up of six centuries, each nominally of eighty legionaries. Each century was led by a centurion. The centurion leading the first century was the most senior (this is Tullus' rank); the centurions were ranked after him, in order of their century: second, third and so on. The cohorts followed the same order of seniority, so that the centurions of the First Cohort, for example, outranked those of the Second Cohort, who were more senior than those of the third etc.

Confluentes: Koblenz.

consul: during the Roman Republic, this position (of which there were two) was the highest magistracy in the land. The consuls were the political and military leaders of Rome for the twelve months of their office. By the time of the early empire, under Augustus, the consuls had become toothless beasts. Considerable honour was still bestowed on the men who served in the positions, as evinced by the emperor taking the post for himself, but they lacked any real power. Although elected, they were in fact appointed by Augustus and subsequent emperors.

contubernium (pl. *contubernia*): a group of eight legionaries who shared a tent or barracks room and who cooked and ate together. (See also entry for legion.)

Danuvius: the River Danube.

denarius (pl. *denarii*): the staple coin of the Roman Empire. Made from silver, it was worth four *sestertii*, or sixteen *asses*. The less common gold *aureus* was worth twenty-five *denarii*.

Donar: the German thunder god, and one of the only tribal deities attested to in the early first century AD.

equestrian: a Roman nobleman, ranked just below the class of senator. It was possible to move upwards, into the senatorial class, but the process was not easy.

falx (pl. *falces*): two-handed, long scythe-like weapons used by the Dacian tribes. Very dangerous! Some historians think that a modification to legionaries' helmets in the second century AD was made to counter the danger posed by these lethal weapons.

Fectio: Vechten.

Flevo Lacus: the Zuiderzee, now the IJsselmeer.

Fortuna: the goddess of luck and good fortune. Like all deities, she was notorious for her fickle nature.

frameae (sing. *framea*): the long spears used by most German tribesmen. They had a short, narrow iron blade and were fearsome weapons. Employed in conjunction with a shield, they were used to stab, throw or swing at an opponent.

frigidarium: an unheated room in Roman bath complexes, with a cold water basin.

Gallia Belgica and Gallia Lugdunensis: these were two of the four Gaulish provinces defined by Augustus. The other two were Gallia Aquitania and Gallia Narbonensis.

Germania: in AD 9, the Romans regarded the area between the Rhine and Elbe Rivers as the province of Germania Magna. East of the Elbe and its tributary the Saale lay Germania Libera, or 'free' Germany.

gladius (pl. *gladii*): by the time of the early principate, the Republican *gladius hispaniensis*, with its waisted blade, had been replaced by the so-called 'Mainz' gladius (named because of the many examples found there). The Mainz was a short steel sword, some 400–550 mm in length. Leaf-shaped, it varied in width from 54–75 mm to 48–60 mm. It ended with a V-shaped point that measured between 96 and 200 mm. It was a well-balanced sword for both cutting and thrusting. The shaped handgrip was made of ox bone; it was protected at the distal end by a pommel and nearest the blade by a hand guard, both made of wood. The scabbard was made from layered wood, sheathed by leather and encased at the edges by U-shaped copper alloy. The *gladius* was worn on the right, except by centurions and other senior officers, who wore it on the left. Contrary to what one might think, it is easy to draw with the right hand, and was probably positioned in this manner to avoid entanglement with the *scutum* while being unsheathed.

Hispania: the Iberian peninsula.

Illyricum (or Illyria): the Roman name for the lands that lay across the Adriatic Sea from Italy: including parts of Slovenia, Serbia, Croatia, Bosnia and Montenegro. Illyricum included the area known as Pannonia, which became a Roman province sometime during the first half of the first century AD.

intervallum: the wide, flat area inside the walls of a Roman camp or fort. As well as serving to protect the barrack buildings from enemy missiles, it allowed the massing of troops before patrols, or battle.

Jupiter: often referred to as 'Optimus Maximus' – 'Greatest and Best'. Most powerful of the Roman gods, he was responsible for weather, especially storms.

Laugona: the River Lahn.

legate (in Latin, *legatus legionis*): the officer in command of a legion, and a man of senatorial rank, most often in his early thirties. The legate reported to the regional governor. (See also the entry for legion.)

legion (in Latin, *legio*): the largest independent unit of the Roman army. At full strength, it consisted of ten cohorts, each of which comprised 480 legionaries, divided into six centuries of eighty men. Every century was divided into ten sections, *contubernia*, of eight men. The centuries were each led by a centurion, each of whom had three junior officers to help run the unit: the *optio*, *signifer* and *tesserarius*. (See also the relevant entry for each.) Every century and cohort had their own standard; each legion possessed an eagle. The legion was commanded by a legate, whose second-in-command was the most senior tribune, the *tribunus laticlavius*. The camp prefect, a former *primus pilus*, was third-in-command; after him – we are not sure in what order – came the five junior tribunes and the *primus pilus*. One hundred and twenty cavalrymen were attached to each legion. (See entries for *tribune*, *primus pilus* and *turmae*.) In practice, no legion was ever at full strength. Sickness and detachments on duty in other places and, in wartime, losses due to combat were some of the reasons for this. Most scholars now therefore accept that Varus' three legions with their associated auxiliary troops numbered around thirteen to fifteen thousand men, rather than the oft-quoted twenty thousand.

legionary: the professional Roman foot soldier. A citizen, he joined the army in his late teens or early twenties, swearing direct allegiance to the emperor. In AD 9, his term of service was twenty years, with a further five years as a veteran. He was paid three times a year, after deductions for food and equipment had been made. Over a tunic, most often of white wool, he probably wore a padded garment, the *subarmalis*, which served to dissipate the penetrative power of enemy weapons that struck his armour. Next came a mail shirt or the famous segmented iron armour, the so-called *lorica segmentata*. Military belts were always worn, and for the most part covered by small tinned or silvered plates. It was common to suspend from the belt an 'apron' of four or more dangling leather, metal-studded straps to protect the groin.

Various types of helmet were in use during the early first century AD, made of iron, bronze or brass, sometimes with copper, tin and/or zinc alloy decorative pieces. The legionary carried a shield for defence, while his offensive weapons consisted of *gladius*, *pilum* and dagger (see entries for the first two). This equipment weighed well in excess of twenty kilograms. When the legionary's other equipment – carrying 'yoke', blanket, cooking pot, grain supply and tools – were added, his load came to more than forty kilograms. The fact that legionaries were expected to march twenty miles in five hours, carrying this immense weight, shows their high level of fitness. It's not surprising either that they soon wore down the hobnails on their sandals. Although it was usual for troops to have to pay for such things themselves, there is a recorded instance of soldiers – after a long, forced march – demanding that the emperor pay for their new hobs. Their demand for 'nail money' was granted! I loved this little snapshot, which led me to weave it into the story.

lituus: the curved bronze badge of office carried by soothsayers. Take a look at a modern bishop's crozier to see that nothing changes!

Lupia: the River Lippe.

Mare Germanicum: the North Sea.

Mars: the god of war. All spoils of war were consecrated to him, and few Roman commanders would go on campaign without having visited Mars' temple to ask for the god's protection and blessing.

Minerva: the goddess of war and also of wisdom.

Mithras: possibly a Persian god, he was born on the winter solstice, in a cave. He wore a Phrygian blunt-peaked hat and was associated with the sun, hence the name 'Sol Invictus': 'Unconquered Sun'. We know little about Mithraism, except that there were various levels of devotion, with rites of passage being required to rise between them. With its tenets of courage, strength and endurance, the religion was popular among the Roman military, especially during the empire.

Mogontiacum: Mainz.

molles: Latin word, meaning 'soft' or 'gentle', and my invention of a derogatory term for a homosexual.

Novaesium: Neuss.

optio (pl. *optiones*): the officer who ranked immediately below a centurion; the second-in-command of a century. (See also the entry for legion.)

phalera (pl. *phalerae*): a sculpted disc-like decoration for bravery which was worn on a chest harness, over a Roman officer's armour. *Phalerae* were often made of bronze, but could also be made of silver or gold. I have even seen one made of glass. Torques, arm rings and bracelets were also awarded to soldiers.

Phoenician: someone from Phoenicia, today's coastal Syria and Lebanon. The Phoenicians were famous travellers and traders; they founded Carthage in the eighth century BC.

pilum (pl. *pila*): the Roman javelin. It consisted of a wooden shaft some 1.2 m long, joined to a thin iron shank approximately 0.6 m long, and was topped by a small pyramidal point. The javelin was heavy and, when launched, its weight was concentrated behind the head, giving tremendous penetrative force. It could drive through a shield to injure the man carrying it, or lodge in the shield, rendering it unusable. The range of the *pilum* was about thirty metres, although the effective range was about half this distance. While it is thought that legionaries may have each possessed a pair of *pila*, it's more likely that they would have gone into battle with one. I have portrayed Varus' unsuspecting legionaries carrying two each, because they were on what was, at the outset, a peacetime march.

praetorium: the commandant's house in a Roman camp. Often situated behind the *principia*, it was built on a grand scale, in the style of a townhouse, with a range of buildings around a square central courtyard.

primus pilus: the senior centurion of the whole legion, and possibly – probably – the senior centurion of the First Cohort. A position of immense importance, it would have been held by a veteran soldier, in his forties or fifties. On retiring, the *primus pilus* was entitled to admission to the equestrian class. (See also the entry for legion.)

principia: the headquarters in a Roman camp, to be found at the junction of the *via principalis* and the *via praetoria*. It was where the administrative centre and where the standards of the units in the camp were kept. Its grand entrance opened on to a colonnaded and paved courtyard which was bordered on each side by offices. Behind this was a huge forehall with a high roof, which contained statues, the shrine for the standards, a vault for the soldiers' pay and perhaps more offices. It is possible that parades took place here, and that senior officers addressed their men in the hall.

Rhenus: the River Rhine.

Rura: the River Ruhr.

Sala: the River Saale.

scutum (pl. *scuta*): an elongated oval Roman army shield, about 1.2 m tall and 0.75 m wide. It was made from two layers of wood, the pieces laid at right angles to each other; it was then covered with linen or canvas, and leather. The *scutum* was heavy, weighing between 6 and 10 kg. A large metal boss decorated its centre, with the horizontal grip placed behind this. Decorative designs were often painted on the front, and a leather cover was used to protect the shield when not in use, e.g. while marching. It's recorded that Varus' legionaries' shields became so wet from the rain that they were hard to fight with.

sestertius (pl. *sestertii*): a brass coin, it was worth four *asses*; or a quarter of a *denarius*; or one hundredth of an *aureus*. Its name, 'two units and a half third one', comes from its original value, two and a half *asses*.

signifer (pl. *signiferi*): a standard-bearer and junior officer. This was a position of high esteem, with one for every century in a legion. Often the *signifer* wore scale armour and an animal pelt over his helmet, which sometimes had a hinged decorative facepiece, while he carried a small, round shield rather than a *scutum*. His *signum*, or standard, consisted of a wooden pole bearing a raised hand, or a spear tip surrounded by palm leaves. Below this was a crossbar from which hung metal decorations, or a piece of coloured cloth. The standard's shaft was decorated with discs, half-moons, crowns and representations of ships' prows, which were records of the unit's achievements and may have distinguished one century from another. (See also the entry for legion.)

Styx: the river in the underworld across which the dead had to travel, paying the ferryman a coin for the passage. The ritual of placing a coin in deceased people's mouths arose from the ancients' perceived need for money after death.

tesserarius: one of the junior officers in a century, whose duties included commanding the guard. The name originates from the *tessera* tablet on which was written the password for the day. (See also the entry for legion.)

testudo: the famous Roman square formation, formed by legionaries in the middle raising their *scuta* over their heads while those at the sides formed a shield wall. The *testudo*, or tortoise, was used to resist missile attack or to protect soldiers while they undermined the walls of towns under siege. The formation's strength is reputed to have been tested during military training by driving a cart pulled by mules over the top of it.

tribune (in Latin, *tribunus*): a senior staff officer within a legion. During Augustus' rule, the number of tribunes attached to each legion remained the same (six), but one was more senior than the rest. This tribune, the *tribunus laticlavius*, was of senatorial rank, and was second-in-command of the legion, after the legate. He was often in his late teens or early twenties, and probably served in the post for one year. The other tribunes, the *tribuni angusticlavii*, were a little older, and of equestrian stock. They tended to serve in their posts for longer, and to have more military experience. (See also the entry for legion.)

trireme: the classic Roman warship, which was powered by a single sail and three banks of oars. Each oar was rowed by one man, who was freeborn, not a slave. These ships had a large crew in proportion to their size. This limited the triremes' range, so their main use was as troop transports and to protect coastlines.

turmae (sing. *turma*): a ten-man cavalry unit. In the early principate, each legion had a mounted force of 120 riders. This was divided into twelve turmae, each commanded by a decurion. (See also the entries for *ala* and legion.)

ursarius (pl. *ursarii*): a legionary who also worked as a bear-catcher. (See also the Author's Note.)

valetudinarium: the hospital in a legionary fort. These were usually rectangular buildings with a central courtyard. They contained up to sixty-four wards, each similar to the rooms in the legionary barracks which held a *contubernium* of soldiers.

Venus: the Roman goddess of motherhood and domesticity.

Vetera: Xanten.

via praetoria: one of the two main roads in any Roman camp. It joined the gateways in the longer sides of the rectangular fort.

via principia: the other main road in a Roman camp. It led from the front gate to the *principia*, which lay on the far side of the *via praetoria*.

vicus: the Roman term for a settlement without the status of a town.

Vindonissa: Windisch.

Visurgis: the River Weser.

vitis: the vine stick carried by centurions. It was used as a mark of rank and also to inflict punishment.

Vulcan (in Latin, Vulcanus): a Roman god of destructive fire, who was often worshipped to prevent – fire!

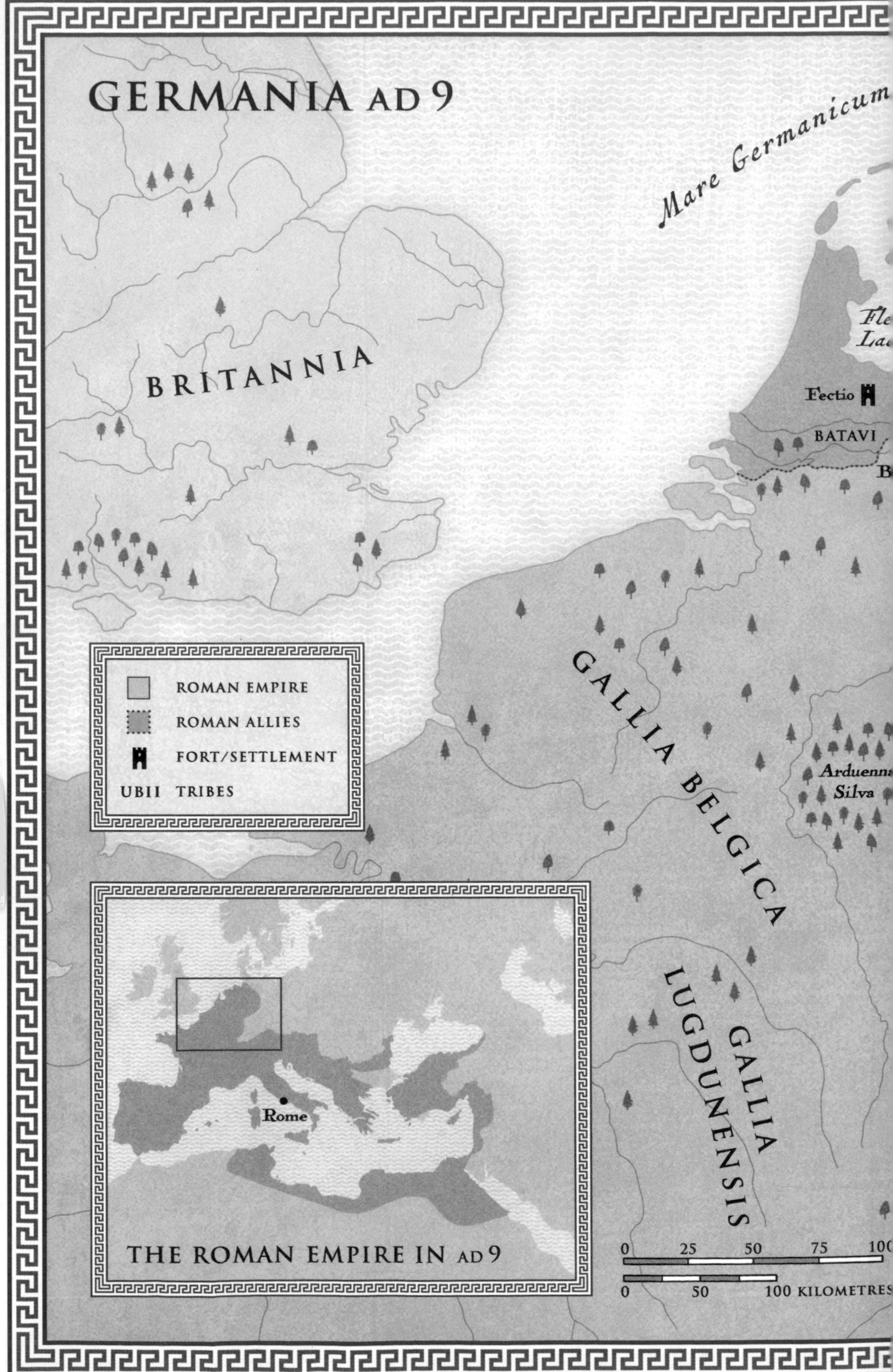
GERMANIA AD 9
Mare Germanicum
BRITANNIA
Fectio
BATAVI
GALLIA BELGICA
Arduenna Silva
GALLIA LUGDUNENSIS
ROMAN EMPIRE
ROMAN ALLIES
FORT/SETTLEMENT
UBII TRIBES
Rome
THE ROMAN EMPIRE IN AD 9
0
25
50
75
0
50
100 KILOMETRES